THE ART OF FIELDING

CHAD HARBACH

The Art of Fielding

FOURTH ESTATE • *London*

First published in Great Britain in 2012 by
Fourth Estate
An imprint of HarperCollins*Publishers*
77–85 Fulham Palace Road,
London W6 8JB
www.4thestate.co.uk

First published in 2011 in the United States
by Little, Brown and Company

1

A catalogue record for this book is
available from the British Library

HB ISBN 978-0-00-737444-1
TPB ISBN 978-0-00-741869-5

Printed in Great Britain by Clays Ltd. St Ives plc

MIX
Paper from
responsible sources
FSC
www.fsc.org
FSC® C007454

FSC is a non-profit international organisation established to promote the
responsible management of the world's forests. Products carrying the FSC
label are independently certified to assure consumers that they come
from forests that are managed to meet the social, economic and
ecological needs of present or future generations.

Find out more about HarperCollins and the environment at
www.harpercollins.co.uk/green

FOR MY FAMILY

So be cheery, my lads
Let your hearts never fall
While the bold Harpooner
Is striking the ball.

— *Westish College fight song*

THE ART
of
FIELDING

1

Schwartz didn't notice the kid during the game. Or rather, he noticed only what everyone else did—that he was the smallest player on the field, a scrawny novelty of a shortstop, quick of foot but weak with the bat. Only after the game ended, when the kid returned to the sun-scorched diamond to take extra grounders, did Schwartz see the grace that shaped Henry's every move.

This was the second Sunday in August, just before Schwartz's sophomore year at Westish College, that little school in the crook of the baseball glove that is Wisconsin. He'd spent the summer in Chicago, his hometown, and his Legion team had just beaten a bunch of farmboys from South Dakota in the semifinals of a no-name tournament. The few dozen people in the stands clapped mildly as the last out was made. Schwartz, who'd been weak with heat cramps all day, tossed his catcher's mask aside and hazarded a few unsteady steps toward the dugout. Dizzy, he gave up and sank down to the dirt, let his huge aching back relax against the chain-link fence. It was technically evening, but the sun still beat down wickedly. He'd caught five games since Friday night, roasting like a beetle in his black catcher's gear.

His teammates slung their gloves into the dugout and headed for the concession stand. The championship game would begin in half an hour. Schwartz hated being the weak one, the one on the verge of passing out, but it couldn't be helped. He'd been pushing himself hard all summer — lifting weights every morning, ten-hour shifts at the foundry, baseball every night. And then this hellish weather. He should have skipped the tournament — varsity football practice at Westish, an infinitely more important endeavor, started tomorrow at dawn, suicide sprints in shorts and pads. He should be napping right now, preserving his knees, but his teammates had begged him to stick around. Now he was stuck at this ramshackle ballpark between a junkyard and an adult bookstore on the interstate outside Peoria. If he were smart he'd skip the championship game, drive the five hours north to campus, check himself into Student Health for an IV and a little sleep. The thought of Westish soothed him. He closed his eyes and tried to summon his strength.

When he opened his eyes the South Dakota shortstop was jogging back onto the field. As the kid crossed the pitcher's mound he peeled off his uniform jersey and tossed it aside. He wore a sleeveless white undershirt, had an impossibly concave chest and a fierce farmer's burn. His arms were as big around as Schwartz's thumbs. He'd swapped his green Legion cap for a faded red St. Louis Cardinals one. Shaggy dust-blond curls poked out beneath. He looked fourteen, fifteen at most, though the tournament minimum was seventeen.

During the game, Schwartz had figured the kid was too small to hit high heat, so he'd called for one fastball after another, up and in. Before the last, he'd told the kid what was coming and added, "Since you can't hit it anyway." The kid swung and missed, gritted his teeth, turned to make the long walk back to the dugout. Just then Schwartz said — ever so softly, so that it would seem to come from inside the kid's own skull — "*Pussy.*" The kid paused, his scrawny shoulders tensed like a cat's, but he didn't turn around. Nobody ever did.

Now when the kid reached the worked-over dust that marked the shortstop's spot, he stopped, bouncing on his toes and jangling his limbs as if he needed to get loose. He bobbed and shimmied, windmilled his arms, burning off energy he shouldn't have had. He'd played as many games in this brutal heat as Schwartz.

Moments later the South Dakota coach strolled onto the field with a bat in one hand and a five-gallon paint bucket in the other. He set the bucket beside home plate and idly chopped at the air with the bat. Another of the South Dakota players trudged out to first base, carrying an identical bucket and yawning sullenly. The coach reached into his bucket, plucked out a ball, and showed it to the shortstop, who nodded and dropped into a shallow crouch, his hands poised just above the dirt.

The kid glided in front of the first grounder, accepted the ball into his glove with a lazy grace, pivoted, and threw to first. Though his motion was languid, the ball seemed to explode off his fingertips, to gather speed as it crossed the diamond. It smacked the pocket of the first baseman's glove with the sound of a gun going off. The coach hit another, a bit harder: same easy grace, same gunshot report. Schwartz, intrigued, sat up a little. The first baseman caught each throw at sternum height, never needing to move his glove, and dropped the balls into the plastic bucket at his feet.

The coach hit balls harder and farther afield — up the middle, deep in the hole. The kid tracked them down. Several times Schwartz felt sure he would need to slide or dive, or that the ball was flat-out unreachable, but he got to each one with a beat to spare. He didn't seem to move faster than any other decent shortstop would, and yet he arrived instantly, impeccably, as if he had some foreknowledge of where the ball was headed. Or as if time slowed down for him alone.

After each ball, he dropped back into his feline crouch, the fingertips of his small glove scraping the cooked earth. He barehanded a slow roller and fired to first on a dead run. He leaped high to snag a tailing line drive. Sweat poured down his cheeks as he sliced through the soup-thick air. Even at full speed his face looked bland, almost bored, like that of a virtuoso practicing scales. He weighed a buck and a quarter, maximum. Where the kid's thoughts were — whether he was having any thoughts at all, behind that blank look — Schwartz couldn't say. He remembered a line from Professor Eglantine's poetry class: *Expressionless, expresses God.*

Then the coach's bucket was empty and the first baseman's bucket full, and all three men left the field without a word. Schwartz felt bereft. He wanted the performance to continue. He wanted to rewind it and see it again in slow motion. He looked around to see who else had been watching—wanted at least the pleasure of exchanging a glance with another enraptured witness—but nobody was paying any attention. The few fans who hadn't gone in search of beer or shade gazed idly at their cell-phone screens. The kid's loser teammates were already in the parking lot, slamming their trunks.

Fifteen minutes to game time. Schwartz, still dizzy, hauled himself to his feet. He would need two quarts of Gatorade to get through the final game, then a coffee and a can of dip for the long midnight drive. But first he headed for the far dugout, where the kid was packing up his gear. He'd figure out what to say on the way over. All his life Schwartz had yearned to possess some single transcendent talent, some unique brilliance that the world would consent to call genius. Now that he'd seen that kind of talent up close, he couldn't let it walk away.

2

Henry Skrimshander stood in line beneath a billowing, navy-and-ecru-striped tent, waiting to obtain his room assignment. It was the last week of August, just three weeks after he'd met Mike Schwartz in Peoria. He'd been on the bus from Lankton all night, and the straps of his duffel bags formed a sweaty *X* across his chest. A smiling woman in a navy T-shirt with a man's bearded face on it asked him to spell his name. Henry did so, his heart thumping. Mike Schwartz had assured him that everything was taken care of, but each moment the smiling woman spent flipping through her printouts confirmed what Henry had secretly known all along, made only more apparent by the groomed green lawn and the gray stone buildings that surrounded it, the sun just risen over the steamy lake and the mirrored-glass facade of the library, the lithe tank-topped girl behind him tip-tapping on her iPhone as she sighed with a boredom so sophisticated that Henry could imagine precisely nothing about her life: he didn't belong here.

He'd been born in Lankton, South Dakota, seventeen and a half years earlier. It was a town of forty-three thousand people, surrounded by seas of corn. His father was a foreman at a metalworking shop. His mom worked part-time as an X-ray technician at All Saints. His little sister, Sophie, was a sophomore at Lankton High.

On Henry's ninth birthday, his dad had taken him to the sporting goods store and told him to pick out whatever he liked. There had never been any doubt about the choice — there was only one glove in the store with the name of Aparicio Rodriguez inscribed in the pocket — but Henry took his time, trying on every glove, amazed by the sheer fact of being able to *choose*. The glove seemed huge back then; now it fit him snugly, barely bigger than his left hand. He liked it that way; it helped him feel the ball.

When he came home from Little League games, his mother would ask how many errors he'd made. "Zero!" he'd crow, popping the pocket of his beloved glove with a balled-up fist. His mom still used the name — "Henry, put Zero away, please!" — and he winced, embarrassed, when she did. But in the safety of his mind he never thought of it any other way. Nor did he let anyone else touch Zero. If Henry happened to be on base when an inning ended, his teammates knew better than to ferry his hat and glove onto the diamond for him. "The glove is not an object in the usual sense," said Aparicio in *The Art of Fielding*. "For the infielder to divide it from himself, even in thought, is one of the roots of error."

Henry played shortstop, only and ever shortstop — the most demanding spot on the diamond. More ground balls were hit to the shortstop than to anyone else, and then he had to make the longest throw to first. He also had to turn double plays, cover second on steals, keep runners on second from taking long leads, make relay throws from the outfield. Every Little League coach Henry had ever had took one look at him and pointed toward right field or second base. Or else the coach didn't point anywhere, just shrugged at the fate that had assigned him this pitiable shrimp, this born benchwarmer.

Bold nowhere else in his life, Henry was bold in this: no matter what the coach said, or what his eyebrows expressed, he would jog out to shortstop, pop his fist into Zero's pocket, and wait. If the coach shouted at him to go to second base, or right field, or home to his mommy, he would keep standing there, blinking and dumb, popping his fist. Finally someone would hit him a grounder, and he would show what he could do.

What he could do was field. He'd spent his life studying the way the ball came off the bat, the angles and the spin, so that he knew in advance whether he should break right or left, whether the ball that came at him would bound up high or skid low to the dirt. He caught the ball cleanly, always, and made, always, a perfect throw.

Sometimes the coach would insist on putting him at second base anyway, or would leave him on the bench; he was that scrawny and pathetic-looking. But after some number of practices and games — two or twelve or twenty, depending on the stubbornness of the coach — he would wind up where he belonged, at shortstop, and his black mood would lift.

When he reached high school, things happened much the same. Coach Hinterberg later told him he'd planned to cut him until the last fifteen minutes of tryouts. Then, from the corner of his eye, he saw Henry make a diving stab of a scorching line drive and, while lying flat on his stomach, flip the ball behind his head and into the hands of the shocked second baseman: double play. The JV team carried an extra player that year, and the extra player wore a brand-new extra-small jersey.

By his junior year he was the starting varsity shortstop. After every game his mom would ask how many errors he'd made, and the answer was always Zero. That summer he played on a team sponsored by the local American Legion. He arranged his hours at the Piggly Wiggly so that he could spend weekends traveling to tournaments. For once, he didn't have to prove himself. His teammates and Coach Hinterberg knew that, even if he didn't hit home runs — had never, ever hit a home run — he would still help them win.

Midway through his senior season, though, a sadness set in. He was playing better than ever, but each passing inning brought him closer to the end. He had no hope of playing in college. College coaches were like girls: their eyes went straight to the biggest, bulkiest guys, regardless of what those guys were really worth. Take Andy Tsade, the first baseman on Henry's summer team, who was going to St. Paul State on a full ride. Andy's arm was average, his footwork was sloppy, and he always looked to Henry to tell him where to play. He'd never read *The Art of Fielding.* But he was big and left-handed and every so often he crushed one over the fence. One day he crushed one over the fence with the St. Paul coach watching, and now he got to play baseball for four more years.

Henry's dad wanted him to come work at the metalworking shop — two of the guys were retiring at year's end. Henry said maybe he'd go to Lankton CC for a couple of years, take some bookkeeping and accounting classes. Some of his classmates were going to college to pursue their dreams; others had no dreams, and were getting jobs and drinking beer. He couldn't identify with either. He'd only ever wanted to play baseball.

The tournament in Peoria had been the last of the summer. Henry and his teammates lost in the semifinals to a team of enormous sluggers from Chicago. Afterward, he jogged back out to shortstop to take fifty practice grounders, the way he always did. There was nothing left to practice for, no reason to try to improve, but that didn't mean he didn't want to. As Coach Hinterberg tried to rip the ball past him, Henry imagined the same scenario as always: he was playing shortstop for the St. Louis Cardinals in Game 7 of the World Series, against the Yankees at Yankee Stadium, ahead by one, two outs, bases loaded. Make the last play and win it all.

As he was putting Zero into his bag, a hand gripped his shoulder and spun him around. He found himself face-to-face — or face-to-neck, since the other man was taller and wearing spikes — with the catcher from the Chicago team. Henry recognized him instantly: during the game he'd tipped Henry the pitch and then called him a name. He'd also hit a home run that cleared the center-field wall by thirty feet. Now he fixed his big amber eyes on Henry with a fierce intensity.

"I'm glad I found you." The catcher removed his huge sweaty hand from Henry's shoulder and proffered it. "Mike Schwartz."

Mike Schwartz's hair was matted and wild. Sweat and dirt streaked his face. The sweat made his eye black bleed down his cheekbones onto his heavy stubble.

"I watched you taking ground balls," he said. "Two things impressed me. First, that you were out there working hard in this heat. Christ, I can barely walk. Takes dedication."

Henry shrugged. "I always do that after a game."

"The second thing is that you're a hell of a shortstop. Great first step, great instincts. I don't know how you got to half those balls. Where are you playing next year?"

"Playing?"

"What college. What college are you going to play baseball for?"

"Oh." Henry paused, embarrassed both by his failure to understand the question and by the answer he would have to give. "I'm not."

Mike Schwartz, though, seemed pleased by this. He nodded, scratched at the dark stubble on his jaw, smiled. "That's what you think."

SCHWARTZ TOLD HENRY that the Westish Harpooners had been crappy for too many years to count, but with Henry's help they were going to turn it around. He talked about sacrifice, passion, desire, attention to detail, the need to strive like a champion every day. To Henry the words sounded beautiful, like reading Aparicio but better, because Schwartz was standing right there. On the drive back to Lankton, while crammed into the jump seat of Coach Hinterberg's Dodge Ram, he felt a kind of desolation come over him, because he figured he'd never hear from the big man again, but when he got home there was already a note on the kitchen table in Sophie's girlish handwriting: *Call Mike Shorts!*

Three days later, after three long conversations with Schwartz, conducted in secret while his parents were at work, Henry was beginning to believe. "Things are moving slowly," said Schwartz. "The whole Admissions office is on vacation. But they're moving. I got a copy of your high school transcript this morning. Nice job in physics."

"My transcript?" Henry asked, baffled. "How'd you do that?"

"I called the high school."

Henry was amazed. Perhaps that was obvious — if you want a transcript, call the high school. But he'd never met someone like Schwartz — someone who, when he wanted something, took immediate steps to acquire it. That night at dinner, he cleared his throat and told his parents about Westish College.

His mom looked pleased. "So Mr. Schwartz," she said, "he's the baseball coach at this college?"

"Um...not exactly. He's more like a player on the team."

"Oh. Well. Hm." His mom tried to keep looking pleased. "And you never met him before last Sunday? And now all this? I have to say, it sounds a little strange."

"Not to me." His dad blew his nose on his napkin, leaving the usual dark streak of steel-dust snot. "I'm sure Westish College needs all the money it can scrape together. They'll stick a hundred gullible suckers on the baseball team, as long as they pay their tuition."

This was the dark thought Henry had been working hard to suppress: that it was too good to be true. He steadied himself with a sip of milk. "But why would Schwartz care about that?"

Jim Skrimshander grunted. "Why does anybody care about anything?"

"Love," Sophie said. "He loves Henry. They talk on the phone all day long, like lovebirds."

"Close, Soph." Their dad pushed back his chair and carried his plate to the sink. "Money. I'm sure Mike Schwartz gets his cut. A thousand bucks a sucker."

Later that night, Henry relayed the gist of this conversation to Schwartz. "Bah," said Schwartz. "Don't sweat it. He'll come around."

"You don't know my dad."

"He'll come around."

When Henry didn't hear from Schwartz all weekend, he began to feel glum and foolish about having gotten his hopes up. But on Monday night, his dad came home and put his uneaten bag lunch back in the fridge.

"Are you feeling okay, hon?" asked Henry's mom.

"I went out for lunch."

"How nice," she said. Henry had visited his dad on his lunch hour many times through the years: regardless of the weather, the guys sat outside on the benches that faced the road, backs to the shop, munching their sandwiches. "With the guys?"

"With Mike Schwartz."

Henry looked at Sophie — sometimes, when he found himself unable to speak, Sophie did it for him. Her eyes were as wide as his. "Well well!" she said. "Tell us more!"

"He dropped by the shop around lunchtime. Took me to Murdock's."

Flabbergasted was maybe not a strong or strange enough word to describe how Henry felt. Schwartz lived in Chicago, Chicago was five hundred miles away, and he'd dropped by the shop? And taken Henry's dad to Murdock's? And then driven back, without so much as telling Henry he'd done it, much less stopping by to say hello?

"He's a very serious young man," his dad was saying.

"Serious as in, Henry can go to Westish? Or serious as in, Henry *can't* go to Westish?"

"Henry can do whatever he wants. Nobody's stopping him from going to Westish or anywhere else. My only concern —"

"Yeay!" Sophie reached across the table and high-fived her brother. "College!"

"— is that he understands what he's in for. Westish is not your average school. The academics are tough, and the baseball team is a full-time commitment. If Henry's going to succeed there…"

…and Henry's dad, who so rarely strung four words together, especially on a Monday night, went on to talk for the rest of the meal about sacrifice, passion, desire, attention to detail, the need to strive like a champion every day. He was talking just like Mike Schwartz, but he seemed not quite to realize it, and in fact he also sounded a good deal like himself, only in many more words, and with, Henry thought, a slightly more generous attitude toward his son's talents than usual. As his dad stood up to carry his plate to the sink, he clapped Henry on the shoulder and smiled broadly. "I'm proud of you, buddy. This is a big opportunity. Grab on to it."

It's a miracle, Henry thought. Mike Schwartz works miracles. After that, he continued to talk to Schwartz on the phone every night, making plans, working out details—but now he did so openly, in the family room, and his dad hovered nearby, the TV on mute, cigarette going, eavesdropping and shouting out comments. Sometimes Schwartz would ask to talk to Jim. Henry would hand his dad the phone, and his dad would sit down at his desk and go over the Skrimshanders' tax returns.

"Thanks," Henry said into the phone, feeling sentimental, on the day he bought his bus ticket. "Thank you."

"Don't sweat it, Skrim," Schwartz said. "It's football season, and I'm going to be busy. You settle in. I'll be in touch, okay?"

"PHUMBER 405," said the smiling woman. She thrust a key and a paper map into his hand, pointed to the left. "Small Quad."

Henry slipped through a cool aperture between two buildings and emerged on a bright, bustling scene. This wasn't Lankton CC: this was college in a movie. The buildings matched—each four or five stories high and made of squat gray weather-beaten stone, with deep-set windows and peaked, gabled roofs. The bike racks and benches were freshly painted navy. Two tall guys in shorts and flip-flops staggered toward an open doorway beneath the weight of a gigantic flat-screen TV. A squirrel tore down out of a tree and bumped against the leg of the guy walking backward—he screamed and dropped to his knees, and the corner of the TV sank into the plush new sod. The other guy laughed. The squirrel was long gone. From an upper window somewhere drifted the sound of a violin.

Henry found Phumber Hall and climbed the stairs to the top floor. The door marked 405 stood slightly ajar, and bleepy, bloopy music came through the gap. Henry lingered nervously in the stairwell. He didn't know how many roommates he'd have, or what sort of roommates they might be, or what kind of music that was. If he'd been able to imagine the students of Westish College in any specific way, he imagined twelve hundred Mike Schwartzes, huge and mythic and grave, and twelve hundred women of the sort Mike Schwartz might date: leggy, stunning, well versed in ancient history. The whole thing, really, was too intimidating to think about. He nudged the door with his foot.

The room contained two identical steel-frame beds and two sets of identical blond-wood desks, chairs, dressers, and bookshelves. One of the beds was neatly made, with a plush seafoam-green comforter and a wealth of fluffy pillows. The other mattress was bare but for an ugly ocher stain in roughly the size and shape of a person. Both bookshelves had already been neatly filled, the books arranged by author name from Achebe through Tocqueville, with the rest of the *T*s through *Z* piled on the mantel. Henry plunked his bags down on the ocher stain and drew his beat-up copy of Aparicio Rodriguez's *The Art of Fielding* out of his shorts' pocket. *The Art* was the only book he'd brought with him, the only book Henry knew deeply: suddenly it seemed like this might be a terrible flaw. He prepared to wedge it between Rochefoucauld and Roethke, but lo and behold there was already a copy there, a handsome hardcover with a once-cracked spine. Henry slid it out, turned it in his hands. Inscribed on the flyleaf, in a lovely calligraphic hand, were the words *Owen Dunne*.

Henry had been reading Aparicio on the overnight bus. Or at least he'd kept the book open on his lap as the dreary slabs of interstate rolled by. By this point in his life, reading Aparicio no longer really qualified as reading, because he had the book more or less memorized. He could flip to a chapter, any chapter, and the shapes of the short, numbered paragraphs were enough to trigger his memory. His lips murmured the words as his eyes, unfocused, scanned the page:

26. *The shortstop is a source of stillness at the center of the defense. He projects this stillness and his teammates respond.*

59. *To field a ground ball must be considered a generous act and an act of comprehension. One moves not against the ball but with it. Bad fielders stab at the ball like an enemy. This is antagonism. The true fielder lets the path of the ball become his own path, thereby comprehending the ball and dissipating the self, which is the source of all suffering and poor defense.*

147. *Throw with the legs.*

Aparicio played shortstop for the St. Louis Cardinals for eighteen seasons. He retired the year Henry turned ten. He was a first-ballot Hall of Famer and the greatest defensive shortstop who ever lived. As a ballplayer, Henry had modeled himself after his hero in every particular, from the gliding, two-handed way he fielded grounders, to the way he wore his cap pulled low to shield his eyes, to the three taps he gave his heart before stepping into the batter's box. And of course the jersey number. Aparicio believed that the number 3 had deep significance.

3. *There are three stages: Thoughtless being. Thought. Return to thoughtless being.*

33. *Do not confuse the first and third stages. Thoughtless being is attained by everyone, the return to thoughtless being by a very few.*

There were, admittedly, many sentences and statements in *The Art* that Henry did not yet understand. The opaque parts of *The Art,* though, had always been his favorites, even more than the detailed and extremely helpful descriptions of, say, how to keep a runner close to second base (*flirtation,* Aparicio called it) or what sort of cleats to wear on wet grass. The opaque parts, frustrating as they could be, gave Henry something to aspire to. Someday, he dreamed, he would be enough of a ballplayer to crack them open and suck out their hidden wisdom.

213. *Death is the sanction of all that the athlete does.*

The bleepy, bloopy music lulled. Henry became aware of a murmurous sound that seemed to be coming from behind a closed door in the corner of the room. He'd thought it was a closet, but now he pressed his ear to it and heard a rush of running water. He knocked softly.

No response. He twisted the knob, and a sharp yelp rang out as the door struck something solid. Henry jerked the door shut. But that was a foolish thing to do—it wasn't as if he could run away. He opened the door again, and again it cracked against something solid.

"Ow!" came a cry from inside. "Please stop!"

The room turned out to be a bathroom, and a person about Henry's age was lying on the black-and-white checkerboard tile, clutching the top of his head. His ashen hair was cropped close, and between the fingers of his canary-yellow rubber gloves Henry could see a cut edged with blood. Water ran in the tub, and a toothbrush lay at his side, frothing with grainy, aqua-flecked cleanser. "Are you okay?" Henry asked.

"This grout is filthy." The young man sat up, rubbed his head. "You'd think they would clean the grout." His skin was the color of weak coffee. He put on a pair of wire-rimmed glasses and surveyed Henry from head to toe. "Who are you?"

"I'm Henry," Henry said.

"Really?" The young man's lunular eyebrows lifted. "Are you sure?"

Henry looked down at the palm of his right hand, as if that might be the place to find some irrefutable sign of Henryness. "Pretty sure."

The young man rose to his feet and, after peeling off one of his bright-yellow gloves, pumped Henry's hand warmly. "I was expecting someone larger," he explained. "Because of the baseball factor. My name's Owen Dunne. I'll be your gay mulatto roommate."

Henry nodded in a way he hoped was appropriate.

"I was supposed to have this room to myself." Owen swept one hand before him, as if spanning a broad vista. "It was part of my scholarship package, as the winner of the Maria Westish Award. I've always dreamed of living alone. Haven't you?"

Henry, actually, had always dreamed of living with someone who owned a copy of Aparicio's book. "Do you play baseball?" he asked, turning Owen's hardback *Art* in his hands.

"I've dabbled in the game," Owen said, and added somewhat mysteriously, "But not like you."

"What do you mean?"

"Last week I received a call from President Affenlight. Are you familiar with his *Sperm-Squeezers*?"

Henry was not. Owen nodded sympathetically. "Not surprising," he said. "It doesn't have much academic traction these days, though it was a seminal—ha!—work in its field. It was a great inspiration to me when I was fourteen, fifteen years old. Anyway, President Affenlight phoned me at my mother's house in San Jose and said that a student of considerable talents had been added to the freshperson class, and that though this was excellent news for the college as a whole, it posed a dilemma for the Housing office. Since I was the only member of the class with a single room, he wondered if I might be willing to forgo one of my scholarship's privileges and take on a roommate.

"Affenlight's a smooth talker," Owen continued. "He spoke so highly of you, and of the more abstract virtues of roommatehood, that I almost forgot to negotiate. Frankly, I find the professionalization of collegiate sport to be a rather despicable phenomenon. But if the administration was willing to buy me that"—he pointed a yellow-gloved finger at the sleek computer that sat atop his desk—"and to throw in a handsome book allowance just to persuade me to live with you, then you must be quite a ballplayer. I'd be honored to throw the ball around sometime."

"They're giving you money to be my roommate?" Henry asked, so incredulous and confused that he barely registered Owen's offer. What could Mike Schwartz have possibly said or done to produce a situation in which the president of Westish called people on the phone and spoke highly of *him?* "Would it be rude...I mean...do you mind if I ask...?"

Owen shrugged. "Probably nowhere near what they're paying you. But enough to buy that rug out there, which is an expensive rug, so please do not put your shoes on it. And enough to keep me in high-quality marijuana for the year. Well, maybe for the semester. Till Halloween, at least."

After that first encounter, Henry scarcely saw Owen. Most afternoons Owen would sweep into the room, remove certain notebooks from his satchel and replace them with certain other notebooks, or remove his handsome gray sweater and replace it with his handsome red sweater, and then sweep back out again with a word: "Rehearsal." "Protest." "Date." Henry would nod and, for however many seconds Owen was in the room, devote himself deeply to whatever assignment lay open in front of him, so as not to seem entirely useless and adrift.

The date was with Jason Gomes, a senior who starred in all of the campus plays. Before long Owen's notebooks and sweaters had migrated to Jason's room. In the mornings, as Henry walked to class, he would see them reading together at the campus coffee shop, Café Oo, Jason's hand laid atop Owen's as they lingered over their espresso and their books, some of whose titles were French. At dinnertime, as Henry sat alone in a dim alcove of the dining hall, trying to look both inconspicuous and content, Owen and Jason would wander in, gather fruit and crackers to sustain them through rehearsals, and wander back out again. After midnight, as Henry drew the shades to go to sleep, he would see them sharing a joint on the opposite stoop, Owen's head tipped sideways to rest on his lover's shoulder. They didn't need to bother with food or sleep, or so it seemed to Henry: they were too busy, too happy, for such trivial concerns. Owen had written a three-act play, "a kind of neo-Marxian *Macbeth* set in an open-plan office," as he once described it, and Jason was playing the lead.

On a couple of weekends that fall, Jason drove home to Chicago or some suburb thereof. For Henry these weekends were a source of relief and joy. He had a friend, at least till Sunday night. Owen would spend the morning reading and drinking tea in his plaid pajamas, sometimes smoking a joint or staring idly at the face of his silent BlackBerry, until Henry, with careful nonchalance, asked whether he might like to go get brunch. Owen would look up over his round-rimmed glasses and sigh, as if Henry were an annoying child. But as soon as they got outside in the autumn air, Owen—usually still in his pajamas, with a sweater over the top—would begin to talk, answering questions Henry would never think to ask.

"It's with my full permission that he goes," he said, looking again at his phone that hadn't made a peep. "My full permission and understanding. We've established parameters for what's allowable behavior, and I'm quite certain that he abides by those parameters. We communicate openly, like adults. And I know that if I went along, it would change the entire nature of the experience."

Henry, who understood who *he* was and not much else, nodded thoughtfully.

"Not that I even *want* to go along, mind you. I really don't. I've said as much and I meant it. And I appreciate his honesty about what he wants at this stage of life. We're both young, he says, and I can't argue with that. But it bothers me nonetheless. For two reasons. Both of them indications of my retrograde sentimentality and general unfitness for modern life, I'm afraid. The first is that his family is there, his parents, his brother, his sister. He ate dinner with them last night. Can you imagine, four other humans who look and act anything like *that*? I want to meet them, I admit it. I want to meet them quite badly. Which is perhaps embarrassing given that it's only been seven...six weeks since we met. God, six weeks. I'm so pathetic. But I know that if my mom lived within driving distance of here, I'd already have forced the two of them into a room together, just for the sake of my own stupid pleasure. You know?"

Henry nodded again, loaded his plate with pancakes.

"You shouldn't eat so much flour," Owen said, taking a single pancake for himself. "Even when I'm stoned I don't eat much flour. The other reason, of course, is that I'm a staunch monogamist. In practice, if not in theory. I can't help it. Do I acknowledge the oppressive, regressive nature of sexual exclusivity? Yes. Do I want that exclusivity very badly for myself? Also yes. There's probably some sort of way in which that's not a paradox. Maybe I believe in love. Maybe I just badly crave my mother's approval. Hang on a sec." Owen jogged back to the hot-food line, spatulaed up four more flapjacks, and slid them onto his plate. "Sorry to babble on like this, Henry. I think I'm immoderately stoned."

After brunch they went to the union to play Ping-Pong. Owen, even immoderately stoned, proved to be a surprisingly good player. His swings were gentle, but he never missed the table, and Henry, who hated to lose at Ping-Pong, had to hustle and grunt and sweat to stay ahead. All the while Owen spoke steadily about love and Jason and the contradictions of monogamy, paying no discernible attention to the game but still carving out subtle drop shots that sent Henry sprawling across the table. Occasionally Henry would interject a comment, to show that he was listening and interested, but for him monogamy was less a contradiction than a glamorous, possibly unattainable goal, the flip side of his virginity, and he kept his comments vague. Inexperience hadn't bothered him much in high school—he was only seventeen, after all—but here at Westish, where everyone was so much more sophisticated, not to mention older, it had already come to seem a rare affliction, one that, though not terribly hard to live with, would be both shameful to reveal and hard to remedy.

Still it felt beautiful to move, to play, and soon Henry was down to his T-shirt, leaking sweat. After each game he felt painfully sure that Owen would put down his paddle—he seemed gently bored, Owen did—but Owen, his high forehead dry, still wearing his sweater over his pjs, would merely murmur, "Well done, Henry," and deliver another cottony serve. They played until it was time for dinner, and afterward they returned to the union to watch the World Series, Henry leaning close to the screen to study the shortstops' moves, Owen lounging on the couch with an open book. Occasionally, roused by a gloomy thought, Owen would pull out his phone and gaze into its face, then tuck it away again.

Henry slept well that night, tired from four hours of Ping-Pong and somehow calmed by the soft snuffle of Owen's breathing. On Sunday evening Owen's phone finally buzzed, and he vanished again.

Even in Owen's absence, Phumber 405 suggested his whole existence so palpably that Henry, as he sat alone and bewildered on his bed, was often struck by the eerie thought that Owen was present and he himself was not. Owen's books filled the bookshelves, his bonsai trees and potted herbs lined the windowsills, and his sparse angular music played around the clock on his wireless stereo system. Henry could have changed the music, but he didn't own any music of his own, so he let it play on. Owen's expensive rug covered the floor, his abstract paintings the walls, his clothes and towels the closet shelves. There was one painting in particular that Henry liked, and he was glad that Owen had happened to hang it over his bed—it was a large rectangle, smeary and green, with thin white streaks that could easily have marked the foul lines of a baseball diamond. Owen's pot smoke hung in the air, mingled with the bracing citrus-and-ginger smells of his organic cleaning products, though Henry couldn't figure out when he smoked or cleaned, since he came home so rarely.

The only traces of Henry's existence, by contrast, were the tangle of sheets on his unmade bed, a few textbooks, a pair of dirty jeans draped over his chair, and taped-up pictures of his sister and Aparicio

Rodriguez. Zero sat on a closet shelf. *Get settled,* he thought, *and Mike will be in touch.* He would have liked to clean the bathroom, as a show of goodwill, but he could never find a speck of scum or grime worth cleaning. Sometimes he thought of watering the plants, but the plants seemed to be getting on fine without him, and he'd heard that overwatering could be deadly.

Though his classmates supposedly hailed from "all fifty states, Guam, and twenty-two foreign lands," as President Affenlight said in his convocation address, they all seemed to Henry to have come from the same close-knit high school, or at least to have attended some crucial orientation session he'd missed. They traveled in large packs, constantly texting the other packs, and when two packs converged there was always a tremendous amount of hugging and kissing on the cheek. No one invited Henry to parties or offered to hit him grounders, so he stayed home and played Tetris on Owen's computer. Everything else in his life seemed beyond his control, but the Tetris blocks snapped together neatly, and his scores continued to rise. He recorded each day's achievements in his physics notebook. When he closed his eyes at night the sharp-cornered shapes twisted and fell.

Before he'd arrived, life at Westish had seemed heroic and grand, grave and essential, like Mike Schwartz. It was turning out to be comic and idle, familiar and flawed — more like Henry Skrimshander. During his first days on campus, drifting silently from class to class, he didn't see Schwartz anywhere. Or, rather, he saw him everywhere. From the corner of his eye he would glimpse a figure that seemed finally, certainly, to be Schwartz. But when he whirled eagerly toward it, it turned out to be some other, insufficiently Schwartz-like person, or a trash can, or nothing at all.

In the southeast corner of the Small Quad, between Phumber Hall and the president's office, stood a stone figure on a cubic marble base. Pensive and bushy-bearded, he didn't face the quad, as might be expected of a statue, but rather gazed out toward the lake. He held a book open in his left hand, and with his right he raised a small spyglass toward his eye, as if he'd just spotted something along the horizon. Because he kept his back to the campus, exposing to passersby the moss-filled crack that ran across his back like a lash mark, he struck Henry from the first as a deeply solitary figure, burdened by his own thoughts. In the loneliness of that September, Henry felt a peculiar kinship toward this Melville fellow, who, like everything else on campus that was human or human-sized, he had mistaken several times for Mike Schwartz.

3

That Thanksgiving was Henry's first holiday away from home. He spent it at the dining hall, working his new job as a dishwasher. Chef Spirodocus, the head of Dining Services, was a tough boss, always marching around inspecting your work, but the job paid more than Henry had ever made at the Piggly Wiggly in Lankton. He worked the lunch and dinner shifts, and afterward Chef Spirodocus gave him a sliced turkey breast to take back to Owen's minifridge.

Henry felt a surge of homesick joy when he heard his parents' voices on the phone that night, his mom in the kitchen, his dad lying on his back in the family room with the TV on mute, ashtray by his side, half-heartedly doing the stretches he was supposed to do for his back. In Henry's mind he could see his dad rolling his bent knees slowly from side to side. His pants rode up to his shins. His socks were white. Imagining the whiteness of those socks—the terrible clarity with which he could imagine it—brought a tear to Henry's eye.

"Henry." His mother's voice wasn't Thanksgiving-cheery, as he'd expected—it was chagrined, ominous, odd. "Your sister told us that Owen..."

He wiped away the tear. He should have known that Sophie would spill the beans. Sophie always spilled the beans. She was as keen to get a rise out of people, especially their parents, as Henry was to placate them.

"...is *gay*."

His mom let the word hang there. His dad sneezed. Henry waited.

"Your father and I are wondering why *you* didn't tell us."

"Owen's a good roommate," Henry said. "He's nice."

"I'm not saying gay people aren't nice. I'm saying, is this the best environment for *you,* honey? I mean, you share a bedroom! You share a bathroom! Doesn't it make you uncomfortable?"

"I sure hope so," said his dad.

Henry's heart fell. Would they make him come home? He didn't want to go home. His total failure so far—to make friends, to get good grades, or even to find Mike Schwartz—made him more loath to go home than if he were having—like everybody around him seemed to be having—the world's most wonderful time.

"Would they put you in a room with a *girl?*" his mom asked. "At your age? Never. Never in a million years. So why would they do this? It makes no sense to me."

If there was a flaw in his mom's logic, Henry couldn't find it. Would his parents make him switch rooms? That would be horrible, worse than embarrassing, to go to the Housing office and request a new room assignment—the Housing people would know instantly why he was asking, because Owen was the best possible roommate, neat and kind and rarely even home. The only roommate who'd want to be rid of Owen was a roommate who hated gay people. This was a real college, an enlightened place—you could get in trouble for hating people here, or so Henry suspected. He didn't want to get into trouble, and he didn't want a new roommate.

His mom cleared her throat, in preparation for a further revelation.

"We hear he's been buying you clothes."

Two weeks prior, on Saturday morning, Henry had been playing Tetris when Owen and Jason walked in, Owen calm and chipper as always, Jason sleepy-eyed and carrying a big paper cup of coffee. Henry closed the Tetris window, opened the website for his physics class. "Hi guys," he said. "What's up?"

"We're going shopping," said Owen.

"Oh, cool. Have fun."

"The *we* is inclusive. Please put on your shoes."

"Oh, ha, that's okay," Henry said. "I'm not much of a shopper."

"But you're not *not* a master of litotes," Jason said. *Lie-toe-tease.* Henry repeated it to himself, so that he could look it up later. "When we get back I'm burning those jeans."

"What's wrong with these jeans?" Henry looked down at his legs. It wasn't a rhetorical question: there was clearly something wrong with his jeans. He'd realized as much since arriving at Westish, just as he'd realized there was something wrong with his shoes, his hair, his backpack, and everything else. But he didn't know quite what it was. The way the Eskimos had a hundred words for *snow,* he had only one for *jeans.*

They drove in Jason's car to a mall in Door County. Henry went into dressing rooms and emerged for inspection, over and over.

"There," Owen said. "Finally."

"These?" Henry tugged at the pockets, tugged at the crotch. "I think these are kind of tight."

"They'll loosen up," Jason said. "And if not, so much the better."

By the time they finished, Owen had said *There, finally* to two pairs of jeans, two shirts, and two sweaters. A modest stack, but Henry added up the price tags in his mind, and it was more than he had in the bank. "Do I really need two?" he said. "One's a good start."

"Two," said Jason.

"Um." Henry frowned at the clothes. "Mmm..."

"Oh!" Owen slapped himself on the forehead. "Did I forget to mention? I have a gift card for this establishment. And I have to use it right away. Lest it expire." He reached for the clothes in Henry's hand. "Here."

"But it's yours," Henry protested. "You should spend it on yourself."

"Certainly not," Owen said. "I would never shop here." He pried the stack from Henry's hands, looked at Jason. "You guys wait outside."

So now Henry had two pairs of jeans that had loosened up slightly but still felt way too tight. As he sat by himself in the dining hall, watching his classmates walk by, he'd noticed that they looked quite a bit like other people's jeans. *Progress,* he thought. *I'm making progress.*

"Is that true?" his dad said now. "You've got this guy buying you clothes?"

"Um…" Henry tried to think of a not-untrue response. "We went to the mall."

"Why is he buying you clothes?" His mom's voice rose again.

"I doubt if he buys Mike Schwartz clothes," Henry's dad said. "I doubt that very much."

"I think he wants me to fit in."

"*Fit in to what?* is maybe a question worth asking. Honey, just because people have more money than you doesn't mean you have to conform to their ideas about *fitting in.* You have to be your own person. Are we understood?"

"I guess so."

"Good. I want you to tell Owen thank you very much, but you cannot under any circumstances accept his gifts. You're not poor, and you don't have to accept charity from strangers."

"He's not a stranger. And I already wore them. He can't take them back."

"Then he can wear them himself."

"He's taller than me."

"Then he can donate them to someone in need. I don't want to discuss this anymore, Henry. Are we understood?"

He didn't want to discuss it anymore either. It dawned on him — as it hadn't before; he was dense, he was slow — that his parents were five hundred miles away. They could make him come home, they could refuse to pay the portion of his tuition they'd agreed to pay, but they couldn't see his jeans. "Understood," he said.

4

It was nearly midnight. Henry pressed his ear to the door. The noises that came from within were sweaty and breathy, loud enough to be heard above the pulse of the music. He knew what was happening in there, however vaguely. It sounded painful, at least for one of the parties involved.

"*Uhh. Uhh. Uhhh.*"

"Come on, baby. Come on—"

"*Ooohhh—*"

"That's it, baby. All night long."

"*uuhnghrrrrnnrh—*"

"Slow down, now. Slow, slow, slow. Yeah, baby. Just like that."

"*—ooohhhrrrrgghhh—*"

"You're big! You're fucking huge!"

"*—rrrrooaarhrraaaah—*"

"Give it to me! Come on! Finish it!"

"*—rhaa…rhaa…ARH—*"

"Yesyesyesyesyesyesyesyesyes!"

"—RRHNAAAAAAAAAGHGHHHH!"

The door swung open from within. Henry, who'd been leaning against it, staggered into the room and smacked against the sweat-drenched chest of Mike Schwartz.

"Skrimmer, you're late." Schwartz wrenched Henry's red Cardinals cap around so the brim faced backward. "Welcome to the weight room."

After hanging up with his parents, Henry had put on his coat and wandered out into the dark of the campus. Everything was impossibly quiet. He sat at the base of the Melville statue and looked out at the water. When he got home the answering machine was blinking. His parents, probably — they'd thought it over and decided it was time for him to come home.

Skrimmer! Football is over. Baseball starts now. Meet us at the VAC in half an hour. The side door by the dumpster will be open. Don't be late.

Henry put on shorts, grabbed Zero from the closet shelf, and ran through the mild night toward the VAC. He'd been waiting three months for Schwartz to call. Halfway there, already winded, he slowed to a walk. In those three months he'd done nothing more strenuous than washing dishes in the dining hall. He wished that college required you to use your body more, forced you to remember more often that life was lived in four dimensions. Maybe they could teach you to build your own dorm furniture or grow your own food. Instead everyone kept talking about the life of the mind — a concept, like many he had recently encountered, that seemed both appealing and beyond his grasp.

"Skrimmer, this is Adam Starblind," Schwartz said now. "Starblind, Skrimmer."

"So you're the guy Schwartz keeps talking about." Starblind wiped his palm on his shorts so they could shake. "The baseball messiah." He was much smaller than Schwartz but much larger than Henry, as became apparent when he peeled off his shimmery silver warm-up jacket. Two Asian pictographs adorned his right deltoid. Henry, who didn't have deltoids, glanced nervously around the room. Ominous machines crouched in the half-dark. Bringing Zero had been a grave mistake. He tried to hide it behind his back.

Starblind tossed his jacket aside. "Adam," Schwartz remarked, "you have the smoothest back of any man I've ever met."

"I should," Starblind said. "I just had it done."

"Done?"

"You know. Waxed."

"You're shitting me."

Starblind shrugged.

Schwartz turned to Henry. "Can you believe this, Skrimmer?" He rubbed his tightly shorn scalp, which was already receding to a widow's peak, with a huge hand. "Here I am battling to *keep* my hair, and Starblind here is dipping into the trust fund to have it removed."

Starblind, scoffing, addressed Henry too. "Keep his hair, he says. This is the hairiest man I know. Schwartzy, Madison would take one look at that back of yours and close up shop."

"Your back waxer's name is Madison?"

"He does good work."

"I don't know, Skrim." Schwartz shook his big head sadly. "Remember when it was easy to be a man? Now we're all supposed to look like Captain Abercrombie here. Six-pack abs, three percent body fat. All that crap. Me, I hearken back to a simpler time." Schwartz patted his thick, sturdy midriff. "A time when a hairy back *meant* something."

"Profound loneliness?" Starblind offered.

"Warmth. Survival. Evolutionary advantage. Back then, a man's wife and children would burrow into his back hair and wait out the winter. Nymphs would braid it and praise it in song. God's wrath waxed hot against the hairless tribes. Now all that's forgotten. But I'll tell you one thing: when the next ice age comes, the Schwartzes will be sitting pretty. Real pretty."

"That's Schwartzy." Starblind yawned, inspected his left biceps' lateral vein in one of the room's many mirrors. "Just living from ice age to ice age."

Schwartz held out a big hand. Henry realized that he wanted him to hand him his glove. No one but Henry had touched Zero in seven or eight years, maybe longer. He couldn't remember the last time. With a silent prayer he placed the glove in the big man's hand.

Schwartz slung it over his shoulder into a corner. "Lie down on that bench," he instructed. Henry lay down. Schwartz and Starblind, quick as a pit crew, pulled from the bar the heavy, wheel-sized plates Starblind had been lifting and replaced them with saucer-sized ones. "You've never lifted before?" asked Schwartz.

Henry shook his head no.

"Good. Then you don't have any of Starblind's crappy habits. Thumbs underneath, elbows in, spine relaxed. Ready? Go."

Half an hour later Henry threw up for the first time since boyhood, a weak quick cough that spilled a pool of pureed turkey onto the rubberized floor.

"Attaboy." Schwartz pulled a ring of keys from his pocket. "You two keep working." He returned with a wheeled yellow bucket full of soapy water and a long-yarned mop, which he used to swab up the mess, whistling all the while.

With each new exercise, Schwartz did a few reps to demonstrate proper form, then spotted Henry and Starblind, barking insults and instructions while they did their sets. "Coach Cox won't let me lift before baseball season," he explained. "It drives me nuts. But if I get too big up here" — he slapped himself on the shoulder — "I can't throw."

The session ended with skullcrushers.

"Come on, Skrim," Schwartz growled as Henry's arms began to quiver. "Make some goddamn noise."

"uh," Henry said. *"gr."*

"You call that noise?"

"Big arms," cheered Starblind. "Get big."

Henry's elbows separated, and the squiggle-shaped bar plummeted toward a spot between his eyes. Schwartz let it fall. The dull thud against Henry's forehead felt almost pleasant. He could taste a cool tang of iron filings on his tongue, feel the throb of a future bruise.

"Skullcrushers," Starblind said approvingly.

Schwartz tossed Henry his glove. "Good work tonight," he said. "Adam, tell the Skrimmer what he's won."

Starblind produced, from some dim corner, a gigantic plastic canister. *"SuperBoost Nine Thousand,"* he intoned in a game show announcer's baritone. *"The proven way to unlock your body's potential."*

"Three times a day," instructed Schwartz. "With milk. It's a supplement, meaning it supplements your regular diet. Don't skip any meals."

The next day, Henry could feel the soreness mounting throughout his dishwashing shift. When he returned to the room, a glass of milk heavy in each hand, Owen was seated behind his desk, dressed in white, picking broken twigs from a baggie.

"What's *that?*" Owen gestured toward the canister, which Henry had left atop the fridge.

"SuperBoost Nine Thousand."

"It looks like it came out of a hot-rod garage. Put it in the closet, will you? Behind the guest towels."

"Sure." Owen had a point: the black plastic tub didn't exactly fit the room's decor. The label's lightning-bolt letters slanted forward, trailing fire behind as they wrapped across a stylized photo of the most grotesquely muscled arm Henry had ever seen. "But first I have to try some."

Owen licked the fringe of a small piece of paper. "Try it how?"

"By mixing one heaping scoop of SuperBoost with eight ounces water or milk."

"You're going to *eat* it?"

Henry twisted the lid off its threads and peeled back the shiny aluminum seal. Inside, half buried in pallid powder like an abandoned beach toy, lay a clear plastic scoop. He dumped both glasses of milk into his quart-sized commemorative Aparicio Rodriguez cup, which Sophie had bought him on eBay for Christmas, and added two heaping scoops of SuperBoost.

Instead of sinking and dissolving, the powder floated on the milk's surface in a stubborn pile. Henry found a fork in his desk drawer and began to stir, but the powder cocooned around the tines. He beat at it faster and faster. The fork clanged against the cup. "Maybe you could do that elsewhere," Owen suggested. "Or not at all."

Henry stopped stirring and lifted the cup to his lips. He intended to down it in one gulp, but the sludgy mixture seemed to leaven in his stomach. When he set down the cup it was still almost full. "Can you see my body's potential being unlocked?"

Owen put on his glasses. "You're turning a little green," he said. "Maybe that's an intermediate step."

Two months later, when tryouts began, Henry didn't look much bigger in the mirror, but at least he didn't throw up anymore, and the weights he lifted were slightly less small. He arrived at the locker room an hour early. Two of his potential future teammates were already there. Schwartz sat shirtless in front of his locker, hunched over a thick textbook. In the corner, smoothing a pair of slacks on a hanger —

"Owen!" Henry was shocked. "What are you doing here?"

Owen looked at him as if he were daft. "Baseball tryouts begin today."

"I know, but —"

Coach Cox appeared in the doorway. He was Henry's height but thick-chested, with a strong square jaw in which he ground a wad of gum. He wore track pants and a Westish Baseball sweatshirt. "Schwartz," he said gruffly as he stroked his clipped black mustache, "how are those knees?"

"Not bad, Coach." Schwartz stood up to greet Coach Cox with a combination handshake-hug. "I want you to meet Henry Skrimshander."

"Skrimshander." Coach Cox nodded as he wrung Henry's hand in a painful grip. "Schwartz tells me you plan to give Tennant a run for his money."

Lev Tennant, a senior, was the starting shortstop and team cocaptain. Schwartz kept telling Henry he could beat him out — it had become a kind of mantra for their evening workouts. "Tennant!" Schwartz would yell as he leaned over Henry, dripping sweat into Henry's open mouth while Henry struggled with the skullcrusher bar. "Beat out Tennant!" Henry didn't know how Schwartz could sweat so much when he wasn't even lifting, and he certainly didn't know how he was supposed to beat out Tennant. He'd seen the smooth, sharklike way Tennant moved around campus, devouring girls' smiles. "I'll do my best, sir," Henry said now.

"See that you do." Coach Cox turned to Owen, extended a hand. "Ron Cox."

"Owen Dunne," Owen said. "Right fielder. I trust you don't object to having a gay man on your team."

"The only thing I object to," Coach Cox replied, "is Schwartz playing football. It's bad for his knees."

Tryouts would take place inside the VAC, but first Coach Cox ordered the assembled crowd out into the cold. "A little roadwork," he instructed them. "Around the lighthouse and back."

Henry tried to tally up the bodies as they filed outside, but everybody kept shifting around, and anyway he didn't know how many guys would make the team. He ran faster than he'd ever run and finished the four miles in the first group, alongside a surprisingly nimble Schwartz and behind only Starblind, who'd sped ahead in the first hundred meters and disappeared from view. The second group included most of the team's established players, including Tennant and Tom Meccini, the captains. Schwartz's roommate, Demetrius Arsch, who weighed at least 260 and smoked half a pack a day between the end of football season and the beginning of baseball, brought up the rear. At least everyone assumed he'd brought up the rear, until Owen cruised into view.

"Dunne!" Coach Cox bellowed.

"Coach Cox!"

"Where the goddamn hell've you been?"

"Doing a little roadwork," Owen reminded him. "Around the lighthouse and back."

"You mean to tell me"—Coach Cox planted a hand between the shoulder blades of Arsch, who was bent over, gasping for breath—"that you can't beat Meat here in a footrace?"

Owen bent down until he and Arsch came face-to-face—Arsch's damp and fragrantly purple, his own composed and dry. "I bet I could beat him now," he said. "He looks tired."

But when batting practice began, Owen knocked one line drive after another back up the middle of the batting cage. Sal Phlox, who was feeding balls into the old-fashioned machine, kept having to duck behind his protective screen. "Get out of there, Dunne," grumbled Coach Cox. "Before you hurt someone."

Henry had never taken grounders on artificial turf before; it was like living inside a video game. The ball never hit a rock or the lip of the grass, but the synthetic fibers could impart some wicked spin. In four days of tryouts he didn't miss a single ball. When the roster was posted, four freshpersons had made the team: Adam Starblind, Rick O'Shea, Owen Dunne, and Henry Skrimshander.

5

Six weeks later, the Harpooners strode across the tarmac at the tiny Green Bay airport, wind whipping their faces, WAD-emblazoned bags slung over their shoulders. Everyone but Henry nodded to the beat of his headphones' music. It was a clear, cold day, the temperature in the twenties, but they were dressed for their destination, no jackets or sweaters allowed. The plane's propellers pureed the air. Dry week-old snow swept across the runway in windblown sine curves. Henry threw back his shoulders and walked as tall as his five-nine frame would allow, just like every road-tripping athlete he'd ever seen on TV. They were headed to Florida to play baseball, all expenses paid.

They were staying at a Motel 4 an hour inland from the Clearwater Municipal Baseball Complex. The older guys slept two to a bed; the freshpersons slept on cots. Henry was assigned to Schwartz and Arsch's room. He lay awake the whole first night, listening to Meat's plane-engine snoring and the tortured cries of the springs as the two sophomores, five hundred pounds between them, battled in their sleep for control of the supposedly queen-size bed. Henry closed his eyes, wrapped the smoky vinyl drapes around his head, and counted the minutes until their first real outdoor practice.

The next morning, a Saturday, they loaded onto the bus and drove to the complex — eight plush and lovely diamonds laid out in adjacent circles of four diamonds each. The dew twinkled in the buttery Florida sunlight. Henry, as he jogged out to short for infield drills, spun and launched into a backflip, staggering only slightly on the landing.

"Damn, Skrim!" yelled Starblind from center field. "Where'd that come from?"

Henry didn't know. He tried to remember the footwork he'd used, but the moment had passed. Sometimes your body just did what it wanted to.

"You should try out for gymnastics," Tennant said. "You're about the right size."

During batting practice, Henry scaled the left-field fence and stood in the parking lot to shag the amazing moonshots that Two Thirty Toover kept hitting. "Welcome back, Jim," Coach Cox cheered, as ball after ball soared easily over the wall. "We missed you."

Mild-eyed Jim Toover had just returned from a Mormon mission to Argentina. Jim was six-six and had a long, powerful swing. They called him Two Thirty because that was when the Harpooners took batting practice before home games. Now Henry was standing thirty feet beyond the fence, and the balls were raining down as if dropped from the clouds. Fans hustled out to the parking lot to move their cars. The teams on adjacent diamonds abandoned their drills to watch.

"But we wouldn't call him Two Thirty," Schwartz told Henry, "if he did it during games."

"What does he do during games?"

"He chokes."

That afternoon, the Harpooners played the Lions of Vermont State. DON'T CROSS THE STATE LIONS, read one long-traveled mother's sign. Henry sat in the dugout between Owen and Rick O'Shea. Starblind had already been penciled into the starting lineup, as the center fielder and leadoff hitter.

Owen took a battery-powered reading light from his bag, clipped it to the brim of his cap, and opened a book called *The Rubáiyát of Omar Khayyám*. Henry and Rick would have found themselves doing shuttle drills and scrubbing helmets if they'd even thought about reading during a game, but Coach Cox had already stopped punishing Owen for his sins. Owen posed a conundrum where discipline was concerned, because he didn't seem to care whether he played or not, and when screamed at he would listen and nod with interest, as if gathering data for a paper about apoplexy. He jogged during sprints, walked during jogs, napped in the outfield. Before long Coach Cox stopped screaming. In fact, Owen became his favorite player, the only one he didn't have to worry about. When practice was filled with miscues, as it usually was, he would whisper mordant remarks to Owen from the corner of his mouth. Owen didn't want anything from Coach Cox—not a starting job, or a better spot in the batting order, or even any advice—and so Coach Cox could afford to treat him as an equal. Much the same way, perhaps, that a priest appreciates his lone agnostic parishioner, the one who doesn't want to be saved but keeps showing up for the stained glass and the singing. "There's so much standing around," Owen said when Henry asked him what he liked about the game. "And pockets in the uniforms."

By the sixth inning against Vermont State, Henry could barely restrain his restlessness. "Kindly desist," Owen said as Henry's knees jittered and twitched. "I'm trying to read."

"Sorry." Henry stopped, but as soon as he turned his attention back to the game his knees started up again. He flipped a handful of sunflower seeds into his mouth and precision-spat the splintered shells into a little pool of Gatorade on the floor. He turned his hat backward. He spun a baseball in his right hand and flipped it to his left. "Doesn't this drive you nuts?" he asked Rick.

"Yes," Rick said. "Cut it out."

"No, not me. Sitting on the bench."

Rick tested the bench with both palms, as if it were a floor-sample mattress. "Seems okay to me."

"Aren't you dying to be out there?"

Rick shrugged. "Two Thirty's only a junior, and Coach Cox loves him. If he does half of what he's capable of, I'll be spending the next two years right here." He looked at Henry. "You, on the other hand, have Tennant worked into quite a lather."

"I do not," Henry said.

"Yeah, sure. You didn't hear him blabbing at Meccini last night while I was lying in my cot, pretending to be asleep."

"What'd he say?"

Rick looked both ways to make sure no one else was listening, then segued into his Tennant impression. "Bleeping Schwartz. Can't stand the fact that I'm the captain of this bleeping team. So what does he do? Digs up that little piece of bleep who catches every bleeping thing you hit at him, that's what. Then trains the little bleep night and day, and proselytizes Coach Cox all bleeping winter about what a fantastic bleeping player he is. Why? So the little bleep can steal *my* bleeping job, and Schwartz, who's only a bleeping sophomore, for bleep's sake, can declare himself the bleeping king of the team."

Owen looked up from his book. "Tennant said *proselytize?*"

Rick nodded. "And *bleeping.*"

"Well, he has reason to fear. Henry's performance has been outstanding."

"Come on," Henry protested. "Tennant's way better than me."

"Lev can hit," Owen said. "But his defense is slipshod. He lacks the Skrimshander panache."

"I didn't realize Tennant disliked Schwartzy so much," said Henry, by which he meant, I didn't realize Tennant disliked *me* so much. No one had ever called him a little bleep before. He'd noticed that Lev treated him coldly during drills, but he'd chalked this up to simple indifference.

"What, you live under a rock?" Rick said. "Those two can't stand each other. I wouldn't be surprised to see things come to a head pretty soon."

"Verily," Owen agreed.

The game was tied in the ninth, Tennant on first base, when Two Thirty stepped to the plate. He screwed his back foot into the dirt, lifted his bat high above his head. Already today he'd hit a single and a double. Maybe Argentina had done him some good.

"Jim Toover!" Owen cheered. "You are skilled! We exhort you!"

Ball one. Ball two.

"How could anyone miss that strike zone?" Rick asked.

Ball three.

Henry looked toward third base to see if Coach Cox would put the take sign on. "Letting him swing away," he reported.

"Really?" Rick said. "That sounds like a bad i—," but his words were interrupted by an earsplitting *ping* of ball against aluminum bat. The ball became a speck in the pale-blue sky and carried deep, deep into the parking lot. Henry thought he heard a windshield shatter, but he wasn't sure. They rushed from the dugout to greet Jim at home plate.

Rick shook his head in astonishment. "Now I'll never get off the bench."

"Indeed!" Owen gave Two Thirty a celebratory smack on the ass with his *Omar Khayyám*. "Indeed!"

With that win the Harpooners, for the first time in anyone's memory, including Coach Cox's, were undefeated. They celebrated at the all-you-can-eat Chinese buffet in the strip mall near their motel. Then, over the next three days, they lost their next five games. Tennant was booting every grounder that came his way. Two Thirty struck out repeatedly. As the losses mounted, Coach Cox stood in the third-base coaching box with crossed arms, digging a moat in the dirt with the toe of his cleat and filling it with a steady stream of tobacco juice, as if to protect himself from so much ineptitude. The mood in the dugout turned from optimistic, to determined, to gloomy, to gloomy with a venomous edge. On the bench during their seventh game, Rick hid his phone in his glove and surreptitiously scrolled through the Facebook photos that their classmates had posted that day from West Palm, Miami, Daytona, Panama

City Beach—album after album of bikinied girls, blue ocean, brightly colored drinks. "So close," he moaned, shaking his head. "But so, so far away."

"Owen," Henry said excitedly, "I think Coach wants you to hit for Meccini."

Owen closed *The Voyage of the Beagle,* on which he had recently embarked. "Really?"

"Runners on first and second," Rick said. "I bet he wants you to bunt."

"What's the bunt sign?"

"Two tugs on the left earlobe," Henry told him. "But first he has to give the indicator, which is squeeze the belt. But if he goes to his cap with either hand or says your first name, that's the wipe-off, and then you have to wait and see whether—"

"Forget it," Owen said. "I'll just bunt." He grabbed a bat, ambled to home plate, nodded politely at Coach Cox's gesticulations, and pushed a perfect bunt past the pitcher. The shortstop's throw nipped him by a quarter step, and Owen trotted back to the dugout to receive congratulations from his teammates. This was Henry's favorite baseball custom: when a player hit a home run, his teammates were at liberty to ignore him, but when he sacrificed himself to move a runner, he received a long line of high fives. "Sweet bunt," Henry said as he and Owen bumped fists.

"Thanks." Owen picked up his book. "That pitcher's not bad-looking."

Throughout the week the Harpooners slept, ate, traveled, practiced, and played as a unit. If they weren't at the fields or their crappy fleabag motel, they were tethered to their decrepit rented bus. The most inconsequential decisions, like whether to eat dinner at Cracker Barrel or Ye Olde Buffet, took hours. "I love it when I have to take a dump," Rick said. "It's the only time I get to be alone."

As the losing continued, the constant togetherness grew tougher to take. On the too-lengthy trips between the diamond and their motel, the juniors and seniors sat in the back of the bus with Tennant, the sophomores and freshpersons up front with Schwartz. Only Jim Toover stretched his endless limbs across the empty seats of no-man's-land; being six-six and Mormon lifted him above the fray.

Meanwhile Tennant's defense was growing worse with each passing day. His face hardened into a haggard, pinched expression, and he radiated a black energy whenever Henry came near. Between games Coach Cox would confer with Tennant quietly, a hand on his shoulder, while Tennant nodded and looked at his shoes. "He's pressing," Rick said after Tennant bobbled a toss at second, botching a sure double play. "Look at his face."

Owen cleared his throat, pressed a hand to his chest. "For at his back he always hears / Henry's footsteps hurrying near."

On Thursday night, Henry and Schwartz reclined in stiff plastic-weave chairs by the scum-topped, unswimmable pool of the Motel 4. As the earth cooled, Henry's senses expanded to take in what they normally missed: the scutter of roaches and geckos over the tile, the flit of moths against the blue security lights, a whiff of distant water on the breeze. Schwartz paged through a phonebook-sized LSAT prep guide, though he wouldn't be taking the LSAT for eighteen months. "You know, it's only my first year," Henry said. "I can wait."

"Maybe *you* can." Schwartz didn't look up. "But the rest of us can't. We're one and seven. We need you out there."

"Maybe if somebody told Lev he didn't have anything to worry about, he'd relax and play better."

"What do you think Coach Cox is saying during their little pow-wows? He spends half his time stroking Tennant's ego, telling him he's the man. But Lev's not stupid. He knows you're the better player."

"But I'm not, really. Tennant's just playing tight."

"He's playing tight because he's a crappy shortstop. He did this last year too. Makes errors and mopes about it. His attitude's abysmal. It has nothing to do with you, Skrimmer. Almost nothing, anyway."

"I hope not."

"It has nothing to do with hope either." Schwartz slapped his LSAT book shut. "It has to do with Coach Cox. I respect Coach a lot, but he's too loyal to guys just because they've been here for a while. Why be loyal to a bunch of losers? I'm sick of losing. This is America. Winners win. Losers get booted. You should be in there, and Rick should be in there, and the Buddha should probably be in there too. If only to get you ready."

"Tennant's a senior," Henry said uncertainly. "I can wait till next year."

"Wait till tomorrow," Schwartz said. "That's all I ask."

The next afternoon, they played Vermont State, the team against which they'd scored their only victory. The Harpooners led 4 to 1 with an inning to play. But the first Lion batter of the ninth stroked a routine grounder to short, and Tennant couldn't get the ball out of his glove. It was just one play, but it seemed to remind the Harpooners that they were losers and destined to lose. Four batters later the game was over. As his teammates filed grimly to the locker room, Henry lingered in the dugout, picking up scraps of trash and gazing at the infield, which looked especially green and regal in the afternoon sun.

When he reached the locker room, Schwartz had Tennant in a head-lock. A steady stream of blood dripped from his nose into Tennant's hair. "Try that again!" he roared as he rammed the crown of Tennant's head into the metal lockers. "Try it one more time!"

"Get him off me!" Tennant pleaded, his voice muffled by Schwartz's meaty forearm. "Get this crazy bastard off me!"

"You crazy bastard!" Owen cheered. "Get off him!"

No one moved to intervene, and the scene hung in an almost peaceful stasis, Schwartz slowly banging Tennant's head against the lockers, until Coach Cox charged in from the coaches' room, his unbuttoned jersey flapping around his white briefs. He and Arsch pried Tennant from Schwartz's grasp.

Henry braced for a tirade from Coach Cox. But Coach Cox didn't scream at all. "Schwartz, go wash your face," he said, his tone that of a weary parent at the end of an exasperating day. Schwartz walked toward the bathroom, head held high, not bothering to check the flow of blood down over his lips and chin. He returned with a wad of toilet paper protruding from one nostril and held his hand out to Tennant. Tennant studied it for a moment before shaking it firmly.

"You two take the night off." Coach Cox cast his gaze around the room. "You loose, Arsch?"

"Like a goose, Coach."

"Henry, you loose?"

"—"

"Henry?"

"Sure, Coach."

Henry heard the story from Rick and Owen during warm-ups: While Henry picked up paper cups from the dugout floor, Schwartz walked past Tennant's locker and whispered something under his breath. Tennant whirled and threw a wild punch that connected with Schwartzy's nose. His head snapped back and blood poured down. "Schwartzy looked pissed for about half a second, while his head was still bouncing around," said Rick. "But then he sort of smiled, like getting socked by Tennant was exactly what he wanted."

"I think it *is* what he wanted," Owen said.

Rick nodded. "Even when he was banging Lev's dome against the lockers, you could tell he wasn't trying to hurt him. Strictly pro forma."

"He orchestrated the whole episode to get you in the game," Owen told Henry. "He even took a punch in the nose for you. You should feel flattered."

It seemed far-fetched to Henry. Then again, Schwartz had promised he'd be in the lineup, and here he was, in the lineup. Two hours later, as he jogged out onto the diamond under the lights, he felt giddy and light-headed. He bounced on the balls of his feet, windmilled his arms, dropped into a squat to slap the ground. Starblind collected a fresh ball from the ump, went into the night's first windup. *"Adam Adam Adam,"*

Henry chanted. He danced a step to the left and back to the right, kicked up each knee, pounded his fist into Zero, leaped, and landed in his crouch.

Ball low. Starblind called time and motioned to him. Henry sprinted to the mound.

"Are we at a dance party?" Starblind asked. "I'm trying to pitch over here."

"Sorry sorry sorry," Henry said. "Sorry."

Starblind looked at him, spat into the grass. "Are you hyperventilating?"

"Not really," Henry said. "Maybe a little."

But when the game's second batter lofted a blooper down the left-field line, Henry turned his back to the infield and took off, unable to see the ball but guessing its landing point based on how it had come off the bat. Nobody else was going to get there; it was up to him. He stretched out his glove as he bellyflopped on the grass, lifted his eyes just in time to see the ball drop in. Even the opposing fans cheered.

Putting Henry at shortstop — it was like taking a painting that had been shoved in a closet and hanging it in the ideal spot. You instantly forgot what the room had looked like before. By the fourth inning he was directing the other fielders, waving them left or right, correcting their tactical miscues. *The shortstop is a source of stillness at the center of the defense. He projects this stillness and his teammates respond.* The Harpooners made only one error, by far their fewest of the trip. Most of their tiny, grating mistakes disappeared. They lost by a run, but Coach Cox was grinning after the game.

The next day, their last in Florida, Henry started at shortstop and Tennant moved to third. Instead of bitter or angry, Tennant seemed relieved. When Henry struck out, as he did too often — his hitting was nowhere near as good as his defense — Tennant cuffed him on the helmet and told him to hang in there. They won the game, and though a 2 and 9 Florida trip wasn't great, an odd kind of optimism was creeping in.

After his freshperson year ended, Henry stayed at Westish to train with Schwartz. They met at five thirty every morning. When Henry could run up and down all the stairs in the football stadium without stopping, Schwartz bought him a weighted vest. When he could run five seven-minute miles, Schwartz made him do it on the sand. When he could do it on the sand, Schwartz made him do it with lake water lapping at his knees. Medicine balls, blocking sleds, yoga, bicycles, ropes, tree branches, steel trash cans, plyometrics — no implements or ideas were too mundane or exotic. At seven thirty, the sun still low over the lake, Henry showered and headed to the dining hall to wash breakfast dishes for the summer-school kids. After his shift he walked to Westish Field, where Schwartz set up the pitching machine and the video camera. Henry hit ball after ball until he could hardly lift his arms. Then they went to the VAC to lift weights. In the evenings they played on a summer team in Appleton.

Henry had never felt so happy. Freshperson year had been one thing, an adventure, an exhilaration, all in all a success, but it had also been exhausting, a constant struggle and adjustment and tumult. Now he was locked in. Every day that summer had the same framework, the alarm at the same time, meals and workouts and shifts and SuperBoost at the same times, over and over, and it was that sameness, that repetition, that gave life meaning. He savored the tiny variations, the incremental improvements — tuna fish on his salad instead of turkey; two extra reps on the bench press. Every move he made had purpose. While they worked out, Schwartz would recite lines from his favorite philosophers, Marcus Aurelius and Epictetus — they were Schwartz's personal Aparicios — and Henry felt that he understood. *Every day is a war.* Yes, yes it was. *The key is to keep company only with people who uplift you, whose presence calls forth your best.* Done: there was only one of those. He was becoming a baseball player.

By the time his sophomore season began Henry had gained twelve pounds. He was still one of the smaller guys on the team, but the bat felt different in his hands, lighter and more lively. He batted .348 and was named the first-team Upper Midwestern Small Colleges Athletic Conference shortstop. In thirty-one games he didn't make a single error. He was still shy in class and around campus—he never went to the bars and rarely to parties; there was too much work to do—but among his teammates he flourished. He loved those guys and felt good in their midst, and now that he was undisputedly the best player on the team, he became something of a leader. He wasn't loud like Schwartz, but everyone listened when he spoke. The Harpooners finished .500 for the first time in a decade.

That summer, inspirited by success, he worked even harder. Instead of five thirty, he got up at five. Instead of five meals a day, he ate six. His mind felt clear and pure. The ball rocketed off his bat. He was coming to understand certain parts of *The Art of Fielding* in a new way, from the inside out, as if the great Aparicio were less an oracle than an equal.

He acquired a protégé too—Izzy Avila, a player Schwartz had recruited from his old neighborhood in South Chicago. Schwartz loved Westish, and he both loved and hated where he came from, and he wanted to help guys get from one to the other. Izzy was a perfect candidate, a gifted athlete and decent student who nonetheless needed the help. His two older brothers had also been gifted athletes—now one lived with their mom and the other was in prison. "He's a little raw," Schwartz said. "He can ride the bench this year, learn some things. Then play second next year after Ajay graduates. Then when you're gone, he's the new shortstop."

Izzy feared and respected Schwartz, but he worshipped Henry. When they took their daily ground balls, he tried to copy Henry's every move. When Henry talked about the subtleties of infield positioning, Izzy, unlike the other Harpooners, understood. When he didn't understand, he studied until he did. They worked relays, rundowns, bunts, feints, pickoffs, double plays. Henry bought him a copy of *The Art of Fielding* for his birthday.

But Izzy wasn't ready, mentally or physically, for Henry's toughest workouts. Henry trained speed with Starblind, the fastest guy on the team. He trained strength with Schwartz, the strongest. When those guys went home, he went to yoga class with Owen. Then he trained some more. He fielded grounders in his mind until he fell asleep. He got up at five and did it again.

By the start of his junior season, he'd become something Westish College had never seen: a *prospect*. He hit a home run in the second game of the Florida trip, another in the fourth game, a third in the sixth. By then the scouts were loitering in their Ray-Bans behind the backstop. Fans showed up too, local baseball lovers who'd heard about the must-see kid with the magic glove. By week's end the team was 10 and 2, Henry was hitting .519, and he'd moved within a single game of tying Aparicio Rodriguez's NCAA record for most consecutive errorless games. The flight back to Wisconsin was one long celebration.

6

In the spring of 1880, Herman Melville, then sixty years old, was working as a customs inspector at the Port of New York, having proved unable to support his family through literary work. He was not famous and earned almost nothing from royalties. His first-born son, Malcolm, had committed suicide thirteen years earlier. Melville's in-laws, among others, feared for his health and regarded him as insane. On a national scale, the horrific, bloody rift he'd prophesied in *Moby-Dick* and *Benito Cereno* (both long out of print in 1880) had come to pass, and, as he had been perhaps the first to foresee, the anguish had not ceased with the end of the war.

Not surprising, then, that the great writer might have found himself growing grim about the mouth, as his best-known protagonist put it; that he might have deemed it high time to get back to sea. Too old, impecunious, and hemmed in by family matters to make any more ocean crossings, Melville settled upon a more modest adventure. The spring thaw came early that year, and in March he boarded a ship headed up the Erie Canal, to tour the Great Lakes and thereby reprise alone a trip he had taken with his friend Eli Fly forty years before. Scholars have made much of Melville's pilgrimage to Jerusalem (1856–57), but this later domestic voyage went unmentioned until 1969, when an undergraduate at Westish College — a small, venerable but already in those days slightly decrepit liberal arts school on the western shore of Lake Michigan—made a remarkable discovery.

The undergraduate's name was Guert Affenlight. He was not, at the time, a student of literature. Rather, he was a biology major and the starting quarterback for the Westish Sugar Maples. He had grown up in the undulant, plainsy part of the state, south and west of Madison, the fourth and by far the youngest son of small-time dairy farmers. He'd been accepted to Westish in part to play football, and though the school, then as now, did not offer athletic scholarships, he was rewarded for his gridiron toils with a cushy job in the college library. Officially he was supposed to shelve books for twelve hours a week, but it was understood that the bulk of that time could be spent studying.

Affenlight enjoyed having the run of the library after hours, and frequently he neither studied nor shelved but simply poked around. Late one evening in the fall of his junior year, he found a thin sheaf of yellowed paper, tucked between two brittle magazines in the library's non-circulating bowels. The faded handwriting on the first page announced that it was a lecture given by one "H. Melville" on "this first instant of April 1880." Affenlight, sensing something, turned the page. A visceral charge went through him when he read the opening sentence:

> It was not before my twenty-fifth year, by which time I had returned to my native New York from a four years' voyage aboard whalers and frigates, having seen much of the world, at least the watery parts, and certain verdant corners deemed uncivil by our Chattywags and Mumbledywumps, that I took up my pen in earnest, and began to live; since then, scarcely a week has gone by when I do not feel myself unfolding within myself.

Upon his first reading, Affenlight failed to untangle the syntax before the semicolon, but that final clause embedded itself swiftly in his soul.

He too wanted to unfold within himself, and to feel himself so doing; it thrilled him, this oracular promise of a wiser, wilder life. He'd never traveled beyond the Upper Midwest, nor written anything a teacher hadn't required, but this single magical sentence made him want to roam the world and write books about what he found. He snuck the pages into his knapsack and back to his room in Phumber Hall.

The stated topic of the lecture was Shakespeare, but H. Melville, excusing himself by the sly pronouncement that "Shakespeare is Life," used the bard as reason to speak of whatever he wished — Tahiti, Reconstruction, his trip up the Hudson, Webster, Hawthorne, Michigan, Solomon, marriage, divorce, melancholia, awe, factory conditions, the foliage of Pittsfield, friendship, poverty, chowder, war, death — all with a scattered, freewheeling ferocity that would have done little to refute his in-laws' allegations of mental imbalance. The more deeply Affenlight imbibed the lecture, hidden away in his dorm room from any influence that might shake him out of his strange mood, the more convinced he became that it had been delivered extemporaneously, without so much as a note. It astonished and humbled him to think that a mind could grow so rich that its every gesture would come to seem profound.

The next day Affenlight left his room and went in search of an appropriate authority. Professor Cary Oxtin, the college's expert in nineteenth-century America, perused the pages slowly in Affenlight's presence, tapping his pen against his chin. Upon finishing, Oxtin declared that though the prose was unmistakably Melville's, the handwriting was not. The lecture must have been transcribed — and who knew how reliably — by some attentive listener. He added that by 1880 Melville counted as little more than a travel writer past his prime, and so it was not implausible that his lecture had been misplaced and that his visit to Westish had passed unnoticed by history.

Affenlight left the pages with Professor Oxtin, who shipped copies of them eastward, to the counters and compilers of such things. Thus they entered the scholarly record. Several months later, Oxtin published a long essay on Melville's Midwestern trip in the *Atlantic Monthly*—an essay in which Affenlight's name did not appear.

At the end of that dismal '69 season—the Sugar Maples won just one game—Affenlight turned in his helmet. Football had been a diversion; he had a purpose now, and the purpose was to read. It was too late to change majors, but each night when his problem sets were finished, he devoted himself to the works of H. Melville. He began at the beginning, with *Typee,* and read through to *Billy Budd.* Then the biographies, the correspondence, the critical texts. When he'd absorbed every word of Melvilleania in the Westish library, he started over with Hawthorne, to whom *Moby-Dick* had been dedicated. Somewhere in there he'd stopped shaving as well—these were the opening days of the '70s, and many of his male classmates wore beards, but Affenlight imagined his as something different: not a hippie beard but an antique, writerly one, of the kind that graced the faded daguerreotypes in the books he was learning to love.

He had also, from his first days on campus, fallen in love with Lake Michigan—having grown up in landlocked farmland, he was amazed by its vastness and the combination of its steadiness and its constant fluctuations. Walking along its shore called forth some of the same deep feelings that his reading of Melville did, and that reading explained and deepened his love of the water, which in turn deepened his love of the books. He resolved to get himself to sea. After graduation, he managed to display enough knowledge of marine biology to win an almost unpaid job—an internship, in today's parlance—aboard a U.S. government ship bound for the South Pacific. For the next four years he saw much of the world, at least the watery parts, and learned how well Melville had captured the monotony-in-motion of life under sail. He woke in the night, every three hours, to record data from a dozen instruments. With the same regularity he recorded his lonely thoughts in graph-paper notebooks, trying as best he could to make them sound profound.

After those four years he returned to the Midwest. He'd turned twenty-five, the Age of Unfolding, and it was time to write a novel, the way his hero had. He moved to a cheap apartment in Chicago and set to work, but even as the pages accumulated, despair set in. It was easy enough to write a sentence, but if you were going to create a *work of art,* the way Melville had, each sentence needed to fit perfectly with the one that preceded it, and the unwritten one that would follow. And each of those sentences needed to square with the ones on either side, so that three became five and five became seven, seven became nine, and whichever sentence he was writing became the slender fulcrum on which the whole precarious edifice depended. That sentence could contain anything, *anything,* and so it promised the kind of absolute freedom that, to Affenlight's mind, belonged to the artist and the artist alone. And yet that sentence was also beholden to the book's very first one, and its last unwritten one, and every sentence in between. Every phrase, every word, exhausted him. He thought maybe the problem was the noise of the city, and his dull day job, and his drinking; he gave up his room and rented an outbuilding on an Iowa farm run by hippies. There, alone with his anxious thoughts, he felt much worse.

He returned to Chicago, got a job tending bar, resumed his reading. With each new writer he began at the beginning and proceeded to the end, just as he'd done with Melville. When he'd exhausted the American nineteenth century, he expanded his reach. By absorbing so many books he was trying to purge his own failure as a writer. It wasn't working, but he feared what would happen if he stopped.

On his thirtieth birthday he borrowed a car and drove up to Westish. Professor Oxtin, thank God, was still alive and compos mentis. Affenlight, with a calm determination that stemmed from desperation, reminded the old man of the capstone that the Melville lecture had placed on his career, and of Oxtin's failure to credit him in the *Atlantic* article. The old man smiled blandly, not quite willing to admit or refute the charge, and asked what Affenlight wanted.

Affenlight told him. The old professor lifted an eyebrow and walked him down to the campus watering hole. There, over beers, he administered an impromptu oral examination that ranged from Chaucer through Nabokov but dealt mainly with Melville and his contemporaries. Satisfied, perhaps even impressed, the old man placed the call.

That September Affenlight trimmed his beard, bought a suit, and began Harvard's doctoral program in the History of American Civilization. There he became for the first time—excepting a few lucky moments on the football field—a star. Most of his fellow students were younger, and none had achieved so desperate a grasp on the literature of his chosen period. Affenlight could drink more coffee, not to mention whiskey, than the rest of them put together. *Monomaniacal,* they called him, an Ahab joke; and when he spoke in seminar—which he did incessantly, having suddenly much to say—they nodded their heads in agreement. Thirty-page papers rolled out of his typewriter in the time it had taken to write a single paragraph of his not-quite-forgotten novel.

At first, Affenlight felt uneasy about his newfound sense of ease. He considered himself a failed writer, nothing more, and there didn't seem to be much honor or grandeur in having read some books. But soon he decided—whether because it was true or because he needed it to be true—that academia was a world worth conquering. There were fellowships to win, journals to publish in, famous professors to impress. Whatever he applied for, he got; whatever he hinted he might apply for, his classmates shied away from. His successes were social as well. He'd always been tall, square-shouldered, and striking; now he had a purpose, an aura, a name that preceded him. *The Cambridge ladies come and go / from Guert's flat at 50 Bow.* That was another joke of his classmates, and it was true.

He wrote his dissertation in the kind of white heat in which he'd always imagined writing a novel—the kind of white heat in which his hero Melville, over six torrid months in a barn in Western Massachusetts, had written the greatest novel the world had ever seen. The dissertation, a study of the homosocial and the homoerotic in nineteenth-century

American letters, turned into a book, *The Sperm-Squeezers* (1987), and the book turned into a sensation: academically influential, widely translated, and reviewed in the *Times* and *Time* ("witty and readable," "augurs a new era of criticism," "contains signs of genius"). It wasn't *Moby-Dick*, but it sold more copies in its first year than The Book had, and it became a touchstone in the culture wars. At thirty Affenlight had been nobody; at thirty-seven he was debating Allan Bloom on CNN.

Just as abruptly, he'd become a father. While preparing the book for publication, he'd been dating a woman named Sarah Coowe, an infectious-disease specialist at MGH. They were evenly matched in many ways: sharp-dressed, sharp-tongued, and devoted to their careers and personal freedoms to the exclusion of any serious interest in so-called romance. They spent ten months together. A few weeks after they broke up — Sarah initiated the split — she called to say that she was pregnant. "It's mine?" asked Affenlight. "He or she," replied Sarah, "is mostly mine."

They named the child Pella — that was Affenlight's idea, though Sarah certainly had the final say. For those first couple of years, Affenlight conspired as often as he could to show up at Sarah and Pella's Kendall Square townhouse with expensive takeout and a new toy. He was fascinated with his daughter, with the sheer reality of her, a beautiful something where before there'd been nothing. He hated kissing her good-bye; and yet he relished, couldn't keep himself from relishing, the total quiet of his own townhouse when he walked in, the scattered books and papers and lack of baby-proofing.

Soon after Pella turned three, Sarah received a grant to go to Uganda, and Pella came to stay with Affenlight for the summer. In August came the news: Sarah's jeep had rolled off an embankment, and she was dead. Pella was half an orphan, and he was a full-time father.

After a perfunctory stint as an assistant professor, during which a series of winks and perks from the administration kept Stanford and Yale at bay, Affenlight was awarded tenure. He never mustered another major project like *The Sperm-Squeezers,* but his lectures were the department's most popular, and the grad students vied fiercely for his favor. He reviewed histories for *The New Yorker,* stockpiled teaching awards, and kept up with his reading. He became the head of the English Department and a fixture on the *Boston* magazine Most Eligible Bachelor list. Meanwhile he raised Pella, or at least stood by while Harvard raised her; the entire school seemed to consider her their charge. He sculled on the Charles to stay in shape. He took the Cambridge ladies to the opera. He thought he would do such things forever.

Then, in February of 2002, while Pella was in eighth grade, the phone in his office rang. Affenlight, rattled by what was proposed, dumped his espresso on a stack of senior theses. The interviews and vetting would take months, but that first phone call so unnerved him that he knew it was going to happen. Never again would he stride through the Yard with a graduate student at each elbow, extending the seminar as the sun went down. Never again would he hop the shuttle to LaGuardia just for kicks. Never again would his recent publication record bedevil his sleep. He was headed home.

7

Guert Affenlight, sixty years old, president of Westish College, tapped an Italian loafer on the warped maple floorboards of his office on the ground floor of Scull Hall, swirled a last drop of light-shot scotch in his glass. On the love seat sat Bruce Gibbs, the chair of the trustees. It was the last afternoon of March, the eighth year of Affenlight's tenure.

Besides Affenlight's desk and the love seat, the room contained two wooden spindle-backed Westish-insignia chairs, two wooden filing cabinets, and a credenza devoted to dark liquor. The built-in floor-to-ceiling bookshelves were filled with leather-bound volumes of and about the American nineteenth century, a drab but lovely sea of browns and olives and faded blacks, alongside neat rows of navy binders and ledgers related to the business of Westish College, and the brushed-steel stereo through whose hidden speakers Affenlight listened to his favorite operas. He kept his more colorful collection of postwar theory and fiction upstairs in his study, along with the handful of truly valuable books he owned — early editions of *Walden, A Connecticut Yankee,* and a few minor Melville novels, as well as The Book. The room contained so many bookshelves that there was space for only one piece of art, a black-and-white handpainted sign Affenlight had commissioned years ago that constituted one of his prized possessions: NO SUICIDES PERMITTED HERE, it read, AND NO SMOKING IN THE PARLOR.

Gibbs's walking stick, which he never called a cane, was propped on the love seat's arm. He sank deeper into the leather, swirled the amber liquid in his tumbler, gazed down at the lone melting cube. "Peaty," he said. "Nice."

Affenlight's scotch was long gone, but to pour another would be to encourage Gibbs to linger. The chill coming off the windowsill at his back reminded him how much he wanted to be out there, at the baseball diamond, before driving down to Milwaukee to pick up Pella from the airport.

Gibbs cleared his throat. "I'm confused, Guert. I thought we'd agreed to postpone new projects until we recapitalized. We got hammered in the markets, we're hemorrhaging financial aid, and"—he met Affenlight's eyes steadily—"there's almost nothing coming in from donors."

Affenlight understood the admonition. He was the fund-raiser, the face of the school; in his first years on the job he'd mounted the most successful capital campaign in Westish history. But the economy of recent years—the collapse, the crisis, the recession, whatever you called it—had both eroded those gains and frightened donors. His influence among the trustees, once almost boundless, was gently on the wane.

"And now," Bruce went on, "suddenly you're putting all these new initiatives on the table. Low-flow plumbing. A complete carbon inventory. Temperature setbacks. Guert, where is this crap coming from?"

"From the students," said Affenlight. "I've been working closely with several student groups." Really, he'd been working closely with one student group. Okay, really he'd been working closely with one student— the same student he wanted desperately to get down to the baseball diamond to see. But Gibbs didn't need to know that. It was true enough that the students wanted to cut carbon.

"The *students,*" said Gibbs, "don't quite understand the world. Remember when they made us divest from oil? Oil *is* money. They complain about tuition increases, and then they complain when the endowment earns money."

"Cutting emissions will be a PR boon," Affenlight said. "And it'll save us tens of thousands on energy. Most of our benchmark schools are already doing it."

"Listen to yourself. How can it be a PR boon if our benchmarks are already doing it? If we're not first movers on this, then we're back in the pack. There's no PR in the pack. Might as well sit back and learn from their mistakes."

"Bruce, the pack's way out ahead of us. Ecological responsibility is basically an industry ante at this point. It's becoming a top-five decision factor for prospective students. If we don't recognize that, we'll get hammered on every admissions tour till the cows come home."

Gibbs sighed, stood up, and hobbled to the window. Management consulting terms like *industry ante* and *decision factor* were the glue of their relationship — Affenlight tried to learn as many of them as possible, and to intuit or invent the ones he hadn't learned. Gibbs gazed out at the Melville statue that overlooked the lake. "If it's a decision factor we'll deal with it," he said. "But I doubt we can afford it this year."

"We should get started now," Affenlight replied. "Global warming waits for no man."

This was true, of course — he'd read the books, he had rightness on his side — but still he feared that Gibbs, or someone, would detect a deeper reason for his urgency. He wanted to do what was right, wanted to prepare Westish for the century ahead, but he also wanted to prove to O that he could do those things. A year, two years, three — the normal time horizons of the college bureaucracy didn't square with his objectives. When it came to impressing someone you thought you might love, a year might as well be forever.

8

Having taken leave of Gibbs, Affenlight crossed the campus as quickly as his long legs would carry him, nodding and smiling at the students he passed, and settled into the top row of bleachers behind first base to watch the Westish Harpooners play the Milford Moose in early-season, nonconference Division III baseball. Shreds of cloud blew past the setting sun, causing shadows to scurry rodentially over the grass. To his right rose the big stone bowl of the football stadium; to his left stretched Lake Michigan, which this afternoon was colored a deep slate blue that perfectly matched his bathroom floor. It was a cold, uncompromising color — he always put on slippers before his four a.m. piss. The visiting Moose were in the field, and each outfielder stood dumb against an expanse of frozen grass. Affenlight couldn't tell, from here, what sort of fellows they were: whether they manned their lonely outposts with dejection or relief.

Even the slight elevation of the bleachers afforded a handsome view of the campus, whose situation here on the lakefront had always been one of its selling points. Affenlight exhaled and watched his lungs' CO_2 float whitely away. His elbows rested on his knees, his long knobby fingers interlocked. His forearms, hands, and thighs formed a diamond-shaped pond into which his tie dropped like an ice fisher's line. The tie, which was silk, sold at the campus bookstore for forty-eight dollars, but he received a free box of six each fall, because the tie depicted the official emblem of Westish College. A diagonally arranged series of tiny ecru men posed against the navy silk, each standing in the prow of a tiny boat. Each held a harpoon cocked beside his head, ready to let fly at a pod of unseen whales. Affenlight also owned the figure-ground-reversal version of the tie, with its navy harpooners bobbing on an ecru sea. These were the Harpooners' colors: the batter at the plate wore a parchment-colored jersey with pin-width navy stripes.

In Affenlight's undergraduate days, when they were still called the Sugar Maples, the Westish teams had worn a rather hideous combination of yellow and red, in homage to the autumn colors of the state tree. The change to the Harpooners was unveiled soon after Affenlight's graduation, and as a direct result of his literary discovery. Near the end of H. Melville's lecture, while thanking his hosts for their hospitality, he'd uttered the following comment, now long committed to Affenlight's memory: "Humbled, I am, by the severe beauty of this Westish land, and these Great Lakes, America's secret sinew of inward-collecting seas." The schools' trustees, not wanting to squander such an eloquent endorsement, erected a statue on campus in Melville's honor in 1972 and had those words inscribed on the base. They also changed the athletic teams' name to the Harpooners, and their colors to blue and ecru—to represent, Affenlight assumed, the lake Melville admired and the age-faded sheets on which his admiration had been transcribed.

At the time this might have seemed like a stretch, not to say a risible act of desperation—to adopt Melville a thousand miles from where he spent his life, ninety years after a visit that lasted a day. But as rebrandings went it had turned out okay. Certainly the new colors looked more dignified on a seal or brochure, and the athletes enjoyed not having their teams named after a tree. And over the years a thriving cult of Melvilleania had developed at the college, such that you could walk across campus and see girls wearing T-shirts with a whale on the front and lettering on the back that said, WESTISH COLLEGE: OUR DICK IS BIGGER THAN YOURS, or you could enter the bookstore and buy a Melville's-bust keychain and a framed poster of the full text of "The Lee Shore" to hang in your dorm room. Quotes from Melville's work were threaded throughout the brochure, the application materials, and the website. A seminar called Melville and His Times was one of the few permanent features of the English Department rotation—Affenlight hoped someday to make time to teach it—and the library had acquired a small but significant collection of Melville's papers and letters. Affenlight tended to be heartened by his hero's academic legacy at Westish and to despair over the ways he'd been turned into commercial kitsch, but he wasn't so naive as to think you could necessarily have the former without the latter. The bookstore did a brisk business in that kitsch; they shipped it all over the world.

The aged scoreboard in left-center field read WESTISH 6 VIITOR 2. The wind flared off the lake in petulant gusts. The few dozen fans on the home side, most of them parents and girlfriends of the players, huddled under afghans and sipped from Styrofoam cups of decaf that had long ago ceased to steam. A few fathers—the ones too tough for decaf, the ones who shot deer—stood in a row along the chain-link fence that abutted the dugout, feet spread wide. Hands thrust deep in their jacket pockets, they rocked from heel to toe, muttering to one another from the corners of their mouths as they cataloged their sons' mental errors. With only a topcoat over his wool suit and no hat or gloves, Affenlight felt underdressed. That lone scotch he'd had with Gibbs was still generating a hint of inner warmth. The Westish batter—Ajay Guladni, whose father taught in the Economics Department—stroked a single up the middle. Mittens muffled the sparse clapping of the fans.

The inning ended, and the Moose trotted off the diamond. Affenlight leaned forward as the Westish players emerged into the frigid daylight to take the field. He took pride in knowing the names of the school's twenty-four hundred students, and even from a distance the faces of the upperclasspersons were familiar to him: Mike Schwartz, Adam Starblind, Henry Skrimshander. But where was the face he'd come to see?

Perhaps he wasn't playing today. Affenlight knew he was a member of the baseball team, but whether he was a starter or a benchwarmer or somewhere in between was a question he'd never considered. How stupid to have sat here, behind the home dugout, so that he couldn't see inside. And yet what else could he do? Move over to the visitors' bleachers and become a traitorous president? How suspicious would *that* look? For now he stayed put. He couldn't see O, but he and O were facing the same way, watching the same white ball zip toward home plate, the same anxious batter swing and miss, and that in itself, that same-way-facing, felt like something.

Whatever happened, he couldn't be late to pick up Pella. To be late would be a bad start, and things were tricky enough without a bad start. He hadn't seen her since she'd dropped out of Tellman Rose, midway through her senior year, to elope with David. That was four years ago, an unthinkably long time. If events had unfolded differently, she'd be graduating from college this spring.

Two nights ago she left a message on his office phone — strategically avoiding his cell, which he might have answered — and asked him to buy her a ticket to Westish. "It's not an emergency," she said. "But the sooner the better." Affenlight bought the ticket with an open return. How long she'd stay, whether things were going badly with David, he didn't know.

Baseball — what a boring game! One player threw the ball, another caught it, a third held a bat. Everyone else stood around. Affenlight looked about, bethinking his options. He had less than an hour. What he needed was a *reason,* an excuse, to circle over to the Milford side and thereby catch a glimpse of the person he was eager to glimpse. He scanned the visitors' bleachers, and his eyes settled on two large, well-dressed men whose attitudes and accessories marked them as distinct from the other spectators. Affenlight, combining what he saw with what he'd lately heard, guessed that they must be professional scouts, here to see Harpooner shortstop Henry Skrimshander, a junior. Which seemed to afford the perfect excuse: he would pay his guests a cordial visit.

He rose from the bench, pulling his tie out of the pond-shaped space between his knees. As he followed the bleachers around the backstop, the corrugated aluminum resounded beneath his loafers. He shook a pair of powerful right hands — insisting that Dwight and L.P. call him Guert, just Guert — and lowered himself beside them. The new patch of aluminum felt far colder through his slacks than the old one.

"So gentlemen," Affenlight said. "What brings you to Westish?"

The one named Dwight gestured toward the shortstop position with his sunglasses, indicating Henry Skrimshander. "That fellow right there, sir."

L.P. and Dwight, it turned out, were ex–minor leaguers not far removed from their playing days. Smooth-featured and polite, business-casual in dress, with slender laptops in their laps and BlackBerries laid beside them on the bleachers, they looked like oversize consultants or CIA agents playing a very reserved sort of hooky. L.P. had his hands clasped behind his head and his legs stretched before him, covering several rows; he would have dwarfed Affenlight if they both stood. Dwight was blond and pale, more densely built than L.P. but not quite as tall. Dwight did most of the speaking, in the chatty, choppy tones of the Upper Upper Midwest — Affenlight guessed Minnesota, or maybe he was Canadian:

"Henry Skrimshander. I tell you what, Guert. A heck of a shortstop. I first saw him play last summer at this tournament down in, boy, I forget where…"

If Affenlight wanted, he could swivel his head to the right, away from the smiling eyes of Dwight, and look down into that distant corner of the Westish dugout and see him.

"…and this pitcher I was there to scout, boy, did he turn out to be a dog, but I was too lazy to get up and…"

If he wanted? Of course he wanted. It was the wanting, the incredible strength of the wanting, that had prevented him so far. Affenlight felt afraid to look — afraid, perhaps, that looking might commit him irrevocably. But to what? Commit him to what?

Now, finally, as Dwight paused for breath, Affenlight indulged the desire that had been simmering in his mind. He snuck a peek into the Westish dugout. *Oh.* His features were indiscernible at this distance, lost in the heavy shadows that shrouded that corner of the dugout. A thin stream of light connected his cap to the book in his lap.

"...that's what scouting is," Dwight was saying, more or less. "Following up on tips and notes, ninety-nine point five percent of which inevitably turn out to be..."

Features indiscernible but contours unmistakable: slender-limbed, right knee flipped girlishly over left, torso gently canted in that direction, bundled up against the cold in a hooded Westish sweatshirt with a windbreaker on top of that. Chin at a downward tilt, studying his book instead of the game. Affenlight felt something young swell up in his chest, a thudding pain interspersed with something sweet, as if he were being dragged by an oxcart through a field of clover. He blinked hard.

Dwight shook his head slowly, as if disbelieving his own memory. "I've seen a lot of baseball, Guert. But never have I seen someone like Henry, in terms of sheer — what would you call it, L.P.?"

L.P. reclined with his elbows spread wide on the row behind him, his wraparound shades disguising his eyes. He answered as if from the depths of sleep: "Prescience."

The maroon-clad batter rifled a one-hopper to short. Henry backhanded it without a flourish and threw him out. The ease and power of the throw startled Affenlight; he himself was several inches taller than Henry and had been no slouch at quarterback, but he'd never thrown a projectile half that hard.

"Henry can flat-out play," Dwight went on. "The only question mark in some people's minds is competition. It's tough to guess a guy's ceiling when he's in such a lousy environment for baseball. No offense, Guert."

"None taken, Dwight." The next batter popped up, and the Harpooners jogged off the field to soft applause. There couldn't have been more than thirty people left in the stands.

"I'll tell you one thing, though. After the way he played in Florida last week, the word is out. That's how scouting works nowadays—you don't discover guys so much as you take the master list and rank them. And Henry's on the master list. The only reason this place isn't crawling with scouts today is it's so dang cold and we're so dang far from a decent airport. But they'll be here."

Airport. Pella. Affenlight checked his watch.

"As of yesterday we had him rated the third-best shortstop in the draft, behind Vance White, who was first-team all-American last year, and this high school kid from Texas who scouts call the Terminator, because he looks like he was built in a lab." Dwight paused. "But after seeing Henry today, I'd have half a mind to take him over both those guys. He's not big enough to be the best, he's not fast enough to be the best, he doesn't have the body or the raw numbers to be the best. He just *is*."

"Beautiful to watch," L.P. opined from behind his shades.

Dwight nodded, his pale-blue eyes and pink-rimmed nose glistening in the cold. "He understands the game like a veteran major leaguer. And defensively there's no competition. Today he ties Aparicio Rodriguez's NCAA record for consecutive errorless games by a shortstop. Fifty-one and counting."

Dwight's BlackBerry bleated. He answered in a hushed, almost childlike voice and wandered off, phone pressed close to his ear. He was wearing a wedding band; Affenlight pictured a perky blond sales rep with a diamond of reasonable size, whispering PG-13 yearnings into her cell phone while she shopped at the Whole Foods in downtown St. Cloud. Perhaps she was wearing one of those complicated toddler holders strapped to her chest. Or perhaps she was pregnant and trying to decide which toddler holder to buy.

Affenlight didn't glance back into the dugout, as if it might diminish the sensation to indulge it again. Or maybe he was just afraid. Either way, he turned his attention to Henry Skrimshander, who was back in the field. His pinstriped uniform was baggy, but it somehow suited him perfectly, suggested his entire existence, like the uniforms of the rowers and doctors in the Eakins lithographs that hung in Affenlight's study. His navy socks were pulled to midcalf. His shoes were dirty white. Before the pitch he stood at ease, glove on his hip, his face round and windburned and open, delivering instructions or encouragement to his teammates with a relaxed smile. But as the ball left the pitcher's hand his face went blank. The chatter stopped midword. In one motion he yanked his navy cap with its harpoon-skewered *W* toward his eyes and dropped into a feline crouch, thighs parallel to the field, glove brushing the dirt. He looked low to the ground but light on his feet, more afloat than entrenched. The pitch was fouled back, but not before he had taken two full steps to his left, toward the place where he anticipated the ball to be headed. None of the other infielders had moved an inch.

"Prescience," L.P. said again.

In the bottom of the eighth, Henry batted for what would almost certainly be the final time. He'd already hit two doubles since Affenlight's arrival, and the Milford pitcher looked reluctant to let him hit another. He walked on four pitches and sprinted down to first. Dwight and L.P. rose in unison and bagged their laptops. "That's enough for us," Dwight said. "We've got a flight to catch." Affenlight offered warm presidential handshakes as the two men departed. The pumpkin sun had impaled itself on the spire of Westish Chapel and begun to bleed. He was so glad Pella was coming, overjoyed, but he dreaded it too — it had been so long since they'd seen each other, and so much longer than that since they'd gotten along. He glanced toward the Westish dugout one last time and felt himself growing sad. *O me, O life.* Perhaps, he thought, with a touch of melodrama, this whole thing was merely an old man's last gasp. A late-life crisis, a doomed passade.

The half inning ended, and the Harpooners took the field for the top of the ninth. On his way out, Affenlight returned to the first-base bleachers to say hello to the last few shivering fans and to congratulate them on the valor of their sons and lovers. He was facing the field, buttoning his topcoat, when the Milford hitter slapped a grounder toward short. Henry closed on it quickly, absorbing it into his glove with the thoughtless ease of a mother being handed her newborn baby. His feet shifted into throwing position, his shoulders torqued, his arm became a blur. The ball left his hand on what looked, to Affenlight, like a true course.

But then, for whatever reason — a gust whipped up off the water, to be sure, but could even the strongest gust do this? — the ball, having already covered a third of its path, veered sharply. It tailed inland, tailing and tailing until Rick O'Shea, the first baseman, could only usher it by with a halfhearted lunge. Affenlight's left hand jerked toward his tie's half Windsor, where the twist of the knot made the little spearmen lie supine, as the ball sailed with frightening velocity into just that corner of the Westish dugout where he'd been directing his attention. The gust gave way to a hush. Mike Schwartz, who'd tossed aside his mask as he hustled down the baseline to back up the throw, stopped dead and swiveled his head in Affenlight's direction.

And then all Affenlight saw were faces, Mike Schwartz's big and nearby and twisted in a suffering grimace, Henry's beyond it round and distant and blank, revealing nothing, as there came, from that corner of the dugout, a muffled but nonetheless sickening crunch, followed by a thud.

Owen.

9

Henry wiped his right hand against his thigh, back and forth, back and forth. His index finger must have slipped off the seams. That must have been what happened. He misgripped the seams, and then his finger slipped, and then a gust of wind kicked up and carried the ball much farther off course than could have happened with finger-slippage alone. Finger-slippage could cause the ball to tail only so far, and wind could cause the ball to tail only so far, but finger-slippage combined with wind probably had some kind of multiplier effect, like smoking pot when you've been drinking. Henry rarely drank and never smoked pot, so he didn't know about the multiplier effect firsthand. But something like that must have happened here, to account for what happened.

Which was that Owen was dead. Henry knew it. He kept wiping his hand against his thigh, back and forth across the cool, starchy warp knit of his uniform pants. Back, forth, back, forth. His index finger itched, just above the top knuckle crease, an itch that wouldn't go away. The spot where the ball slipped off.

Owen was dead. No one had said so yet, but Henry knew. He didn't need to go over there, by the paramedics and umpires and coaches who were crowded into the dugout around the body. He could stay right here on the infield, by himself. He squatted down, rubbed the itchy index finger against his thigh. Against the red-brown dirt of the infield.

The throw had struck Owen full in the face. He was reading a book, his battery-powered light clipped to the brim of his cap; he never saw it coming. His head snapped back and cracked against the concrete wall behind him. Bounced, like a ball made of bone. After the bounce he hung there, wobbly but upright, for a frozen moment, his eyes huge and white. He seemed to be staring straight out at Henry, asking him some wordless question. Then he slumped to the dugout floor, where Henry couldn't see him.

Schwartzy, who'd been hustling down the first-base line to back up the play, charged down into the dugout. So did Coach Cox. A tall man in a suit — could it have been President Affenlight? — hopped the short fence beside the dugout, barking into a cell phone as he did so. The two umpires followed President Affenlight down the dugout steps. The five of them were down there now with the paramedics, crouched over Owen. Over Owen's body.

It had been such an easy play, a topspin bounder two steps to Henry's left. When he let go of the throw it felt fine, routine, indistinguishable from hundreds of other throws, all of which had been perfect.

The ballpark lights came on. Henry hugged himself and shivered. Behind him the scoreboard remained lit. Ninth inning. One out. WESTISH 8 VISITOR 3. The players from both teams chomped their sunflower seeds or wads of gum and looked on in silence, though of course the silence did no good. Henry wished they would scream, throw their heads back and scream bloody murder until the paramedics strapped Owen to their pale-blue surfboard-looking thing and carried him to the morgue. That would at least have been something.

Schwartz emerged from the dugout and walked across the field — big, bowlegged, unhurried. He was still wearing his chest protector and shin guards, his backward cap. He turned to face the same direction as Henry, laid a hand on Henry's shoulder.

"You okay?"

Henry bit his lip, looked at the ground.

"The Buddha's out cold."

"Cold?" This seemed like an odd way to tell someone that someone else had died. Odd but effective. What's colder than death?

"Cold," Schwartz confirmed. "You put quite a lick on him. He's going to be hurting tomorrow."

"Tomorrow?"

"You know. Day after today."

The two of them stood there, side by side in the yellowish, unreal light of the diamond that made distant objects seem near. After a while Schwartz said, "At least those two scouts left before things hit the fan."

That thought had occurred to Henry, though he was glad not to be the one to voice it. The paramedics carried Owen out of the dugout, lowered the gurney's collapsible legs into an *X,* and wheeled him toward the ambulance. The fans and Milford players clapped. When things like this happened on TV, the strapped-down athlete always lifted a hand to the crowd to show that he'd be okay. To show that the human spirit could triumph over any hardship. Owen did no such thing. President Affenlight clambered into the ambulance behind the gurney, and the ambulance screamed away.

The umpires and coaches gathered at home plate, conferred for a few moments, and exchanged handshakes. As he walked back toward the rest of the team, Coach Cox beckoned Henry and Schwartz with a wave. Schwartz put a hand in the small of Henry's back, guided him toward the huddle.

"We decided to call the game." Coach Cox smoothed his clipped black mustache, spoke in clipped black words. "So good win. I know you're worried about Dunne. But we can't have twenty of us dinking around the hospital. Go home, shower up. As soon as I hear anything, I'll send out word. Understood?"

Rick O'Shea raised his hand. "Off day tomorrow?"

Coach Cox pointed at him. "O'Shea. Watch yourself. Three o'clock practice. Now let's get out of here before we freeze our asses off." As the players dispersed he squeezed Henry's shoulder. "I'm headed to the hospital. You need a ride?"

"We'll go in my car," Schwartz told him. "So you can hit the road afterward."

Coach Cox lived in Milwaukee, two hours south, and commuted through the season. "Goddamn Dunne," he muttered, stroking his mustache. "Him and his goddamn books."

Henry waited off to one side, goose-bumped and shivering, while his teammates collected their equipment. They slapped him wordlessly on the back and set out across the early-spring mud of the pitch-dark practice fields, toward the campus proper. When they were no longer visible, even to Henry's 20/15 vision, he took a deep breath and headed down the dugout steps.

The dugout was low and long and dark. The concrete walls exuded an ominous coolness, like the hold of an arctic ship. A narrow beam of fuzzy-edged light streamed through a few feet of grayness and illuminated a small patch of wall. Owen's reading light, still clipped to his Harpooner cap. Henry clicked it off and zipped the cap-light combo into Owen's bag. Then he slung one big bag over either shoulder — Owen's with the number 0 stenciled on the side, his own with the number 3. Halfway up the dugout steps he thought to check for Owen's glasses. He unslung the bags, dropped to his knees, and felt around the sticky floor in the darkness beneath the bench: Small mucky puddles of tobacco spit. Tooth printed wads of gum. The plastic caps of Gatorade bottles, their spiny underedges like tiny crowns of thorns. Plain old clumps of mud. Owen's glasses had been kicked all the way to the far end of the bench. Henry picked them up and wiped the lenses clean against his jersey. One arm wobbled on its hinge.

When he and Schwartzy arrived at St. Anne's, President Affenlight was pacing up and down the ER waiting room, head bowed. He devoured the checkerboard floor with six strides, turned, and did it again. Schwartz cleared his throat to announce their entrance.

Affenlight's expression, weary and disarmed when he thought he was alone, changed instantly to a bright presidential smile. "Michael," he said. "Henry. Glad to see you."

Henry hadn't expected President Affenlight to know his name. They passed each other often on the sidewalks of the Small Quad, because Phumber Hall was right beside the president's quarters, but they'd spoken only once, on Henry's very first day at Westish, while Henry was blending in with the tent poles at the Freshperson Barbecue, nibbling his fourth or fifth hot dog:

"Guert Affenlight." The older man sipped his drink, held out a hand.

"Henry Skrimshander."

"Skrimshander?" Affenlight smiled. "It'll be the seven hundred and seventy-seventh lay for you, I'm afraid." He was wearing a silver tie that matched his hair. His sleeves were rolled midway up his forearms—the way they hung unwrinkled from shoulder to cuff, their lines crisp and pristine, suggested a man at ease with his surroundings. When Sophie had asked Henry to describe Westish, the first image that came to mind was that of Affenlight's perfectly rolled-up sleeves.

"Any news?" Schwartz asked now.

"He woke up for a moment in the ambulance," Affenlight said. "Out cold, and then suddenly his eyes popped open. He said, *April*."

"April?"

"April."

"April," Henry repeated.

"The cruelest month," Schwartz said. "Especially in Wisconsin."

"April." Henry parsed the word into sounds so small their sense disappeared, as if he'd wandered into the wide spaces that separate the solid parts of a molecule. "Starts tomorrow."

Coach Cox walked into the waiting room. Like Henry and Schwartz, he hadn't changed out of his Harpooner pinstripes. He carried, two to a hand, bulging white bags that bore the golden arches. "Any word?"

"He's in having a CAT scan," Affenlight told him. "They want to make sure there's no bleeding in the brain."

"Goddamn Dunne." Coach Cox shook his head. "If anything happens to him I'll kill him." He plunked the bags down on the round faux-wood table in the corner. "I brought dinner."

Schwartz and Coach Cox settled in at the faux-wood table and unwrapped their Big Macs. Henry loved fast food, but tonight the smell made him queasy. He sank down on a stiff couch and looked up at the TV bolted high on the wall. On-screen a statuary Christ, shot tight in a bright swath of light, hung upon the cross. His chin slumped against a bony, toga-sashed shoulder. ORGAN MUSIC, read the closed-captioning. Cut to biplane angles of an equatorial island: sapphire water, pink beach, the firework tops of palm trees. ISLAND DRUMBEAT.

"Here," said Coach Cox. "Keep your strength up."

Henry let the french fries sit there in his hand. The televised colors, the swift jolting movements from shot to shot, didn't help his stomach. He hadn't seen a TV since October, when the World Series ended.

President Affenlight stopped pacing and sat down on the couch. Henry tipped the flimsy red carton toward him. Affenlight, with a nod of thanks, drew out a fry. The gesture reminded him of his smoking days, which had—more or less—ended with his return to Westish. Upon taking the job, he'd come to this very hospital for a checkup, his first in fifteen years, as was required by his new insurance. He'd expected accolades and hushed admiration from the doctor; he'd recently guest-rowed on a Harvard varsity eight at practice and hardly cost the team a beat. What he got instead was a vehement, statistics-laden lecture. His family history—his father had suffered two heart attacks; his older brother George had died of a so-called coronary event at sixty-three— was as cautionary as they come. His LDL of 200 placed him squarely in the danger zone. His age-old three-pack-a-week smoking habit amounted to a suicide note. The doctor, having played up the pathos of all this to extract from Affenlight a promise not only to quit smoking but to cut back on red meat and alcohol, sent him away with prescriptions for Lipitor, TriCor, and Toprol-XL. Sentenced to a life of pills. He was also supposed to take a baby aspirin every day.

What proved hardest about forgoing his vices wasn't the loss of the vices themselves but the fact that some young punk of a doctor had insisted he forgo them. Baby aspirin indeed. Apparently this was how a man got treated after fifty, even if he was the picture of health. George's death had saddened Affenlight without frightening him much; George was eighteen years his senior, and their relationship had always been removed and avuncular. But it was true that they shared their genetic predispositions, and after a stint of somewhat juvenile resistance Affenlight resolved to comply, or mostly comply, with the doctor's regimen, while making sure to preserve a margin for his freedoms. He took his meds and his baby Asa five days a week, with longer breaks in the summer, as if they were a job from which he required time off; he'd kicked the cigarettes except for the occasional sneaky singleton; and he thought twice before ordering a steak or a second scotch, though especially in the case of the scotch, thinking twice and declining were different things. Whether he was better off for all that was an open question, but he certainly felt fine.

On the TV, young men wearing short-sleeved black shirts and clerical collars filed down the steps of a turboprop, squinting into brilliant sunlight. WELCOME TO *TEST OF FAITH*, said the program's host, his hands thrust pensively in his clam diggers' pockets. BEFORE THESE TWELVE MEN ARE ORDAINED AS PRIESTS, THEY'LL HAVE TO GO THROUGH SOMETHING A LOT MORE TEMPTING THAN FORTY DAYS IN THE DESERT. Cut to drab yearbook photos of girls in plaid jumpers with braces, bangs. THESE YOUNG LADIES ALL WENT TO CATHOLIC SCHOOL. THEY ALL LIST "FAITH" AS AN IMPORTANT QUALITY IN A FUTURE HUSBAND. OH, AND ONE MORE THING — color-soaked flash-cut montage of tanned and sweat-beaded stomachs, cleavage, thighs — THEY'RE ALL REALLY, REALLY HOT.

Are they? Affenlight wondered. The girl-women scampered around a beach house in various states of preparative undress, wriggled into sundresses, shook out their hair. He took another fry. They possessed a veneer of hotness, certainly, a sheen of sexual health. You could call them clean, chromatic, shapely, sun-kissed, and, yes, even *hot*—but you could never call them lovely, not in the way that Owen was lovely.

A baby-faced novitiate sat in the interview chair and thumbed through a well-thumbed Bible. His sad Hispanic eyes found the lens. RODERIGO: WHY? I FEEL THAT THE LORD HAS SENT ME HERE. THAT HE MEANS TO TEST MY FAITH, JUST AS HE TESTED HIS SON. Cut to ice-blue kidney-shaped swimming pool. Roderigo playing water volleyball with three women: peach bikini, striped bikini, cream bikini. Roderigo's necklace's gold crucifix swinging toward his shoulder as he rises for a spike.

"TV's strange," Henry said.

Affenlight slid out another fry, wondering what else Henry found strange. Was it strange for a college president to show so much concern for a student? To run out onto a baseball field? To ride in the back of an ambulance? To watch bad TV, chain-munching french fries, waiting for news?

"How long have you known Owen?" he asked.

Henry stared up at the screen. "We've been roommates since freshperson year."

Roommates! Yes, of course, Affenlight remembered now: how he'd been enlisted by Admissions and Athletics, three years ago, to convince Owen to take on a roommate. The roommate was a late admit and supposedly some kind of baseball phenom. Affenlight had rolled his eyes and complied; he didn't like special treatment for athletes, and he didn't see how one player could help such a bungling baseball program. Now the phenom was Henry, being courted by the St. Louis Cardinals.

Back then Affenlight knew of Owen only because he'd chaired the selection committee for the Maria Westish Award. He admired the elegance of the young man's essays, the breadth of his reading; he championed his application, though other candidates had higher test scores and GPAs. But that had been strictly business, or had seemed so at the time. He'd always avoided entanglements with students, and entangling with a male student had never crossed his mind.

Then, two months ago, the campus environmental group had requested a meeting. A dozen students crowded into Affenlight's office. They lectured him on the evils of global warming. They presented a ten-page list of colleges that had pledged to become carbon neutral by 2020. They demanded energy-efficient lighting, facility upgrades, a biomass plant built out beyond the practice fields, fired by woodchips. "You're getting me too late," he said when they'd finished. "Where were you back when we had money?" Three-quarters of those schools would renege on their pledge; the other quarter were filthy rich. Besides, a dozen students—was that all they could muster? Where were the petitions, the rallies, the outrage? A biomass plant for a dozen students? The trustees would giggle.

While thinking these things, he'd been riveted by Owen, who leaned against the door, hands in the pockets of his baggy sweatpants, while his cohorts gesticulated and shouted. When he spoke his voice was soft, pacific, but the others fell silent; even in their most strident moments they were waiting for him to intervene.

Later that night, while still thinking about Owen, thinking about why he was thinking about Owen, he received an e-mail:

Dear Guert,

Thank you very kindly for meeting with us today. I found it edifying but more cacophonous than might have been maximally productive. I don't wish to impose on your busy schedule, but perhaps we could schedule a smaller meeting to determine which initiatives might be fiscally possible?

Sincerely,

O.

A *Dear Guert* and a one-initial signature, coming from a student, would normally have annoyed Affenlight. In this case, for whatever reason, it felt more like intimacy than presumption. Since then he and Owen had met several times, had put together a plan, and a plan for achieving the plan. Owen's group would collect the student signatures; Affenlight would rally the faculty and lobby the trustees.

Had Owen caught him staring and known what it meant? Was that why he'd written that e-mail? The eyes behind those wire-rimmed glasses seemed to miss nothing. In their subsequent meetings, Owen was self-assured and patient and sometimes teasing; Affenlight was rapt and eager to please. After nearly thirty years of student-teacher interactions, he'd found himself on the wrong end of a crush. After a few weeks the word *crush* no longer covered it.

Affenlight drew another fry from the carton. Henry's eyes were squeezed shut — he wasn't asleep but seemed rather to be wincing, perhaps in memory of his errant throw. His face was ghostly pale, still dusted with infield dirt. He was in full uniform, except for his cap. His glove sat on one knee. "It'll be okay," Affenlight said. "He'll be okay."

Henry nodded, unconvinced.

"He's a wonderful young man," said Affenlight.

Henry's chin squinched, as if he might cry. "Schwartzy," he said, "do you have a ball on you?"

Schwartz, having finished his dinner, had pulled out his laptop and begun typing away, a stack of note cards at his elbow. Now he reached down into his backpack and flipped a baseball to Henry. Henry spun the ball in his right hand, slapped it into the glove. The gesture seemed to enable him to speak. "I keep seeing it over and over in my head," he said miserably. "I've never made a throw like that. A throw that bad. I don't know how it happened."

Schwartz stopped typing and looked up, his face bathed in the cool submarine glow of his laptop screen. "Not your fault, Skrimmer."

"I know."

"The Buddha's going to be okay," Schwartz said. "He's already okay."

Henry nodded, unconvinced. "I know."

"Goddamn Dunne." Coach Cox kept his eyes on the bikini-clad Catholic girls on TV, who were testing the novitiates' faith with back rubs. "I'm going to wring his scrawny neck."

A door opened. "Guert Affenlight?" called a young woman in pale-blue scrubs, reading the name off her clipboard.

"Yes." Affenlight stood and straightened his Harpooner tie.

"My name is Dr. Collins. Are you a relative of Owen Dunne?"

"Oh, no," Affenlight said. "His family, actually, is from, um..."

"San Jose," Henry said.

"Right," Affenlight said quickly. "San Jose." He'd felt such stupid pride at having the doctor call his name, as if he were the person nearest to Owen. The doctor turned to address herself to Henry:

"Your friend isn't doing too badly, all in all. The CT showed no epidural bleeding, which is what we worry about in this kind of case. He has a severe concussion and a fractured zygomatic arch—that is, a cheekbone. His functions appear normal. The arch will require reconstructive surgery, which I imagine we'll try to do right away, as long as we've got him here." Dr. Collins, who despite the purple fatigue marks under her eyes looked no older than twenty-five, paused to pluck at the V of her scrub top, above which her skin was Irishly pink and mottled. Affenlight saw, or imagined he saw, her tired eyes settle on Henry in an interested way.

"Can I see him?" Henry asked.

Dr. Collins shook her head. "His concussion's pretty severe, and we're going to keep him in the ICU tonight. He seems to be suffering some short-term memory loss, which we assume will clear. Tomorrow you can see him all you like." She patted Henry consolingly on the arm.

Affenlight's cell phone shivered against his thigh. The number was unfamiliar, with a 312 prefix, but he knew who it would be. He made an apologetic gesture toward the doctor, who didn't notice, and walked into the hall. "Pella. Kiddo. Where are you?"

"Chicago. I made my connection. We're about to board, so I should be right on time." Her voice sounded thin and crackly through the payphone static. "I thought maybe we could go to Bau Kitchen."

This was Pella's favorite restaurant in Milwaukee, the place where they'd celebrated her sixteenth birthday. If Affenlight had been zipping down I-43 toward the airport, an Italian opera tucked into the Audi's CD player, he would have been heartened by this suggestion, which seemed like a gesture of peace. Instead he was bound to be late, and he couldn't help wondering whether Pella had already sniffed out his neglect, or what was bound to seem like neglect, and had decided to punish him with solicitude. "That's a wonderful idea," he said. "But I'm afraid I'm running a little late."

"Oh."

Disappointment, fragility, the phrase *picking up where we left off*— these things and more came streaming through the phone line's silence. "I'm at the hospital," Affenlight said, trying to ward them off. "We've had an accident at the school. I'll be there as soon as I can."

"Sure," Pella said. "Whenever."

As he hurried out, Affenlight paused long enough to buy a pack of cigarettes—Parliaments, his old standby—from the hospital gift shop. A hospital that sold cigarettes: he rolled this notion in his head, wondering whether it spelled doom or hope, while he thrust a twenty at the gray-haired woman behind the counter. He shoved the pack in his pocket and tried to leave without his change, but she summoned him back and insisted on counting out, with excruciating and perhaps remonstrative slowness, a ten, five ones, and several coins. Coach Cox drove him to his car, and he rocketed down the empty interstate, *Le Nozze di Figaro* blasting, windows down.

10

Pella left San Francisco with only a floppy, cane-handled wicker bag that contained whatever remained from her last trip to the beach nine months ago, a useless assortment of crap—sunglasses, tampons, gummy worms, sand—to which she'd added nothing but her wallet and a black bathing suit, designed for serious swimming.

As the plane slipped up the narrow industrial corridor that connected Chicago to Milwaukee, the darkness of Lake Michigan spread beyond the starboard windows, she was already beginning to regret not having packed a suitcase. It was the kind of overly emphatic gesture she was famous for, at least in her own mind, and should have outgrown by now. Maybe she'd thought it would make the break with David cleaner, easier, more decisive: *See, I don't need you. I don't need anything. Not even underwear.* She hadn't bothered to remember that there was nowhere decent to shop near the so-called city of Westish, Wisconsin.

How stupid she felt, to feel this bad, to feel her life lying around her in ruins, and yet to have no story to tell about it. Sure, in some abstract sense it was a story, or would someday become one... Yes, I was married once. I dropped out of high school, ran off with an architect who'd come to lecture at my prep school. I was a senior, had just turned nineteen. David was thirty-one. At the end of his week at Tellman Rose, I slept with him. One of us was going to sleep with him, and as the reigning alpha female I had first dibs. I had dated older guys—high school guys when I was in junior high, college guys when I was at Tellman Rose, a few starving-artist types on trips to Boston or New York—but David was something new to my experience. A man, full stop.

A bit of a weenie, perhaps—petulant, conniving, prim. But that's a retrospective analysis. At the time I just saw the charm and cultivation, the dark twinkling eyes above the brown beard, the immense learning. And more than those things, I saw the virtue. He was a man who lived by a code. He thought classical learning was important, and so he'd become an excellent classical scholar, though it was only indirectly useful to his practice. Which was itself a model of virtue: an attempt to create classically beautiful buildings that were, you know, green. This wasn't a man who watched TV, went to the gym, wasted time. He didn't eat meat and he drank only to show off his knowledge of wine.

I was attuned to his every move as he delivered his afternoon lectures, as he held forth at various luncheons and dinners, to which I always managed to be invited. Clearly I had a daddy thing going on, even more than usual. He possessed the three qualities I associated most closely with my father—learned, virtuous, flummoxed by me—and he displayed them all much more conspicuously, not to say pretentiously, than my dad ever had. My dad was cool. David was like my dad but not cool at all. One of the TR girls, not my main rival but the one I feared most, because she was as smart as I was, referred to me as Pellektra. I couldn't complain; it was too spot-on, her tone too light. *You're only Jung once,* I replied. *Enjoy it.*

Because of David's virtue, his virtuous self-image, I had to present myself as the seducer. Which I did, a project that culminated the night before his departure. I felt as if I'd deflowered him, not because he was inept compared to other guys—again, he was thirty-one—but because he maintained that facade of virtue until the last. *You're awfully stiff,* I said right before we kissed—my last best double entendre of the night.

A week later was spring break. I'd just gotten into Yale. My friends and I were going to Jamaica to drink. We were at the Burlington airport, already drinking. David walked in. He had a bag over his shoulder, two tickets to Rome in his hand. *Shall we?* he said. He was sweating, plotting, a turtleneck under his jacket, anxious about my answer — not cool.

My break was a week long, but we stayed in Rome for three. Afterward we flew to San Francisco, where David's latest project was located; I felt elated, like I'd bypassed Yale and young adulthood and graduated straight into the world. When I recall those first weeks with David among the crumbling buildings of Rome, weeks of feeling deliciously older than old, giddy with my own seriousness, it's probably no accident that I can't think of my life without using the word *ruined*.

Pella, per instructions, finished her whiskey and returned her seat back to the upright position. Okay, you could tell *that* part like a story, a creative-writing assignment, could even toss in a florid last line to keep people on their toes, but that was because it wasn't the real story. By which she meant it wasn't an answer to the questions she feared most: Who are you? What do you do? Well, what do you *want* to do?

No, the past four years — and especially the last two — had passed in something like a dream, and nobody wanted to hear about your dreams. She'd done nothing. At some point she'd realized that the marriage was a mistake, but she'd been unable to admit it to herself. She'd cut herself off from the source of her distress, which happened to be her entire life. Consequently she became helplessly depressed, and David hadn't minded, because when she was helplessly depressed she depended on him and was therefore unlikely to leave him for someone her own age, which was always his greatest fear.

And so the months had mounted, Pella lying in bed in their sunstruck loft, dragging herself to the Rite Aid and the psychiatrist and back again, David alternately peeved and given purpose by her somnolence. There were events, fights, excursions, but none of it mattered, none of it penetrated the thick fog under which she lived. *I ruined my life in Rome and lived in a fog in San Francisco.* Their sex life dwindled, and neither of them mentioned it. "They" were fine. She had to get better. Why was one in quotes and not the other? David prescribed regimens to help her sleep at night: no caffeine, no TV, no electric lights. Each night she would go to bed beside him and then, the instant his breathing changed, get up and go to the kitchen to begin her nightly vigil of slowly drinking whiskey and chewing sunflower seeds while enduring the sheer excruciating boredom of being alive.

Eventually, inevitably, she'd landed in the hospital, with heart palpitations from the mix of drugs she was taking—over-the-counter sleep aids, antianxietals, prescription painkillers, in almost random configurations, in addition to the whiskey and her antidepressants. In the hospital they put her on suicide watch. She hadn't been trying to kill herself, though that was easy to say in retrospect, now that she felt a tiny bit better. Her thinking about death had always been inextricable from her thinking about her mom; there was pain and pleasure, fear and comfort there, mixed in roughly equal parts. "It's the Affenlight men who die young," her dad had said long ago, in a weird attempt to reassure the nine- or ten-year-old daughter he'd never quite known what to do with. "The women live forever." Though this had been borne out in particular historical cases, she couldn't believe it applied to her or, God forbid, to him. It was hard to imagine her father as anything but immortal, her own purchase on the world as anything but tenuous.

Not long after the hospital incident she'd been given a new, experimental SSRI—a tiny sky-blue pill called Alumina, presumably to connote the light it would bring into your life, though Pella couldn't help seeing the word *Alumna* and interpreting it as a snide remark on her failure to finish high school. She Sharpied out the label and called it her sky-blue pill. But it worked, it worked, better than anything ever had. She started to read again. She felt a little better; she was able to think about her life. It was confusing to have leaped precociously ahead of her high-achieving, economically privileged peers by doing precisely what her low-achieving, economically unprivileged peers tended to do: getting married, staying home, keeping house. She'd gotten so far ahead of the curve that the curve became a circle, and now she was way behind.

In recent months, her panic attacks came less often and lasted less long. After David fell asleep she bundled up and went out on their plant-filled terrace with a flashlight and sat in a lawn chair and read through the chilly San Francisco night, downtown and the bridges twinkling in the distance. She could feel her strength slowly returning, being marshaled for some maneuver or another; she didn't know what it was. Then at five o'clock Tuesday morning, David in Seattle on business, she found herself dialing her dad's number. She hadn't seen him since she met David, hadn't spoken to him since Christmas.

Pella chomped her gum as the plane descended. Then she headed for the baggage claim, not because she had any baggage — except for that failed marriage, ka*ching!* — but because that was where she and her dad used to meet, when she made trips from Tellman Rose. She stretched out across three plastic chairs and watched the carousel mouth disgorge a series of compact black bags with wheels. Her dad had said he'd be late — how dully typical of him — but he hadn't said how late. The black bags all disappeared, were replaced by a new set from a new flight, and then another. Was there an airport bar nearby? Probably, but she was too tired to look. It saddened her that her dad was willing to start on this note. The carousel bags blurred together, and she closed her eyes.

"Excuse me," said somebody, somebody male. The guy smiled suavely. "You probably shouldn't fall asleep here," he said. "Somebody might steal your bag."

"I wasn't asleep," Pella said, though clearly she had been.

The guy smiled some more. Everyone's teeth were so white these days, even in Milwaukee. He gestured to the carousel. "Can I help you with your bags?"

Pella shook her head. "I like to travel light."

The guy nodded intently, as if this were the most fascinating thing he'd ever heard. He held out his hand, introduced himself. Pella told him her name.

"My, what a lovely name. Is that British?"

"Wull I don't rightly know, luv," she said in her worst Cockney. "Would ya like it ta be?"

The guy's brow furrowed, but he recovered. "So. Where are you headed?"

"Home." What was it with guys in suits? They acted like they ran the world. Pella saw her dad striding through the long concourse, tie dangling. "And there's my fiancé now," she said.

The guy looked up at the approaching late-middle-aged man, back at Pella. His brow furrowed again. He'd wind up with wrinkles. "You're not wearing a ring," he pointed out.

"You've got me there." Her dad looked wounded, disoriented, lost— he was about to walk right past when Pella leaned out and plucked at his sleeve. "Hey," she said. Her heart was hammering away.

"Pella." They faced each other, separated by one final yard of fibrous blue carpeting. Four years. Pella fiddled with her sweatshirt zipper. Her dad's forearms lifted from his sides in an apologetic, almost helpless gesture of welcome, palms upturned. "Sorry I'm late."

"That's okay." Obviously there was an evolutionary advantage to thinking your own family attractive—it made the members more likely to protect one another against outside threats—but Pella couldn't imagine *anyone* failing to find her father handsome. He'd entered his sixties, a decade usually associated with decline—but apart from a weary confusion in his eyes, he looked just as she remembered, his thick gray hair streaked with silver, his skin mahogany-ruddy in that way that lent credence to rumors of Native American ancestry, shoulders as square and upright as a geometry proof.

"The prodigal daughter," she said as they embraced in a quick, stiff clinch.

"You've got that right."

Pella sniffed his neck as they separated. "Have you been smoking?"

"No, no. Me? I mean, I might have had one in the car. It's been a long day, I'm afraid...Do we need to collect your luggage?"

Pella frowned at her wicker bag. "Actually, this is all I brought."

"Oh." Affenlight had been hoping she might stay for a while; the ticket, after all, had been one-way. But a lack of luggage didn't bode well. He didn't dare ask; better to enjoy the present. Perhaps if the question of leaving never came up, she'd forget to want to leave. "Well then. Should we hit the road?"

I-43, after passing through the northern Milwaukee suburbs, cut due north through vast stretches of flat, yet-unplanted fields. Clouds obscured the moon and stars, and the southbound traffic was sparse. Off to the right lay Lake Michigan, invisibly guiding the highway's course. Pella expected an immediate grilling—*How long are you staying? Have you broken up with David? Are you going back to school?*—but her father seemed anxious and preoccupied. She wasn't sure whether to feel relieved or insulted. They spent most of the ride in silence, and when they spoke, they spoke in monosyllables, more like characters in a Carver story than real live Affenlights.

The president's quarters, cozily appointed in academia's dark wood and leather, were located on the uppermost floor of Scull Hall, in the southeast corner of the Small Quad. The Westish presidents of the twentieth century had all lived downtown, in one or another of the elegant white houses that flanked the lake, but Affenlight, the first president of the twenty-first, had decided to revive the quarters' original purpose and reside among the students. It was just him, after all. This way his office lay just a staircase away from his apartment, and he could sneak down at dawn for a quiet stint of work, dressed in whatever, before Mrs. McCallister arrived and the day's appointments began.

He poured them each a whiskey, his with water, Pella's without. "I suppose this is legal now," he said as he handed her the glass.

"Takes half the fun out of it." Pella arranged herself in a square leather chair, drew her knees up to her chest. "So how's business?"

Affenlight shrugged. "Business is business," he said. "I don't know why they keep hiring English professors for these jobs. They should get guys from Goldman Sachs or something. If I have ten minutes a day to think about something besides money, I consider myself lucky."

"How's your health?"

He drummed on his sternum. "Like a bull," he said.

"You're taking your medicine?"

"I take my walk by the lake every day," Affenlight said. "That's better than medicine."

Pella gave him a distressed maternal look.

"I take them," he said. "I take them and take them. Though you know how I feel about pills."

"Take them," Pella said. "Are you seeing anyone?"

"Oh. Well . . ." *Seeing,* actually, was just the word for it. "Let's just say there aren't many enthralling women in this part of the world."

"If there are any, I'm sure you'll hunt them down."

"Thanks," Affenlight said dryly. "And you? How's David?"

"David's fine. Although he'll be less so when he finds out I'm gone."

"He doesn't know you're here?" This revelation trumped the lack of luggage; Affenlight resisted the urge to stand and pump his fist.

"He's in Seattle. On business."

"I see."

Lately it seemed to Affenlight that the students were growing younger; maybe he was just getting old, or maybe adolescence was stretching out longer and longer, in proportion with the growing life span. Colleges had become high schools; grad schools, colleges. But Pella, as always, seemed intent on shooting ahead of her peers. She looked older than he remembered, of course—her cheeks less round, her features more pronounced—but she also looked older than twenty-three. She looked like she'd been through a lot.

"Are you tired?" he asked, remembering not to say *You look tired.*

She shrugged. "I haven't been sleeping much."

"Well, the bed in the guest room is great." Mistake: he should have said *your room*. Or would that have seemed too eager? Anyway, onward: "And the darkness out here is something to behold. Totally different from Boston. Or San Francisco."

"Great."

"You can stay as long as you like. Of course."

"Thanks." Pella finished her whiskey, peered into the bottom of her glass. "Can I ask one more favor?"

"Shoot."

"I'd like to start taking classes."

"You would?" Affenlight stroked his chin and considered this happy news. "That should work out fine," he said, trying to keep his tone as neutral as possible; to betray too much enthusiasm might backfire. "The deadlines for the fall have passed, of course, but you can register for the summer session as a visitor, and if we sign you up for the next SAT date, I'm sure I could convince Admissions —"

"No no," Pella said quietly. "Right away."

"What's that?"

"I . . . I was hoping I could start right away."

"But, Pella, the summer *is* right away. It's already April."

Pella chuckled nervously. "I was thinking about tomorrow."

"Tomorrow?" Every nerve in Affenlight's spine quivered, half with love of his daughter, half with indignation at her presumption. "But, Pella, we're halfway through the semester. Surely you can't expect to hop right in."

"I could catch up."

Affenlight set down his drink, drummed his fingers on the arm of the chair. "I don't doubt that you could. You're an excellent student when you choose to be. But it's not simply a matter of catching up. It's a matter of courtesy. As a professor, I can tell you I wouldn't be pleased to be suddenly told —"

"Please," Pella said. "I could just audit. I know it's not ideal."

Those first two years after Pella's mother died: call them an adjustment period. He tried day care—expensive day care—but as soon as Affenlight grew accustomed to the fact that Pella was *his,* the sons and daughters of his fellow professors seemed like wan, elitist company. Better to throw her in with hoi polloi, to let her lift them up—but no, that would be even worse. He'd wanted to take her to another country, Italy, or Uganda, or *somewhere,* where it might be possible to raise her properly; he wanted to buy a tract of land in Idaho or Australia, with hills and streams and trees and rocks and birds and mammals, where Pella could roam and explore and he could trail behind, watching her grow; alternately he wanted to drop her at an orphanage and get back his life.

But something happened, to her and to him, when Pella learned to read. He would struggle out of bed after a late night's work to find her already awake and dressed, in the breakfast nook of their townhouse on Shepard Street, reading from some or another novel—Judy Blume, Trixie Belden, her abridged *Moby-Dick*—or else some picture-laden science book culled from the stacks of Widener. She read with colored pencil in hand, copying the best sentences and sketching members of her favorite phyla onto sheets of construction paper. A few last Cheerios, floating in a bowl beside her elbow, impressed Affenlight as symbols of utter independence.

When interrupted by a polite paternal throat-clearing, Pella would look up from her book and wipe a coppery curl from her eyes, her expression oddly reminiscent of the one Affenlight's dissertation adviser would assume when Affenlight appeared unannounced at his office door, and that Affenlight always thought of as *studius interruptus.* Still groggy and somewhat cowed by his daughter's industry, he would tousle her hair, start the coffee, and head back to bed. If the school authorities wanted her that badly, he reasoned, they could come a-knocking.

The next half dozen years were halcyon ones for Affenlights *père et fille.* *The Sperm-Squeezers* went through several reprints. Pella became a perpetual truant from the Cambridge public schools, and a kind of Harvard celebrity. She wandered the Yard with her backpack, handing out sketches and poems to the students who stopped to chat. The members of each new freshman class, neurotically eager to compete with one another in any and all endeavors, fought mightily for Pella's affection, and within the Freshman Union it became a mark of status to have her at your lunch table. She sat quietly through Affenlight's packed lectures on the American 1840s, as well as his graduate seminar on Melville and Nietzsche, and she seemed to draw few distinctions between herself and the graduate students, except that the graduate students were forever eager to please Affenlight, whereas she did so without effort, and so could afford to think for herself.

When Affenlight took the job at Westish, he and Pella decided that she would not come with. Instead she enrolled at Tellman Rose, an unconscionably expensive boarding school in Vermont. Academically, this made sense; Pella was finishing eighth grade at the time—around age eleven she'd started attending Graham & Parks every day—and Tellman Rose was far superior to any high school in northern Wisconsin. But beneath that rationale lay the obvious, unspoken truth that the two of them, by that point, could barely coexist in Boston, and Affenlight shuddered to think what would happen in a foreign, isolated place like Westish. Most of Pella's friends were older, and she claimed their freedoms for herself. She came home later and later at night, sometimes so late that Affenlight couldn't stay awake to see what was on her breath.

One day during that eighth-grade spring, Pella mentioned that she was thinking about getting a tattoo.

"Of what?" Mistake: it didn't matter.

"The Chinese character for nothingness. Right here." She pointed to one of her coltish hip bones.

"No tattoos until you're eighteen."

"*You* have one."

"I've been eighteen for a while," Affenlight countered. "Besides, tattoo parlors are illegal in Massachusetts." This wasn't a great argument, depending as it did on a geographical contingency—what if they'd lived someplace else?—but at least it posed a logistical difficulty.

Two weeks later, he walked into the kitchen and found Pella standing before the sink, rather pointedly wearing a tank top in chilly March weather. "Hi," she said.

On her left arm was a black-ink tattoo of a sperm whale rising from the water. Its long square head twisted back toward its tail, as if it were in the process of thrashing some helpless whaling boat. The surrounding skin was pink and splotchy. "Where did you get that?" he asked.

"Providence."

"How did you get to Providence?" Affenlight was shocked. Not by the fact that she'd defied him — as soon as she'd said the word *tattoo* he'd known she would defy him — but by the tattoo itself. It was a perfect mirror image of his own. Even the dimensions were identical, uncannily so. They could have stood side by side, pressed their upper arms together, and the ink would have lined up perfectly.

Even now it was hard to parse what Pella had done. His tattoo, then thirty years old, now close to forty, had always been a secret, sacred, sentimental part of him. Was Pella defying him on the surface while allying herself with him more deeply, more permanently, underneath? She had always loved The Book, as they called it, and she probably loved her father too, somewhere in there. This was a bond the two of them now shared. Their hair, their eyes, their complexions, were nothing alike — Pella looked unreasonably like her mother — but this was proof, proof of something, a kinship even deeper than blood...

Unless she was, for lack of a better phrase, fucking with him. She might have been fucking with him, playing around with things that were terribly, even preposterously, important to him. Pointing out the very preposterousness of his feelings for her, for The Book, for everything. *Everything you've ever done is nothing, old man. Anyone could have done it, every bit. I've already done it, and I'm fourteen.*

Affenlight had never been so angry. When she was young he'd never dreamed of using corporal punishment, but now he wanted to shake her, to shake every bit of insolence and cruelty, if that's what it was — of course, it might have been something very different—out of her body and onto the floor.

Instead he walked into his study and softly closed the door.

In a sense, that was the end of their relationship. Affenlight went off to Westish, Pella to Tellman Rose. She canceled half of her scheduled visits, claiming school or swimming commitments. Her grades were good, but every few weeks the phone would ring, and it would be an administrator, wanting to discuss some "incident."

And now here she was, asking to take classes at Westish, to be re-admitted to his fatherly care. Affenlight opened his top desk drawer, pulled out his daybook. "What kind of classes did you have in mind?"

"History." Pella straightened in her chair. She wanted to prove she was serious. "Psychology. Math."

Affenlight's eyebrows lifted. "No painting?"

"Dad, please. I gave that up forever ago."

"No lit classes?"

Pella yawned and fidgeted with her zipper. She looked exhausted—purple circles beneath her eyes, a small tic pulsing at the corner of her mouth. "Maybe one."

Affenlight made a few notations, clapped the book closed. Pella yawned again. "You should hit the sack," he said. "I'll see what I can do."

11

Henry flipped the light switch, dropped his equipment on the rug, sank down on the edge of his unmade bed. He kicked off his shoes and almost instantly fell asleep. But the phone was ringing. He had to answer the phone. It might be about Owen.

"Skrimmer."

"Schwartzy." They'd last seen each other ten minutes ago, when Schwartz dropped him off by the loading dock of the dining hall.

"Have you eaten?"

"No. Not since lunch."

Schwartz gave a paternal sigh of reproof. "Gotta eat, Skrimmer."

"I'm not hungry." ·

"Doesn't matter. Have a shake. What time are you running stadiums?"

"Six thirty." Henry lay on his back, eyes shut. "Hey. I forgot to ask. Any news from schools?" Schwartz was applying to law schools, top-notch places like Harvard and Stanford and Yale. Tucked into Henry's bag was a bottle of Ugly Duckling, the big guy's favorite bourbon, to give him when the good news came. Henry hoped it would be soon — the bottle wasn't all that heavy, but he'd been lugging it around for weeks.

"Mail only comes once a day, Skrimmer. I'll keep you posted."

"I heard Emily Neutzel got into Georgetown," Henry offered. "So maybe soon."

"I'll keep you posted," Schwartz repeated. "Have a shake. I'll see you at breakfast."

Henry got up—last time, this—and pulled a pitcher of pilfered dining-hall milk out of the fridge, added two scoops of SuperBoost. Ever since he'd arrived at Westish he'd been trying, trying, trying to gain weight. He'd grown an inch and put on thirty pounds; he could do forty pull-ups and bench-press alongside the football players. But still the knock against him was his size. Teams wanted monsters in their middle infields, guys who could blast home runs; the days when you could thrive as a pure defensive genius, an Omar Vizquel or Aparicio Rodriguez, were over. He had to be a genius *and* a monster. He had to eat, and eat, and eat. He lifted weights so he could chug his SuperBoost, so he could lift more weights, so he could chug more SuperBoost, lift, chug, lift, chug, trying to gather as many molecules as possible under the name Henry Skrimshander. An economy like that wasn't very efficient—it produced, to be honest, an awful lot of foul-smelling waste, which caused Owen to light matches and shake his head in dismay. But it was what he had to do.

Hours after the game, he was still wearing his jockstrap and cup— not a pleasant feeling. He pried them away from his crotch, stripped naked, climbed into bed. His legs and feet, gritty from sliding and diving on the infield, chafed against the sheets.

The phone again. He needed to answer the phone: it would be news about Owen, or someone looking for news about Owen.

"Henry Skrimshander?"

"This is Henry." Not a teammate—a woman's voice. Probably the doctor.

"Henry, this is Miranda Szabo of SzaboSport Incorporated. I hear congratulations are in order."

"What for?"

"What for? How about for putting yourself on par with the great Aparicio Rodriguez? Today was the day, right?"

"Oh. Well, I mean, it's...yes, today." When a game ended midinning, which happened most often because of rain, the official statistics reverted to the last finished inning. Officially, then, the Harpooners had beaten Milford 8–3 in eight innings. Officially, the top of the ninth inning had never happened. Officially, he'd never made an error.

"Splendid," said Miranda Szabo. "Listen, I'm sorry to call so late, during your private time, but I'm out in L.A., closing a deal for Kelvin Massey."

"Kelvin Massey? The Rockies' third baseman?"

Miranda Szabo paused for a perfect, haughty half beat. "Kelvin Massey, the *Dodgers'* third baseman. But don't tell Peter Gammons, that snoop."

"I won't," Henry promised.

"Good. The press can't know till tomorrow. We're still putting the finishing touches on this little objet d'art. Fifty-six million over four years."

"Wow."

"How's that for a recession special? Sometimes I impress myself," Miranda Szabo admitted. "But let's stay focused. Henry, I keep my ear to the ground, and lately your name is all I hear. Skrimshander, Skrimshander, Skrimshander. Like a tongue twister, only better. More mellifluous."

"Wow. Thanks."

"Everybody's asking, *Where'd this kid come from?* And nobody knows."

"I'm from Lankton, South Dakota."

"Exactly my point. Nobody knows where you're from, but everybody knows where you're going. Straight to the top of the draft charts. I'm hearing third round, I'm hearing higher."

"Higher?"

"Higher's what I'm hearing. Third, second, who knows? Now Henry."

"Yes?"

"Listen to me closely. You're a busy person trying to balance baseball and academics at a reputable institution. We may not know each other well, but I know enough about you to know that much. And I also know that you're about to get a whole lot busier. Do you know what the average signing bonus was for a third-round pick last year?"

"Uh, no." Until very recently, Henry's thoughts had been focused on next year's draft, not this year's—both juniors and seniors were eligible—and his goal for next year's draft was to get himself picked in the fiftieth round, or maybe the forty-ninth if he was lucky. He'd barely even bothered to daydream about a signing bonus. He had no idea what the five-star guys, the high school hotshots and the sluggers from Stanford and Miami, got paid.

"Guess," urged Miranda Szabo.

"Um. Eighty thousand?" It felt embarrassing, greedy, to name such a big number, even in indirect connection to himself.

"Close. You forgot the three. Three hundred eighty thousand."

"Holy shit." How long did it take his dad to earn that much? Six years? Seven? "Oops. Sorry. I didn't mean to swear."

"Swear away, sailor. Now, that doesn't exactly put you in Kelvin Massey territory, but it's a reasonable sum of money, and I think it's the least you can reasonably expect, come June. And that means people are going to want a piece of you. It's a crossroads, a complex time. You're going to need someone working for your best interests. You're going to need representation."

"An agent?"

"Exactly right. You're going to need an agent. Someone to help you navigate this crossroads, personally and fiscally. Selecting representation is a big decision, Henry, and not one to be taken lightly. Your agent has to be an extension of yourself. Just like your glove, when you're out there in the field. Do you trust your glove, Henry?"

"Sure."

"Well, you have to trust your agent just as much. Your agent, if your agent's a good agent, doesn't just draw up terms and disappear. Your agent becomes the fiscally minded, detail-cognizant you. So that *you*—the Henry-you, not the Miranda-you—can focus on baseball. And academics. Do you follow me, Henry?"

"I think so."

"Have you been contacted by other parties interested in providing representation?"

"Um, no."

"You will. Believe me. The mere fact that you're on the phone with Miranda Szabo means that everybody and their mother will be calling to offer representation. Happens every time."

"How will they know you called me?"

"They just will," Miranda Szabo said, and sighed at the predictability of it all. "These people are animals."

Henry's thoughts swung in odd orbits over the next few hours, as he lay in bed listening to the groan of Phumber's ancient heat vents. It was strange not to be able to hear Owen's breathing. Midnight came, and one o'clock and two, and though he wasn't quite awake he remained aware of the passage of time, the quarterly toll of the chapel bells. Unlike most of his classmates, who pulled all-nighters and slept through their early classes, he hardly ever saw or heard this time of night. He trained too hard and awoke too early, and it was a rare weekend kegger that found him leaned against a wall, politely holding a cup of beer that would be poured into the bushes on his walk home. The windows were cracked open, because it was always warm in their garret room. An occasional glitter of voices rose up from the quad below, an occasional gust of wind shuddered the panes. The latter drifted into Henry's head and became the gust that helped to blow his throw off course. He wished he could have seen Owen tonight. Just for a moment, just a peek of Owen asleep in his room in the ICU. Then he'd know that Owen was okay. It was one thing to be told by the doctor, another to see it for yourself. In Henry's half dreams Owen stared out at him, in the frozen instant before he slumped to the dugout floor, his popped-wide eyes asking, *Why?*

Why, in Henry's experience, was a question an athlete shouldn't ask. Why had he made such a terrible throw, so bad that Rick couldn't even get a glove on it? Was it because of the scouts? He'd tensed up because of the scouts? No, that made no sense. For one thing, the scouts weren't even there, they'd left after the eighth, and he'd seen them go. And anyway he had no fear of scouts in his heart, at least not that he could detect. Was it because he didn't want to break Aparicio's record, be the one to wipe his name from the record book, because Aparicio was Aparicio but he was just Henry? Maybe. But he could at least have tied the record before he messed up; then their names would be side by side. Then again he *had* tied the record; the error hadn't counted. He'd have a chance to break it next game. If he didn't want to break it, he'd have to mess up again. Maybe he'd mess up again. This was why you didn't ask why. *Why* could only mess you up. But he'd be fine in the morning, as long as Owen was okay.

Schwartz would be glad about Miranda Szabo. Thrilled. Ecstatic. Henry had been worried about what would happen next year, after Schwartz graduated and went off to law school on the East Coast or the West. But maybe he'd be gone too, off to the minor leagues a year ahead of schedule, with money in his pocket. It was bittersweet to think about leaving, he loved it here, but baseball was baseball, and it was fitting that he and Schwartz might leave together. Without Schwartz there *was* no Westish College. Without Schwartz, come to think of it, there was hardly even any Henry Skrimshander.

12

On Schwartz's law school applications, as on most posted documents, he listed his home address like this:

MICHAEL P. SCHWARTZ

VARSITY ATHLETIC CENTER

WESTISH COLLEGE

WESTISH, WI 51851

He rented a campus-slum two-bedroom house on Grant Street with Demetrius Arsch, his cocaptain on the football team and backup catcher on the baseball team, but rarely set foot inside it. During the day there were classes and practices to attend, plus Henry's regimen to oversee, and at night he worked on his thesis — "The Stoics in America" — here on the top floor of the VAC, in a dark-carpeted conference room that he long ago appropriated as his personal office. Schwartz held no official position within the Athletic Department, but he'd donated so much time and effort over the past four years that no one begrudged him his key to the building. Books with brittle, snapped bindings and missing pages, collected via his nationwide ILL dragnet, stood in drunken piles all along the long oval table, surrounded by a sea of color-coded note cards, wire-bound notebooks, and empty coffee mugs that had been converted to spit cups. He'd quit chewing tobacco two years ago, but it aided his concentration so much that, as he entered this final thesis crunch, he'd had to make some exceptions. With a good dip in, plus a couple Sudafed for luck, he could crank out nine or ten pages in a night. He wasn't into Adderall.

Schwartz cherished these private, diligent hours. All day long, no matter how hard he worked, no matter what he accomplished, a voice in his head berated him for his laziness, his sloth, his inability to concentrate. His concerns were trivial. His knowledge of history was shallow. His Latin sucked, and his Greek was worse. How did he expect to grasp Aurelius and Epictetus, inquired the voice, when he could barely string two Latin words together? *Vos es scelestus bardus.* Only here, long after midnight, while everyone else was sleeping, when nothing was expected of him, could Schwartz convince himself that he was working hard enough. These hours felt stolen, added to his life. The voice fell quiet. Even the pain in his knees subsided.

Tonight, though, didn't seem destined to contain much calm. First the Buddha's injury, and now, as Schwartz stepped out of the VAC elevator and into the corridor lit only by a red EXIT sign at either end, he could see a bulge in the manila envelope he'd affixed to his office door as a makeshift mailbox. He pressed his fingertips to the sandy yellow paper: sure enough, there was something inside, something that — he drew it out, heart thundering — bore the blue insignia of Yale University.

Schwartz prided himself on his honesty. If one of his teammates was dogging it, he busted that teammate's balls, and if one of his classmates or professors made a comment that seemed specious or incomplete, he said so. Not because he knew more than they did but because the clash of imperfect ideas was the only way for anyone, including himself, to learn and improve. That was the lesson of the Greeks; that was the lesson of Coach Liczic, who'd banged on the Buick's window.

That happened two years after his mom died of cancer. He was living by himself. He'd never met his dad — his parents had been engaged at one point, but his dad drank and bet on sports and left before Schwartz was born. When the woman from Children and Family Services came by a month after his mom's funeral, he'd told the woman he was about to turn eighteen. The woman's paperwork clearly said otherwise, but he was already six feet tall, weighed a hundred eighty pounds, and had little trouble buying cigarettes and sometimes even beer. "Come on," he'd said as he stood in the apartment doorway, arms folded across his chest, the dog yapping behind him. "Do I look like I'm fourteen?" Baffled, the woman left, and though it wouldn't have taken much investigation to prove him a liar, she never returned.

His aunt Diane's family lived nearby, and Schwartz went there often for dinner. In retrospect it seemed strange that Diane let him live alone like that, but then again she and her husband had three little kids and a too-small apartment, and it wasn't only strangers who equated Schwartz's size with maturity. His mom had socked away a little money, which paid the rent.

His school—on Chicago's South Side, near the Carr Heights projects—had metal detectors at every entrance and armed guards in the halls. The rooms had no windows, and the bolted-down desks could barely contain Schwartz's massive frame. Even though he was white, his teachers eyed him warily; they seemed intent on averting some vague but imminent disaster. AVERT DISASTER, in fact, would have been a perfect school motto—the purpose of the place, as far as Schwartz could tell, was to keep three thousand would-be maniacs sedated by boredom until a succession of birthdays transformed them into adults. Schwartz couldn't stand it, and the bank account was running low. In November of his sophomore year, as soon as football season ended, he stopped going to class. He got a job at a foundry—he was six-two by then, same as now, and people were more likely to ask his bench press than his age. He worked second shift, learned to drive a forklift, lugged tons of alloys from one end of the shop floor to the other. When his probationary period ended he was making $13.50 an hour, plus overtime. Some nights he drank cheap beer or Mickey's till dawn by himself. Other nights he took girls he'd gone to school with to seafood restaurants that overlooked Lake Michigan. When he woke early enough he went to the library and read the financial news — he thought that once he'd saved a few grand he might switch to third shift and trade stocks online during the day.

No one from the school commented on his absence until the following August, when football season rolled around. A gentle drizzle dampened the pavement as he left work and headed for his car — an expansive, rust-eaten Buick without a rear bumper, which he'd bought with his first few paychecks. Work covered him with sweat and metallic soot. He climbed into the Buick and dug under the seat for a beer. It was Thursday, just shy of the weekend. He pulled out a warm, linty can. As he cracked it, one of the assistant coaches of his high school team rapped on the passenger's-side window. Schwartz leaned over and unlocked the door. The coach wedged himself into the seat and asked Schwartz what the hell he was doing. Didn't he think he should quit acting like a goddamn spic and get his ass back in school?

Schwartz was looking at the pouch of the coach's sweatshirt, which sagged with the sharp weight of what was obviously a gun. He sat up tall behind the steering wheel and eyed the coach steadily. "That place is a prison," he said.

"And this isn't?" The coach chuckled and jerked a thumb toward the long low foundry building. He was one of the varsity assistants; Schwartz, who'd captained the JV the year before, couldn't even remember his name.

"This is just a shithole," Schwartz said. "Not a prison."

The coach shrugged. The gun-form rose and fell on his gut. "Have it your way," he said. "But this shithole doesn't have a football team." He climbed out of the car and was gone. Schwartz finished his beer as his crappy wipers slashed through the beading rain.

The next day, he went to school and then to practice. He hadn't been afraid of the gun. But the gun as a gesture impressed him. It seemed to indicate, if not love, at least the possibility of such a thing. The coach hadn't left him alone; hadn't assumed that he knew what he was doing. Instead he bothered to get in Schwartz's face, to tell him exactly what he thought of him, in the most forceful way he knew how. Nobody else — relatives, teachers, friends — had ever done such a thing for Schwartz, before or since. He'd vowed to do it for other people.

But lately he'd been lying, even to Henry. Especially to Henry, since Henry kept asking. Zipped tightly into the inside pocket of Schwartz's backpack were five torn envelopes he'd already received from law schools. Each contained a letter that began with a terrible phrase: *We regret to inform you … We cannot at this time … Unfortunately, our applicant pool …*

Schwartz turned on the hallway light and held up the envelope, but it was made of quality paper, the fibers thickly woven, and he couldn't see a thing. Maybe a quality envelope meant good news; maybe they sent thin translucent ones to the losers who didn't get in. He rested it on his palm, gauged its weight, though he'd heard that the thick/thin envelope test was mostly bullshit. He tapped it against his palm to see if he could sense the shifting of a reply postcard — *I, Mike Schwartz, humbly accept your kind offer.* Impossible to tell.

This envelope contained his final hope. If you wanted to use a trite analogy, he was oh for five, and now, with two down in the ninth, he had one last chance to redeem himself. Yale had the most competitive admissions in the country, but the other schools he'd applied to were nearly as exclusive, and his thesis adviser was an honored alumna. Schwartz, at all other times in his life, did not believe in fate, but maybe fate was on his side. Maybe those five rejections were a ruse to ratchet up the suspense.

At any rate, it was absurd to stand here wondering. The decision had been made weeks ago by a bunch of deans; it could not be changed. *Open the envelope, you putz,* Schwartz thought. *See what's inside, react, get back to work.*

He slid a fingernail under a corner of the glue, but that was as far as he could force himself to go. He sat down against the wall, let the letter fall between his thighs. The cartilage in his knees was torn to shreds, the result of too many hours behind home plate, too many sets of squats with too much weight, the bar bowed over his shoulders like a comma. The muscles in his back clenched and pulsed in painful, unpredictable rhythms. He unclasped his backpack, fished for his bottle of Vicoprofen, tossed three in his mouth. He tried to avoid Vikes while thesis-writing, but tonight was a special occasion. The whirlpool was what he needed; a good soak would soothe him and give him strength. He stepped back onto the elevator and pressed B2, the letter clenched between his teeth.

There was a brand-new whirlpool on the second floor, for which Schwartz had raised the funds, but still he preferred this one, a battered iron contraption in the subbasement beside the locker room. It was pitch-black down there, but his feet led him straight to his locker. As he twisted his combination lock in its casing, right left right, he could sense a gentle depression, like the hollow of a girl's neck, each time he reached the right number. He pulled a towel down from the top shelf—it smelled almost clean—and lowered himself to the splintered bench behind him. He laid the letter at his right hand. The cold-water pipes dripped; the hot-water pipes reeked of singed grime. He bent down slowly, like an old man, to remove his pants and boots and socks. The concrete floors, which sloped gently to grated drains, felt slick beneath his bare feet from dozens of coats of paint.

Locker rooms, in Schwartz's experience, were always underground, like bunkers and bomb shelters. This was less a structural necessity than a symbolic one. The locker room protected you when you were most vulnerable: just before a game, and just after. (And halfway through, if the game was football.) Before the game, you took off the uniform you wore to face the world and you put on the one you wore to face your opponent. In between, you were naked in every way. After the game ended, you couldn't carry your game-time emotions out into the world—you'd be put in an asylum if you did—so you went underground and purged them. You yelled and threw things and pounded on your locker, in anguish or joy. You hugged your teammate, or bitched him out, or punched him in the face. Whatever happened, the locker room remained a haven.

Schwartz wrapped the towel around his waist, found the letter—it radiated energy into the darkness—and wended his way around lockers and benches to the whirlpool room. He flipped a switch: a bare, cord-dangled bulb cast wobbling dusty light into the room. He preferred total darkness in the whirlpool, but he needed to be able to see his fate. He flipped another switch. After a beat the whirlpool gave a reluctant shudder and groan, and the water began to churn, kicking up an odor of stagnant chlorine.

He dropped his towel and climbed gingerly into the tub, positioning his lower back before the push of a jet. His chest hair waved to the surface like marine flora straining toward the light. What this school needs, he thought, is a full-time masseuse. He allowed himself a brief understanding of the masseuse: her merciless hands probed his neck muscles; her breath fluttered warmly in his ear; through the thin fabric of her blouse a nipple pressed, perhaps on purpose, against his shoulder blade. The fantasy went nowhere; his penis stayed dormant beneath the water, curled in on itself like a small brown snail.

When next he glanced at his watch, it read 3:09. He liked it to run forty-two minutes fast—a gently irrational habit, like wearing your watch into the whirlpool—which meant it was nearly 2:30. If he wanted some good working hours before dawn, he needed to head upstairs, throw in a dip, start writing. Heat and steam were loosening the envelope glue; all he needed to do was flick up the flap and peek inside. Instead he leaned out of the tub and turned on the old paint-splattered radio that rested on the cracked tile floor. He sank back into the water and listened to classic rock as the corners of the envelope softened and curled.

It's no big deal, he thought. If it doesn't work out, there's always next year. A year means nothing in the long haul. You'll go back to Chicago, work as a paralegal, volunteer at the circuit court. Sure, you studied for the LSAT for two full years, but you can always study more. You'll scrape together the cash for a rich kids' prep course and nail the god-damned thing to the wall. You'll win in the end, because you'll refuse to lose. You're Mike Schwartz.

But that was precisely the problem: he was Mike Schwartz. Everyone expected him to succeed, no matter what the arena, and so failure, even temporary failure, had ceased to be an option. No one would under-stand, not even Henry. Especially Henry. The myth that lay at the base of their friendship—the myth of his own infallibility—would be shattered.

"Looks like April's comin' in like a lion," the wee-hours DJ was say-ing. "Heavy snowfall in Ogfield and Yammersley counties right now. It should reach the Westish area within the hour, so plan on a messy com-mute. So much for global warming, hey?"

Schwartz checked his watch, subtracted forty-two: almost five o'clock. He hadn't wasted so many good hours, at least while sober, in years. Seized by a sudden, overwhelming urge to talk to Henry, he hauled himself from the tub, felt his way through the dark locker room to his stack of folded clothes, and pulled his phone from the pocket of his jeans.

"G'mornin'." Henry picked up on the second ring, sounding only a little groggy. It was part of their routine; Schwartz could call Henry at any time, or vice versa, and the other would answer quickly and casually, ready for whatever, never mentioning the oddness of the hour. Because what was sleep, what was time, what was darkness, compared to the work they had to do? Usually, of course, it was Schwartz who did the calling.

He settled back into the tub. "Skrimmer," he said. "Feeling better?"

Henry stifled a yawn. "I guess so. Where are you?"

"At the VAC, soaking my back. There's a snowstorm moving in. I thought you might like to get your stadium in before it hits."

"Okay. Thanks."

Schwartz glanced down at the letter in his hand. When he dialed the phone, he'd been unsure why he wanted Henry on the line; now he realized he wanted to tell him the whole story. Then they could open the envelope together, share the agony or the ecstasy or whatever. Let the Skrimmer prop *him* up for once. "Listen," he said. "I've been meaning to—"

"Hey!" Henry sounded suddenly wide awake. "Something weird happened when I got home last night." He began to recount his conversation with Miranda Szabo.

"Third round?" Schwartz repeated. "She said third round?"

"That's what she said. *Third round or higher.* Do you think it was a prank call? I kept imagining one of the softball players on the other end, with Rick and Starblind sitting in the background laughing."

Schwartz held the letter up to eye level, turned it in his hand. He brought it to his nose and sniffed the loosening glue. He knew what Henry expected of him right now, but it took a good half minute to find words that sounded like words he might say. "It's real, Skrimmer. This is what life's going to be like from now on. This is what we've been working toward for the past four years."

"Three years."

"Right. Three years." Humidity had detached the flap from the envelope. Schwartz lifted it gently, until he could see the handsome, promising ecru of the paper folded inside. "So the key," he continued, "is to stick to the plan. You can't control the draft. And if you can't control it, it's not worth your time. You can only control how hard you work today."

"Right," Henry said.

"If it happens this year," he said, "great. If not, it'll happen next year." Schwartz let his eyelids fall shut before reaching into the envelope: the trifolded letter, protected from the room's moisture, felt crisp and promising. Henry was saying something about Peter Gammons, the baseball analyst, but his voice sounded far away. The metal walls of the tub shuddered against Schwartz's shoulders. He undid the folds of the letter.

"Hello?" Henry said. "Schwartzy?"

13

Henry's breath clouded faintly before his face. Beneath his wind-breaker and sweatshirt and thermal top, over his T-shirt, he was wearing his weighted vest. No snow yet, but the clouds sagged low, like an awning about to collapse. He switched from a walk to a trot and passed from the Small Quad to the Large. Here the buildings were bigger, especially the tinted-glass library and the chapel, which loomed at the north end. The stripped trees shivered in the wind. A single light shone from an upper-floor window of the VAC: Schwartzy's office.

The stadium, a cavernous stone horseshoe with Roman arches, was built a century ago, and its size indicated some strange ambition. Even for the homecoming game, it was never more than a quarter full. Four mornings a week, Henry came here and charged up the deep, wide concrete steps that served as bleachers, down the shallower ones that served as stairs.

Inside the stadium's near-enclosure, the silence smelled different. He didn't bother to stretch — just bounced on his toes a few times, rocked back and forth, and charged up through the dark. The stone bleachers were knee-high and deep, and each step required a leap. A leap of faith, since it was so dark he could barely see the next one. The cold air shocked his lungs. The first time he ever did this, a few months after his arrival at Westish, he slipped and chipped a tooth on Section 3, then sank to the ground after Section 9, wishing he could puke, while Schwartz whispered unflattering remarks in his ear. That was when Schwartz still ran stadiums, the big guy surprisingly nimble. Before his knees got too bad.

Each step sent a frozen jolt up Henry's spine. Step. Step. Step. What was Schwartz thinking, sending him out here at this hour, in this weather? He liked rising early but this was absurd, more night than morning, no flicker of dawn or stirring of birds to keep him company. Just black cold and those clouds pressing down. He'd hardly slept, worrying about Owen, replaying that throw in his head. Of course if Owen'd been watching the game instead of reading, it wouldn't have happened, but that didn't stop Henry from feeling responsible. Then, beyond what he'd done to Owen, there was the simple frustration of messing up in the field, something he hadn't done in so long he'd forgotten that it was possible. Perfection was what he was after out there. At least those scouts had left before it happened.

After an interminable ascent, he reached the top row and slammed a gloved hand against the big aluminum 1 bolted to the back wall. He gave it a good whack, but the frigid atoms barely resounded at all. When he turned, he was standing atop a steep precipice that fell off into darkness. He kept his back against the wall as he edged, as quickly as his quivering legs would let him, toward the staircase between Sections 1 and 2. He could practically touch the rumpled quilt of cloud overhead.

He minced quickly down the stairs between sections—the descent, though easier on the legs, was the scary part—using his windbreaker sleeve to wipe his nose. His ears burned. At the bottom he turned and gave a little skip and duck, like a high jumper beginning the approach. "Come on!" he growled aloud in Schwartz's voice, trying to rally himself as he shoved off and headed grimly back to the top, dragging one weary leg before the other, slamming a squeezed fist into the frozen metal 2.

Just do half, he told himself on the way down, shaking his limbs in a full-body shiver. Half a stadium, seventeen sections, and then home to a hot shower, so hot it'd feel cold on his numb skin, and some hot chocolate from Owen's hot pot, and anything else that's hot. And then burrowing back beneath the sheets, the warm hot sheets, until physics class, which was still five hours away.

But then around Section 5, his legs began to loosen, his lungs to unclench. Better thoughts flowed through his brain. He picked up the pace. The blood worked through his body, trapping warmth between the layers of his clothes. His feet landed more lightly on the stone.

First he took off his gloves and flung them aside. Two sections later, he grabbed his Cardinals cap in one hand so he could peel off his windbreaker with the other, jamming the cap back on as he tossed the windbreaker. It floated up, bloated by the wind, before settling on the steps. Heat radiated off Henry's face. Salty snot ran down over his upper lip. A majestic fart propelled him to the top of Section 12, just at the springing of the stadium's curve. He slapped the sign as if high-fiving a teammate. It gave back a game shudder. He was cruising now, darkness be damned, stripping off his sweatshirt and his long underwear top without breaking stride. He moved through the dark, glad of the dark, part of the dark. He was down to his vest and T-shirt, wielding his own heat. A warm pocket of dark in the large cold dark.

14

Before Pella had lain down, she'd taken her swimsuit from her wicker bag and spread it on the David side of the bed, a reminder of what this day would contain. Now she undressed, put on the suit, dressed again. She hadn't really slept; it was three thirty in the morning, San Francisco time. The suit was a little snug — okay, it was a lot snug — but it was what she had. She twisted quickly past the bureau mirror, timing the movement to a blink. If no one saw her, including herself, it didn't matter what she looked like.

She could hear footsteps in the kitchen, the protest of the espresso machine as it pressed a few last drops, but it was too early even to exchange pleasantries with her dad. She slipped down the stairs and onto the quad, where a heavy, soggy snow was beginning to collect on the grass. She put up the hood of her sweatshirt and, in a gesture that seemed downright exuberant, since it wasn't strictly necessary, tied the strings into a bow.

Pella hadn't been in the water in forever, and yet, when she'd contemplated the possibility of coming to Westish to stay with her dad, the one agreeable thought that kept popping into her head was of swimming laps at dawn. She'd been a varsity swimmer, specializing in the butterfly, at Tellman Rose. During school vacations, while visiting her dad, she worked out at the VAC in the early mornings, when the only other people in the pool were old guys whose hairless legs poked out of their short piped trunks. Science professors, she assumed; the kind of lovably obdurate old men who bicycled everywhere, ate seven small meals a day, and were plotting to live to a hundred twenty. Her dad, though not a habitual swimmer, was a little like that too. At sixty, he seemed no more than halfway finished with this world.

Pella shuffled across the parking lot with her head down, trying to keep the wind-angled snow out of her eyes. As she climbed the steps of the VAC, she stumbled over what turned out to be a leg—the bare hairy leg of an enormous, almost naked person. Sleep deprivation, apparently, had caused her to hallucinate a naked lumberjack. The lumberjack was sitting on the steps in a snow-white towel, staring sadly ahead as wet snow gathered in his hair, his beard, his chest hair. Even when Pella tripped over his leg and had to plant her hands on the concrete to keep from planting her face, he didn't acknowledge her presence. She rolled over onto her butt, wound up sitting beside him on the steps.

"Nice towel."

No response.

"Are you okay?" she asked.

The massive shoulders shrugged up and down. Pella had never seen, nor hallucinated, so much flesh at such close range.

"Are you locked out?" she said. "Because I think they're supposed to open at six. It must be just about—"

"Door's open." The lumberjack heaved a heavy sigh. "You don't look familiar," he said wearily, still staring straight ahead. "Are you a freshperson?"

"No. Although I guess, in a way, you could kind of say—I'm just visiting," Pella concluded. "What about you?"

"Mike Schwartz." His right hand reached across his body for her to shake, though his head stayed turned toward the parking lot, the stone bowl of the football stadium, the darkness of the lake beyond.

"Pella," she said, leaving off her surname. She felt a pleasant anonymity, born of the swirling snow and Mike Schwartz's apparent indifference to her presence, which she was afraid her father's name might dispel.

"Like the city," he said.

"Yep."

"Sacked by the Romans in 168 BC."

"Somebody's been doing his homework."

Like an apparition—everything looked like an apparition in this weather, in this hoary predawn light—an elderly man rode up on a bicycle, dismounted niftily, and docked the bike in a skeletal rack at the foot of the stairs. His wispy hair was dusted with snow. He unhooked a small canvas duffel from his handlebars and trotted up the VAC stairs, nodding as he passed. To judge by the old man's affably neutral expression, you'd think Mike Schwartz sat on these steps in a towel every morning, greeting industrious gym-goers. Which was true, for all Pella knew. "Aren't you cold?" she asked.

"Cold is a state of mind."

"Well, my state of mind is freezing." Pella stood and brushed the snow from her thighs. "It was nice to meet you, Mike."

That was when he finally turned his head and looked at her for the first time. Pella saw that his eyes were a lovely, light-bearing color, like the lucid amber in which prehistoric insects were preserved. They contained a look of injured confusion, as if she had promised to sit there all day and was suddenly reneging on the deal. She felt, for a moment, as if her soul were being evaluated in some unusually profound way. Then he glanced down at her breasts. Pella crossed her arms. She felt annoyed that he'd looked, ruining the moment; doubly annoyed that she was wearing her unflattering flattening suit beneath her hoodie.

"I didn't get in," he said heavily.

"Get in what?"

He pointed between his shower-thonged feet, where an envelope was being buried by the snow. "Law school."

"That's why you're sitting here in a blizzard? Because you got rejected from law school?"

"Yes."

"Your loincloth's kind of riding up, there."

"Sorry." He adjusted the towel. "You know, you're the only person I've told about this. It's a confidence. You should pat me on the shoulder and say, *There, there.*"

"Sorry." She patted him on the shoulder. "There, there. So why would you want to go to law school anyway? Law school people are the dullest of the dull."

"I was thinking of becoming governor."

"Of Wisconsin?"

"Illinois. I'm from Chicago."

"Aren't you Jewish?"

"There are currently three Jewish governors," he said solemnly. "But yes."

His tone, as he'd announced this lofty ambition, didn't seem ironic. In fact, it didn't seem to admit the possibility of the existence of irony. "Well," she said, "there's always next year."

"Yeah."

Pella couldn't stop shivering—she hadn't even brought any socks from San Francisco—but for some reason she didn't want to leave. The sky was lightening beneath the clouds, and the snow had buried the muddled browns of early spring. Mike, his elbows planted on his knees, gazed down glumly at his clasped hands.

"So how do you like Westish?" she asked.

"I love it," he said. "It's my home."

He was so ingenuous, so honest, so physically massive—somehow the combination was wildly endearing. She sat down again. She felt moved to make a counter-confession, to distract him from his sorrow. "My dad's the school president," she said.

"Affy? He's your dad?"

"Yeah."

"Then I guess you heard what happened at our game yesterday."

Pella had not. Mike recounted the story. "Your dad even rode with

Owen in the ambulance on the way to the hospital," he said. "He really helped calm Henry down."

Pella didn't know who Owen and Henry were. "I guess that's why my dad was so late to the airport last night."

"He didn't tell you why? Hm. Maybe he likes to perform his Good Samaritan duties on the sly."

"I thought you were Jewish."

"So are the Samaritans. More or less."

The lumberjack governor was proving less stupid than Pella initially guessed. He was still staring out into the parking lot. "I can't believe Affenlight's your dad," he mused. "That guy gives a hell of a speech."

"I know."

"He's the reason I came to school here. Not that I had a lot of options. But I drove up here for prefrosh weekend, and he gave a speech I'll never forget. About Emerson."

Pella nodded. She knew the Emerson riff by heart, but Mike clearly wanted to tell it, and if that would cheer him up she was willing to listen.

"His first wife died young, of tuberculosis. Emerson was shattered. Months later, he went to the cemetery, alone, and dug up her grave. Opened the coffin and looked inside, at what was left of this woman he loved. Can you imagine? It must have been terrible. Just a terrible thing to do. But the thing is, Emerson *had* to do it. He needed to see for himself. To understand death. To make death real. Your dad said that the need to see for yourself, even in the most difficult circumstances, was what educa—"

"Ellen was nineteen," Pella interrupted to say. She hated the namelessness of women in stories, as if they lived and died so that men could have metaphysical insights. "One of the cures the doctors prescribed for tuberculosis back then was 'jolting.' Which meant going for high-speed carriage rides on deeply rutted roads. Months, weeks before she died. Coughing up blood all the way."

"Wow," Mike said. "That's awful."

"Yeah, right?" Pella stood again, repeated the motion of brushing the snow from her thighs. "Well, I'd better go swim my lap." She turned toward the door, more or less expecting Mike to follow, but he stayed put, staring out at the gathering snow. "Hey," she called back. "Maybe you should put some pants on."

He nodded absently, absorbed in some thought she couldn't decipher, about law school, or her father's speeches, or his injured teammate. "I might do that."

15

Pella wasn't in the guest room when Affenlight, post-espresso, peeked in. Perhaps this should have seemed worrisome—he expected her to vanish for good at any moment—but mainly he felt relieved not to have to explain or lie about where he was going. Which was to the hospital.

It was early, a thick snow was falling, and the hallways of St. Anne's were quiet. Affenlight obtained the room number from a nurse and knocked softly on the jamb. No response. Tentatively, he pushed open the door. Owen seemed half asleep; his eyes lazily followed Affenlight into the room. Two narrow tubes snaked up his ashen arm.

"Hi," Affenlight said.

Owen lifted his eyebrows in reply. He looked beautiful, beautiful, beautiful, in the way that a shattered dynastic vase might be beautiful, the ivory pieces unearthed and glued so the delicate plum filigree once again retraced its original circling paths after a lapse of centuries. Or was that an awful analogy? Owen did seem strangely ancient, after all, and possessed of an Asian delicacy, though not of Asian descent; the colors of plum and ivory could have come from his bruises and blood-sapped skin; and of course he'd been damaged now, and this evidence of his fragility could only increase his beauty . . .

At any rate, he somehow managed to look quite beautiful, even with the left side of his face grotesquely swollen and distended. Affenlight hesitated. His impulse to move toward the bed and offer some kind of comforting touch, to bless and thank Owen for being okay, was counteracted by the fear that whatever gesture he made might seem exaggerated and artificial. Finally he walked past the bed, feeling as if he were committing some tiny but still unforgivable crime of caution, and sat down in the chair beside the window.

Owen began to open his mouth, then grimaced and stopped. On the second try he carefully parted his lips and breathed the words through a slim gap between his teeth, without his usual elocutionary precision: "Guert. How did the meeting with the trustees go?"

Affenlight smiled. "Pretty well," he said. "I think we're on track."

"My hero." Owen winced with every word. He was looking toward Affenlight, but his eyes didn't seem to focus properly.

"Don't talk if it's painful," Affenlight told him. "I just wanted to say hello."

"I like talking." He paused with the obvious pain of talking. "What happened to me?"

"You don't remember?"

"The doctor said a ball hit me. But I don't remember batting."

"You were in the dugout. Henry made a bad throw."

"Henry did? Really? Are you sure?"

"Yes."

"Well, it's always the ones you least suspect." Owen let his eyes fall shut. "I don't remember anything at all. Was I reading?"

Affenlight nodded. "I warned you. It's a dangerous pastime."

The side of Owen's mouth farther from his injury lifted into something resembling a smile.

"It's good to see you," Affenlight said.

"I can't imagine why. I'm sure I look abysmal."

"No."

"It's good to see you too. Though I can't, really. Are my glasses around?"

Affenlight realized that this, more than the swelling and bruising, more than the slash of black stitches where the seams of the ball sliced his cheek, was what made Owen look so different, so vulnerable and lovely: for the first time in their acquaintance, he wasn't wearing his glasses. "They didn't make it into the ambulance," he said. "Most likely they're broken."

"Ah."

"Do you have another pair?"

Owen nodded. "Back in my room."

"I'll bring them to you," Affenlight offered.

"No, no," Owen said. "You're busy. I'll have Henry do it."

"It's no trouble. I need to swing back this way anyway." Affenlight fished for something else to say, before Owen could remark on the obvious falseness of this statement. St. Anne's lay five empty miles from West-ish. "I'll get a key from Infrastructure. Is there anything else you need?"

Owen thought about it. "I have a bit of pot. In my top dresser drawer."

Affenlight laughed. "I doubt I could get it past the guards." He pulled himself up out of his chair — he could bear to do so now that he'd sched-uled a return visit. On the way to the door a wave of courage swept over him, and he pressed his hand to Owen's smooth forehead, above his ban-dages and bruises. Owen's eyes stayed closed. His flesh felt surprisingly warm, and Affenlight's first impulse was to call the nurse. Then he real-ized that it wasn't the heat of a fever, just the average animal warmth of youth. Embarrassed, he removed his hand and thrust it in his jacket pocket. He didn't want to know how his touch felt to Owen — cold and stale, no doubt. No wonder he'd finally fallen in love — now that he had so little warmth of his own left to give. He truly was a fool. He moved toward the door, feeling defeated.

"You'll bring my glasses?"

"Of course."

"It's pretty boring here. And I'm having trouble focusing. A thought slides into my head, it slides right out again. Perhaps when you come you could read me something."

And just that easily, Affenlight was renewed.

16

The plows had been working since before sunrise, and the midday sun was warm. The roads were nearly clear. Henry had brought everything he could think of that Owen might need: schoolbooks, spare glasses, red sweater.

"It's funny, isn't it?" he said in the car. "I was freaked out about what would happen next year, after you left. But now I might not be here either." He hesitated, glanced at Schwartz, and brought out the thought that had been working on his mind all day. "I was thinking, if I did wind up getting a good signing bonus, like Ms. Szabo said, we could use it to pay your law school tuition. So you wouldn't have to go any further into debt."

Schwartz white-knuckled the steering wheel. "Skrimmer..."

"It wouldn't be a loan," Henry said. "More like an investment. After law school, you'll be making serious money. So we could just—"

"*Henry*. How much money do you have in the bank?"

Henry tried to remember what he'd spent on his last SuperBoost run. "I don't know. Four hundred?"

"Then that's what you've got." Schwartz swung the huge hood of the Buick around a snowbank and into the hospital parking lot. "No matter what some hotshot agent says."

"Sure," Henry said. "I was just thinking—"

"Don't think." Schwartz, bleary and beleaguered, cut the engine. "If anybody else calls you, agents, scouts, whoever, tell them to call Coach Cox. Understood?"

"Sure," Henry said.

When they found the room, Owen was asleep. "He's on a lot of meds," the nurse told them. "Even if he was awake he wouldn't be making much sense." The left side of his face, from the undercurve of his eye socket down, was hugely swollen. Henry stared at the blooming bruises, the ugly muddy mix of purples and browns and greens. He'd done that to his friend. Either the swelling or the broken cheekbone was interfering with Owen's breathing, and he sucked in air with a gasping honk. Henry left the stack of belongings beside the bed.

When they arrived at practice, Coach Cox was yelling at Starblind.

"Starblind!"

"Yes, Coach?"

"Did you get a haircut?"

"Uh, no, Coach."

"Don't pull that crap with me. I saw you at eight o'clock last night. You were shaggy as a dog."

Coach Cox had only two hard-and-fast rules: (1) show up on time, and (2) don't get your hair cut the day before a game. Haircuts threw off a ballplayer's equilibrium, because they subtly altered the weight and aerodynamicity of his head. It took, according to Coach Cox, two days to adjust. This posed a problem for Starblind, whose extreme sensitivity to the smallest fluctuations in his own attractiveness led to frequent emergency visits to his stylist.

"You want to ride the bench tomorrow?"

"No," Starblind said sullenly.

"Then you'd better give me twenty shuttle drills after practice. Get that equilibrium unkinked."

Starblind groaned.

"Groan some more, it'll be thirty." Coach Cox motioned to Henry. "You got a minute?"

"Sure, Coach."

They stepped out into the hallway. "I got a call from the UMSCAC commissioner," Coach Cox said. "Apparently the league wants to make a little fuss over your streak."

"Oh," Henry said. "That's not necessary."

"Goddamn right it's not. But Dale seemed set on it. Publicity opportunity and all that." Coach Cox stroked his mustache and fixed Henry with a big-news kind of expression. "Somebody over there managed to get Aparicio Rodriguez on the phone, and he said he'd be willing to be here for it."

"Aparicio?" Henry whispered. "You're joking."

"He said he'd like to meet the man who's tied his record."

Henry's ears began to ring. Aparicio, his hero, winner of fourteen Gold Gloves, two World Series. The greatest shortstop who ever lived.

"Apparently he comes to the States every year about this time, to work with the Cards' infielders. And he's offered to come up here before he heads back to Venezuela. Which'll probably be the last weekend of the season, against Coshwale."

Coach Cox caught Henry's eye and looked at him sternly. "Now, I don't want this to be a distraction, for you or anybody else. If we stay in the hunt, those Coshwale games are going to be huge."

"Don't worry," Henry assured him. "Nothing distracts me."

"I know." A smile crossed Coach Cox's face. "Things are happening for you, Skrimmer. Things are goddamn happening."

After practice, Schwartz and Henry headed up to the makeshift, nylon-netted batting cage in the gym on the VAC's fourth floor. Schwartz filled the pitching machine and then stood behind Henry with crossed arms, grunting, harrumphing, occasionally offering a word of instruction. Henry drove ball after ball through the middle of the cage. His goal, as always, was to meet the ball so squarely that it retraced its path and reentered the mouth of the pitching machine, sending the big rubber wheels spinning in the opposite direction, as if reversing time. He'd never quite done it, in all these hundreds of sessions, but he continued to believe it was possible.

"Hips," Schwartz said.

Ping.

"That's it."

Ping.

"Don't drift."

Ping.

Ping.

Ping.

Every Friday after their BP session, in season and out, Henry and Schwartz drove to Carapelli's, sat in their usual booth, and ate whatever appetizers Mrs. Carapelli brought them, followed by an extra-large house special pizza with extra sauce, extra cheese, and extra meat. Afterward Schwartz nursed a single slim glass of beer, Henry a mammoth SuperBoost shake, and they talked about baseball until Carapelli's closed.

But tonight Schwartzy turned on foot toward his and Arsch's house. "Where're you going?" Henry said.

"Home."

"But it's Friday."

Schwartz stopped, looked down at his gnarled fingers. His mitt hand's forefinger nail, nipped by a Milford player's backswing last night, had turned purple-black and would soon fall off. He'd run out of money, but that wasn't the reason he didn't want to go to Carapelli's. The last thing he wanted to do was sit there acting happy about the Skrimmer's impending fame. He still hadn't told him about Yale. And Harvard. And Columbia. And NYU. And Stanford. And U of C. "I'd better stay in tonight," he said. "Thesis crunch."

"Oh," Henry said. "Okay." He'd been waiting to deliver the news about Aparicio until they arrived at Carapelli's, where it could be savored properly. But it could wait until tomorrow—and it would have to, because Schwartz was already moving across the lot, his collar turned up against the cold.

17

Affenlight climbed the stairs of Phumber Hall, nervously fingered the key in his jacket pocket. His quarters were next door in Scull Hall, an almost identical building in many respects, same warping stairs and latticed windows on the landings, same hard-to-describe odor of lake water soaked into hundred-year-old stone, but he felt a world from home. Loud music played behind several of the doors. Presumably the students were at dinner, but they let the music play anyway. The proctors needed to emphasize conservation—talk to Dean Melkin about that. Dirty dishes sat on the windowsills. White dry-erase boards hung on the doors, black markers attached by corkscrewing cords. The boards were filled with scrawled phone numbers, quotes, directions. On one, a stick-figure man faced a stick-figure woman. An arrow pointed to his shoulder-high tumescence—THESIS, it read. Another pointed to the blacked-in hair between her legs—ANTITHESIS. Well, thought Affenlight, that about covers it.

Most of Phumber's residents were freshpersons, still frantic with their recently acquired freedoms. The top floor felt more sedate. No noise, no dishes, no vulgar cartoons. Only two doors, one to either side of the narrow landing. Affenlight faced the leftward one and knocked. He wanted Henry Skrimshander not to be home, so that he could be alone among Owen's things—not to snoop, mind you, but just to *be*—and so was glad when he got no answer. Voices rose up through the stairwell. He stuck the key in the lock and ducked into the room.

Soothly it belonged to Owen: orderly and full of books, with a memory of marijuana in the air. In many ways it was better appointed than Affenlight's: there were thriving plants, paintings on the walls, slim silver electronics. Messiness was confined to one unmade bed.

No lingering, he thought. No paging through books. Get what you came for and go. He scanned the room's surfaces for a pair of eyeglasses. It was clear which desk was Owen's—the tidier of the two. As Affenlight leaned across it his wrist brushed against the mouse that was tethered to Owen's computer. With a whir the screen came to life. He couldn't help but look. Open in the internet browser was a picture of a man, a muscled, bronzed, hairless, oiled twentysomething man, sprawled in a wooden chair with one hand cupped over the tip of his erect and outsize penis like it was the gearshift of Affenlight's Audi. Affenlight clapped the laptop closed, tried to name the potted herbs that were growing along the windowsill. Mint. Basil. And was that thyme? Yes, thyme.

The first definable feeling that worked its way up to his brain was disappointment. Owen would never want me, he thought. If this is what Owen wants, then Owen would never want me. Maybe he'd been thinking of Owen as a creature of the mind, a pure spirit to be mixed with his own, but that wasn't quite right, was it? Because Owen had a body too, and a need for bodies—and when it came to that, how did Affenlight feel about Owen's body? Did he want Owen in a sexual way? Because that website, that photograph—that was sexual. That was what he was getting himself into, or trying to get himself into. Not that Owen wanted him. But if Owen did want him—if Owen wanted his aging, pasty, great-for-sixty, okay-for-forty, unthinkable-for-twenty body, which was seeming more unlikely by the second—then would he want Owen's body in return? He thought he did, had fantasized about it, sort of, but compared to the sharp lines of that photograph his fantasies were all caresses and quiet confidences, sweetness and abstraction.

Two sets of questions swirled through Affenlight's mind—one set to do with Owen's erotic desires, the other with his own. He'd never thought of either of them in connection with hard-core pornography. And yet there was the website, right there. A part of Owen's life, in whatever small way; and now, because he'd broken his no-snooping dictum, a part of his. He lifted the lid of the laptop, prepared himself to look and to gauge his reaction. There were footsteps on the stairs again—but this time they passed the third-floor landing.

BY THE TIME HENRY MADE it to the dining hall, the salad bar had been cleared, the stainless-steel bins in the entrée line pulled from their stainless-steel frames and dumped. He found a campus phone, called Rick O'Shea to see if he wanted to go to Carapelli's.

"Sorry, Skrimmage," Rick said. "Starblind and I ate a while ago. Where's the big guy?"

"Working on his thesis."

"Figures. Listen, I've got Grandma O'Shea on the other line. She's telling me why Clinton was *almost* a better president than Jack Kennedy. See you bright and early, okay?"

Henry walked back into the dining hall, where he poured himself two glasses of skim milk. He'd have to double up on SuperBoost and be satisfied with that.

Chef Spirodocus came clip-clopping out of the kitchen on his wooden clogs, staring down at his clipboard. "Hey, Chef Spirodocus," Henry said.

Chef Spirodocus looked up from his clipboard reluctantly, his fat-pinched eyes slow to focus. In general he didn't like to talk to students. But when he saw it was Henry, he nodded. "Young man. When are you coming back to work?"

"Soon." Henry mostly enjoyed working in the dining hall. Chef Spirodocus drove a lot of work-study kids to quit with his speeches and tirades about how food was art, the kitchen a studio, the dish a canvas, and could you make art on a messy canvas? —but for Henry that kind of discipline fit right into his routine. And yet. If he got drafted, if he got paid to play baseball, he wouldn't have to do it anymore. "I think."

A mistiness entered Chef Spirodocus's small black eyes. "I could use you." He lifted an awkward hand to pat Henry's shoulder. "Your fellow students are idiots."

Back in Phumber Hall, Henry set his glasses of milk on the floor of the stairwell and rooted in his bag for his keys. He found them, then realized the door wasn't locked—odd, since Owen was at the hospital. He pushed the door with his hip and picked up the milk. As he turned into the room, he caught movement from the corner of his eye. Startled, he dropped one of the glasses. It landed where Owen's Tibetan rug met the floorboards, exploded into glinting shrapnel. Milk splattered his sweatpants and desk chair and half the rug.

"Henry." President Affenlight took two quick strides into the center of the room. "My goodness. I'm sorry."

"President Affenlight. Hey. Sorry. You surprised me."

"And rightly so." President Affenlight began gathering up shards and dropping them into the wastebasket. "What a boneheaded move on my part."

"No use crying over it, right?" Henry slung his bag on the bed and grabbed a towel from the hamper. "Here, let me do that." It was weird to find the president in his room, but it was weirder to watch him crawl around on his hands and knees, scanning the rug for invisible slivers.

"I'm very sorry," President Affenlight said. "I was just, well, you see, the hospital called my office this afternoon. Apparently they listed me as Owen's contact person, since I arrived at the hospital first. They needed someone to bring over his glasses."

"His glasses? That's weird. I dropped them off before practice."

"Ah. Well, that would explain my difficulties finding them."

"I left them next to the bed. At least I think I did. I hope they didn't fall out of the bag."

"I'm sure it was just a misunderstanding," President Affenlight said quickly. They knelt on either side of the sopping towel, separating pieces of glass from fibers of rug. Henry tried to think of something to say. President Affenlight seemed sad, or lonely, or something, though maybe it was just the context, the two of them hunched here on the floor. "Your tie," Henry said as the silk point of the president's tie dipped down into a milk puddle.

"Hm? Ah. Thanks."

When they stopped finding slivers, President Affenlight stood and buttoned his coat. "Sorry again to bother you, Henry. I owe you a glass of milk sometime."

Henry couldn't think of anything to say to President Affenlight, but he also sort of didn't want him to leave. Maybe it wasn't the president who was lonely — maybe it was him. "What do you call it," he asked, "when you assume somebody else has the same problems as you?"

"Projection," Affenlight said.

"Right. Projection. Do you ever have that problem?"

"You mean, do I ever project my problems onto other people?"

"Yeah."

Affenlight smiled. "Why, do you?"

"I asked you first."

"Sure," said Affenlight. "Doesn't everybody?" As Affenlight departed, the door swung shut behind him, and his expensive shoes made bright noises on the stairs.

Henry mixed his remaining milk with three scoops of SuperBoost, whipped it into a thick sludge, and ate it with a spoon. Not much of a dinner, but what could you do? He'd been up since before dawn, and he didn't have the energy to leave the room again. He opened his physics book and tried to study, but what he saw was the path of that ball, from his fingertips to Owen's face, over and over. The phone rang.

"Henry."

"Owen! How are you?"

"Much better, thanks."

Henry knew Owen would say precisely this, regardless of how he felt, but it was good to hear it anyway. As they chatted he could tell Owen wasn't quite himself — his words came slowly, and at moments he forgot where a sentence was headed. The one time he became animated was when Henry told him about his conversation with Miranda Szabo. *"Three hundred eighty thousand dollars?"* Owen said. "My God. That's ridiculous. But tremendous. It's ridiculously tremendous."

"That's the average," Henry said. "But high school guys usually get more than college guys. Maybe I'd get two-fifty."

"A premium for a lack of education? That's the most ridiculous news yet." Owen was getting worked up; it made him enunciate better.

"The high school guys have more leverage," Henry explained. "They can refuse to sign and go to college instead."

"Bah! Two can play that game. We'll sign you up for the GRE, threaten to send you to grad school. They'll crack. Oh, they'll crack so fast..."

"Hang on a sec?" Henry said. "We've got another call." He clicked over.

"Henry? This is Dwight Rogner. I'm an area scout with the St. Louis Cardinals. Great game yesterday. I was freezing my butt off, so I cut out a little early. But I heard you tied Aparicio's record. Congratulations."

"Um...thanks."

"I'll level with you, Henry. I saw you play last year, and I was impressed, but I figured you were a couple years away. Another of our guys saw you over the summer, and he said the same. Our attitude was, wait and see."

"Right," Henry said. "Wait and see."

"Then last week I started hearing it from our scout in Florida. 'Dwight, where you been hiding this Skrimshander kid? He's better than Vance White.'" Vance White, Henry knew, was the University of Miami's all-American shortstop. "You've made huge strides since last season, Henry. Huge. You just turned twenty, right?"

"In December."

"Heck, you're a baby. A lot of guys straight out of high school are nineteen. That's great. It gives you time to develop. Now mind you, it's still early, and a lot could happen before the draft. But you're shooting up our board. We'd love to see you in a St. Louis uniform. Too bad we've already retired your number."

"I know." And Dwight knew that he knew. That was why he wore number 3—because Aparicio had worn it for the Cards for eighteen seasons.

"Have you signed with an agent?" Dwight asked.

"No."

"Well, I'm technically not allowed to talk about stuff like this. But you should know, just between us, that our front office likes you a lot, and we're looking for signable players in the early rounds—guys who aren't looking to break the bank. So you should keep that in mind when choosing an agent. A hyperaggressive agent—your Scott Borases, your Miranda Szabos—can really hurt your draftability. If you know what I'm saying."

"Sure."

"It's not uncommon," Dwight went on, "for a team and a player to come to an informal agreement before the draft. For instance, we might come to you and say, Henry, we'll agree to take you in the first round, with our number twenty-six pick, if you'll agree to sign for reasonable money. Say, six hundred thousand or whatever."

The call-waiting was beeping again, Owen calling back, but Henry wasn't going anywhere. "First round?" he said softly.

"That's just between you and me," said Dwight. "But yes. First round."

"Wow."

"It's a lot to take in," Dwight said. "And it's a bit premature. Lots of time till the draft, lots of things could happen. But our GM wanted me to open up a dialogue.

"This is the perfect place for you, Henry. With the right support you could become the next Aparicio. Personally, I think everyone involved — you, me, the front office — should do everything possible to make sure you wind up wearing a St. Louis Cardinals cap."

Henry reached up and touched his brim. "I'm wearing one right now."

18

Schwartz sprawled on the couch in his boxer shorts and cracked his second forty of Crazy Horse. He never drank during the season, especially on the eve of a game, but today was a special day. The Day of Not Getting In. His penis slipped through the slit of his boxers into the open air. He flipped it speculatively from side to side a few times, but it felt insensate, like something that belonged to somebody else. Come mid-June he'd be unemployed and homeless, with a degree in history and eighty thousand dollars in student loans coming due. The Crazy Horse, all six dollars and ninety-four cents' worth, had gone on whichever of his credit cards wasn't maxed. He couldn't remember the last time he jerked off.

If he didn't get out of the house he'd turn to the handle of Smirnoff in the freezer. A pleasant idea, to get thoroughly and mercifully blotto, but the bus was leaving for Opentoe at seven a.m. He flipped open his cell phone out of habit, but he couldn't call Henry, not after standing him up for dinner. Or rather, he *could* call Henry, but he didn't feel like it. He scanned the bookshelves for the campus directory. It seemed unlikely that Affenlight's home number would be listed, but there it was in black and white. Yet another benefit of the small liberal arts college.

President Affenlight answered. "Good evening, sir," Schwartz said. "This is Mike Schwartz."

"Michael. What can I do for you?"

"First of all, I wanted to let you know that Owen is doing much better. It looks like he'll be coming home this weekend."

"Marvelous," President Affenlight said. "Thanks for letting me know."

"And thank you for all of your help yesterday." Schwartz could feel himself overenunciating to compensate for the Crazy Horse. "The whole team really appreciated it."

"You're welcome. But of course I was just doing my job. Have a good night, Michael."

"I was also wondering whether I might speak to your daughter for a moment."

"My daughter? Do you know her?"

"We met this morning."

"Ah. Well, I believe you've come to the right place. Hold on just a moment."

President Affenlight held the phone away from his mouth. "Pella," he called. "Telephone." There came a pause in which Pella yelled something back. "It's not David," Affenlight replied. "It's Mike Schwartz."

Pella picked up the phone a half beat later. "You didn't freeze to death."

"How was your swim?"

"I lasted a lap and a half. Then I had to lie down on the deck. The lifeguard came over to administer CPR, but I waved him off."

"Sounds rough."

"I prefer to start slow," Pella said. "Gives me room for improvement." She began a new thought, something about the snow. Schwartz slugged down the rest of his forty and cut her off.

"I was wondering whether you were free tonight."

"Free? Heavens, no. After a cappella practice I'll be volunteering down at the soup kitchen while I finish my paper on the theme of revenge in *Hamlet*. Then my sorority has a mixer with the Alpha Beta Omegas, my bulimia support group is getting together for dessert, and after that I have a date with the captain of the football team."

"I'm the captain of the football team."

There was a long pause.

"Oh. Well, in that case. What time can you pick me up?"

"YOU'VE GOT SCHOOL SPIRIT," he remarked as he took her sweatshirt and hung it on a wooden peg in the front hallway of Carapelli's. "A true Harpooner."

Pella glanced down at her outfit: a navy Westish polo shirt beneath an off-white Westish sweater, the same jeans she'd worn on the plane. "Sorry," she said. "There weren't many choices at the bookstore."

"No, no," Mike said. "You look great."

"Thanks. So can I ask you a question?"

"Shoot."

"Do you always have a beard?"

Mike touched his cheek as he slid into the booth. "It's supposed to be motivational," he said. "While I finish my thesis. Kind of an I'm-so-busy-writing-I-don't-have-time-to-shave thing."

"Does it work?"

"Not lately. I take it you're not much into beards."

Pella shrugged. "My ex has one."

"David."

"How'd you know that?"

"I heard you mention him to your dad. While we were on the phone."

A woman waddled over the red carpet toward their table, her arms open in greeting. "I thought you boys weren't ev—" Seeing Pella, she shrieked and spun toward Mike as if to shield him from harm. "Where's my Henry?"

"Henry sends his love, Mrs. Carapelli," Mike said. "He had to study tonight."

"Studying! That doesn't sound like my Henry." Mrs. Carapelli gave Pella a sniffy, formal, I-will-be-your-server look as she slid a menu in front of her. The menu itself seemed to be an insult—she didn't give Mike one. "Would you care for anything to drink, ma'am?"

Pella looked to Mike. "Should we order wine?"

"Uh...sure."

"We don't have to."

"No, no. A bottle of your finest white." Mike gave Mrs. Carapelli a reassuring pat on the shoulder as she spun on a sturdy heel and stomped away.

"Mrs. Carapelli doesn't seem eager to attract new business," Pella said.

"Don't take it personally. Henry and I have been coming here every Friday for years."

"But tonight he had to study?"

Mike planted an elbow on the table, ran a big hand over his widow's peak. "I'm having a hard time talking to Henry right now."

"Tell me about it," Pella said. But as Mike began to speak—haltingly at first—her heart sped up in that familiar, terrible way. At the bar a thirtysomething couple was dandling hands, their legs intertwined beneath their stools. The woman wore a red dress that clashed with the huge, ornately framed oil painting that hung above their heads, on which darker reds and golds were slathered in thick, light-catching layers like a bad Van Gogh. Pella felt little beads of sweat forming along her hairline. Not right now, she thought. Her panic attacks had grown less intense in recent months, and she knew how to withstand them, but this would be a less-than-ideal time. She considered excusing herself to go to the bathroom, but that would have been rude, since Mike was midparagraph and picking up steam, and besides, the bathroom seemed impossibly far away, across the dining room and down a corridor and around a corner and through a door, and it was bound to have some sort of terrible citrusy odor, citrus mixed with shit...

Mike had stopped talking, his head cocked at a concerned angle. "Are you okay?"

Pella nodded, squeezing her hands together under the table.

"Are you sure? You seem a little pale." He looked at her with those light-bearing eyes, laid his hand on her upper arm, just for a moment. Pella tried to remember whether she'd taken her pills this morning, both the birth-control one and the sky-blue one. But actually she'd stopped taking birth control however many months ago. Get yourself together, girl. "I'll be okay," she said. "Just keep talking."

By the time Mike finished his History of Henry, the wine was nearly gone. He looked so upset that it raised Pella's spirits, as if one corner booth at Carapelli's could hold only so much distress.

"So," she said, taking a small square of the extremely large pizza and setting it on her plate. "Let me see if I have this straight. Ever since you met Henry, you've been his mentor. Teaching him what to eat, what classes to take, how to hit a speedball, whatever. Henry doesn't move from point A to point B without thinking, *How would Mike want me to do this?*"

"We usually call it a fastball."

"Fastball. And now your work is paying off. You were right about the kid—what you saw in him three years ago, everyone else is seeing now. But it's not making you happy, the way you thought it would. In fact, you're starting to resent the ungrateful bastard."

Mike frowned. "Henry's grateful."

"But not grateful enough. Without you he'd be working in a factory right now. And instead he's about to realize his dream. And make a boatload of money to boot."

Mike folded his hands beneath his chin. Pella felt relieved to sit across from someone who was willing to act so unreservedly glum in her presence, as if she weren't there. David never did that—David's eyes were always right on her, probing, admiring, assessing, enjoying. That was what he called love. "It makes me feel like an asshole," Mike said.

"What?"

"To not be happy for him."

"You are happy for him."

"But to the extent I'm not, it's irrational. I had a plan for Henry, and it worked. I had a plan for myself, and that one didn't. I shouldn't take it out on him."

"Well, feelings aren't rational."

Mike folded two squares of pizza into a kind of sandwich and tossed them in his mouth. His woes didn't seem to affect his appetite. "You're talking to a man who's writing a two-hundred-page paper about Marcus Aurelius."

"How old are you?" Pella asked.

"Twenty-three."

"Same here. And not only am I not going to law school this fall, I haven't even graduated high school. I quit when I met David."

"Love at first sight, huh?"

Pella shrugged. "I thought so then. Now I just think I was intent on doing something big. Something nobody else my age was doing. David came to my prep school to lecture. He wasn't an academic, but he read Ancient Greek better than my instructor. He also had a wife, but I didn't know that at the time." She looked up to see how Mike would react to the revelation of the wife.

Mike's eyes were wide. "He knew Greek?"

She nodded.

"And you know Greek?"

"Sort of."

He touched his beard. "Wow."

"It was senior year," Pella said. "I'd just been accepted to Yale — my dad taught at Harvard when I was a kid, so I wanted to be just like him while pretending to be the opposite. Beforehand I was worried I wouldn't get in. But after I did get in, it started to seem so boring, you know? Half my class was going to Yale. But a bad starter marriage — that was at least five years ahead of the curve."

Was she rambling? She'd talked so little lately that it was hard to tell.

"David lived in San Francisco," she said, skipping ahead a bit. "I flew back with him and we moved into this loft he was renovating. I didn't find out about the wife for a while — the two of them were separated. By that time I was pretty much committed to staying."

Mike grunted in an impressed-sounding way. "How'd that go over with the president?"

"About like you'd expect. First he'd call and lecture me, tell me I was ruining my life. Then came the silent treatment, which lasted about a year, although it was hard to tell who was administering it to whom. Since then he sends me a Westish application once a month."

"And now here you are."

"And now here I am." She looked at Mike, who was looking at her. "I might be here for a while."

"Good," he said. "For me anyway."

Pella, embarrassed, pinged her thumbnail against her empty wine-glass. She'd had three little squares of pizza at most. It was the biggest pizza she'd ever seen, and even with Mike's valiant eating they hadn't finished it. "Is it fun?" she asked shyly.

"Huh?"

"College, I mean."

He shrugged. "I'm not much for fun."

Both of the young waitresses looked like Carapelli offspring, dark and voluptuous where their mom was dark and fat. One of them slid the check onto the table as she moved down the row of booths, collecting glass shakers of parmesan cheese and red-pepper flakes. Mike dug in his wallet, pulled out a blue credit card, and laid it on top of the check. Then, after squinting at the blue card quizzically for a while, he pulled out his wallet again and traded it for a gray one.

He smiled bravely, but the gray card didn't appease him either. As they talked he kept stealing glances at it. "Wait here," he finally said, sliding out of the booth and scooping up card and check.

"Is everything okay?"

"Everything's perfect," he said. "I'll be right back."

Pella wanted to crawl under the table—here she didn't have a dime to her name, and she'd thoughtlessly ordered a bottle of wine, and to top it off she'd barely touched the pizza. Talk about independent. She slunk down in her chair, pulled the collar of her polo shirt—purchased, of course, with her father's Visa card, which was sitting on the dresser in the guest room right now and which she easily could have brought with her—tight around her throat.

"I'll pay next time," she said as Mike approached, carrying his jacket and her sweatshirt. "I, um, forgot my wallet."

Mike smiled. "Don't be silly. I invited you."

"Still," Pella said. Mike wasn't pink-cheeked, not like the rest of these Westish kids. He seemed simultaneously old and young—sort of like she felt. "This might sound strange," she said, "but it's been forever since I hung out with someone my own age."

"How does it feel?"

"Not bad." She nodded, slipping her arms into her sweatshirt as Mike held it for her. "It feels not bad."

They'd driven to the restaurant, though it was only ten or so blocks from campus—a chivalrous gesture on Mike's part, to keep her out of the cold, or else he just wanted to show off his beastly boat of a car. On the way back they took a different, longer route along the lakefront, past the lighthouse. Waves crashed on the breakers, sending up curtains of surf The black of the water, which stretched as far north and south as the eye could see, graded imperceptibly into the black of the starless sky. "I forgot how much it looks like the ocean," Pella said, cracking open her window to see how it smelled.

"Everything but salt."

"When we lived in Cambridge, my dad was always driving us down to the ocean. Even in the middle of winter, he'd find some excuse." A spritz of mist came through the open window, along with an odor of rotting fish.

"I should have warned you," Mike said. "That window's impossible to roll up. Here." He blasted the heat and angled the vents toward Pella. They had already wrapped around the lighthouse and were headed, very slowly, back toward the campus, the lake now on the Mike-ward side of the car. Pella felt that flicker of sad foreclosure she always felt at the end of an outward voyage.

"We have three options," Mike said. "We can go to Bartleby's, which is a bar. We can go to my house, which is a mess. Or we can drive around until my car breaks down, which will be soon."

Would it seem forward, not to say slutty, to go to his house? Pella wasn't sure what the college dating norms were like these days—whether accepting three squares of pizza and half a bottle of syrupy chardonnay amounted to a sexual bargain. In any case, it seemed like Mike had a set of dating norms all his own. She didn't want to seem slutty or forward, but, just as on the steps of the VAC this morning, she felt reluctant to leave his company.

"I vote for your house," she said.

"Consider yourself forewarned."

The house was appointed in classic collegiate squalor: garbage cans on the porch, busted spindles in the railing. A storm door hanging from a single hinge, a peeling slab of tape on the mailbox lid that read: SCHWARTZ/ARSCH.

"I'd turn on the lights," he said as he reached back to lead her by hand through the dark living room, "but that would be embarrassing."

Pella could smell dried beer and another sickly odor, like spoiled milk. The sticky floorboards clung to the soles of her shoes. "How do you ever pick up any girls," she whispered, "living in a place like this?"

"I don't."

She let the lie slide. They passed through a low archway into a second room, perhaps a dining room, though the table beneath the chandelier appeared to be a Ping-Pong table. Even stronger than the smell of beer in here was the burnt dusty odor of a used bookstore's basement, where paperback copies of *The Catcher in the Rye* and *Rabbit, Run* and Leon Uris novels cost a quarter. "Books," Pella said.

"Too many."

"What's that noise?"

"My roommate."

Pella felt, again, both older and younger than the situation required. She'd skipped this whole era of roommates and beer pong and Salvation Army furniture—it wasn't necessarily something you wanted to go back to once you'd lived in a clean decorated place of your own. And yet being here, with Mike's huge hand wrapped around hers, she sensed a certain long-felt pressure lifting from her sternum. She imagined hiding out for a year or two, pacing her way through the brittle paperbacks, and finally emerging, rested and fine. Though someone would have to wash the floors. "Do you think he's okay?" she asked, meaning the roommate.

"He's a bit of a snorer. You'll get used to it."

"When?"

"A few weeks, at the most. Do you want anything to drink?"

"No."

Old. Young. Old. Young. They entered a room that was mostly consumed by a low bed, and Mike let go of her hand to shut the door. Pella sat down on the bed's edge. A fat stack of books slid off the mattress and crashed to the floor. *"Sorry,"* she whispered.

"Don't be."

She took off her shoes, lay down with her head on the pillow, and closed her eyes. She hadn't had sex with anyone but David in four years, and she couldn't remember the last time she'd had sex with David. A year ago, at least. If she'd once been a precocious, a promiscuous girl, she wasn't anymore. The world had caught up to her and passed her by. Every sorority girl who lay down in this bed probably had more "experience," arithmetically speaking, than she. She heard Mike fumbling in the dark, then the snap of a match. The blackness behind her eyelids grew slightly green. "A candle," she said, her eyes still closed. "Very suave."

"Thanks." Another stack of books was removed from the bed, and then she felt Mike lie down beside her. The heaviness of his body depressed the mattress, rolling her toward him. He whispered her name, which struck her, for some reason, as amazingly strange. Maybe he was just making sure he remembered it. She could feel the softness of his beard — denser, softer than David's — against her forehead. The candle flickered and waved, the snoring came faintly through the wall. She nestled into the line of his body, smelled the sweet sweaty odor of his neck, and fell asleep.

19

The Harpooners rumbled down a poorly maintained highway toward Opentoe, Illinois, for their noon doubleheader. Half the team slept. The other half stared out the windows at passing farmland, DJ-sized headphones clamped over their baseball caps. The cloud-clotted early light filtered through the bus windows and smeared itself on the drab pebbled olive of the seats. Schwartz's temples throbbed with half a hangover. Eighty ounces of Crazy Horse wasn't part of his usual pregame regimen. Still, he felt better than he had yesterday. Two games today, a rest day tomorrow, and after that, perhaps, another datelike evening with you-know who. He wanted to try not to think about her, not even her name; wanted to keep the fact of her existence tucked in the back of his mind, like an extra thousand dollars in your bank account. Bad example: his bank account was officially kaput, his credit card killed off by last night's dinner. If he wanted to buy a coffee at a rest stop, he'd have to ask Henry to spot him. Henry, all of a sudden, could afford it.

Okay, one quick thought about Pella: for someone who was supposedly a fierce insomniac, she certainly slept soundly. He'd neglected to set either his alarm or the backup alarm on his watch, and he didn't wake this morning until Arsch drummed on the bedroom door and announced that he was ready to go. Which meant they were already late, because Arsch always overslept. Schwartz twisted out of Pella's grip, threw on a pair of sweatpants, swept his dirty uniform back into his equipment bag (the Harpooners did, or were supposed to do, their own laundry), and headed for the door. On the way out, he paused to sweep a curl out of Pella's eyes, not sure whether to wake her or not. She didn't move a muscle. Maybe she'd stay there all day, sleeping and sleeping, her breathing the only sound in the house. The thought pleased him.

Now he pulled out his laptop and brought his thesis up on the screen. He felt, for the first time since he received his first rejection letter, like he might be able to work.

"High school!" called Izzy, pointing out the window at a long windowless structure of turreted gray brick.

"High school," agreed Phil Loondorf.

Steve Willoughby leaned across the aisle to check it out. "That's a prison," he said. "That's a full-on correctional center."

As the bus shuddered past the building, a block-lettered sign confirmed that it was indeed the Wakefield Correctional Center.

"No fair!" Izzy said. "Steve saw the sign!"

"No I didn't. Look at that place. It's got sniper towers."

"Who cares, man? So'd my high school."

"That's a point for Willoughby," Henry said.

"Oh *man*." Izzy slumped down in his seat. "Buddha wouldn't give him that."

"I'm not the Buddha," Henry said, and that was that. In the absence of Owen, the usual arbiter of High School or Prison, Henry had agreed to serve as guest referee. Whichever freshperson scored the most points en route to Opentoe was exempt from equipment duty for the afternoon. "That makes the score two to one to one," Henry announced. "To zero, since Quisp is asleep."

"Who's better?" Izzy asked Steve and Loondorf. "Henry or Jeter?"

"Oooh. Tough call."

"I gotta take Jeter."

"Henry's better on D, at least."

"On D, sure. But Jeter's a better hitter."

"Henry in five years, or Jeter?"

"You mean Jeter now, or Jeter in five years? 'Cause he'll be washed-up by then."

"He's washed-up already."

"Jeter five years ago. Henry in five years."

"Are you guys insane?" Henry whacked Loondorf on the back of the head. "Shut up."

"Sorry, Henry."

Every guy on that bus, from Schwartz down to little Loondorf, had grown up dreaming of becoming a professional athlete. Even when you realized you'd never make it, you didn't relinquish the dream, not deep down. And here was Henry, living it out. He alone was headed where they each, in the privacy of their backyard imaginations, had spent the better part of their boyhoods: a major-league diamond.

Schwartz, for his part, had vowed long ago not to become one of those pathetic ex-jocks who considered high school and college the best days of their lives. Life was long, unless you died, and he didn't intend to spend the next sixty years talking about the last twenty-two. That was why he didn't want to go into coaching, though everyone at Westish, especially the coaches, expected him to. He already knew he could coach. All you had to do was look at each of your players and ask yourself: What story does this guy wish someone would tell him about himself? And then you told the guy that story. You told it with a hint of doom. You included his flaws. You emphasized the obstacles that could prevent him from succeeding. That was what made the story epic: the player, the hero, had to suffer mightily en route to his final triumph. Schwartz knew that people loved to suffer, as long as the suffering made sense. Everybody suffered. The key was to choose the form of your suffering. Most people couldn't do this alone; they needed a coach. A good coach made you suffer in a way that suited you. A bad coach made everyone suffer in the same way, and so was more like a torturer.

For the last four years Schwartz had devoted himself to Westish

College; for the last three he'd devoted himself to Henry. Now both would go on without him. *Thanks for everything, Mikey. See ya around.* After draft day, Henry would have plenty of people telling him what to do. An agent, a manager, a battery of coaches and instructors and teammates. He wouldn't need Schwartz anymore. Schwartz didn't know if he was ready for that — ready to not be needed.

Izzy, who was sitting a row ahead of Henry, draped himself over the back of the seat to command Henry's full attention. "If you went to the majors next year," he mused, "then I'd be the starting shortstop. That'd be crisp. But you wouldn't be here."

"It wouldn't be the majors," Henry reminded him. "Not even close. I'd be in rookie ball out in Montana or somewhere. I'd be riding a bus like this every day."

Schwartz nodded to himself, pleased at this levelheadedness.

"Even in the minors you get mad pussy," Izzy said. "I'm talking *mad* pussy, yo."

"Sounds great." Henry gazed absently out the window, spun a baseball in his right hand.

"Guys want to fight you too. You walk into a bar and some guy clocks you with a bottle. I read it in *Baseball America.*"

"Why would anyone want to fight Henry?" Loondorf looked hurt.

"Because he's a ballplayer."

"So?"

"So he's a baller. He's got cash, chains, crisp clothes. He's got a hat that says Yankees and it's the real deal, yo. He didn't buy it at no yard sale. He walks into a bar and girls are like *damn.* Dudes get jealous. They want to get in his face, prove they're somebody."

"They want to take down the man," Steve said helpfully.

"That's right. Take down the man."

Loondorf shook his head. "Henry doesn't even *go* to bars."

Henry slid into the seat across from Schwartz. "Weird without Owen here."

Schwartz nodded. It wasn't all that weird: the Buddha just read in silence on the bus and arbitrated the occasional High School or Prison dispute.

"Any word from your schools?"

"Not yet."

"I wish they'd hurry up."

"Me too."

"I've been carrying this around for weeks." Henry reached into his bag and produced a bottle of Duckling bourbon. "I figured I'd be ready when the good news came."

A too-precise longing zipped down Schwartz's spine. Duckling was his favorite, and he'd been craving it lately, in the absence of any money with which to buy a bottle. "Skrimmer —," he began, but wasn't sure how to continue. Henry didn't have a fake ID, nor did they sell Duckling anywhere near campus. He must have gone to considerable trouble.

"Just take it now," Henry said, pressing the bottle into Schwartz's hands. "I'm sick of carrying it around."

"I can't," Schwartz said.

"Call it a Passover present."

"It's *chametz*."

"It's what?"

"If I observed Passover I'd have to throw that in the trash. Or let the goyim steal it."

"Oh." Henry thought hard. "Then it's an early graduation present."

Schwartz was starting to get annoyed. He couldn't tell Henry right now. The little guy had enough on his mind — an errorless game today meant he would break Aparicio's record, and there were bound to be plenty of scouts in the stands. Once Miranda Szabo called you on the phone, you were big-time, and you had to perform.

"It can't be long now," Henry said. "I told you about Emily Neutzel and Georgetown, right?"

Schwartz ground his teeth together. The bus slowed to take the

Opentoe College exit. The other Harpooners bobbed their heads to their pregame playlists, whittling down their thoughts to the ones that would help them win. Henry was still holding the bottle. "That stuff's expensive," Schwartz said gruffly. "You should keep it."

"What am I going to do with a bottle of whiskey?"

"Drink it on draft day. Celebrate your newfound fame and wealth."

The tone of this was wrong, mean, and a confused look crossed Henry's face. In his mind it was Schwartz who'd be drinking bourbon on draft day, clinking a toast against Henry's SuperBoost shake as they celebrated their departure from Westish into a bigger, better world. Henry tucked the bottle back inside his bag. He turned in his seat to gaze out the window.

Christ, thought Schwartz. He should have told the Skrimmer straight up, each time a letter came. Now he'd maneuvered himself into a real damned-if-you-do-or-don't. The only reason not to tell him right now was to avoid distracting him right before the game—but he'd already distracted him by being so brusque and rude. Might as well come clean.

"I didn't get in." It came out sounding heavier, more melodramatic than he'd planned.

Henry looked at him. "What?"

Try to be lighter this time. "I didn't get in."

"Where?"

"Anywhere."

Henry shook his head. "That can't be right."

"It ain't right. But it's true."

"You heard from Harvard?"

"Yup."

"You heard from Stanford?"

To keep him from going through the whole list, Schwartz reached into his bag and pulled out the stack of envelopes. Henry flipped through them. He didn't read the letters, just glanced at the fancy seals by the return addresses, ticking off each of the six in his mind. He handed the stack back to Schwartz, looked at him desolately. "Now what?"

The bus ground to a halt in the Opentoe lot. The Harpooners rose from their seats, stretching and yawning.

"Now," said Schwartz as upbeatly as he could muster, "we play ball."

20

Pella realized she'd been asleep for a very long time. The clock by the bedside — by Mike's bedside — read 1:33, and daylight streamed through the uncurtained window. It was pleasant and scary both, to think about where her mind had been for the past twelve hours or so. She wished she knew exactly what time she'd fallen asleep, so she could record her accomplishment, quantify her journey: I slept for *this long!*

Mike was nowhere to be found, and she remembered nothing of his departure. She hadn't taken any sleeping pills — just half a bottle of wine, barely more than doctors recommended. She headed to the bathroom, which was surprisingly clean, at least compared to the rest of the house. She peed and, for kicks, opened the cabinet above the sink: it contained nothing but a stick of deodorant, an athlete's foot ointment, and a tube of toothpaste. Amazing creatures, men. She yanked aside the shower curtain and found, inside the elegant old claw-foot tub, a battered beer keg, the metal top clouded with mildew. At least they had a shower curtain.

It would have been nice of Mike to leave a note — *"Back soon!"* — but she hadn't seen one in the bedroom, and there wasn't one in the kitchen either. Ah, well. She could live with the omission, given how sweet he'd been to let her, a near stranger, pass out in what had no doubt been the exact center of his little bed, so that he had to scrunch his big body against the wall.

On the kitchen counter, behind a scatter of sticky notes and tented-open books, sat a coffeemaker. The glass pot didn't contain any egregious mold. She decided to brew a fresh cup and drink it here, before heading back to her dad's place. He'd probably be pissed; she hadn't told him she wasn't coming home.

In the pantry, among economy-sized boxes of cornflakes and gigantic tubs of something called SuperBoost 9000, she found filters and a five-pound can of generic coffee. Everything in bulk: that appeared to be the Mike Schwartz philosophy. The Affenlights, on the other hand, were coffee snobs. She peeled back the plastic lid and sniffed at the coffee, if you could call it that — it was the pale-brown color of woodchips but not as fragrant. It would do.

She dumped the old coffee into the sink, where it diffused in the cloudy water, cascading down over the lips of stacked dishes. So far so good. But when she tried to rinse and refill the glass pot, she couldn't work the lip underneath the faucet. She tried to shift the dishes to make the faucet more accessible, but they were stacked in a precarious, Jenga-like pyramid, glasses on the bottom, and she was afraid the whole shaky construction would collapse with a ringing crunch.

The thing to do, really, would be to wash the dishes. In fact, she was feeling a strong desire to wash the dishes. She began loading them onto the countertop, so that she could fill the sink with water. The ones near the bottom were disgusting, the plates covered with water-softened crusts of food, the glasses scummed with a white bacterial froth, but this only increased her desire to become the conqueror of so much filth. Maybe she was stalling, because she didn't want to face her dad after not having come home all night.

As she squeezed liquid soap into the stream of hot water, an objection crossed her mind: What would Mike think? It was a nice gesture, to do somebody else's dishes, but it could also be construed as an admonishment: "If nobody else will clean up this shithole, I'll do it myself!" In fact, some version of that interpretation could hardly be avoided. She turned off the water. Even if she and Mike had been dating for months, unprovoked dishwashing might be considered strange. Meddlesome. Overbearing. Unless she'd dirtied the dishes herself: that would be different. Then the dishes *should* be done, and the failure to do them might pose its own problems.

But the dishes weren't hers, and she and Mike weren't dating. They hadn't even kissed. Therefore the doing of dishes could only seem weird, neurotic, invasive. Mike's roommate—Mr. Arsch, from the mailbox—would take one look at the order she'd imposed and say something penetrating, something along the lines of "Dude, is that chick psycho or what?" And Mike would shrug and never call her again.

She looked down into the white bubbles. Steam rose off the water, brushed her cheeks and chin. Her hand rested on the four-pronged hot-water knob, which felt warm to the touch. She really, really wanted to wash the dishes. Once, late at night, not long after she'd moved to San Francisco, she'd really, really wanted to cut up a slightly mushy avocado and rub the pit in her palms. It was an ecstasy-type desire, though she hadn't taken ecstasy. She made David drive her to three supermarkets to find the right avocado. She told him she was craving guacamole—a more acceptable urge, if just barely. Luckily he'd fallen asleep while she was rolling the slimy pit in her palms, pretending to make guacamole. In the morning, having buried the chips and the yellow-green mush in the kitchen trash, she claimed to have eaten it all. She still had no idea how to make guacamole.

That episode stood out in Pella's mind as a benchmark of small but irresistible desire, but if anything she wanted to wash these dishes even more. She could see in advance the scrubbed white color of the fresh-bleached sink, the rows of overturned pots lying on the counter to dry. Maybe Mr. Arsch wouldn't think she was psycho. Maybe he'd be thrilled. Who wouldn't want a maid who worked for free? Maybe Mr. Arsch was sad, just as she'd been sad, and that was why the kitchen was such a mess. Maybe a scrubbed-out sink would be the boost he needed. Slovenliness correlated highly with despair—the inability to exert influence over one's environment, et cetera. Speaking of despair, she hadn't yet taken her sky-blue pill. She'd probably have a cracking headache in about five minutes. Better enjoy this respite while it lasted.

While these thoughts were spinning through her sleep-buoyed brain, she had scrubbed several plates and laid them on the counter in a fanned-out formation to dry. A fistful of flatware was calling her name. Whatever retribution awaited, she'd left herself little choice but to finish the dishes. She squinched her rag between the fork tines and rubbed.

By the time she finished she'd worked up a sweat, and she needed her sky-blue pill far more than a cup of coffee. On her way out she lingered in the doorway for a long minute, admiring the empty sink.

21

As the Harpooners filed off the bus, each of them slapped the black rubber seal above the door for luck. Driving four hours south made a difference in the weather; birds were chirping, and a loamy smell of spring hung thick in the air. Loondorf began to sneeze. The clouds were breaking and shrinking, leaving marbled patches of stonewashed blue between them. The Opentoe players, clad in their threadbare brown-and-green uniforms, were liming the foul lines and raking the basepaths like old homesteaders.

"Same old Opentoe," Rick O'Shea noted, scratching his incipient beer belly as he blinked the sleep from his eyes. "Same ugly-ass jerseys."

Starblind nodded. "Same jerks." Opentoe College had some sort of evangelical mission that involved perpetual kindness and hopelessly outdated uniforms. The Harpooners hated them for it. It was unspeakably infuriating that the one school in the UMSCAC that spent less money on its baseball program than Westish always managed to kick their ass. The Opentoe players never talked even the mildest forms of smack. If you worked a walk, the first baseman would say, "Good eye." If you ripped a three-run triple, the third baseman would say, "Nice rip." They smiled when they were behind, and when they were ahead they looked pensive and slightly sad. Their team name was the Holy Poets.

Usually Owen began warm-ups by leading the team in a series of yoga stretches. Today Henry took his place, omitting Owen's stream of commentary ("Pretend that your shoulders have dissolved, good, no, let them dissolve entirely...") and instead just proceeding from one stretch to the next. The Harpooners followed along by rote as they scanned the bleachers. There weren't any girls, Opentoe was weak on girls, but more and more scouts kept arriving, each new scout announcing himself as such by either his laptop or his cigar, depending on his generation, and by shaking hands with the rest of the scouts.

After they stretched, Arsch took Starblind down to the bullpen to begin loosening up to pitch. The rest of the Harpooners jogged into position for infield/outfield drills. Schwartz, who saved his body for games by practicing as little as possible, retreated to the dugout. Today was going to be a long one: in his rush to leave the house, he'd left his Vicoprofen behind. Now, like a true addict, he emptied his bag, side pockets and all, strewing the contents on the bench. The sweep yielded two chipped and dusty Sudafed, three Advil, and a promising white spheroid that turned out to be a mint. He threw it all in his mouth, germs be damned, and downed it with a slug of lukewarm Mountain Dew.

He ambled to the bullpen to check on Starblind's progress. The ball struck the heart of Arsch's mitt with a loud report.

"How's he looking, Meat?"

"He's poppin' it, Mike. Really poppin' it."

"Deuce?"

"Poppin' it."

"Change?"

"On a string," Arsch declared. "He's poppin' them all."

After a few more pitches Starblind wandered toward them, working his right arm in rapid, manic circles. Starblind entered a crazed, almost incommunicado state when he pitched. If you didn't know better, you'd swear he'd done oodles of coke. "Look at 'em," he said, jerking his head toward the scouts, who were still arriving.

Schwartz shrugged. "Rest of the season'll be like this. Might as well get used to it."

"Get used to what?" Starblind snorted. "Those guys see Henry and zero else. I could give up ten or strike out twenty. Doesn't make a shit bit of difference."

"Makes a difference to me," Schwartz said mildly.

Coach Cox called the Harpooners together. "Here's the batting order. Starblind Kim Skrimshander, Schwartz O'Shea Boddington, Quisp Phlox Guladni. Let's work the count, keep our wits about us. Mike, anything to add?"

Not only had Schwartz forgotten his pills but he'd also neglected to pick out a quote. That's what you got for going on a date the night before a game. He'd have to extemporize. He leaned into the center of the huddle and surveyed his teammates, testing each with a mild version of The Stare. "Brook," he said, fixing his eyes on Boddington, one of the team's few seniors, "what was our record your first year?"

"Three and twenty-nine, Mike."

"O'Shea. What about yours?"

"Um . . . ten and twenty?"

"Close enough. And last year? Jensen?"

"Sixteen and sixteen, Schwartzy."

Schwartz nodded. "Don't forget it. Don't anybody forget it." He looked around, cranked The Stare to about a five on a ten-point scale. He looked at Henry, Henry looked at him, but nothing useful passed between them. Schwartz took off his cap and wiped the sweat from his forehead. He felt a little off, a little odd, like he was playing himself on TV. He could hear his own voice bouncing around in his head.

But the troops were nodding, waiting, their faces pulled into expressions of grim resolution: they loved Schwartz's fire and brimstone. They lived for it. They were going to imitate it for their grandkids. He kept going: "All those losing seasons. And not just for us. For all the guys who came before us too. A hundred and four years of baseball, and Westish College, *our* college, has never won conference. Never."

"Now we're a different ball club. We're eleven and two. We've got all the talent in the world. But look at those guys in the other dugout. Go on, look at them." He waited while they looked. "You think those guys care what our record is? Hell no. They think they're going to walk all over us, because we're from Westish College. They see this uniform and their eyes light up. They think this uniform's some kind of joke." Schwartz thumped himself on the chest, where the blue harpooner stood alone in the prow of his boat. "Is this a joke?" he snarled, throwing in some curse words. "Is that what this is?" His voice softened in preparation for the denouement; it was important to vary your volume and your cadence. "Let's teach them something about this uniform," he said. "Let's teach them something about Westish College." He scanned the huddle. His teammates' jaws were clenched, their nostrils flared. Most of their eyes were hidden behind sunglasses, but the eyes he could see looked ready to go. Even he felt a little heartened.

Henry stuck a batting-gloved hand into the center of the huddle, palm down. Everybody else followed suit. "Owen on three," he said. "One-two-three—"

"*Buddha.*"

STARBLIND WALKED, Sooty Kim bunted him to second, Henry roped a single past the pitcher's ear. Schwartz crushed a moonshot into left-center field. Opentoe's park had no outfield wall in the usual sense—just a faraway chain-link fence to separate it from the soccer field. A faster or better-medicated man would have made it to third or even scored, but Schwartz could only trot to second, press both hands to the small of his back, and stand there wincing while Rick and Boddington made outs. Two–nothing, Westish.

Meat was right. Starblind was popping his pitches like Schwartz had never seen. The only balls put into play were weak pop-ups or squibblers back to the pitcher. Schwartz heard a couple of Holy Poets cursing under their breath as they swung and missed. The curses were different from his own, but the currents that ran beneath their *shucks* and *biscuit* and *featherhead* were equally dark. Then their cheery looks returned, whether because a world of deeds and miracles surrounded them even when they lost, or because they were playing Westish and were therefore bound to win.

Between pitches Schwartz snuck glances at the crowd of scouts sitting three-deep behind the backstop, their wraparound shades disguising their thoughts. If there wasn't one from every major-league team, it was damned close. He almost wished that Starblind wouldn't pitch so well, so the Poets would put more balls in play, so the Skrimmer could show off his defense.

In the bottom of the fourth, finally, an Opentoe batter laced a low shot into the hole between short and third. Henry broke toward it with typical quickness, snapped it up cleanly on the backhand side. As he set his feet to throw, though, the ball seemed to get stuck in his glove. He had to rush the throw, which flew low and wide of the bag. Rick O'Shea stretched to his full length and scooped it out of the dirt, lifted his glove to show the ump he had the ball.

"Safe!"

"What?" Rick, enraged, jumped like he was hornet-stung. "I scooped it!" he yelled, waving the ball. "I scooped it clean!"

The ump shook his head. "Foot came off the bag."

"No way!"

Schwartz couldn't say for sure whether Rick's foot had stayed on the bag or not. Normally he might not have argued, but Rick seemed adamant—and if the runner was safe, the play would be ruled an error. Henry's streak would be over, Aparicio's record unbroken. He turned to the plate umpire. "D'you see that, Stan?"

"Not my call."

"You're in charge out here."

Stan shook his head.

"I'll be right back." As Schwartz walked toward him, the field ump resumed his crouch, hands on thighs, peering in toward home plate as if the next pitch were about to be thrown. This was his way of saying, *Don't approach me.* Schwartz approached. "Close play."

The ump kept his hands planted on his thighs, humorlessly ignoring Schwartz. "Stan said I could come out here," Schwartz told him.

"Good for Stan."

Schwartz glanced at Henry, who was earnestly smoothing the dirt with his cleat, head bowed. "The throw had him," he said.

The ump stayed in his crouch and stared straight ahead.

"Stand up and talk to me like a man," Schwartz said.

"Watch yourself."

"You watch yourself. You blew the call and you know it."

"I don't know who you think you are, kid, but you've got till the count of one to get out of my face."

"Kid?" Schwartz repeated. He lowered his chin to stare down into the watery eyes of this pathetic, ineffectual man.

Whether the umpire did it on purpose, or was fumbling his words because it unnerved him to have two hundred thirty pounds of Schwartz looming over him, or simply because such things were inevitable when you put two faces so close together, a fleck of spittle flew out of his mouth and struck Schwartz on the cheek. A red cloud descended over Schwartz. He never should have told Henry about law school. "You little pissant," he hissed. "Your real job sucks, your wife doesn't, so you come out here and boss around a bunch of college kids every weekend, to make you feel like a man, a big fucking man, a big fucking little man, and now you're going to *spit* on me? Do you have *any idea* who you're fucking with? I'll tear you apart. I'll tear you up and eat your godda—"

The next thing he knew Coach Cox had him around the waist and was leading him off the field, calmly chomping his gum while Schwartz twisted halfway around so he could keep screaming at the umpire. The ump fiddled with his ball-strike counter and pretended not to listen. Schwartz stopped midsentence. The red cloud behind his eyes began to lift, and he wondered what all he'd said. Of course he'd been ejected. He glanced back toward Henry, who offered a tiny lift of his shoulders. Schwartz never should have told him, not right before a game.

Schwartz shifted his gaze to the scoreboard in right field. There it was, plain as day, that green light winking in the distance beneath the letter *E*. Somebody said a few words over the loudspeaker, announcing the end of Henry's streak. The whole crowd, including the scouts and the players from both teams, rose as one and began to applaud.

22

Affenlight slipped out of his office, a slim volume of Whitman tucked into his inside jacket pocket like a concealed weapon. He headed toward his car, staying close to the bleached-stone walls of Scull Hall so he couldn't be seen from the windows above. Scull Hall, though similar in size and design to the other buildings on the Small Quad, was supposed to look slightly more distinguished, housing as it did the president's office and quarters, and to that end the narrow strip of earth between the foundation and the sidewalk had already been churned and fertilized and planted with spring bulbs. The damp soil, sprinkled with tiny white nutritional pellets, sent up a pleasingly dense black odor. He'd told Pella he needed to work until four, whereupon they'd drive to Door County to buy her some new clothes.

He drove fast and parked the Audi. The glass doors of St. Anne's parted to grant him entrance. Affenlight dropped his cigarette butt into a trash can and thought of Pella's mother, who'd spent her life—or at least the part during which he'd known her—among the sick and dying, but never seemed to suffer a moment of physical or psychological weakness. Perhaps she was blessed with a hardy constitution, or perhaps she couldn't afford to complain or feel pain when she had so many fragile bodies to tend to. When Affenlight caught the flu or fell into one of his grim moods, she would frown and ignore him. He'd dismissed this as a lack of sympathy, and even perhaps a form of stupidity, but maybe it was wisdom instead. Had he learned—would he ever learn—to discard the thoughts he could not use? It remained an open question, how much sympathy love could stand.

When he walked into Owen's room, Owen was sitting up in bed, and a very composed-looking African-American woman in a tailored suit was sitting in his—in Affenlight's—chair, though she'd dragged it closer to the bed than Affenlight would ever have dared. "President Affenlight," Owen said, his voice improved since yesterday. "What a nice surprise."

The woman rose and extended her hand. "Genevieve Wister." Her tone and smile suggested some sort of ownership of the room. A doctor, then, or a physical therapist—they probably dispensed with uniforms on the weekend. Her skirt was cut just above the knee. Her heels, though low, made it virtually impossible not to notice the long sleek muscles of her calves.

"Guert Affenlight."

She continued to clasp his hand, several beats past what Affenlight had anticipated. "A personal visit from the school president," she said, her tone occupying some hard-to-identify spot between wry and impressed, "after a bump on the head. I've always known that Owen was in good hands here at Westish, but this surpasses everything."

Always known? Affenlight looked from Genevieve Wister to Owen Dunne, and back and again. Owen nodded, as if in response to an audible question. "My mother," he explained.

"Ah." It occurred to Affenlight that if someone aimed a gun at his chest right now, Whitman would take the bullet. The little green-clad book rested against his heart like a hidden ridiculous earnestness. What had he been thinking, bringing poems, poems about sturdy lads, supple lads, lads who lay athwart your hips? It wasn't just ridiculous; it was criminal.

Even as he thought this, his spirits dipped at the loss of the chance to read to Owen. He'd been dreaming of it all morning. But Whitman! What was he thinking? Reading aloud was already borderline intimate, one voice, two pairs of ears, well-shaped words—you didn't need to press your luck. He should have brought Tocqueville. Or William James. Or Plato. No, not Plato.

He released Genevieve Wister's hand and bathed her in the most charming, mother-schmoozing smile he could muster. Still, he felt jittery, as if addressing an authority-wielding elder rather than someone twelve or fifteen years younger than he. "The surname threw me," he said apologetically.

"When I divorced Owen's father, I decided that 'Owen Wister' wasn't such a good idea."

"Ah," Affenlight said again dumbly. What a strange thing love was! You met an excruciatingly beautiful creature, one who seemed too well formed to have sprung from sperm and egg and that whole imperfect error-prone process—and then you met his mother.

"Good news," Owen said. "They're setting me free today."

"You won't have to travel so far to visit, President Affenlight," Genevieve joked.

"Wonderful," Affenlight said. "That's wonderful." The longer he looked, the more attuned he became to the resemblances between mother and son. At first the differences in their skin color had fooled him. Owen's—apart from his parti-colored, metallically bright bruises—was close in hue to Affenlight's own, though ashen where Affenlight's was ruddy. Genevieve, on the other hand, was extremely darkly complected in a West African way. Owen's black, Affenlight thought. He'd known this, of course, but seeing his mother made it plain.

Genevieve's features were sharper, more forceful than Owen's, but their dark eyes were nearly identical, and the true similarities were in their bodies: the same modest, gently sloping shoulders, the same soft limbs and long graceful fingers. The way she sat down on the edge of the bed, gesturing Affenlight toward the vacated chair with a slight, lively movement of her palm, might have been something she'd learned from countless hours of observing her son. Or, of course, the other way around.

"I really can't stay," Affenlight said. "I just dropped by to ensure Owen was being well cared for. Clearly"—he offered Genevieve a solicitous smile—"he is."

"Well, you're very kind to take such an interest," Genevieve said.

"My pleasure." Affenlight took out his handkerchief to wipe his brow. He hadn't felt this awkward in a social situation since—well, since last night with Henry, in Owen's room. But before that it had been a long time.

"Perhaps you'd let me make a small show of thanks? Owen and I would love it if you could join us later for dinner."

"Oh, I couldn't possibly," Affenlight said quickly, but maybe that bordered on rudeness. "That is, I'd love to, and you're extremely kind to offer, but unfortunately—well, not unfortunately, of course—my daughter's just arrived from San Francisco. In fact"—he glanced at his watch—"I'm late to meet her ri—"

"Your daughter?" Genevieve said. "How perfect! I thought you were going to claim a business engagement. The four of us can dine together. My treat."

Why, why hadn't he claimed a business engagement? Affenlight appealed silently to Owen, but Owen, propped against his pillows, looked as amused and detached as if he were watching a movie. "It's not every day my mother comes to town," he pointed out.

Genevieve nodded. "I'm allergic to the Midwest."

"So's my daughter," Affenlight allowed, and something in his tone—he heard it as readily as Owen and Genevieve did—marked this as an acceptance of the invitation. "There's a French place near the campus," he said. "Maison Robert. It's a little down at the heel, but the food is good."

"That sounds perfect," Genevieve said.

As Affenlight inched toward the door, she stood up and extended her arms in a pre-embrace posture. Affenlight tried to minimize the contact and make it more of an air-hug, but she wrapped him up familiarly. Their chests sandwiched the Whitman. "What's that?" Genevieve asked, releasing him and tapping the book's cover through Affenlight's jacket fabric.

"Nothing," said Affenlight hastily. "Just a little reading material."

"May I?" Genevieve clearly was one of those people who didn't mind touching other people. Before Affenlight could twist away, she reached behind his lapel and extracted the book. "Owen, look — Walt Whitman. Your favorite."

"Whitman's not my favorite," Owen said. "Too gay."

"Oh, stop," said Genevieve, with a wave of her book-holding arm. Affenlight thought about snatching the book back, but it was way too late. "You used to *love* Whitman."

"Sure, when I was twelve." Owen glanced at Affenlight. "Whitman appeals to the newly gay. He's like a gateway drug."

"I'm sure he appeals to all kinds of people," Genevieve said. "He's the poet of democracy."

The unhurt corner of Owen's mouth turned upward in a smile. "Is that what they're calling it now?"

Affenlight needed a cigarette more than he ever had when he smoked half a pack a day. What year did they finally ban smoking in hospitals? What happened if you did it anyway? He both did and didn't want Owen to figure him out — like that dirty picture on Owen's laptop, the possibility of being figured out made things more real, more thrilling and terrifying — but what he certainly did not want was for Owen to figure him out in front of his mother. Affenlight was glad that Genevieve had said what she said about the poet of democracy; otherwise he would have said it, or something like it, and felt like a fool.

"All through high school you loved Whitman," Genevieve said. "What's the one about the tree? The oak tree?" She opened the book and began to scan the table of contents.

"Please, put that thing away," said Owen as if it were a soiled diaper. He coughed and, avoiding as well as possible the blood-stiffened, drug-slackened side of his mouth, began carefully to declaim the poem: "I saw in Louisiana a live-oak growing, / All alone stood it, and the moss hung down from the branches…"

Affenlight's heart grew calm at the sound of Owen's voice reciting the familiar words. So much of one's life was spent reading; it made sense not to do it alone. And he'd always loved the poem, admired in the narrator exactly what the narrator admires in the oak tree—manifest independence—even while the narrator insists on his thorough dependence on his friends.

Halfway through, Owen broke off. "Bah," he said. "My head."

Affenlight couldn't help himself. He cleared his throat and picked up where Owen left off, stumbling over only the phrase "manly love." "For all that," he concluded, unable to keep from shifting into a slightly higher oratorical gear, "and though the live-oak glistens there in Louisiana, solitary, in a wide flat space, / Uttering joyous leaves all its life, without a friend, a lover, near, / I know very well I could not."

"Bravo," cheered Genevieve. She handed Affenlight his book.

Affenlight smiled sheepishly. He felt both good and exposed. He wondered briefly about the precise etymology of the word *flush:* you flushed when you were happy and exhilarated, you flushed when you were humiliated, and you flushed a bird from cover before you shot it. He looked at Owen to see if he could see what Owen thought of his recitation, but Owen's eyes were closed, not in a sleepy way but like Sherlock Holmes at the opera, ears alert, a gentle smile on his lips.

"Well," said Affenlight, "I suppose I'd better be off. Pella and I will see you tonight."

"What a lovely name." Genevieve clasped Affenlight's hands warmly in farewell. "Who knows, O? Maybe this Pella Affenlight will turn out to be your ideal woman. She certainly has a dashing enough father."

"Don't make me laugh," Owen said, eyes still closed. "It hurts my face."

23

There were no more than two hundred people in the Opentoe ballpark, players and scouts included, but they made a lot of noise. They stood and stomped the bleachers, the cheers grew louder instead of dying out, and he realized they weren't going to stop. He lifted his head guardedly and looked at Schwartzy, who was standing on the lip of the dugout, his expression drained and pissed but not unhappy, clapping his Schwartz-sized hands together. Henry blinked hard a few times. Elastic PE equals one-half K L squared, he thought. Gravitational PE equals mgh.

Schwartz pointed to the brim of his cap. Henry looked at him dumbly. Schwartz did it again, and this time Henry understood. He lifted one hand and tipped his cap. The cheering swelled and peaked and ended. Schwartz trudged back to the bus. Arsch hurriedly put on pads and a chest protector and lumbered out to take his place behind the plate.

Two innings later, Henry made another error. It resembled the first one: he fielded a routine grounder, double-pumped, and pulled Rick off the bag with a low wide throw. He pounded his fist in his glove, pulled his hat down as low as it would go. What the heck was happening? Was there something wrong with his arm? No, his arm felt strong, his arm felt fine. Don't overthink it. Just let it fly.

After the game ended—the Harpooners won 8 to 1—he headed toward the bus to talk to Schwartz, but he was intercepted by a broad-shouldered blond guy in a dress shirt with a Cardinals logo. His nostrils were rimmed by a rheumy pink glow. "Henry," he said as they shook hands, "Dwight Rogner. We spoke on the phone. Nice game out there."

"Wish I could've played a little better."

"Don't sweat those errors," Dwight said. "Gosh, you've made two mistakes in two and a half years? We all should be so lucky. I played in the minors for nine years, batted twice in the majors. And I'll tell you something — pretty much every guy I ever shared a locker room with wound up becoming either an alcoholic or a born-again Christian. Booze or God. That's what this game does to you. The name of the game is failure, and if you can't handle failure you won't last long. Nobody's perfect."

Henry nodded. Dwight, his rheumy eyes twinkling merrily in the cloud-strafed sunlight, shook his hand again. "So we'll talk again soon," he said. "Okay?"

"Okay," Henry said.

A few other scouts — Orioles, Phillies, Cubs — stopped over to say hello, and then Henry joined his teammates, who were arranged on the grass in a rough circle, relaxed and cheerful after the win, eating turkey sandwiches. Rick O'Shea lifted his valve-topped sports drink above his head. "To the Skrimmer," he said, "whose name shall be listed alongside that of the great Aparicio, for as long as we all shall live."

"Hear! Hear!"

"Go Henry."

"Attaboy, Skrim."

Instead of occupying the center of the circle, as he usually did, Schwartz lay a little ways off, doing stretches for his back — either he didn't want to be bothered or he only wanted to be bothered by Henry. Henry, not sure which was the case, approached with hunterly care.

"Hey."

"Hey," Schwartz said.

"Sorry you got tossed."

"Bastard spit on me." Schwartz swung his knees to the other side of his body. "Sorry I didn't tell you sooner about my apps."

"Maybe there was some mistake," Henry suggested. "Maybe they messed up your LSAT scores or something."

Schwartz shook his head. "I'm the only one who messed up my LSAT scores."

"You did well, I thought."

"I did okay."

"And your extracurriculars, captain of two teams. Everything you've done for Westish. Everything you've done for *me*."

Schwartz stretched his legs out, massaged his kneecaps. "I don't think they give me credit for that."

They sat there for a while, saying nothing, the day cool and blue around them.

Schwartz hauled himself up from the grass, his ligaments popping and creaking in protest. "Let's go," he said. "Get a new streak started."

THE HARPOONERS WON the second game 15 to 6. Only two balls were hit to Henry. Both times he double-clutched and made a soft, hesitant throw. Instead of rifle shots fired at a target, they felt like doves released from a box. He didn't know which way they'd go, and he watched in suspense as each, somehow, found its way into the distant nest of Rick's first-baseman's glove.

That evening, on the long ride back to Westish, he dozed against the shimmying side of the bus, a sweatshirt tucked beneath his cheek against the cold. His teammates bounced from seat to seat, gleefully scheming, poised between a successful day and what promised to be, since tomorrow was a rare day off, a successful night.

"Melanie Quong," somebody said.

"Kim Enderby."

"Hannah Szailes."

The names were plans and prayers and poems all at once. Henry's right arm reeked of Icy Hot. An image surged into his mind and repeated itself at a rate both dizzying and monotonous — an image of a white ball veering off course and drilling Owen in the cheekbone, and of Owen's white startled eyes as he stared out at Henry before slumping to the dugout floor. He did some math. In the space of fifteen innings he'd made the five worst throws of his college career — the one that hit Owen, the two errors in the first game today, and the two ungainly throws in the second game. All five came on routine and in fact almost identical plays: hard-hit balls more or less right at him, so that he had plenty of time to plant his feet and find Rick's glove before making the throw. Simple plays, of a kind he hadn't botched since puberty. Clearly there was something wrong with his mechanics. Tomorrow he'd sleep in, catch up on the homework he'd neglected since Owen's injury. Monday at practice he'd work out the kinks in his delivery. The problem, like most problems in life, probably had to do with his footwork.

24

Pella leaned closer to the bureau mirror, planting her elbows as she forced a silver earring—bought by her dad this afternoon—through the thin slit where her piercing used to be. She hadn't bothered to wear earrings in many months or to bring any with her from San Francisco. A minim of bright blood cradled the edge of the slit and then subsided. She felt almost lovely, in her new lilac-colored dress, which was scoop-necked and sleeveless, and hung very simply and straight. She'd been admiring it this afternoon, at a little shop in Door County; her dad offered to pay for it, a sweet gesture marred only by the shame Pella felt at her own utter lack of resources. She needed to figure out how to fend for herself. Still, she felt pretty good. The eggplant bags beneath her eyes were shrinking. Her hair shone in the lamplight and, freshly washed, felt soft against her neck.

Her father's face appeared beside hers in the mirror, as if they were posing for a family portrait, except that the elder Affenlight looked distinctly agitated. "Is this tie okay?" he asked, fiddling with the flat taper of his half Windsor. The familiar burnt apple butter scent of his cologne filled the room.

"Sure," Pella said. "All of your ties are nice."

Affenlight frowned and continued improving the already perfect knot. "But maybe I have a nicer one. Look"—he lifted the tie with a spindled finger so its silver-and-burgundy stripes hung beside his face—"see how the color brings out these capillaries in my cheeks? I look like a washed-up alcoholic."

"Oh, you do not." Pella forced the second post through and turned to eye her dad directly. "You have the skin of a ten-year-old. Not to mention the brain. Since when are you quite *this* vain?"

Affenlight pretended to pout. "I'm an emissary of the college. It's my duty to make a good impression on the tuition-paying parents."

"Mm-hm. Single female parents in particular."

Before he could respond, his phone trilled. He pulled it from his pocket and two-stepped into the hallway. "Genevieve, hello!"

Pella went back to the mirror. David would return from Seattle tonight. How long would it take him to figure out where she was? Not long — she had no friends, no other relatives, just these two looming figures, her dad and David, to bounce between. David's first impulse would be to think that she had run off with someone her own age, just as he'd always believed she would do, and he'd ransack the loft for clues. But there were no clues. When he picked up the phone to find her, there would be only one number to dial.

She could hear her dad on the phone in the hall, bantering. Ten to one when this Genevieve showed up she'd be a lot hotter than your average mom of a twenty-one-year-old. Pella wasn't sure why she had to be dragged along on what seemed like a double date, but she wanted to indulge her dad, to prove that they could be friends again. Plus, of course, he'd bought her this dress.

Affenlight, looking more agitated than ever, poked his silver-gray head around the jamb of Pella's door. "Change of plans!" he said. "Make drinks!" The head vanished.

The head reappeared. "Drinks!" it added.

Pella smoothed her dress, allowed herself one last approving glance in the mirror, and went to the study to pour two scotches, one with ice and one without. She delivered the former to the kitchen, where her father was dicing chives with manic staccato knife strokes. "What's going on?" she asked. "When did you change your tie?"

Affenlight looked down at his baby-blue tie. "You don't like it?" he said with childlike disappointment.

"I like it," Pella said. "But I think you're very strange."

Affenlight nodded distractedly and resumed hacking at the chives with one hand. Meanwhile he grabbed his scotch with the other and belted back two-thirds of what had been a very full tumbler. A bright matrix of pinpricked sweat stood out against his flushed mahogany forehead. "What's going on?" Pella asked.

"Owen's won the Trowell."

"The what?"

"The Trowell. It's a fellowship. He'll be studying in Tokyo next year."

"Well, that sounds good. Right?"

"Fantastic." Affenlight grabbed a tomato from the wooden bowl beside the sink and halved it with a powerful *thwack*. "Many of our students have applied," he said as he speedily minced the tomato to a pulp, "but none have won. It's a very prestigious fellowship. Imagine — Owen gone to Tokyo!"

"What are you making, there?" Pella gestured toward the red puree blooming across the cutting board.

"Hors d'oeuvres."

"I thought we were going out to dinner."

"Owen's not up to it. Poor fellow, he's been through a lot these past few days. Genevieve thought a restaurant might be too hectic for him. She suggested she and I have dinner, just the two of us, but I thought that wouldn't be fitting, seeing as how we have Owen's news to celebrate. So I invited them here."

"For hors d'oeuvres."

"Right." Affenlight drained his drink and sank down on one of the stools that flanked the little kitchen's butcher-block island. He gazed around the room with plangent, uncomprehending eyes. He looked, for a moment, wildly old — a decade older than his literal age, two decades older than his usual self. "Tokyo," he murmured. Pella took the knife from his hand and laid it on the counter. She peeked into the refrigerator: limes, butter, and pert white bags of coffee beans. "I'll walk over to the dining hall," she said. "Maybe they can whip us up something."

25

A Saturday evening gloom hung in the air of the dining hall, and it seemed that the revelry happening elsewhere on campus had left a sad vacuum here. Dinner was no longer being served, and the vomit-green chairs contained only a few lonesome stragglers, gazing down at textbooks as they slowly forked their food. A gigantic clock glowered down from the far wall, its latticed iron hands lurching noisily to mark each passing minute. *Go somewhere else,* the noise seemed to say, *anywhere but here.*

Pella passed through the open doorway to the kitchen. A small but substantial man, built low to the ground like an Indian burial mound, was scraping mashed potatoes into a giant baggie. He had wide fleshy features, flared nostrils, and acne scars under his eyes. He wore a flopped-over, caved-in chef's hat. "Closed," he said forlornly, without glancing up, before Pella could open her mouth. "Closed."

"I know. I'm sorry to bother you. I was hoping that maybe—"

"Closed." He pronounced it softly, as a sad but ineluctable truth, and clanged his mashed-potato scooper against the rim of the pan.

"I know, it's just…"

He didn't even say the word this time, just shook his bent head from side to side and clanged the potato scooper against the pan's rim again, somehow producing a long somber *O* sound that matched his voice's timbre: *Cl-OOOOOOO-sed.*

"Right," Pella said. "The thing is, see, President Affenlight sent me." She paused and tugged on one of her tender, freshly pierced earlobes, waiting to see what effect her father's name would have. The mound-shaped man lifted the bag of mashed potatoes to eye height and performed a subtle wrist move that spun the bag slowly on its vertical axis, winding the neck into a long tight strand. "President Affenlight," he said, a weary shrug in his voice. "Chef Spirodocus." His tone indicated that it was an open question as to which of these was the loftier title; that despite the loftiness of their titles they were both just men; and that because they were men they would surely die. He opened a tremendous refrigerator and tossed the bag inside.

Behind him, in the kitchen proper, a small Latino man was blasting a huge pan with a pressurized hose. Wet chunks of charred gunk kicked up and spattered his shirt. Pella imagined the inside of the pan slowly coming clean, black giving way to gleaming silver as the fierce stream of water worked its way through the caked-on layers of sauce or soup or — as the menu card propped on the counter beside her said — Southwestern Veggie Lasagna. The guy didn't exactly look happy, his eyes glazed over and his face slick with sweat, but Pella envied the clarity of his purpose. Dirty → Clean. A hose like that, she thought, would make a good addition to Mike and Arsch's kitchen.

"So...," she said, unsure where she stood with Chef Spirodocus, who had unspooled another bag from a giant roll and resumed the spooning of potatoes, "President Affenlight and I—he's my father, I'm his daughter—are having guests, unexpected guests, and we were wondering, if it wasn't too much trouble, whether you might have something lying around that we could maybe use as an appetizer."

"*Lying around?*" repeated Chef Spirodocus broodingly. "*Use* as an appetizer?"

He balanced his potato scooper on the edge of the pan, pressed the heels of his hands to the countertop, and fixed his flesh-pinched eyes on Pella for the first time. He struck Pella as a deeply democratic man, a man of the people, and she wished that she were wearing her usual uniform of hooded sweatshirt and frazzled hair and bags under her eyes, instead of this pretty lilac dress and earrings and makeup. She fidgeted with a sliding bra strap.

"A thousand people." Chef Spirodocus encompassed kitchen, serving line, and dining room with a broad sweep of a stubby arm. "Every day. For a thousand people, you cannot do things right. You must simply do them. Do you understand?"

Pella started to say that yes, she understood, but he had already spun on a wooden-heeled clog and vanished into the kitchen. Without those heels he would really be impressively short. Minutes passed. He didn't come back. Pella was pretty sure she'd been abandoned, but she didn't have a plan B, so she just stood there watching the Latino dishwasher blasting away with his power hose, his face purpled by exertion.

She'd given up on appetizers but was still standing there blankly when Chef Spirodocus returned, a brimming shopping bag in his stubby arms. Atop whatever else was inside sat an unbaked loaf, redolent of cinnamon, with currants or raisins on top. "Put that in the oven as soon as you get home," he said. "Serve it with the coffee."

"Wow," Pella said. "Wow. Did you make this right now?"

"A chef never tells." Chef Spirodocus's face turned pleasant for the first time; it seemed to sink and soften. He reached up to give Pella a clumsy pat on the back. "Tell your father I did my best. I had no time, I had no notice, but I did my best. Okay?"

"Okay," Pella said. "Thanks so much, Chef Spirodocus. My dad will really appreciate it."

She turned to leave but found herself rooted to the navy-and-ecru-tiled floor. The tiny desire-voice in her chest was chanting something, softly and incoherently; she stopped and tried to listen.

After a while Chef Spirodocus looked up from his potatoes. "Something else?"

"Um…" Pella rocked from one foot to the other. "I was just

wondering, you know, whether you hired people to work in the kitchen. To wash dishes and such."

"Do I hire people to wash dishes?" Chef Spirodocus repeated wondrously, with a sad shake of his head. "Yes."

"So you're hiring right now?"

"I am hiring always."

"Could I have an application?"

His eyebrows lifted. "For whom?"

"For me."

Chef Spirodocus's eyes took in her white flat sandals and pale legs and crisp dress and whatever else he happened to find. Pella felt his gaze linger, not on her breasts, as men's gazes tended to do, but on her fluked tattoo. "You've worked in a kitchen?" he asked.

"No." The word left her mouth and hung dead in the air. "I'm an extremely hard worker," she added quickly, and wondered whether there was any way in which this could possibly be considered true.

"I have an opening on the breakfast shift," Chef Spirodocus said. "It begins at five thirty. Monday to Friday."

"Five thirty?" Pella said.

Chef Spirodocus nodded with infinite sadness. "I understand. It's far too early."

"It's early," agreed Pella. "I'll see you Monday."

26

Affenlight, who was keeping watch through the kitchen window as he mopped up the wet red mess he'd made of the tomatoes, saw Genevieve and Owen emerge from Phumber Hall and, hand in hand like the most comfortable of couples, make their way across the foreshortened strip of spring-damp lawn that separated Phumber from Scull. The sight sent a misguided pang of jealousy through him, not unlike the one he'd suffered when he found out that Henry Skrimshander was Owen's roommate. Imagine that: jealous of the boy's mother, for holding his hand. He checked his tie and his cuffs in the hallway mirror and headed downstairs ahead of the bell.

Genevieve released Owen's hand and squeezed both of Affenlight's, planted kisses on both his cheeks. "Guert! Can you believe it?"

"Barely," Affenlight said.

"On one hand I think, Darling, why do you have to go to *Japan?* Is it really necessary to abandon your poor mother entirely? But I'm so proud. And really, Tokyo's not much farther from San Jose than Westish is."

"And warmer," Affenlight agreed. "Much more pleasant to visit."

"Oh, don't be modest," Genevieve said. "Your campus is so quaint, so ... nineteenth century. I'm embarrassed that it took O landing in the hospital, of all things, to finally get me to visit." She ran her hand through her hair, which was cut so short it should have been butch but instead looked sleekly feminine. She was wearing the same navy skirt and white blouse as this morning, but a few subtle changes—a jangle of silver bracelets, an undone blouse button—had altered their impression entirely. She fixed Affenlight with a look: "I'll have to come back when I can stay longer."

"Parents are always welcome," Affenlight said cautiously. He extended his hand to Owen, felt an electric thrill as their palms clapped together. "Congratulations, young man. You're the first Westish student to win a Trowell."

Owen smiled with the good side of his mouth. "Well, the Trowells have only been handing them out since eighty-two," he said with laconic pride. The handshake lasted.

Upstairs, Affenlight opened a bottle of wine, showed Genevieve to the bathroom, and encouraged Owen to take off his shoes and put his feet up on the ottoman. "Please," he said. "Don't stand on ceremony here." Affenlight tucked a pillow behind Owen's head, on the back of which stood a massive, bandage-covered lump. He heard again the ugly thud of that beautiful head slamming against the cement back of the dugout. "How are you feeling?"

Owen nodded gingerly. "I've felt worse."

"When?"

"Well, never. But I could imagine feeling worse." A fuchsin semi-circle rimmed his eye socket; the swelling spread all the way down to the blood-stiffened corner of his lip, so that his words emerged slowly, slightly thickened, from one side of his mouth. "I get dizzy," he said. "I've been having some trouble remembering things. Hard to tell if it's the concussion or the drugs." He paused. "And I hear these awful toneless ringing sounds."

The Westish Chapel bells were tolling eight o'clock. "Every hour?" Affenlight said.

"Just about." Owen laid his hands on the gentle swell of his belly and closed his eyes. "I did feel worse once, I suppose. When Jason broke up with me."

Jason. The name broke over Affenlight like a wave. "Jason?" he asked.

"Jason Gomes. Do you remember him?"

It took Affenlight a moment to place the name. "Ah, yes. Jason was one of our best students."

Owen nodded. "And your best-looking."

"I don't remember that part."

"Oh, I'm sure you do," Owen said coyly. "He was much better-looking than I am. He might even have been better-looking than you." Owen scratched his chin, his tone evaluative and probably slightly teasing. Affenlight blanched. If Owen thought Jason was slightly better-looking than Affenlight but much better-looking than Owen, then Owen thought that Affenlight was better-looking than Owen. Which was a compliment. But to be compared unfavorably to an ex-boyfriend: that was a slight. But the conditional had been used: *might even have been.* It was like an SAT for gay flirting. Not that gay flirting differed from straight flirting. But if it didn't differ, why was Affenlight so bad at it? Genevieve had returned and was perusing Affenlight's bookshelves, her back turned, sipping her wine.

"It hurt that much?" Affenlight asked quietly, meaning the breakup.

"I was so distressed I refused to eat. Henry had to force-feed me." Owen opened his eyes and looked at Affenlight. "I don't like getting my heart broken."

Before Affenlight could digest this, Genevieve arranged herself beside him on the couch, crossing those dynamite legs in his direction. "Guert, this is quite a place."

"Do you like it?"

She looked around, her chin lifted thoughtfully. "I do," she decided. "But it's certainly very..."

"Academic?" Affenlight suggested.

"I was going to say *undergraduate.* Or *masculine.* But I suppose your daughter can help with the latter, at least. Where is she, by the way?"

"She went out to forage for some snacks for us."

"She'd better not be going to any trouble." Genevieve waggled a finger at Affenlight. "The whole point of this evening was for *me* to thank *you* for taking such good care of Owen."

"Nonsense. You two are the guests of honor. You've traveled all this way, and Owen has done Westish proud. News of the Trowell goes out worldwide—it's the sort of thing that makes a school president look good."

"The school president looks pretty good already." Genevieve smiled. Affenlight smiled back. Was he straight flirting? The legs seemed to demand it. Or maybe it wasn't the legs but the fact that he had no other way to relate to women. What could you do if you couldn't flirt, charm, and flatter? You could keep the conversation lofty and erudite, but in Affenlight's experience this was usually perceived as flirting too. Luckily Owen seemed to have dozed off. Though maybe he was just pretending.

For a split second Affenlight thought that Genevieve's hand was tickling his thigh; despite himself he flinched, kicking the coffee table and sloshing wine out of his glass. It turned out to be his cell phone buzzing in his pocket. Genevieve, by way of response, patted him on the thigh. "Easy," she said, plucking at the crease in his light-wool slacks. "You okay?"

"Ha-ha. Yes, of course. Sorry about that," Affenlight said. "My phone." He slipped the infernal device partway from his pocket and checked the caller ID. A 415 area code—Pella, he thought, but Pella had left her phone in San Francisco. David, then, returned from wherever he'd been, returned to find his wife's phone on the kitchen table, the call log stuffed with his own unrequited calls. Bewildered now; apoplectic soon enough. Affenlight let it ring.

27

Any doubts Pella might have had about the provenance of her father's strange behavior dissolved when she entered the study to find a beautiful black yoga-sculpted woman nestling—or maybe not quite nestling but sitting pretty close for a near–total stranger—against him on the couch. Her skin was youthful, her hair cropped short, her legs and eyelashes insanely long. The legs, as she uncrossed them and rose from the couch to greet Pella, flashed in sensual arcs like polished Brancusi birds.

"Pella! So nice to meet you." Genevieve squeezed Pella's elbow and smoothly took the bag of groceries from her, as if they'd accomplished this exchange hundreds of times. Pella, in the presence of this sleek being, felt frumpy and floury again. She crossed her arms to protect the pasty sag of her breasts and biceps, vowed to hit the pool with new vigor tomorrow.

"Pella, this is Owen," Affenlight said. "Owen, Pella."

Owen smiled with half his face and lifted a palm in greeting.

"Congratulations on your fellowship," Pella said.

"Thank you." The unsmiling half of his face was hugely swollen, covered in purple bruises, and he was wearing a bizarre getup of white undershirt and red pajama pants dotted with black-and-white yin-yang symbols. But what struck her most was how slender and gentle he looked: she knew he played baseball and was expecting an enormous jock like Mike.

"Pella and I will be in the kitchen." Genevieve carried the food that way as if the apartment were her own. "You men try to entertain yourselves."

Pella trotted behind obediently. Genevieve opened all the right cabinets, finding serving dishes Pella didn't know existed, and busily began transferring Chef Spirodocus's concoctions—falafel, hummus, vegetables, something wrapped in grape leaves, something that smelled of fennel—from their plastic cartons. Pella tried to think of some way to help. Finally she spotted the cinnamon-currant loaf sitting on the counter, where Genevieve had set it, and stuck it in the oven.

"Now," Genevieve said, pouring herself another glass of wine, "as long as we're women in the kitchen, can we indulge in a bit of women-in-the-kitchen gossip?"

"Sure." Pella squinted at the oven display. Three hundred degrees? Four hundred? She decided to split the difference.

"You should probably preheat that." Genevieve touched Pella's elbow to lessen the force of the order.

"Of course." She punched the button that said PREHEAT.

"Maybe without the loaf in there?"

"Ah." Pella withdrew the pan and set it on a burner. Back home in Buena Vista she had a restaurant-quality six-burner self-cleaning stainless-steel range, yet she didn't even know how not to char food that someone else had made. That seemed like some kind of metaphor for her life, or modernity, or something.

"Perfect," said Genevieve. "So. Your dad's not married anymore?"

"He never was," Pella said, more eagerly than she intended. It'd been a long time since she'd talked about boys; it was fun, even if the boy was her dad.

Genevieve nodded. "He has that perpetual-bachelor thing going. Responsible without being mature. And this apartment—it's like an English major's dorm room but with first editions instead of paperbacks. Where does he spend the summer?"

"Here."

"The poor man." Genevieve's hair was shorter than Mike's, but she had an analogous way of passing her hand over it when nonplussed. Though maybe it wasn't analogous at all—Genevieve's was a breezy feminine grooming motion, whereas Mike's was always accompanied by a sad exhalation. In which case, thought Pella, I'm looking for excuses to think about Mike. Which would mean that I like him. But maybe I don't want to like him. She poured some wine into her empty whiskey tumbler and tabled the question—she'd come to Westish to try her hand at being *un*attached.

Genevieve was looking at her intently.

"Pardon?" said Pella.

"I'm sorry. Did that question offend you?"

"Which question?"

"It would never have crossed my mind," Genevieve said quickly, sounding apologetic, "except that when O was in high school he read your dad's book—I forget the title—and was so enamored of it. I think that's how he first heard of Westish, by Googling Guert Affenlight."

"Ah," said Pella. "Is my dad gay."

Genevieve was watching her anxiously, as if awaiting forgiveness.

"Actually," Pella said, "the book has very little to do with homosexuality per se. It's more about the cult of male friendship in nineteenth-century America. Boys' clubs, whale boats, baseball teams. Emotional nourishment before the modern era of gender equality."

"Pseudo-equality, you mean."

Pella smiled. "Pseudo-equality. I think my dad's lonely," she added. "When we lived in Cambridge he always had a girlfriend, two girlfriends, however many. But none of them stuck around very long. I think it was too soon after my mom died." Pella paused. In fact she had little idea how her dad felt about her mom's death, and this simple sentence she'd always, as a child, believed—*It was too soon*—now came out sounding like a lie.

"Anyway," she concluded with overt cheer, because Genevieve was looking at her with oh-no-your-mom-died sympathy, "he could use a girlfriend."

Genevieve tipped the bottle's dregs into her glass. "I'll take that as a blessing."

Pella, happy to play along, drew a sign of the cross in the air between her and Genevieve. She retrieved the champagne that her father had jammed into the freezer, and they carried the food and champagne into the study.

"To Owen," her dad said, raising his glass aloft. "May he prosper in the Land of the Rising Sun, as he has in the Land of the Falling Snow."

"How sweet," Genevieve said. "Hear! Hear!"

"We'll miss him" — Affenlight's voice fell to a forlorn note — "but we'll soldier on." Pella thought this a bit much; her dad must be pretty keen to get between Genevieve's legs. Not that he could really be blamed. Few women made it into their forties with legs like that.

They clinked glasses. "Only a sip for you, kiddo," Genevieve said, leaning forward to squeeze her son's toes. "You're on all that medication." She turned to Pella. "I never asked what you do in San Francisco."

"Do? Um, well, you know..."

"Wait, don't tell me. You're a graduate student. In" — Genevieve pressed her fingertips to her temples and closed her eyes — "something stylish. Something artistic. Something like... *architecture*." She opened her eyes. "How did I do?"

Had David left that deep an imprint on her? Pella reached across her body to scratch a nervous itch along the flukes of her tattoo. "You're close," she said.

"I knew it! How close?"

"Genevieve, you're being gauche." Owen yawned, opening his mouth cautiously because of the swelling, and rubbed his belly. "It's only Americans who insist on asking everyone what they do."

"Well, we *are* Americans, dear."

Pella distributed the remaining champagne, filling Owen's flute to the brim as thanks for his intervention. He winked at her, took a long slow sip, and let his eyelids flutter closed. He had beautiful eyelashes, like his mother. Pella wondered at the blithe comfort that allowed him to doze off like that, in the company of the president of his college, in his pajamas. She was developing an admiration for him.

"Let the punishment fit the crime," her dad said. "Genevieve, what do *you* do?"

"I'm an anchorperson," Genevieve said. "On the San Jose evening news."

"Ah!" said Affenlight. "A celebrity in our midst."

"It's really not very glamorous. Sit around all day staring at the internet, then spend an eternity in hair and makeup—that's why I shaved my head, so I could skip a step."

Genevieve paused to give Affenlight an opportunity to tell her how good her hair looked, but Affenlight barely noticed. Was Owen really asleep? he wondered. Or was he just *pretending* to be asleep, in order to monitor Affenlight's behavior toward Genevieve? That would be like Owen—to control the room with his torpor.

"Your hair looks lovely," he said several beats too late.

Genevieve beamed, ran a hand breezily over her scalp. "Tell my producer. I thought he was going to fire me. But I'm black and I've been there forever."

"Indeed," Affenlight said.

Owen's good eye popped open. "What's that?"

"What?"

"Outside. Listen."

Affenlight leaned forward. "I don't hear anything."

"Probably the wind," Genevieve said, but then it came again, a patter that rattled the windowpane, like a handful of tossed pebbles. Affenlight went to the window and peered down into the dark quad. Unable to make out whoever or whatever was below, he pushed open the hinged windows and, half a moment later, staggered backward, spilling champagne as his hand shot up to clutch his jaw. A round object, more rock than pebble, dropped to the study's floor. "Who's there?" he yelled.

"Hi, President Affenlight. It's Mike Schwartz. I was, uh, aiming for the weather vane."

Affenlight rubbed his jaw. "You missed."

The gray form three stories below — he was standing in what, tomorrow morning, would be the shadow of the Melville statue — lifted his arms in a cruciform gesture of apology. "I guess I'm a little tired. We played two games today."

"Both wins, I hope."

"Yes, sir."

"Well done. You gentlemen are doing us proud this year." As Affenlight stepped back from the window, he tested the small lump that was forming at his jawline. "Good night, Michael."

"Uh, President Affenlight?"

"What is it?"

"I was wondering whether I could speak to Pella."

Affenlight looked at Pella, who nodded her assent. Aha, thought Affenlight. "Should I lower her down in a bucket," he said to the window, "or would you prefer to come upstairs?"

"I'd be happy to come up, sir."

"Make it snappy," Affenlight growled, his tone a kind of half-serious homage to the surliness of fathers toward their daughters' suitors. "The champagne's getting warm."

MIKE SCHWARTZ ENTERED THE ROOM muttering apologies, wearing a penitent frown between his beard and his baseball cap. He stopped short when he saw Owen. "Buddha. You're out of the hospital."

"I am," Owen agreed. "Mike, this is my mother. Genevieve, this is Mike Schwartz, the moral conscience of Westish."

Genevieve rose from the couch to shake Mike's hand, legs flashing below her navy skirt. "Now I just need to meet the famous Henry," she declared. "And my trip will be complete."

Affenlight, who'd gone to the kitchen, returned with tumblers and bottles on a tray. "Invite Henry over," he said. "I thought we might try some scotch, in honor of Owen's news."

"Yes, call him!" Genevieve said. "I've been talking to Henry on the phone for *years,* he's practically my second son, and yet I've never met him. It's really atrocious."

Mike shook his head. "He's probably asleep already. The Skrimmer had a rough day."

Owen asked what happened, and Mike delved into the story at greater length than Pella cared to follow — a bad throw, another bad throw, and so on.

"Poor Henry," Genevieve said. "Sounds like he could use a drink."

It was good scotch, meant for sipping, but Pella poured herself an extra belt and burrowed down into the couch. Mike, Owen, Genevieve — it seemed like everyone she met wanted to talk about Henry. On her way out of the dining hall she'd seen a copy of the weekend *Westish Bugler* lying on an unbussed table. "Henry Goes for 52," read the block-lettered headline, and beneath it ran a half-page photo of a guy on a field, throwing a ball. His hat was pulled down to his eyes and he looked like any guy on any field, throwing any ball.

When a lull came in the conversation, she touched Mike's elbow and flashed her comeliest come-hither look. Although technically it was more of a let's-go-thither look. He had certainly earned some romance points by tossing pebbles at her window, even if the toss turned out to be an athlete's forceful throw, the pebble a rock, the window her dad's face. He'd tried, in his courtly but awkward, bearlike way — he'd been thinking about her. And he had those eyes, those lovely amber eyes...

Those eyes met hers with a total lack of comprehension. "What?" he said, halting the conversation and turning everyone's heads toward them.

"Maybe we should get going."

Mike looked at her dumbly. "Why?"

"You know . . . we were going to watch that movie? That movie you wanted to watch?"

"Are you serious?" he said. "And pass up a chance to sample the presidential scotch collection? I've been waiting years for this."

"Oh, please stay!" Genevieve chimed in. "I'm leaving in the morning."

That settled it. Affenlight, pleased by Mike's mention of his scotch collection, brought out three more bottles. They tested each in turn, murmuring, *Ooh, peaty . . . ahh, smoky!* as they made small noises of pleasure. They toasted Genevieve's visit, Pella's arrival, Owen's Trowell, Henry in his absence. Mike, looking happier than Pella had yet seen him, roamed the room, browsing the endless shelves, until he found The Book itself—the oversize, hand-set, Arion Press *Moby-Dick* that her dad had bought for a thousand dollars in 1985 and was now worth thirty times more, not that you could assign a value to such a dear and beautiful thing . . . Soon Mike and Owen and Genevieve were gathered around, admiring The Book, listening raptly as Affenlight launched into the tale of Melville's trip to the Midwest, his own discovery of the misplaced and tattered lecture, and the subsequent story of how the Melville statue and the name Harpooners came to be.

Pella stayed put on the couch. She had a complicated attitude toward her dad's performances. Deep down she loved to listen to him and thought he should have been a truly famous man—president of Harvard, at least, or a small but influential post-Soviet country. But the way he cranked up the charm at certain moments and then basked in the adulation of his audience annoyed her. She knew this was precisely a professor's job—to build a repertoire of lectures, refine them over time, and perform them as charismatically as possible. To never seem sick of your own voice, for the sake of others. And yet. You could take the same class only so many times.

When the lecture ended Mike wrapped a big paw around Pella's hand, smiled at her gently. Her annoyance faded as she glimpsed

Westish College through his eyes. To her it was a run-down, too-rustic safety school to which her father had banished himself; to Mike it was everything, his home and family, the place into which he'd poured every bit of himself, and which, as soon as the semester ended, planned to boot him out forever. He'd been trying to find a new home, a law school that would take him in, but it hadn't panned out. If home was where your heart was, then Westish was Mike's home. If home was where they had to take you in no matter what, then it was hers. She squeezed his hand.

AFTER ONE MORE SCOTCH, the evening passed its fulcrum. Mike fell asleep in his chair, his bowling-ball shoulders heaving politely, one bearded cheek squashed against an open palm. Affenlight caught Pella gazing at his sleeping form. She'd never gone for jocks — they were too straitlaced, too prone to follow orders — but Affenlight sensed that this one stood a pretty good chance. David had left three messages on Affenlight's cell in the past two hours.

Genevieve's shoulder was pressed against his own, but her attention had been diverted to Pella; the two of them were looking at Schwartz and whispering girlishly. Affenlight excused himself to carry glasses to the kitchen. He picked up a dishtowel and brushed some crumbs off the countertop. He flipped on the light above the sink. He flipped it off again. He was loitering, and he didn't know why, or at least could pretend he didn't know why, until Owen walked into the room and leaned against the crumbless counter.

"Can I ask you a question?"

"Please."

"Genevieve seems rather smitten with you."

Affenlight feigned a smile. "As an erstwhile English professor, I should probably point out that that isn't a question."

"I'll be more direct. You're not intending to sleep with my mother, are you?"

Through the archway, not five yards away from where Affenlight was standing, Genevieve's slim dark legs projected from the couch, her top foot bobbing gently as she dangled her sandal between two toes. "No," Affenlight said. "I'm not."

"Good."

Owen looked at Affenlight intently, and Affenlight felt—well, Affenlight felt like an idiot. What would happen next? He slung his dishtowel over his shoulder, he pulled it down and wound it around his hand like a boxer's wrap. Not since the night he found out that Pella's mother had died, his daughter's visit suddenly transformed from a novelty, a running departmental joke, into a permanent way of life, had Affenlight felt so overwhelmingly helpless.

"You're leaving," he said, meaning not for the evening but for Japan. "Soon."

"Yes."

"We'll miss you."

Owen smiled. "Who's we?"

Affenlight didn't answer. He was a little taller than Owen, but the way they leaned against the counter made their eyes exactly level.

"You might have to endure me awhile longer," Owen said. "Dr. Sobel asked me to teach playwriting to the summer-school kids."

Three extra months—it wasn't the forever Affenlight longed for, but it was something. He nodded, showing part but not all of his relief at this. "Beautiful summers here."

"So I hear."

"Fishing. Some very good fishing."

Owen smiled. "Sounds barbaric."

"We could go sometime," Affenlight ventured. "On a Saturday morning."

Owen smiled again. "As long as we don't kill any fish." His socked toes brushed against Affenlight's cordovan loafer. "Or any worms, of course."

The moonlight made a little patch on the battered linoleum, which Affenlight had always meant to replace and which now seemed awfully embarrassing. What would happen next? Owen leaned toward him, one eyebrow lifted in an expression of benign irony, his eyes near blind like a prophet's. Closer and closer still, taking care to avert the sore, swollen side of his face. The moon slipped behind clouds, and the pall over the linoleum became uniform. Affenlight's heart galloped and seized. The phone in his pocket buzzed again. The kiss landed tenderly, toward the corner of his mouth.

28

Sunday morning, quietest time of the Westish week. The dining hall didn't serve breakfast. The chapel held no early service. The VAC didn't open until eleven, the library until noon.

Spring was coming for real, and the chirps of robins and sparrows curled toward the upper reaches of the football stadium. From high above came the nasal honks of gulls. One word kept bobbing to the surface of Henry's mind. He spat it out on the broad stone steps. It came back again, insidious, bright as a neon sign. *Motherfucker.* He spat it out and back it came. When he hit the top he knuckle-popped the sign, number 17, dodged along the stone bowl's rim to the next row of steps, triple-timed it down. The south end goalpost's paint looked dull and chipped. *Goalposts need paint, motherfucker.*

He was running as hard as he could, vest cinched tight, sprinting to the top and chop-stepping down, saving nothing. He thought of engines running hot, burning the oil spilled on their blocks. When his vision blurred and sweat stung his eyes, he thought of the salt as wrongness, impurity, error — spill it onto the concrete and watch it evaporate. *Offer it up, motherfucker.*

He wanted to chase down the holy vacancy that marked his best workouts, to sense his body as a hollow drum. Wanted to let the cool gray-blue of the lake and the green-brown-gray of the campus enter and open his lungs. But he was too agitated, too pissed off. He finished the stadium, his second, and started back the other way. Stair-pounding pain shot up through his anklebones to his shins. He quickened his pace.

He finished his third stadium with a halfhearted war whoop and turned to survey what he'd done. He hadn't quieted his mind, but at least he'd reduced his legs to quivering, twitching, thoughtless things. The sun lifted high above the lake. A pair of circling birds swooped toward unseen prey and, finding nothing, braked their heels against the water. The dew lay heavy on the football field's scattered patches of living grass, green welts amid the rutted mud. There against the far goalpost leaned Schwartz, sipping coffee from one of two steaming paper cups he held. He wore WAD sweatpants, shower thongs, a flannel workshirt whose untucked tail flapped in the wind. Henry collected his scattered clothing and hopped the short stone wall that separated the stands from the field.

"You're crazy, you know that?" Schwartz held out a paper cup. "It's supposed to be your day off."

Henry's nostrils sucked in the wonderful chemical sweetness of powdered hot cocoa, but he couldn't catch his breath well enough to take a sip. "Couldn't sleep."

"Me either."

They walked across the practice fields toward the VAC, the sun warm against their necks, Schwartz's flip-flops slurping noisily through the mud. From the VAC they collected their gloves, a bat, a bucket of balls, and a broomstick. They headed out to the baseball diamond.

First base was held in place by a metal post that fit into a long, square-edged hole in the ground; Henry pulled out the base, tossed it aside, and wedged the broomstick into the hole. It tilted a few degrees off the vertical. He slapped it with his hand to check its steadiness, drained the sweet dregs of his cocoa, and jogged out to shortstop.

"How's the wing?" Schwartz yelled. The wind was whipping off the water; it was hard to hear.

Henry worked his shoulder in its socket, gave Schwartz a thumbs-up.

"Take it easy," Schwartz called. "Last thing we need is a dead wing."

"What?"

"*Easy!*"

Schwartz held up a ball. Henry nodded, dropped into his crouch. The first ball shot up high on his backhand side, snapped sharply into his glove. After a long night of thinking, it felt good to be out here doing. He planted his back foot, brought the broomstick into his sights, whipped his arm. The ball cut through the crosswind and struck the broomstick solidly.

There were fifty balls in the bucket. Seventeen hit the broomstick. The others described a tight arc around it, like the knives of a circus performer around the assistant's sequined body. "Feeling better?" Schwartz asked as they gathered their stuff and headed for the dining hall.

"Not bad." Henry nodded. "Not bad at all."

TUESDAY, MUSKINGUM. The sky was a madhouse of riotous cross-blown clouds, the low ones wispy and torn-cotton white, the high ones gray with sullen underbellies shading to ominous black. Nobody in the stands but scouts and dutiful girlfriends. The Muskingum players wore long-sleeved shirts beneath their powder-blue jerseys. The Harpooners' arms were bare. Schwartz insisted on it: a psychological advantage could be gained by pretending to be impervious to the weather. By pretending to be impervious, you became so.

Henry checked his teammates to make sure they were shaded correctly, waved Ajay a step to the left. "Sal Sal Sal," he chanted. "Salvador Dalí Dolly Parton Pardon my French." Infield chatter wasn't exactly cool at the college level, but Henry couldn't help himself. He pounded his fist into the tender pit of his glove. "Dot your *i*s, cross your *t*s, spread a little cheese. Spread a little Muenster, spread a little Swiss."

Sal cranked into his awkward staccato windup. Henry dropped into his shallow crouch. *Hit it to me,* he prayed. *Hit it to me.* Redemption time. The pitch was a forkball right where Schwartzy wanted it, low and outside. Henry broke from his crouch even before bat met ball with a tinny reverberant *ding*. At the last second the ball skidded off a lump tucked in the grass. He shifted his glove and fielded it cleanly—no such thing as a bad hop if you were prepared.

He clapped his right hand over the captive ball, spun it to find the seams. He cocked his arm, locked his eyes on Rick's glove. His arm was moving forward, there wasn't time to think, but he was thinking anyway, trying to decide whether to speed up his arm or slow it down. He could feel himself calibrating and recalibrating, adjusting and readjusting his aim, like an army sniper hopped up on foreign drugs.

As soon as the ball left his hand he knew he'd messed up. Rick O'Shea tried to scoop it out of the dirt, but it hit the heel of his glove and skittered away. Henry turned his back to the infield, looked up at the roiling clouds, mouthed his new favorite word: *Motherfucker.*

Schwartzy called time and trudged out to the mound, beckoned to Henry. "You okay?" he asked, his catcher's mask tipped back on his head, eye black already smearing down into his beard.

"Fine," Henry said curtly.

"You sure? Wing's not sore or—"

"Wing's fine. I'm fine. Let's just play, okay?"

"Okay," Schwartz said. "Nobody out. Let's get 'em."

Now Henry had another error to atone for. *Hit it to me,* he thought fiercely. *Hit me the ball.* "Sal-Sal-Salamander," he chanted, pounding his glove in disgust. "Drop that forkbomb. Let me and Ajay turn a little two-step."

Sal threw another forkball, a good one. The batter cracked a sharp shot to Henry's left. He snagged it and twisted toward Ajay, who was breaking toward the second-base bag. The distance called for a casual sidearm fling—he'd done it ten thousand times. But now he paused, double-clutched. He'd thrown the last one too soft, better put a little mustard on it—no, no, not *too* hard, too hard would be bad too. He clutched again. Now the runner was closing in, and Henry had no choice but to throw it hard, really hard, too hard for Ajay to handle from thirty feet away; it handcuffed him, glanced off the heel of his glove and into short right field.

After the inning Henry sought out Ajay to apologize.

"Forget it." Ajay smiled. "How many times have I done that to you?"

Rick O'Shea clapped Henry on both shoulders. "Don't sweat it, Skrim. Happens to the worst of us."

"Bats bats bats!" somebody yelled, drumming on the wooden rear wall of the dugout.

"Bats bats bats! Let's get 'em back! Bats bats!"

Schwartzy hit a home run. So did Boddington. An inning later, Henry smacked a bases-clearing triple. The umpires stopped the game after six innings, with the Harpooners ahead 19–3. The mercy rule was meant to be merciful to the team getting beat, but no one could have felt more relieved than Henry. For the first time in his life he wanted not to be on a ballfield. He blinked back miserable tears the whole way home, pressed against the shuddering side of the bus.

"You've got to relax out there," Schwartzy told him. "Relax and let it come."

"I know."

"Just let 'er rip, like you're firing at the broomstick. Break Rick's hand if you've got to."

"Okay."

The usual depressing landscape unspooled outside, cows and billboards, fireworks stores and adult emporia. Schwartz picked his words carefully. "Why don't you take it easy tomorrow?" he suggested. "Skip your run, slack off during practice like I do. No use grinding yourself down."

"I'm fine."

"I know you're fine. I'm just saying we're not in prep mode anymore. We've got fifteen games in the next twenty days. We've got to conserve our strength."

The next time Schwartz looked over, Henry's eyes were closed, his forehead tipped against the grimy window. Schwartz could tell by the nervous tug at the corner of his right eye that he wasn't really asleep, but he didn't call him on it.

Schwartz could feel what was happening, or one thing that was happening: he was distancing himself from Henry, and he was using Pella to do so. That was why he hadn't even mentioned Pella to Henry yet. For years he'd kept no secrets from Henry; now he'd kept two in a matter of weeks.

It was a bad thing to do: to distance himself from Henry, to cut the Skrimmer adrift while pretending nothing had changed — and to do so, when you got down to it, because he couldn't handle Henry's success.

He couldn't do it, not to Henry. Look what was happening already. Maybe it was hubris for Schwartz to blame himself, but it didn't matter. He would do whatever he could to get Henry straightened out. If that meant picking up the phone at four a.m. while in bed with Pella, then so be it. If that meant spending the next two months thinking of nothing but Henry and how to help him, so be it. Pella could wait. His life could wait. Henry needed him, and the Harpooners needed Henry. That was all he had to know.

29

T oday," said Professor Eglantine darkly as she stood before the chalkboard, feet splayed like a ballerina, and twisted her bony, bracelet-freighted arms into a series of pretzeled contortions while she stared at the tape player provided by the A/V Department, "in lieu of our usual business, I hope you'll be so indulgent as to listen with me to a recording of the dear dead anti-Semite Thomas Stearns Eliot, reading aloud his longish poemlike creation *The Waste Land,* and meanwhile to meditate on the ways in which Modernism rejects, retains, or possibly even transforms the traditional elements of orality we've been discussing throughout the semester."

Henry never entirely understood Professor Eglantine, but he took this to mean there wouldn't be much discussion. He slumped in his chair, relieved. He was perched in the top row of the tiny amphitheater between Rick and Starblind, the three of them tucked into too-small desks with piano-shaped tops and presiding in their game-day shirts and ties over the smaller, less athletic members of the class. Rick's kelly-green bow tie drooped like mistletoe above a huge expanse of rumpled white oxford, armpit stains visible as he yawned and stretched. Starblind looked ready for Wall Street or maybe Hollywood, in a glossy gold tie and a shirt the shimmering vermilion of leaves in late October. Henry wore what he always wore: beat-up blue shirt, navy-and-ecru Westish tie. He and Rick wore their Harpooner caps. Starblind, who only covered his gel-slick blond hair while on the diamond, did not. Shirts and ties were a Mike Schwartz dictum of which Coach Cox did not approve. "What's wrong with a sweatshirt?" he'd grumble as the Harpooners filed into the locker room. "Goddamn college boys."

Henry took his physics labs during fall semester, so they wouldn't interfere with baseball season. In the spring he stuck to jock-friendly guts and courses for which Owen or Schwartzy already owned the books. Transforming the Oral Tradition, English 129, cross-listed as Anthropology 141, was the latter. It wasn't easy enough to qualify as a gut, but Rick and Starblind were both in the class, and Schwartzy had "edited" Henry's paper on the *Iliad* to the tune of an A+.

The classroom faced east and was often flooded with light at this hour, but today the lake churned gravely and it looked like rain. Henry felt a thought creep into his mind, the kind of thought he'd never had before or imagined having: *I hope we get rained out.*

"Marie! Marie!" Eliot squealed, in what seemed like a hopeless bid for Henry's attention. Starblind scribbled a note on a piece of paper, laid it on Henry's desk:

!?!

This could mean only one thing, coming from Starblind. Henry scanned the room for the girl in question: a female newcomer seated beside Professor Eglantine. She had kinky, shoulder-length, wine- or bruise-colored hair. She looked older than a student but too young to be a professor. She could have been a grad student, but there weren't any grad students at Westish. She looked precisely like the kind of girl — or maybe he should call her a woman — the kind of woman Henry knew nothing about. She had a wide and heart-shaped face, and she was chewing one of her sweatshirt's strings, not out of nervousness, because nervousness was not an emotion likely to be felt by a person who looked like that, but for some other, better reason. Probably she was chewing on the string because she was concentrating hard on this incomprehensible poem and thinking profound thoughts about Modernism of which Professor Eglantine would approve.

Starblind wrote again: *I'd transform her orality. Seen her before?*

Henry gave a slight shrug to indicate no.

She's no prefrosh. She's 25, 26.

Slight nod.

A little worse for wear, but still . . .

Henry didn't respond to this one.

Eggy's girlfriend?

Henry rolled his eyes. Only in Starblind's sex-crazed imagination did Professor Eglantine have a twentysomething lesbian lover whom she invited to class.

You're useless. Wake up Rick.

Henry, using an absolute minimum of movement, elbowed Rick. He didn't like to talk during Professor Eglantine's class, not because he'd get in any trouble but because Professor Eglantine seemed as sensitive as a skinned knee, she frequently cried during class at the beauty of various poems, and Henry worried about disappointing her.

Rick's chin jerked up. He wiped a glistening wisp of drool from the corner of his mouth. "Wuh?" he asked. Henry pointed to the top item on the piece of paper: *!?!* Rick furrowed the big pale brow beneath his sandstone hair-shelf, looked around the room. Unfurrowed, furrowed, looked around some more. "Holy criminy," he whispered, picking up Henry's pencil. Eliot droned on. Professor Eglantine lifted her eyes ceilingward as she flicked her paper-thin fingers in rapt arcs like a conductor. The mysterious girl/woman chewed her sweatshirt string and speed-kicked the toe of one running-shoed foot with the heel of the other, in a way that would have looked nervous if she wasn't who she was. Whoever that was. Rick crossed out *25, 26* and wrote *22*, tapped the pencil against his chin, crossed out *22* and wrote *23*. Starblind pointed to *Seen her before?*

Almost didn't recognize. Tellman Rose. 1 yr ahead of me. Pella Affenlight.

Affenlight, Affenlight?

Rick confirmed this relation with a nod. *WILD,* he wrote. *Also crazy.*

Meaning what? Been there?

Not me.

Shocking, Starblind wrote.

Rick ignored the insult. *Ran off with dude who came to lecture on Greek architecture.* He went back and inserted *old bearded* before *dude.*

Heard she had a bunch of kids.

Starblind glanced across the room, nodded thoughtfully. *Could explain the tits.*

Henry was mostly ignoring this exchange, which had spilled over its original scrap of paper to cover a full page of his five-subject notebook. Mostly he was looking out the window, wondering whether it would rain. He could feel some part of himself willing it to rain. He'd never quite discarded the childhood belief that he could alter the course of distant or natural events with his mind. Westish Field was already early-April soggy; fifteen minutes of steady rain would probably suffice to postpone the game. The sky was growing darker by the second. A grainy electric grayness accumulated in the room, matching in tone the scratch and crackle of the old cassette player. When T. S. Eliot began to read the part about what the thunder said, Henry, who'd skimmed his homework and knew the thunder was coming, nonetheless assumed it to be a sign of his own unconscious influence. *Da da da shantih shantih shantih* and soon the sky would crack open and rain would whip the field and he wouldn't have to go out there and try to throw the ball today. But instead the room's light brightened half a shade as Eliot's voice crackled into quietness, and Professor Eglantine dismissed the class. He and Rick and Starblind shouldered their backpacks and headed for the exit.

"Henry?" said a female voice — quiet, cautious, inquisitive, but no less startling for that. Henry froze in the doorway. Doomful scenarios skipped through his brain. It was Professor Eglantine, addressing him directly for the first time all semester: he should at least have read his

Iliad paper after Schwartzy rewrote it. Schwartz had a tendency to show off, to throw in old foreign words with letters Henry couldn't even find in Microsoft Word. Cheating would get him kicked off the team and maybe out of Westish. It couldn't prevent him from being drafted, only continuing to play like crap could accomplish that, but teams did take into account what they called "character"—all week he'd been staying late after practice to take weird multiple-choice personality exams administered by scouts from different teams.

If one of your teammates told you he had raped someone, what would you do?

What's your favorite thing about money?

If you were an animal, what kind of animal would you be?

It was sheer laziness not to have reread the paper and rephrased the parts that sounded like Schwartzy; he was usually much more careful about that kind of thing.

"Henry?" said the voice again, nearer now, even more tentative, and Henry realized it wasn't Professor Eglantine at all but rather Pella Affenlight, standing there bookless. "Are you Henry Skrimshander?"

Henry nodded dumbly.

She told him her name. "I figured you had to be Henry. Mike's told me a lot about you."

"Oh." Henry felt a touch disappointed. He'd been ready to believe this exotic stranger just happened to know who he was; he'd been in the local news a lot lately. "You know Mike?"

"Well, yeah..." Now it was Pella who seemed disappointed. "I guess he hasn't mentioned me."

"Of course he's *mentioned* you," Henry said vaguely, though Schwartz hadn't. "I just...I've had a lot on my mind."

"So I hear."

Rick and Starblind were watching this exchange without, thankfully, being able to hear it. Henry shot them a stern, desperate, get-out-of-here look over Pella's shoulder. Starblind licked his index finger lasciviously and made a little tally mark in the air. Finally they wandered off toward the north doors. Henry headed the other way. Pella Affenlight matched his steps, all the way through the dining-hall line and back outside, where they settled with their trays near the Melville statue. On sunny days this was a popular spot, because you could look out at the water without leaving the quad, but today the sky was a low gray dome, and they had Melville to themselves. Henry sipped a glass of skim milk, which the outdoor light made feebly blue, and waited for Pella to speak.

"It must be nice," she said, "to be so good at something."

Thunder shuddered somewhere to the northeast. "Um," Henry said, embarrassed.

"Am I embarrassing you? I don't mean to."

"It's okay."

"I'm just wondering what it's like, to be so good at something and *know* it. For a while in high school I thought I wanted to be an artist, but I gave it up, because I could never convince myself that I was good enough."

Henry, not sure what to say, made an interested noise meant to encourage her to continue.

"I mean, I made some okay paintings, but nothing I made had any *life* to it. You know? Finally I just said fuck it. I decided I didn't like painting so much as I liked covering myself in paint and drinking a lot of coffee. So now I just do that once in a while." She jabbed her fork at her dish of chickpeas and ducked her head and laughed. If you could have said with any certainty that someone like Pella Affenlight was capable of nervousness, you might have called it a nervous laugh. She looked up at Henry. "So?"

"So what?"

"So what's it like to be the best?"

Henry shrugged. "There's always somebody better."

"That's not what Mike says. He says you're the top—what is it, short-stop?—in the entire country."

Henry thought about it for a moment. "It doesn't feel like much," he said. "You really only notice when you screw up."

Pella nodded, finished chewing. "I know what you mean."

Out over the lake, the clouds were pulling apart into pale-gray gauze, blueness shining through from behind. The sky was lightening lumen by lumen. On how many rainy game days had Henry stared out a class-room or bus window, wishing for exactly this kind of reprieve? But now his stomach churned at the thought of having to play.

When he arrived in the locker room, Schwartzy and Owen were dis-cussing the Middle East. Henry was late; the discussion had already entered its terminal stage.

"Israel."

"Palestine."

"*Israel.*"

"Palestine."

"*Israel!*" Schwartz roared. He slammed the heel of his hand into the steel of his locker.

Owen shook his head and whispered, with no less conviction, "Palestine."

It was Owen's first appearance in the locker room since his injury. "Owen," Henry said. "How's your face?" It was funny how glad he could feel to see his roommate, even though they were roommates and saw each other all the time. And yet over the winter holidays or during the summer, when Owen went to Egypt, as he'd done last summer, or home to California, as he'd done the summer before, Henry didn't miss him much at all. The more he saw him, the more he missed not seeing him.

"Getting better," Owen said. "I'm still having some trouble with my studies, though. The words swim around."

"Are you going to play today?"

"No, no. I'm out until these bones heal. A month, they say. I came to support my comrades."

"Buddha!" cheered Rick O'Shea as he ambled out of the bathroom with his belt undone. "What's the matter? You missed seeing me naked?"

"I'm not into fat guys," Owen said.

"Fat? That's not fat. Just a little moss on the ol' rock." Rick hoisted his T-shirt and slapped his doughy midsection. "Here, feel."

"Ugh. Get away from me."

"Suit yourself." Rick tugged his shirt down, clapped Henry on the back. "Hey Skrim. How'd it go with Pella Affenlight? Looked like she was really feeling your fabric."

Henry glanced around, worried that Schwartzy would hear and get the wrong idea, but Schwartz had already dragged his banged-up body down to the trainer's room to get taped and wrapped. Izzy's impish face appeared around a row of lockers. He tilted his head to one side as he unpinned a gleaming diamond stud from his ear: no jewelry allowed during games. *"Feeling his fabric?"* he said. "What kind of phrase is that?"

"Whaddya mean, what kind?" Rick said. "It's just a phrase. It means she's into him. She's down. She's feeling his fabric."

Izzy shook his head. "That's not a real phrase."

"Sure it is. It's a phrase in the culture."

"Estúpido." Izzy tossed the earring from one hand to the other, spat into one of the grated floor drains. "You made it up, man. Admit it."

"Did not."

"Did too."

"Not."

"Too."

"So what if I did?" Rick's face was bright pink with exasperation. "How do phrases get started anyway? You think they're all written down in a book somewhere? Somebody has to make them up!"

"Somebody," said Izzy. "Not you."

"Why, because I'm not black? What's so great about black people anyway?"

"We're more authentic," Owen said.

"Irish people are authentic. Look at this chin. You think this chin's not authentic?"

"It's a pretty good phrase," Henry said. "I might use it sometime."

Rick smiled, grateful for the kind of pleasant intervention Henry could always be counted on to provide. "Thanks, Skrim."

Izzy spat again. *"Estúpido."*

Coach Cox poked his head into the room. "Dunne! How the god-damn hell are you?"

"Much improved, Coach Cox."

"Well, you look like hell. Skrimmer sure did a number on that cheek. Skrim, you got a minute?"

"Sure, Coach."

They left the locker room and wandered the corridors of the VAC. The medieval fencing club was scrimmaging in one of the all-purpose rooms, off hands tucked behind their backs as they danced along lines of masking tape. They wore chain-mail vests and what looked to Henry like pirate hats. The lights were off in the other AP room. A winsome music of chimes and woodwinds issued from the room's speakers as the students sat cross-legged on the floor. "If you feel the need to pass gas," said the instructor cheerily, "it's important that you do so."

A lopsided leather medicine ball lay in the hallway. Coach Cox gave it a dull kick as they passed. He wasn't much for heart-to-hearts. "So," he said.

Henry nodded. "Yeah."

"Been a rough week. But you can't get down."

"I know."

"Just relax out there. Scouts or no scouts. Let 'em sit there, type on their fancy laptops, talk on their fancy phones. Relax and play your game."

"Right," Henry said. "I will."

"I know you will." Coach Cox gave him an awkward pat on the back. "We're with you, Skrim."

By the time Henry returned to the locker room, banter had given way to preparatory solemnity. Each Harpooner sat half or mostly uniformed in front of his locker, nodding along with his iPod's pregame playlist. Schwartz used an ancient cassette-tape Walkman; only Henry didn't listen to music at all. Izzy twisted his wristbands so the Nike insignia were aligned just so. Sooty Kim buttoned the bottom two buttons of his jersey, unbuttoned one, buttoned two more, unbuttoned one. Detmold Jensen worked at his glove's leather with tiny pinking shears, snipping off a superfluous centimeter of lacing. Henry went to the bathroom, which was still thick with the ordurous odor of Rick O'Shea, and urinated a long clear stream. He soaped his arms and hands with industrial candy-pink liquid soap, rinsed clean.

His stomach was rumbling queerly. It always clamped down before a game, not from nervousness exactly — it was more like self-containment, a narrowness of purpose that made the idea of putting anything into his body seem bizarre. Today, though, something was amiss. He could taste bile in the back of his throat. He went into a stall, locked the door, knelt down with his face to the bowl. He'd heard of major leaguers who threw up because of nerves. It wasn't necessarily a sign of weakness or any kind of big deal. Still, he hoped no one could hear him. He hiccuped once, twice, dryly. He wasn't sure how to hasten the process along. He stuck his index finger into his mouth and rooted around with it, rubbed his tongue, prodded the place where his tongue met his palate. His finger tasted like the pink soap, whose color suggested sweetness but which was warm and horrid. The taste made his stomach churn worse. Finally his finger found the right spot. His gut lurched, he gagged, and his lunch cascaded into the bowl in one long spilling fall. Slumped there on the floor, he felt better, almost sleepy. A happy surge of chemicals hit his brain.

He headed back to the locker room. He was behind schedule now, but he took care not to rush his own ritual preparations, the double- and triple-checking of jockstrap, cup, sliding shorts, pants, Cards T-shirt, jersey, sanitary socks, stirrups, belt, batting gloves, glove, and cap. He tested each part of his body for looseness: wrists, fingers, toes, all the anonymous muscles that surrounded his chest cavity and made up his neck and face. He untied his laces and retied them to the ideal tightness, so that the tops of his feet were pressured but not pinched. He followed his teammates outside.

"They're *baaaa-aaack,*" Izzy said, meaning the scouts. Supereconomy rental cars stood in a row in the parking lot, their bright paint jobs dulled by the closet-gray day. Mixed in among them were a few bald-tired sedans, their foot wells littered with fast-food bags and Styrofoam cups. These were the two kinds of scouts: scouts who rented, and scouts who owned.

During warm-ups Henry's arm felt light and pliant, lively as a bird — but it didn't matter how you felt during warm-ups. You had to perform when the pressure was on. He hit a double in the first and a long, long home run in the third. But when an easy grounder came his way he hesitated, threw low and wide of first so that Rick had to scoop it out of the dirt. Three innings later, he did it again, only this time Rick couldn't make the scoop. Another error, his fifth in a week; they were piling up like bodies in a horror movie.

After the game, the sports editor of the *Westish Bugler,* Sarah X. Pessel, approached him with her tape recorder. "Hey Henry," she said. "Tough game."

"We won."

"Right, but personally."

"I had four hits."

"Right, but defensively. It seems like you've been struggling. Couple more shaky throws today."

"We're fifteen and two," Henry said. "That's the best start in school history. We just have to keep improving."

"So you're not worried about the way you've been throwing the ball?"

"Fifteen and two," he repeated. "That's what counts."

"What about your personal future? Doesn't that count too? With the draft just eight weeks away?"

"As long as the team's winning, I'm happy." Whenever Henry set some kind of record, or was named somebody's Player of the Week or Month, Sarah would ask him for a comment, and he would tell her, with the practiced blandness of an all-star, that he'd gladly forgo the plaques and stats and trophies, would even be happy to ride the bench, if it meant that the Harpooners, after more than a hundred years of trying, would finally win a conference title. Until today, he'd always been certain he meant it.

"Do you know who Steve Blass is?" Sarah asked.

"Never heard of him," Henry lied. Steve Blass was an all-star pitcher for the Pirates in the early '70s. In the spring of 1973 he suddenly, inexplicably, became unable to throw the ball over the plate. He struggled for two years to regain his control and then, defeated, retired.

"What about Mackey Sasser?"

"Never heard of him." Sasser was a catcher for the Mets who'd developed a paralyzing fear of tossing the ball back to the pitcher. He would double-, triple-, quadruple-, quintuple-pump, unable to believe it was okay to let go. Opposing fans would loudly, gleefully count the number of pumps. Opposing players would run around the bases. Total humiliation. When it happened to Sasser, they said he had Steve Blass Disease.

"Steve Sax? Chuck Knoblauch? Mark Wohlers? Rick Ankiel?"

If Sarah X. Pessel hadn't been a girl, Henry might have socked her in the face. Her middle name probably didn't even start with X; she probably just liked the way it looked in her byline. "None of those guys were shortstops," he said.

"Don't get mad at *me,* Henry. I'm just doing my job."

"You're in college, Sarah. You work for the *Bugler.* You don't get paid for this."

Sarah looked pointedly out at the field, back at Henry. "Neither do you."

30

Like many Midwesterners, Mrs. McCallister started the workday early. By four fifteen she'd put in an hour of overtime and headed home to her half-acre garden and a multicourse dinner cooked by Mr. McCallister, whose fall from a tree stand three deer seasons ago had smashed his left hip and forced him to retire. Now he grew vegetables in the McCallisters' garden, cooked them into sauce for his homemade pasta. Often Mrs. McCallister would slide a plate onto Affenlight's desk at noontime; even reheated in the office microwave, it always tasted exquisite.

It became Owen's habit to drop by Affenlight's office around four thirty, post–Mrs. McCallister, on days when the Harpooners didn't have a home game; because of his injuries he wasn't yet traveling or practicing with the team. Owen would enter without a word, shut the door behind him, and slide out from under his messenger bag, the strap of which held a rainbow pin, a pink-triangle pin, a black-and-white *taijitu* pin, and pins that read CARBON NEUTRALITY NOW, PAY A LIVING WAGE, and WESTISH BASEBALL. Then he lay down on the love seat, which wasn't quite long enough to lie down on and too stiff to be comfortable anyway, but Owen didn't seem to mind. He slipped off his shoes, crossed his slender ankles on the love seat's far arm, and closed his eyes, fingers interlaced atop the soft swell of his childlike belly. The only sign of wakefulness would be the slow, thoughtful tap of his thumb pads against each other. He wanted Affenlight to read to him.

This was what Affenlight wanted too. The original pretense for these sessions was that the aftereffects of Owen's concussion made it hard for him to focus. Now, two weeks removed from Owen's injury, Affenlight wasn't sure whether this was still the case — often Owen would turn his head and follow along on the page anyway — but he didn't want to break the spell by asking. He rose from his desk chair, which was too antique and massive to move around, and shifted to one of the spindle-backed Westish-insignia visitors' chairs, which he drew up close to the love seat. Owen extracted his homework from his bag and handed it to Affenlight — on this particular day, the last two acts of *The Cherry Orchard* and a turgid dramaturgical essay from a poorly xeroxed course packet. Affenlight began to read.

"Don't you think this is strange?" Owen murmured sometime later, as Affenlight turned a page.

"What?"

Owen rubbed his belly, eyes still serenely closed. "You know. The way we do this every afternoon. I lie here, and you read to me, and we talk."

"I'm sure it's very unusual," Affenlight agreed. "I've certainly never done anything like it."

"That's not what I mean." Owen swung up to a sitting position, opened his eyes, and fixed them on Affenlight. "What I mean is...it's almost as if you didn't like me."

"I do." Affenlight reached out and brushed his fingertips against the little knob of bone at the base of Owen's skull, but the gesture seemed insufficient, if not utterly false. He felt schoolboyish, intimidated. Since that first tentative moment on the moonlit linoleum, they had not touched.

"I don't know if you know what you're doing."

Part of Affenlight felt peeved at Owen for interrupting or dismissing his bliss. Because it *was* bliss, he felt, to be here with Owen and to read to him, even when he was reading dry-as-dust sentences from a poorly xeroxed course packet. Of all the activities two people could do together in private, Affenlight had a special fondness for reading aloud. Maybe this was part of his instinct for solitude and self-enclosure; a way to reveal himself while hiding behind someone else's words. Maybe he should have gone into acting. He'd often thought that Pella would make an excellent actress.

Owen slid closer to him and leaned toward him and took his face in two hands and kissed him, a proper and unambiguous kiss but also a soft and careful one, as he tilted the damaged part of his face away. Affenlight realized in what was as close to an epiphanic flash as he'd ever dared to come that there were many ways of living that had never been named or tried. The chapel bells tolled a long slow song of six o'clock. His tongue, Owen's tongue, two tongues. At least he wasn't quite so old that he didn't have lips to kiss. He thought of Whitman's adhesion: the liking of like for like. Although he and Owen were not much alike and in a way kissing Owen was much like kissing a woman, you could close your eyes and find the same softness, same brush of noses, same thick wetness of the inner walls of cheeks. Except with women Affenlight leaned forward, and now he leaned back.

Owen slipped out of his sweater, which was seafoam green, soft to the touch, with a hole at one elbow. Affenlight traced his fingertips up and down Owen's bare arm below his T-shirt. The two of them kissed again, kept kissing, and it was, still, surprisingly like what happened between a man and a woman — although, thought Affenlight, perhaps I'm the only person in the world naive enough to be surprised by this — and then Owen cupped one hand over the bulge that had appeared in the inseam of Affenlight's herringbone slacks. Affenlight flinched. Owen stopped and looked at him. "Are you okay?"

Was he okay? He was nervous, certainly. Even frightened. If Owen were a girl, Affenlight would have been worried about the politics, the ethics, the power relations of the situation—that was largely *why* it had never happened with a girl—but here there was too much else to worry about, and it was clear where the power lay: with Owen. Affenlight felt dazed, vertiginous. But he'd come this far, and there seemed no reason to stop right here. He nodded.

"Are you sure?"

"Yes."

Owen undid the slacks' clasp and unzipped the zipper, dainty silver tooth by dainty silver tooth, with a guileful smile on his face, a very complex smile, mischievous and beatific and maybe a tiny bit malicious, a beautiful smooth-skinned person—did he ever even shave?—who would not necessarily grow old but would certainly someday die. He used his hands to work out the intricacies of slacks and undershorts and brought Affenlight out into the open—*Affenlight,* strange synecdoche!—and bent and kissed him on the tip of the penis in a womanly way. And kissed for a few more seconds before looking up. "I guess I can't," he said, lifting his head, the smile categorizable now, rueful and tender and a little wry. He tapped a finger against his injured jaw. "I can barely open my mouth."

"That's okay." Affenlight said, and meant it, though his voice sounded strange and hoarse. He picked Owen's sweater off the couch and began to fold it, matching sleeve to sleeve. He pinched the medial crease and draped the sweater over his forearm, all the while feeling a swell of delight at the fastidiousness of this delay, so different from the frenzied garment-rending of cinematic lovers. He'd long ago learned that he found a twinge of erotic joy in the act of buttoning a girlfriend's jacket, zipping her sweater to the chin, bundling her up against the northern cold of Westish, New Haven, Cambridge, Westish again. After folding the sweater neatly he placed it on the warped wooden floorboards between Owen's two-toned shoes, which looked like the saddle shoes of old, and, with the limberness of a man no older than forty, the soundly thrumming heart of seventeen, slid down from his chair and knelt upon it, a hand on each of Owen's knees. Kneeling, whatever the circumstances, could hardly fail to remind him, however ironically, of childhood bedside prayer, the old Latin Mass—he'd hardly been since Vatican II—and, given the hour, vespers; *ad cereum benedicendum,* as they used to say.

31

Henry and Starblind stood facing each other, pounding out curls with heavy dumbbells in perfect rhythm, Henry's right arm moving with Starblind's left, Starblind's right with Henry's left, as if each was gazing into a mirror. Starblind's eyes flicked down to check out Henry's blood-gorged biceps as if they were his own; Henry reflexively did the same.

Little Loondorf groaned and squirmed on the flat bench. Izzy hovered over him, shouting, "Come on, Phil! Take the pain, *vendejo*. The pain is like gas!"

"The pain is like *a* gas," counseled Schwartz. He supervised from a metal folding chair, a newspaper in his lap and towel-wrapped ice bags on both knees. "It expands to fill up whatever space you give it. So we shouldn't fear pain. A lot of it doesn't hurt much more, or take up more psychic space, than a little bit. Viktor Frankl."

"Come on, *vendejo!* The pain is like a gas!"

Henry and Starblind reached their hundredth curl. The dumbbells dropped from their weakened grasps and bounced off the rubberized floor. "Let's go down to the track," Henry said.

Starblind ran a sweat-slick hand through his hair. "Now? You're nuts."

"Let's go."

Starblind sighed that sigh of his—a long, exasperated, put-upon sigh, as if other humans had been designed especially to annoy him. As if he hadn't dumped Anna Veeli, second-hottest girl in the school, to go out with the hottest, Cicely Krum. They headed for the door.

The track was empty. The moon hung early in the violet sky. "Hundreds," said Henry.

"How many?"

"Twenty."

"That's crazy. I've got to pitch this weekend."

"Fine. Twenty-five."

"Whatever's up your ass," Starblind said, "leave it there."

They took off through the dusk. Starblind won the first one easily. He had sprinter's speed, an extra gear to kick it into; the track coach was always begging him to show up, untrained, for important meets. They walked to the next set of lines on the track, took off again.

"Two–zip," Starblind said.

Henry nodded. He had never beaten Starblind in any of their many races, whether up the stadium steps or here on the track or side by side on adjacent treadmills in the dead of winter, their sneakers slapping faster and faster against the fraying woven rubber of the treadmill belts as the motors creaked and moaned, their shaky index fingers jabbing the buttons that added tenths of miles per hour, sweat flying around the room like water off wet dogs.

Starblind won the next two, each time opening a wide gap in the final fifteen meters. "How do my shoe bottoms look?" he asked. "Clean?"

Henry grunted. True, he'd never beaten Starblind—but they hadn't had a full-on race in a long time. He was fitter than he'd ever been. "That's four," he said.

Starblind won the fifth and the sixth and the seventh. Henry hung on his shoulder like a bad angel. As they walked toward the starting line for race number eight, Starblind was gasping for air, his rib cage heaving up and down. Henry kept his inhalations quiet and shallow: hide your weakness, hold your advantage. If he wanted to beat Starblind it wouldn't be by speed. He would have to break his will.

He took a lead in the eighth, but Starblind came roaring past. *Mother-fucker,* Henry thought. He wanted to grab Starblind by the collar of his sleek silver shirt and jerk him back, fling him down on the track, stomp on his chest. He had no special reason to be pissed at Starblind, but he wanted to *hurt,* wanted to hurt somebody, and Starblind was right here, asking for it.

"How many is that?" Starblind asked, as if he didn't know.

"Eight."

"Already?"

They flew side by side down the track, legs flailing like a ragged four-legged beast. "Tie," Henry said firmly.

"What? Fine. Tie." You had to hand it to Starblind—he trained hard, he was in great shape. But now he was leaning forward, hands on knees, gasping for air. Trying to buy a little time before the next sprint. He was dead meat.

Henry won the next one. And the five after that. His lungs rose high in his throat. His legs shook. They'd never run this many sprints at this pace, especially not midseason. He put his hands on his hips and tipped back his chin. His dizziness made the dusk-dark clouds wheel madly through the sky. *Come on,* he thought. *Hang on.*

He won the next two, heart pounding, stomach heaving. He eked out the next one by a nose. Henry nine, Starblind eight, with one tie. Star-blind looked bleach-pale, his footsteps wobbly and erratic as they headed toward the next starting line. Henry almost asked if he was okay, if maybe they shouldn't quit early—but that wasn't how the game worked. Starblind could take care of Starblind.

Henry lost the nineteenth race on purpose. Tie score. That way Star-blind would still have a chance to win and would have to push himself to the last. They walked up to the line. Henry summoned every bit of strength he had left, pounded down the track with a spent-but-still-game, far-from-giving-up Starblind right alongside him. *Empty yourself completely,* Henry could hear Schwartz saying. *Empty yourself.*

He unleashed a war cry and accelerated, outran his breath. He left a dark gap between himself and Starblind. Starblind slowed a few yards short of the finish, coughing hard. He staggered forward, planted his hands on his thighs, spilled his stomach onto the track. Henry, light-headed, hands on hips, was trying to ward off nausea himself. He wandered away to give Starblind some privacy. Out over the lake a hard white spray kicked high off the breakers and caught some source of light. A moth banged against Henry's arm, banged against his shoulder, finally lit on his wet chest. He cupped a hand over it. Furry wings fluttered against his palm. Starblind was still crouched down, making piteous puppyish noises. It felt good to make somebody else puke for a change.

32

A re you okay?"

"Sure."

"No, really. You look stricken. Like you might be ill."

"I'm fine," Affenlight said. He and Owen were side by side on the love seat now, Owen's left leg flipped over Affenlight's right, their arms curled around each other's shoulders.

"If you're not okay just tell me."

"Shhh." Affenlight's stomach did feel a little funny, but he wasn't about to say so.

"Do you want me to leave?"

"No," Affenlight said. "Not at all." But he wasn't displeased when Owen withdrew his leg and arm to leave a space between them on the love seat. He even felt relieved. He didn't want Owen to leave, but he didn't really want him there either.

Owen eyed him warily, tied the drawstring on his martial artist's pants. "Maybe this wasn't such a good idea."

"I'm fine," Affenlight said. "Just give me a second."

"I don't want you to do things you don't want to do. I don't want to force you."

"You didn't. You aren't." Affenlight's stomach grumbled nastily. He felt confused and inarticulate. He wished Owen would go, just for a little while, but he couldn't stand to see him walk out the door.

"If you're straight, you're straight," Owen said. "C'est la vie."

Well, wasn't he? It was true that Affenlight thought of himself as straight. Or, at least, he didn't think of himself as gay. But he also knew he'd never be with a woman again. Or another man either. He was only so old, but it seemed he'd reached the final movement of his sexual life — from here on out, he'd be with Owen or no one. No one or Owen.

"Say something," Owen said.

"I'm not sure what to say." Affenlight noticed his right hand clutching his stomach in a way that indicated discomfort. He tucked the hand under his thigh. "I've never done that before."

"Well, sure," Owen said. "That's obvious."

Affenlight blanched. Not only was what he was doing strange and shameful and somehow wrong — wrong not in any conventional ethical sense but simply because he felt so strange and scraped and speechless now — not only all that, but he wasn't any good at it either. "It was that bad?"

"It was fine."

"Fine?"

"Better than fine. It was wonderful. Are you sure you're okay?"

Affenlight nodded, looked at Owen beseechingly. He wanted Owen to comprehend everything he lacked the courage or clarity of mind to say outright right now, to read it in his eyes without being told, to comprehend it without getting mad, but that was too much to ask of anyone, even Owen. Or maybe Owen understood precisely how he felt, and that was the problem. Owen stood up, patted Affenlight's shoulder consolingly, and walked out of the room.

After a few minutes Affenlight's stomachache passed. He went to the window. Dusk was falling. A soft spring rain was filling the flower beds, a soft wind trembling the new-leafed trees. No lights came on in Phumber 405. Where had Owen gone if not to his room? To dinner, perhaps. Or the library. Or the arms of another, better, more appropriate lover. Affenlight missed him already. Why couldn't he have acted more normal, hid his confusion until it passed? Why couldn't he have explained himself to Owen? Didn't love sometimes have to explain itself?

Affenlight resolved, there at the window in his darkening office, to take himself out of the running for Owen's affections. Not that he was in the running, after today. Owen wouldn't be back, and that was for the best. Owen would be happier with someone his own age, someone better at being gay. Affenlight would call Pella, take her to Maison Robert for dinner—that was the sort of thing he should be doing anyway. The two of them had spent so little time together. His stomachache had been a sign.

He went to his desk, dialed the phone upstairs to see if Pella was there, listened to the first two rings. The office door reopened. There stood Owen, his damaged face bathed in lamplight, his soft, one-sided smile more saintly than anything an old master ever did. Affenlight placed the phone back on the hook just as Pella said hello. "I thought you'd gone," he said.

"Gone? Without my shoes?" Owen nodded toward his saddlebacks, which were right there beside the love seat, heels aligned. Stupid, foolish Affenlight! "I went to make some coffee." He handed Affenlight a steaming mug. IF MOMMA AIN'T HAPPY, AIN'T NO ONE HAPPY, read its weathered pink lettering. "Should we have a cigarette?"

Affenlight smiled. This was the thought that had been eluding him, the little switch deep in his head that needed to be flipped to restore him from his vague fears to his actual physical life: after sex, after oral sex, with your saintly lover, your saintly twenty-one-year-old lover, your saintly twenty-one-year-old male lover, you should get to smoke a cigarette. Of course! Things were simpler than they seemed. Repeat it like a mantra, Guert: Things are simpler than they seem.

"Smoking in the parlor," he said, nodding up at the hand-painted sign as he slapped his overcoat pockets for his cigarettes, "is expressly prohibited."

The routine became entrenched: After they did whatever they did that day, Owen would go out into the hallway and return eight minutes later, always bearing the same two steaming mugs from the particleboard shelf above the coffeemaker: KISS ME, I'M IRISH for himself, IF MOMMA AIN'T HAPPY for Affenlight. They sipped their coffee and smoked a cigarette, chatted, read Chekhov together, passing the book back and forth once Owen's headaches subsided. The kitschy mugs had been culled, over the years, from Mrs. McCallister's home kitchen cupboards. It might have sounded silly, but Affenlight loved the way Owen always picked these same two mugs and even, presumably, went so far as to rinse them in the sink when they were dirty. Such consistency suggested, or seemed to suggest, that Owen found their afternoons worth repeating, even down to the smallest detail. This was the dreamy, paradisiacal side of domestic ritual: when all the days were possessed of the same minutiae precisely because you wanted them to be.

Affenlight told Mrs. McCallister that he'd resumed a daily exercise regimen and so needed to keep the late-afternoon hours clear of appointments. He laid awake nights thinking of Owen, half listening for Pella to come home from Mike Schwartz's house, always relieved when he heard the clap of her flip-flops on the stairs. He arose before dawn, walked his usual route along the lake he loved, went to the office to plow through the work he'd been neglecting. He rarely slept and he rarely tired. His heart in his chest felt dangerously full, swollen and tender, like a fruit so ripe it threatens to split its skin. He wanted every day and every moment, the moments with Owen, the moments between Owen, to last and last and last. In his life he'd passed through long periods of gratefulness and good cheer, but he'd scarcely even imagined this level of thorough contentment with things as they were. His chronic restlessness had fled. He wanted nothing new. He wanted only to hang on to what he had. It was almost excruciating. Everything that floated through his life's width—a sunny day or a sudden cloudburst, an e-mail from an old colleague, a conversation with Pella that didn't turn into a fight—seemed loaded with such poignance that he found himself on the verge of country-music tears, and could cope with his own ridiculousness only by making fun of himself. Affenlight, you maudlin old coot. Affenlight, you fool.

33

On the ferry ride back from Wainwright, Schwartz sat by himself, listening to the battered old tape of carefully chosen Metallica and Public Enemy songs he listened to before every game. The game had ended, ended badly—he was listening not to pump himself up but to drown out his thoughts. The sun was down, and a cold steady wind flowed through the unsealed joints of the old ferry cabin. He'd popped three Vikes with a handful of Advil, bundled up as best he could, and was preparing to recede from consciousness.

Somehow, despite the blaring music and his closed eyes, he sensed a presence at his shoulder. He thought it would be Henry, but it turned out to be Coach Cox.

"You seen the Skrimmer?" Coach Cox asked.

"I think he's out on deck."

"On deck? It's frickin' freezing out there." Coach Cox sat down, rubbed his hands together, blew into his cupped palms. Schwartz took off his headphones and shut the book he hadn't been reading. The rest of the team was belowdecks by the snack bar, playing poker for packets of salt. "You talk to him?" Coach Cox asked.

"A little."

"He's hanging in there?"

Schwartz shrugged. "Seems like it."

"His wing's okay?"

"Wing's fine."

Coach Cox stroked his mustache, pondered the situation for a while. "Well, hell."

Bottom of the ninth. Two outs, runner on second. Westish ahead 7 to 6. Loondorf threw a good heavy curve, and the batter rapped a ground ball right at Henry. All he had to do was throw it to first and the game was over. Instead he patted the ball into the palm of his glove once, twice, again, side-skipping toward first as if not-so-secretly wishing he could side-skip all the way there and hand the ball to Rick. He patted the glove a fourth time and, needing to hurry because the runner was nearing first, uncorked a way-too-high, way-too-hard throw that Rick barely bothered to leap for. It cleared the low fence behind first base and, because there weren't any bleachers or fans to stop it, skidded across the street that abutted the park and rattled into the wheel well of somebody's truck. The tying run scored. The next batter singled to end the game, the Harpooners' first loss in weeks.

"He looked good before that last throw," Coach Cox said. "I thought he had it turned around."

"Me too."

"Listen." Coach Cox's gruff voice sanded the gaps in the wind. "I heard you were low on cash."

"Who told you that?"

"Nobody told me. Something I heard."

"Did Henry say that?"

Coach Cox shrugged. "Let me loan you a few bucks," he said. "Man's gotta eat."

Schwartz had a ten-meal-a-week pass for the dining hall. Lately he'd been eating ten meals a week, plus whatever he could sneak out in his backpack, which wasn't much. The check-in ladies had never warmed to his charms — his size, an asset in other situations, roused their suspicion. Pella brought him ham-and-cheese sandwiches after her dishwashing shifts. She also offered to take him to dinner on her father's credit card.

Schwartz gobbled down the sandwiches but declined the dinners out. It was embarrassing, having your girlfriend provide for you. Mostly their dates consisted of holing up in Schwartz's room, eating saltines and drinking Lipton tea while they read their books. Sometimes on dollar-pitcher night they went to Bartleby's. Now that they'd started having sex he was spending a couple bucks a day on condoms. Condoms were expensive. Not that he was complaining.

"I don't need any money," he said.

"Bullshit." Coach Cox began peeling hundreds off a fat wad held folded by a rubber band. He slipped some number of them against Schwartz's palm.

"I can't," Schwartz said.

"The heck you can't. Stick it in your pocket."

Since long before Schwartz's time, it had been rumored that Coach Cox had a couple million dollars socked away somewhere. "He fits the profile," Tennant used to say. "Never wears anything but free WAD gear. Eats all his meals at McDonald's. Drives a car with three hundred thousand miles on it. I'm telling you, the guy's loaded."

Schwartz had never been sure one way or the other. Coach Cox hardly ever talked about anything but baseball. A third baseman in high school, he was drafted by the Cubs and played a few years in the low minors, retired at twenty-two because, as he put it, "I didn't have the stuff. Hell, I couldn't even fake the stuff." He moved to Milwaukee, became a line repairman for the phone company, got married, had a kid, became the Westish baseball coach, had another kid, got divorced, quit the phone company, and opened his own two-truck operation. Which, if you believed Harpooner lore, had netted him millions.

Their palms were pressed together, neither of them holding the bills that were in between. It was a risky standoff, given the wind. Schwartz wavered. With money, he could take Pella to dinner tomorrow night. He could make up for all the tea-and-cracker meals they'd had, not to mention the nights he'd canceled their tea-and-cracker plans to go hit ground balls to Henry under the lights of Westish Field. He could take her to Maison Robert, the overpriced French place he'd only ever been to with his history adviser. They could drink wine. He closed his hand, just a little.

Coach Cox stood up and exited the forecabin. The bills threatened to slide out of Schwartz's grasp; he slipped them into the pocket of his windbreaker, riffling their edges with his fingers to get a sense of his newfound wealth. There were a lot: nine or ten. He closed his eyes and surrendered to the slow roll of the waves like liquid Vicodin.

It might've been a few seconds later, or an hour, but suddenly Henry stood in front of him, his pale-blue eyes filled with what could only be called anguish. His lower lip quivered and his soft chin squinched into a web of small rolling lines as he tried to keep from crying. "Skrimmer," Schwartz said.

"Hey." Henry's voice cracked miserably; he coughed to clear his throat.

"You okay?"

Henry nodded. "Yeah."

"You played well today." Schwartz removed his headphones from around his neck and tucked them into his jacket pocket. "Arm looked strong, everything looked strong. We're right where we need to be."

"I cost us the game."

"One lousy play," Schwartz said. "We should have been up twelve by then."

"But we weren't." Henry sat down beside Schwartz, bounced back up as if the aluminum scorched his ass. He clapped both hands to the top of his age-blackened Cardinals cap like a long-distance runner warding off a cramp. "What can I do?" he said. "What can I do?" His voice was quiet and disbelieving; awed, even, at the circumstances in which he found himself.

He bent his head back toward the ceiling and breathed out a short pained sigh or moan. He dropped his hands, worried them in quick circles, clapped them to the top of his head again. His movements were spastic and strange, the movements of a person whose thoughts have become toxic.

"It's okay," Schwartz said, "we're okay," but Henry's feet had already carried him through the cabin's rickety metal storm door, which banged behind him, and out onto the deck. Schwartz hauled himself to his feet to follow. By the time he got outside Henry was out of sight. Schwartz leaned heavily against the railing. The darkness was total, neither a star nor a sliver of moon alive in the sky. The Vicodin, though it did almost nothing to mute the pain in his shins and knees, coursed through his brain in a wonderfully gentle way. All he wanted was to be home, off his feet, curled like a child in bed with one hand on the soft little swell of Pella's belly.

A cabin door opened, and the dark outline of a person appeared. The figure yawned loudly, muttered a few pleasant curses, and, using the still-open door as a shield against the wind, struck a match, revealing the meaty, splotchy, amiably dissolute face of Rick O'Shea, his lips cupped around a home-rolled cigarette. "Schwartzy?" he puffed, squinting into the darkness and letting the door bang shut behind him. "That you, pal?"

"It's me."

Rick ambled over and leaned against the railing, blew a pensive smoke-shape into the night. "Bitch-tit of a game."

Schwartz nodded.

"You talk to Skrim?"

Before Schwartz could decide how to answer, a patter of footsteps became audible in the distance and another figure hove into view, this one with its silhouetted hands atop its head, silhouetted elbows spread like wings. The head nodded up and down, keeping time with unheard music. As it drew closer, Schwartz could hear short sharp breathing that bordered on hyperventilation.

"Skrimmer." Schwartz laid a hand on the slick fabric of Henry's warm-up jacket, but Henry kept moving without slowing down. "I'm just walking," he said breathlessly, still nodding. "I'll just walk."

"You okay, Skrim?" Rick asked. "You got a cramp or something?"

"Just walking," Henry said. "I'll keep walking."

He continued down the deck toward the stern and was absorbed into the darkness.

Rick took one last drag before flicking his cigarette butt over the rail. The orange flame bounced once, twice, against the hull and vanished. "Panic attack," he said.

"What do we do?"

"My mom usually drinks a couple screwdrivers. She says the orange juice has a soothing effect." Rick, seized by a thought, took off after Henry. Schwartz tried to follow, but his legs wouldn't let him.

Before long Rick and Henry reappeared, walking fast, Henry still nodding with his hands locked atop his head, Rick with his face tucked close to Henry's own, whispering. Schwartz stepped aside to let them pass.

A few laps later, Henry's arms fell down by his sides, and Rick flashed Schwartz a thumbs-up sign. They made seven or eight more orbits, each at a slower pace than the last, as Henry wound down like a toy. When they finally stopped, the ferry was in sight of the dock.

34

Later that night, Schwartz and Pella lay in Schwartz's bed. Even with some postgame painkillers in his system, even with the deadness that entered his legs after a game, he'd never had trouble before. Pella tried to coax him as they kissed, her fingertips trailing lightly along the flap of his boxers, but it was no use. "It's okay," she said. "Why don't you tell me about it?"

"About what?"

"You know. Henry."

"It's bad," Schwartz said. "I'm starting to worry that it's bad. The last couple of games, he seemed to be getting over it. But today — today was bad."

"Are you sure he's not hurt? Maybe he hurt his arm and he's afraid to tell anyone."

"His arm's fine. You should see the throws he makes at practice. Or even in games, on the bang-bang plays. When he doesn't have time to think about it. His arm is a triumph of nature."

Pella said nothing. The stertor of Meat's breathing came softly, almost soothingly, through the wall. "It's always the easy plays," Schwartz said, "the balls hit right at him. You can see the gears spinning: *Am I gonna screw this up? Maybe I'm gonna screw this up.* I just want to grab him by the shoulders and shake it out of him. He's creating this whole problem out of nothing. Nothing."

Pella nestled closer, again passed her hand against the front of his boxers. In the three-quarters dark of the bedroom he could see the extra-dark protrusion of her nearer nipple beneath the sheet. There wasn't an inch of her body that he didn't desire. She didn't like her legs, thought they were short and stubby, her ankles too thick to be feminine—sheer stupidity, from Schwartz's point of view. If anything he wanted there to be more of her, more and more Pella to anchor him to the world.

Since the first time they'd had sex they'd never not had sex. But tonight it wasn't happening. He was too tired, too tense, had popped one too many pills on the ferry. It was bound to happen eventually, this slip toward domesticity—was a normal and natural and even poten-tially comforting development, but Schwartz could tell this wasn't the night for it. Pella would think they weren't having sex because he was worried about Henry. That was the last thing he wanted her to think, even if it was true.

She had said it was okay, but here she was, persisting. She slid her fingers inside the flap of his boxers and tickled the crease where his pel-vis met his thigh. Schwartz tried to feel it. Missiles, redwoods, the Wash-ington Monument. *Come on,* he thought, *one time.*

He had a few stray Viagra in the bottom drawer of his broken-down dresser beneath his jeans. No shame in that, was there? Sometimes—okay, usually—you were drunk when you brought someone home. Sometimes the girl was too klutzy, or too shrill, or just plain not that sexy. Sometimes you needed a little extra. Part of the relief of meeting Pella was the way he responded to her so fully, so fundamentally—he'd forgotten the pills were even there. But he wished he'd taken one tonight.

Pella withdrew her hand to his belly, outside his T-shirt. Schwartz searched her little sigh for evidence of exasperation—he found some, but if you corrected for paranoia it might as easily have been a yawn.

"It's a block," she said. "Like writer's block. Or stage fright."

"Yes."

"Maybe he should be seeing somebody."

"He is seeing somebody," Mike said. "Me."

"You know what I mean. A professional."

Schwartz bristled. "Henry wouldn't go for that."

"He would if you told him to."

"It would scare him. He'd think there was something wrong with him."

"Well, isn't there?"

"He'll be fine. He just needs to relax."

Pella's fingers brushed his boxers again. "Maybe you should relax a little."

Schwartz flinched. "What's that supposed to mean?"

"What's what supposed to mean?"

"About me needing to relax."

"Nothing. You just seem kind of tense tonight."

It was the *tonight* that got Schwartz. He'd been tense all month. Hell, he'd been tense all his life. What was so goddamn remarkable about *tonight*?

"I'm not tense."

"Fine," Pella said. "Whatever."

The smallness of the bed enforced an awkward closeness. Schwartz was wedged between Pella and the wall. In lieu of a shade, a dirt-gray sheet hung down over the window, barely dimming the lights of the neighbor's garage.

Since moving out of the dorms he'd only occasionally brought a girl back here—better to go to the girl's place, with all those pillows and photo albums and unguessable scents, the fresh sheets on the bed and the carefully labeled class binders stacked on the shelf. In the room of a girl at a place like Westish, the presence of family was almost always palpable, not just in the framed photographs but in the careful replication of a childhood room, updated for post-adolescence; the holdover stuffed animals, the condom box or plastic pastel birth-control wheel left in plain view in tribute to the parent who wasn't there to object. Those absent families soothed Schwartz; for a few hours, he imagined them as his own.

"He should see a psychologist," Pella said. "A behavioral therapist. Someone who deals with athletes. He wouldn't have to free-associate about his mother or anything."

"Maybe that's what he needs. To free-associate about his mother."

"I'm being serious," Pella said.

"So am I," said Schwartz, but he wasn't. For some reason Pella's attempted intervention was really pissing him off. He tried to find a softer, more sincere way of speaking. "Okay, a therapist. But who's going to pay for that?"

"Couldn't Henry's family help out? I mean, he stands to make a lot of money, right? It'd be an investment."

"The Skrimshanders don't have money to *invest*," Schwartz said. "His dad's not a college president."

"I didn't imagine that he was."

"I'm not sure you can imagine anything else."

"Don't pick a fight with me! Why are you picking a fight with me?"

"Sorry."

They lay in silence for a while. Finally Pella said, "I've been planning to sell my wedding ring. Henry could use part of that money. As a loan."

As soon as the words left Pella's lips, she knew that they were a mistake. It was a genuine offer, genuinely meant—but it came at precisely the wrong time, and she could already tell by Mike's face how it would be interpreted: She was trying to insert herself into his relationship with Henry. She was implying that she, or a therapist, could help Henry where he could not. She was brandishing her superior financial status. She was reminding him that though they both had crackers and tea for dinner, she didn't have to.

"Henry has enough loans," he said.

"Then I could just give him the money. Or give it to you, and you could arrange it with the therapist. Henry wouldn't have to know how much it cost."

"I'm sure it would cost plenty."

"Well," Pella said, "it's a pretty expensive ring."

Something flared in Schwartz's chest. He'd Googled Pella's husband, had seen the photograph on his firm's website: The Architect leaning back from his drafting table, mechanical pencil in hand, fixing the camera with a tight, tolerant smile. He looked like a dork in his cashmere sweater and neatly groomed beard, but he had money and read Greek and was *married,* for Chrissakes, to Pella. However much she disparaged him, he was part of a world of casual privilege that she could return to at any time. "I'm sure it is," he said. "I'm sure it cost a fortune."

"You want to know how much it cost?" Pella matched the sharpness in his voice and raised it one. "It cost fourteen thousand dollars. Does that make you feel better?"

"I feel great," said Schwartz. "I feel like fourteen thousand bucks."

"Ha."

Down the block someone was dribbling a basketball. Each bounce reverberated through the corrugated drainpipes that cut beneath the ends of driveways, connecting one section of culvert to the next. "Forget it," Schwartz said. "We don't need your money."

"I wasn't offering it to *you,*" Pella said. "And anyway I don't know why you're being so contrary. If Henry hurt his elbow, he'd go to the doctor, right? And you'd make sure he had the best doctor money could buy."

"We're not talking about Henry's elbow. We're talking about his head."

"It's an *analogy,*" Pella said, as if he might not have heard the word before. "And a fair one. But you're not trying to be fair, are you?"

Goddamnit, Schwartz thought. If only they'd had sex everything would be fine. The Viagra was right there in the drawer by the jeans; so close and yet so far.

"Would it upset you," Pella said, "if Henry saw a shrink and it helped?"

"What kind of question is that?"

"You can't be afraid that it *won't* help—that would be absurd, because nothing else is helping. You're afraid that it *will* help. What scares you is that he'll get drafted and go pro and be fine. Better than fine. He'll be happy as a clam and he won't need you anymore. But as long as he's at Westish, as long as he's a mess, then you're still running the show."

Schwartz stared up at the dirt-gray sheet that the breeze was making billow and dance just above his nose. "That's bullshit." It *was* bullshit, he knew it was bullshit, but it was plausible bullshit, and to hear it spoken aloud sapped the air from his gut.

Pella wasn't quite finished. "What you two need is couples counseling. Classic codependency. The neuroses and secret wishes of one partner manifesting themselves in the symptoms of the oth—"

"Oh, shut up."

"I will, don't worry. First I have to tell you something." Her eyes softened in a way that surprised him. "David's coming."

"*David* David?"

"That's the one."

This cast the whole evening—their failure to have sex, the arguing after—in a new light. Schwartz had been willing to take the blame, to offer up Henry and exhaustion and Vicodin as excuses. But Pella had her own thing going on. Look at her waltzing in here, kissing him, climbing on top of him, and then saying, *It's okay baby it's okay, don't worry about it,* when really it was her own hesitation he'd sensed, her own body that was sending off warning signs. Really, she was worried about David coming. Or worse, glad.

"When?"

"Soon."

"How soon?"

"I don't know . . . maybe tomorrow?"

"Maybe," Schwartz repeated. He meant to be sarcastic, but it came out sounding incredulous and pathetic. He tried again: *"Maybe?"*

"Tomorrow," Pella admitted. "He'll be here tomorrow."

"Where will he stay?"

"In a hotel."

"Where will you stay?"

She smacked him on the shoulder in a way that was supposed to be playful, but it had real force behind it. "Where do you think? At my dad's."

"Not here."

"I can't. Not tomorrow."

"Because of your husband."

"He's only my husband because we're not divorced yet."

"So why's he coming?"

"He's in Chicago on business. Or so he claims. Anyway, it was stupid of me to think that I could slink off and that would be that. We need to sit down and talk things out. Closure, et cetera. He's been calling my dad's place ten times a day."

"I'll talk to him."

"Yeah, right," said Pella. "That's just what'll calm him down. If he knows *we're* fucking around."

"Is that what we're doing? Fucking around?"

"You know what I mean."

"I'm not sure I do."

"What do you want me to say? Fine, we're fucking around. Or were, until tonight."

Schwartz wasn't sure whether this was a comment about their failure to have sex or a declaration that they were breaking up. His phone, which was lying on the cardboard box that passed for a bedside table, began to skitter and dance. Pella stiffened from head to toe. There was no way he was going to take Henry's call, not right now — but the fact of the call was itself the crime, and not answering helped nothing. The phone gave a final shudder and fell silent.

"I don't know why I ever decided to come here," she said.

"So leave. What's stopping you?"

"Don't worry, I'm leaving." Pella was out of the bed, zipping her sweatshirt over her otherwise naked torso. Schwartz felt a blast of regret at the disappearance of all that beautiful bareness. She turned in the doorway with fire in her eyes. "You love to make life difficult, don't you? Mike Schwartz, Nietzsche's camel. The weight of the world on his big ol' shoulders. But guess what? Not everybody wants to maximize their pain. Some people have enough trouble making it from one day to the next. I'm sorry I went to prep school, okay? I'm sorry I never worked in a factory. Sure, I dropped out of high school. I wash dishes in a dining hall. But that's just slumming, isn't it Mike? That's not *real,* it's not real *suffering,* it's not the fucking South Side. For which I apologize. I'm sincerely fucking sorry my father went to grad school instead of drinking himsel—"

"I thought you were leaving."

"I'm already gone."

The bedroom door slammed, as did the front door. Then came the angry tambourine jingle of the front gate flying open and knocking back against itself. Schwartz turned on a light and tried to read, but he couldn't concentrate, so he popped two Vikes that were earmarked for tomorrow and wandered out into the hall.

A thin crease of light came from beneath the shut bathroom door. The toilet flushed and Arsch's wide pink body, even wider than Schwartz's, filled the door frame. He scratched his balls through his boxers. "You all right?" he asked, squinting without his contacts.

Schwartz shrugged. He had to drag up words from somewhere deep within: "Could be worse."

"Could always be worse." Arsch disappeared into his bedroom and came back with a stack of his mother's chocolate-walnut-ginger cookies. "Nuke 'em for a few seconds," he said. "There's milk in the fridge."

"Thanks."

Arsch scratched his balls some more, squinted. There was something comforting not just about his kindness but also about his physical girth, which suggested the existence of forces larger than Schwartz — forces that, if they weren't quite capable of protecting Schwartz, at least didn't need his protection. "I ain't tripping 'bout no bitches," Meat said, quoting the rap song of the moment. "I just worry 'bout the game."

"Thanks," said Schwartz again. Meat's door clicked shut, and the bedsprings wailed mightily through the wall.

The house was abandoned again. Schwartz felt his way past the beer-pong table en route to the kitchen. *What you missed about these bitches / Is they all can feel my fame. / My sick hits make 'em ticklish / Till they screamin' out my name.* God, the stuff you filled your head with, no matter how hard you tried. It wasn't exactly Milton; it wasn't even Chuck D. Really, he should make them switch the jukebox at Bartleby's from hip-hop to poetry. Then you could drop in your dollar, punch up 10-08, "When I have fears that I may cease to be," and soak up some Keats while you drank your beer.

The kitchen, compared to the rest of the house, was eerily immaculate, the sink shining beneath its sink light and almost restored to its original lima-bean color. Pella had gotten in the habit of scrubbing it every time she came over, and so Schwartz had taken to scrubbing it so she wouldn't have to, and lately it seemed that even Meat had gotten into the act by scraping stains off the linoleum — old chewed gum from previous tenants, more recently spat tobacco — and rinsing out the garbage can. Schwartz microwaved the cookies for thirty seconds, popped one in his mouth, poured a quart of milk into a souvenir Chicago Bears glass, drank it down, and polished off the remaining cookies by the light of the open fridge. Arsch, that mensch, had bought a twelve-pack of Schlitz; Schwartz grabbed two and walked into the musty living room and sat down on the couch in the dark. It was a stupid idea, jukebox poetry, but he liked it anyway. He wished he could tell it to Pella, if only so that she could laugh at him and call him a Chicago conservative.

They'd never fought before; she was good at it, if the point of a fight was to injure the other person. Beneath his anger he could sense a faint counterweight of satisfaction at the knowledge that this kind of pain could happen, that a girl, a woman, could mean enough to him to hurt him, and this raised the possibility that Pella was right, that he preferred to suffer and was happiest while suffering. But that could only be true if you added "for a reason." He liked to suffer for a reason. Who didn't? But all his reasons were falling apart. He ticked them off in his mind: law school, thesis, Henry, Pella.

He wasn't a kid from the projects anymore. If he drank himself to death like so many Schwartzes before him, or otherwise managed to screw everything up, he'd have no one to blame but himself. He didn't have excuses. What he had were *options,* Yale Law notwithstanding. He didn't get into law school only because he hadn't applied to any of the hundreds of schools that would have him. He had all these tools, rhetorical and analytic and critical tools, tools for self-reflection, rich friends, references, respectability. Hell, he even had a thousand bucks in his jacket pocket. He went back to the kitchen for two more beers.

Pella could cruise through James or Austen or Pynchon at seventy pages an hour and remember everything, like she'd been born to the task. He loved to watch her do it, reading glasses perched on the tip of her nose, her thoughts independent of him.

She misunderstood his life. It wasn't that he wanted everything to be difficult but that everything *was* difficult. Forget money. He wasn't smart the way she was. The only thing he knew how to do was motivate other people. Which amounted to nothing, in the end. Manipulation, playing with dolls. What wouldn't he give to have talent of his own, talent like Henry's? Nothing. He'd give it all. Those who cannot do, coach.

A car drove slowly down Grant Street, pumping through its sub-woofer the rumbling bass line of the same inane song Schwartz had just been singing. He forced himself not to remember any more words. He finished the beers and returned to the kitchen for two more. He spread his hundred-dollar bills on the coffee table, and there was a lighter sitting there, and he thought about it for a good long while, picking up a bill and waving the flame beneath it. The bill's bottom edge darkened slightly, but he wasn't quite drunk enough, or dumb enough, or something.

35

Pella wanted to go to Bartleby's and scotch herself into a stupor, but she found herself in the middle of Grant Street with nothing between the soles of her feet and the pebbly pavement, exactly the kind of too-emphatic gesture for which she'd always been famous, at least in her own mind, and so there was nothing to do but head back to Scull Hall. The football-player bouncers would have let her in without shoes, because she was a girl, and not just any girl but Mike Schwartz's girlfriend — ha-ha — but it would have been disgusting to walk around barefoot on those floors, slick with beer and the memory of mopped-up vomit, and it would leave her feeling worse than she already felt.

Damn that Mike Schwartz! How many nights in the past few weeks had he agreed to meet her somewhere, only to phone at the last second and say, *Sorry sweetheart, honeypie, darling, noodlepuss, kiddo, dear — sorry, but Henry and I are at the gym, Henry and I are at the diamond, Henry's feeling down, Henry and I are watching video, Henry and I are chatting,* saying it just like that, saccharine and matter-of-fact and with just a smidgen of condescension, as if she were *almost* capable of understanding the overwhelming importance of every last scrap of Henry's moods and needs.

And had Pella said boo about any of it? Never. Had not said, for instance, that Henry was an adult or nearly adult person who could fend for himself; nor had she said that being occasionally unable to throw a baseball from one place to another with perfect accuracy didn't exactly qualify as tragic; nor had she said—for instance—that Henry would start throwing the ball better when he felt like throwing the ball better, and maybe everybody should just leave him alone for a while and let whatever was going to happen happen. It was amazing the way people hemmed each other in, forced each other to act in such narrowly determined ways, as if the world would end if Henry didn't straighten himself out *right now,* as if a little struggle with self-doubt might not make him a better person in the long run, as if there were any reason why he shouldn't take a break from baseball and teach himself to knit, to play the cello, to speak Gaelic—but no, God no, he had to work hard and stay focused and grind it out and keep his chin up and relax and think positive and keep plugging away, subscribe to every stupid cliché Mike or anyone else could throw at him, working and worrying until he started having panic attacks, for Christ's sake, which wasn't tragic either but was far from a promising sign.

Poor Henry. As if anybody cared what happened to him, a silly kid with a silly problem. Everyone's problems were silly in the long run, silly when compared with global warming, despeciation, some birdborne or waterborne disease that was lying in wait to flatten us all, silly when compared to the brute fact of death, but Henry's problem was just plain silly. And yet she'd wasted plenty of hours on Henry's problem, turning it in her mind, hoping like hell it would go away, so that Mike could spend less time thinking about Henry and more time thinking about her. Because she liked him.

Or *did* like him, she thought as she stamped her way across the dark damp grass toward the wide mirrored windows of the library—liked him, past tense. Because why should she like him? A month since they'd met, and he still hadn't trimmed that stupid beard. She hated beards. "I *hate* beards," she spat aloud, and cuffed the skinny knotted trunk of a staked campus sapling with an open-handed slap. *"Hate hate hate."* The fact that she'd run away from a man with a beard into the grip of another man with a beard proved that nothing would ever change, *she* would never change, and life wherever she lived it was bound to be the same unchanging shitstorm, because she was there.

Two boys sat smoking on the library steps, watching in amusement as she gave the tree angry roundhouse slaps with alternate hands. "Me next!" one of them yelled.

"No man, me! I like it rough."

Pella turned around to flip them off. They grinned and waved. She wound up to give the tree one last cleansing whack, but she swung too hard and, instead of cuffing the trunk with her palm, her middle finger struck the knotty bark awkwardly. As she jammed the finger into her mouth, she screamed something indiscreet that ended in *me*.

"Yeah baby!"

"Thought you'd never ask!"

The finger was either sprained or broken. She headed toward the two boys, not really seeing them in a swarm of livid red buzzing, one wearing a knit winter cap and the other bareheaded, their backpacks laid beside them on the uppermost step. Because she was a girl they didn't stand up to fight or to run away but just watched her dumbly, their idiot faces titillated and amazed.

"Hey," one of them said. "It's Schwartzy's girlfriend."

There was probably no right thing for them to say just then, but that was the wrong thing. She flew up the steps at an angle, spitting curses. The boys snapped up their backpacks and dashed inside the library. They laughed and bumped fists when they saw she wouldn't follow.

She passed along the long cool concrete side of the library into the Small Quad, which was dark and cozy and void of noise. Her finger felt stiff and inarticulate. It pulsed with blood and pain. The chapel bells tolled four times, and she realized it was the middle of the night. She couldn't have gone to Bartleby's even if she'd tried. As she paused there in the dark, she became aware of a figure — mugger? rapist? baboon? — moving up and down in a nearby tree, making heavy-breathing noises.

"Henry? Is that you?"

Henry, startled, dropped from the tree and staggered a step backward. "Hey."

"What are you doing?"

"Pull-ups."

"How many can you do?"

He shrugged. "You can always do one more."

She studied his face for some of the enormous strain Mike claimed he was under, but found none. His breathing returned to normal. He flexed his wrists absently. He had the blank-eyed look of a well-drilled Marine. Pella felt a fleeting sense of fear, as if he might assault her somehow. "Sort of like Zeno's paradox," she said. "I mean, with the pull-ups. If you can always do one more, how can you ever stop doing pull-ups?"

Henry shrugged. "You can't."

"Right. I guess that's why you're out here at four a.m."

He didn't answer. She caught herself fiddling with her sweatshirt zipper — a dangerous tic, since she wasn't wearing anything underneath. She zipped it as high as it would go.

"What happened to your finger?" he asked.

"Nothing. I beat up a tree."

"Do you want some ice? There's an ice machine in the basement of my dorm."

"That's okay. I'll just get some at my dad's."

"Okay."

A light came on in her father's apartment. He kept odd hours lately, waking as early as three thirty or four and heading down to his office soon after. Perhaps it was a sign of age, some kind of male menopause. Throughout Pella's childhood he'd been a tenured professor who clung to grad-student habits, working deep into the night and then rousing himself, bleary-eyed, caffeine-deprived, his rich brown beard uncombed, to see her off to school.

She didn't feel like getting caught coming home at dawn, disheveled and barefoot and swollen-fingered. Maybe she could sneak in while he was in the shower. "I'll leave you to your pull-ups," she said to Henry. "I've got a big day ahead of me."

"Me too," Henry said. As she unlocked the side entrance to Scull Hall, he jumped up, latched onto a branch, and began another set.

Her dad, already shaved and dressed, was sitting in the kitchen nook, sipping his daybreak espresso. "Pella," he said as she entered the room, "can I talk to you for a moment?"

"No."

"Let me rephrase that, then." His manner was Gruff Let-Down Dad, as if this were eighth grade and she'd skipped curfew again. "Please, my darling daughter, have a seat. I'll make more coffee."

"I have to work in an hour," Pella said. "I don't have time for a heart-to-heart. Sorry."

She filled a baggie with ice from the freezer, wrapped it in a dish-towel, applied it to her finger.

"What's that?" said Affenlight. "Let me see."

Pella took some pleasure, however juvenile, in holding up her middle finger toward her father. An ugly finger too—fat and blood-stiffened, with a purple bruise spreading outward from the second knuckle.

"Oh my. Sweetie. What happened?"

"Nothing. I jammed it."

"Well, keep ice on it. Maybe you should take the day off work."

"It's fine."

"Fine? Pella. Look how swollen it is. I'll call the dining hall and tell them you won't be in. Then we'll go over to Student Health to get that looked at."

"It's too late to schedule somebody else."

Her father's long, uninjured, academically pristine fingers dwarfed his espresso cup. "Don't be stubborn. You can take one day off."

"I'm thrilled to have your permission, El Presidente. But I'd just as soon do my job, thanks."

"Really, Pella. I applaud your work ethic, but—"

"Who asked *you* to applaud my work ethic?" she said too loudly. "Are you my boss?"

Her dad looked taken aback. "Well, no," he said. "Of course not. But your health is more important than a few hours of mindless labor in the dining hall."

Pella cringed. She wanted her presence in the dining hall to be *necessary*. Was that too much to ask? Mike thought her job was slumming, because of who her dad was. Her dad thought it was a show of faux independence, and that she should be practicing Latin or whatever. Neither had said so, but she could tell. Unless she was just paranoid, living in her head again, but you always lived in your head and you had to go with what you felt.

"Who cares if it's mindless labor?" Red flares snapped behind her eyes like they had on the library steps. "What's *not* mindless labor? Writing papers? Ha! But at least that's not an embarrassment, right? I'm the president's daughter, for God's sake. The last thing I should be doing is scrubbing pots with a bunch of immigrants—"

"*Pella*—"

"Don't *Pella* me." She yanked out a chair and plunked down at the nook table. The space underneath could barely accommodate their four legs, her father's elegant suit-clad ones and her own flabbier, less majestic pair. "So," she said sharply, "what did you want to talk to me about?"

"It's nothing," Affenlight said. "It can wait."

"Why wait?" She laid her hand on the table and rested the towel-wrapped bag of ice on top. The pain was like a fuel. "You don't like me spending the night at Mike's house."

"We can talk about it later."

"We'd rather talk about it now. Here's my position. I'm an adult. I'll sleep wherever I like."

Her father looked at her. Obviously she'd already hurt his feelings, not least by implying that he was some kind of tacit racist. But the flares were still snapping behind her eyes.

"Now you give your position."

"Pella, please—"

"I'll start you off. You think I'm being disrespectful. You think because I'm living here and not paying rent I should be subject to the rules I was subject to as a child. You think I'm a child even though I've been married for four years."

Affenlight inspected the grains at the bottom of his demitasse. The room was silent. Then the refrigerator's hum ceased, making it more silent. "See?" Pella said. "Isn't this fun?"

Her dad closed his long fingers around the demitasse and made it disappear, an ominous-seeming kind of parlor trick. He looked at her sadly with his deep gray eyes. "Pella," he said. "I love you. If you want my advice, and I realize that you don't, I'd say don't rush to get involved with anyone. Take a little time away from men."

"This whole campus is nothing but men." The *I love you* had done its trick; the bitterness washed out of her voice. "Really fucked-up ones."

Her dad smiled. "Guilty as charged."

The ice was making her second and fourth fingers numb. "Mike and I broke up."

"I'm sorry."

"And David's coming tomorrow. I mean today."

"David?" Affenlight stiffened in his chair as if he'd heard an intruder.

"He claims he's in Chicago on business. Not that I believe him. He's never gone to Chicago on business before. But he knows I'm here and he wants to come and I told him it was a bad idea and he insisted. So he's renting a car and driving up. Today. And then when he leaves he'll be gone forever."

"Okay," Affenlight said.

"And I need your help to get through it. Okay?"

Affenlight nodded. "Of course."

Pella pushed back her chair, picked up her melting ice bag, and kissed her father on the temple. "I'm sorry I'm so mean."

"You're not mean," he said. "There's Advil in the bathroom."

She popped a few Advil and washed her face with one hand. She went into the guest room and undressed slowly and awkwardly, inching her sweatshirt's sleeve past her injured digit. At least she didn't have a T-shirt or bra to wriggle out of—that was her reward for leaving them at Mike's house. Every cloud had a silver lining, right? She had to be up in an hour, but at least she wouldn't have trouble falling asleep. Another silver lining.

She went to the window to pull the curtains shut. Dawn was approaching. She thought the quad was empty, but then a figure dropped from a tree branch and landed in a shallow crouch, knees splayed. It seemed hard to believe he could still be out there, but there he was. He jangled his wrists, shaking the pain or the tension out of his arms. He walked clockwise around the trunk five times, counterclockwise five more. He clapped his hands together, just once, and jumped up to grab the limb again.

36

Shortly after dawn, eight Schlitzes in, Schwartz walked to the VAC under low-slung clouds, not feeling drunk or sober. He took the elevator up to his office and unlocked the cabinet that stored the navy binders and reams of expensive watermarked paper he'd bought back in September. The conference table where he worked looked disastrous, littered with coffee mugs full of dip spit, protein-bar wrappers, note cards bearing hundreds of choice quotes and turns of phrase he'd never deployed. The introduction wasn't finished, much less the bibliography. Back in December, on the basis of his research and outline, his adviser had assured him he'd win the History prize.

He used his school ID to jimmy the lock on the office of Duane Jenkins, the athletic director. There was a high-speed, high-quality printer there, for flyers and posters and press releases. Schwartz slid his watermarked paper into the tray, connected his laptop, and began printing his rough-draft chapters in twelve-point Courier, the official font of idiot jocks.

As the Courier-besmirched pages spooled and printed, in triplicate, he picked up Jenkins's phone.

"Skrimmer," he said. "Why aren't you in class?"

"Why are you calling me," Henry countered, "when I'm supposed to be in class?"

"You can have an off day, Skrim…" God, Schwartz was sick of his own shtick.

"...but I can't have a day off. I know." Henry sounded annoyed; he was sick of it too. Schwartz couldn't remember him ever skipping class before. He wanted to broach the topic of Henry's panic attack, but the distance between them seemed too great. "Feeling any better?"

"I'm fine," Henry said. Which was part of the problem: Henry always said he was fine. Generally Schwartz considered this the proper attitude — say you're fine and you're fine. It was what made Henry such a perfect pupil. Except now, when nothing was fine. Probably Pella was right that he needed a therapist, but there wasn't time for that anyway. Twenty-four hours to Coshwale, twenty-four hours to Henry Skrimshander Day.

"Meet me at the VAC in ten minutes," he said. "No need to change."

ON A SHELF IN HIS OFFICE Schwartz kept a long row of DVDs of Henry taking batting practice. Labeled and arranged by date, they formed a complete record of Henry's progress as a hitter under Schwartz's tutelage, week by diligent week, from his freshperson season till now. Together they'd spent hundreds of hours watching these tapes, breaking down and rebuilding Henry's swing frame by frozen frame. If you had the editing equipment and time to kill, you could take a frame from each day's session and splice them together chronologically, so that the Henry who awaited the pitch would be skinny and indefinite, the bat wavering timidly above his bony right elbow, while the Henry who finished the swing, following through with such forceful purpose that the bat head wrapped around and struck him between the shoulder blades, would be chiseled and resolute, his eyes hardened, his curls shaved down to a military half inch. The making of a ballplayer: the production of brute efficiency out of natural genius.

For Schwartz this formed the paradox at the heart of baseball, or football, or any other sport. You loved it because you considered it an art: an apparently pointless affair, undertaken by people with a special aptitude, which sidestepped attempts to paraphrase its value yet somehow seemed to communicate something true or even crucial about The Human Condition. The Human Condition being, basically, that we're alive and have access to beauty, can even erratically create it, but will someday be dead and will not.

Baseball was an art, but to excel at it you had to become a machine. It didn't matter how beautifully you performed *sometimes,* what you did on your best day, how many spectacular plays you made. You weren't a painter or a writer—you didn't work in private and discard your mistakes, and it wasn't just your masterpieces that counted. What mattered, as for any machine, was repeatability. Moments of inspiration were nothing compared to elimination of error. The scouts cared little for Henry's superhuman grace; insofar as they cared they were suckered-in aesthetes and shitty scouts. Can you perform on demand, like a car, a furnace, a gun? Can you make that throw one hundred times out of a hundred? If it can't be a hundred, it had better be ninety-nine.

At the far left of the shelf of DVDs was a single unlabeled videocassette. Schwartz slid it out with a finger and popped it into the ancient VCR.

"What's this?" Henry asked.

"You'll see."

Schwartz watched this tape alone sometimes, late at night, the way he reread certain passages of Aurelius. It restored some nameless element of his personality that threatened to slip away if he didn't stay vigilant.

The camera, that day, had been positioned on a tripod behind home plate. A thin stripe of chain-link backstop cut at an angle across the frame. The sun glared white against the lens, bleaching out one side, so that when Henry ranged to the camera's right his white undershirt and finally his entire scrawny body dissolved in a ghostly burst of light.

Henry watched himself field a few grounders and whip them to first. "Is this from Peoria?"

Schwartz nodded.

"Weird. Where'd you get it?"

"My Legion team. We taped all our games." After Henry finished fielding on that scorching afternoon, Schwartz had checked the camera and found its red light still lit. He wanted a record of what he'd seen — proof to other people, and especially to himself, that he hadn't exaggerated Henry's talent or hallucinated him altogether. So he commandeered the tape, watched it several times, mailed a copy to Coach Cox. It had served, more or less, as Henry's Westish application.

Henry didn't know the tape existed. Schwartz couldn't quite say why he'd kept it to himself for the past three years — as if there were a part of Henry that belonged more to him than it did to Henry. That he didn't want to share, not even with Henry.

"Weird," Henry said again. "Look how skinny I was. Somebody give that kid some SuperBoost."

"Just watch."

Henry tossed a baseball from hand to hand, gazed at the screen. "What am I watching for?"

"Just watch, Skrim."

"I thought maybe you'd noticed something."

"Maybe *you'll* notice something," Schwartz snapped. "If you shut up and watch."

Henry looked hurt. He stopped tossing the baseball, stared at the screen.

"Sorry," Schwartz muttered. He was doing so unforgivably little to help his friend. Hitting extra grounders, repeating stupid bromides like *relax* and *let it fly* — it amounted to moral support, nothing more. Once Henry stepped out on the field, he was totally alone.

There was that aloneness on the screen: that implacable, solitary blankness on Henry's sweat-streaked face as he backhanded a ball and fired it into the glove of his pudgy first baseman. Not that Henry withdrew from his teammates; in fact, he was more animated on the diamond than anywhere else. But no matter how much he chattered or cheered or bounced around, there was always something frighteningly aloof in his eyes, like a soloist so at one with the music he can't be reached.

You can't follow me here, those mild blue eyes seemed to say. *You'll never know what this is like.*

These days, when Henry walked onto the diamond, those eyes were saying the same thing, but with a rising undercurrent of terror. *You'll never know what this is like.* Baseball, in its quiet way, was an extravagantly harrowing game. Football, basketball, hockey, lacrosse — these were melee sports. You could make yourself useful by hustling and scrapping more than the other guy. You could redeem yourself through sheer desire.

But baseball was different. Schwartz thought of it as Homeric — not a scrum but a series of isolated contests. Batter versus pitcher, fielder versus ball. You couldn't storm around, snorting and slapping people, the way Schwartz did while playing football. You stood and waited and tried to still your mind. When your moment came, you had to be ready, because if you fucked up, everyone would know whose fault it was. What other sport not only kept a stat as cruel as the error but posted it on the scoreboard for everyone to see?

It took ten minutes to watch the tape straight through. Schwartz rewound it to the beginning, and they watched it in slow motion. Then regular speed again. Then slo-mo one more time. Sudden spring rain drummed against the flat metal roof of the VAC. The kid on the screen fielded ball after ball, intent and tireless, engulfed in his half-bored rapture.

"Can we go now?" Henry's foot tapped nervously on the carpet. "I'm hungry." He wasn't, really; he had very little appetite these days, but he wanted to get out of there. It was weird, even creepy, how intensely Schwartz was focused on the video — as if he wanted to will that skinny, thoughtless kid back into being. As if Henry were dead instead of sitting right there. *I'm right here,* he thought.

"One more time," Schwartz said. "Just once more." They watched it again, and still Schwartz's finger hovered over the rewind button. To Schwartz the kid on the screen seemed like a cipher, a sphinx, a silent courier from another time. *You'll never know what this is like.* But Schwartz had been trying for years, and he kept trying now. If he could crawl inside that empty head, crack open the oracle of the kid's blank face—*expressionless, expresses God*—maybe then he'd know what he should do.

Henry headed to lunch, Schwartz to Glendinning Hall with his anti-climactic stack of binders. When he got home he went through three razors shaving off his thesis beard.

37

"Here," Hero had said during the breakfast shift, "I fix."

Pella waved him off. "Forget it. It's fine." Really her finger didn't feel too bad; it was stiff and purplish but not overly painful from moment to moment. Every once in a while she'd jam it on a pot or plate or the beveled lip of the sink, and a yelp of pain would escape her. Chef Spirodocus had told her she could go home, but she didn't want to go home—she wanted to sort silverware into bins, blast bacon fat from shallow pans. After breakfast ended she wanted to restock the so-called salad bar with ketchup and syrup and blueberry yogurt, skim the yellow crust off the mayonnaise, replenish the ice that underlay the stainless-steel tins. Today was Friday, her double-shift day. She wanted to work. She didn't want to think about last night with Mike or tonight with David. She wanted to be here among the rolling Portuguese and the tinny salsa that wailed from somebody's radio, the mingling roars of the trash compactor and the power washer, water everywhere, the added roar of Chef Spirodocus when he got upset. She wanted to keep moving, to stay right here in the heart of the noise. She had built up a tiny bit of momentum in her life, going to lectures and swimming and working, checking out books from the library, falling asleep when her head hit the pillow. She'd caught herself thinking that spending four years at Westish might not be the worst thing in the world. But she could also sense how tenuous this progress was, how easy it would be to slow down and shut down and wind up back where she started, in bed all day but unable to sleep, terrified by the day and doubly terrified by the night, never picking up the phone, comforted only by the thought of never needing comfort again.

"Here." Hero beckoned her impatiently. With a cleaver he lopped off a length of white woven first-aid tape, wound it around her injured and ring fingers so the two were bound firmly together. "No jams."

"Hmph," said Pella, impressed. She looked tough, like a football player. After a few hours of steam and soapy hot water the tape's glue dissolved and Hero cut another length. She made it through both of her shifts without jamming her finger again. Then, the lunch dishes done, her uniform covered in food slop and dishwasher scum, her skin by a sheen of sticky gold grease, she sank down at a round faux-wood table in the empty dining hall with a fresh bag of ice for her finger. The afternoon light through the tall mullioned windows was itself deepening to a greasy gold. David would be arriving soon.

Between shifts Chef Spirodocus had thrust a stiff envelope into her hand. Now she pulled it from her pocket, feeling oddly nervous as she folded and tore the perforated edges. And there it was—an honest-to-God paycheck, made out to Pella Therese Affenlight. The government had taken out taxes: Social Security, Medicare, state, federal. They added up to $49.83. Her first direct contribution to trash collection and public schooling, the maintenance of highways and libraries, the killing of people in war.

She kept looking at the check, though there wasn't much to see. She and David used to spend more on dinner. But it wasn't nothing, especially here in the middle of nowhere, especially when your meals and rent were free. And it was *hers*. She wouldn't have to ask her father for money anymore. She could buy some underwear to replace what she'd left at Mike's.

She needed to shower and change, David showed up early for

everything, but instead she poured herself a Sprite from the drink dispenser and sat back down to admire the check some more. She still planned to sell her ring, but this was something better. Like Ishmael said: *Being paid—what will compare with it!* It was embarrassing, how proud of herself she felt. The check proved that she'd been alive these weeks, that she'd accomplished something, however trivial. This was why people grew so attached to earning money, even money they didn't need. This was how they justified themselves. This was how they kept score.

Chef Spirodocus clomped out of the kitchen in his backache-relieving clogs, frowning down at his clipboard. "Pella," he said. "You're still here." He pronounced it as a great truth of which she might be unaware.

"Still here." Pella slid the check off the table with her good hand, tapped its edge against the table's underside. Chef Spirodocus sat down across from her. "You should go home," he said. "You look tired."

In Pella's experience this was a way of telling a woman she looked bad, old, past her prime. "You mean I have bags under my eyes."

Chef Spirodocus looked up from his clipboard. "Bags? What bags? I mean you worked hard and became tired. Go home. Drink a glass of wine with your boyfriend."

"My *boyfriend*," Pella said, "is at baseball practice."

Chef Spirodocus waved his stubby fingers. "So find a new one. A girl like you can choose." He set down his clipboard and looked at her with a solemn expression. "You're a fine employee," he said, his voice thick with feeling.

"Thank you."

He waved his fingers again, as if to brush away the casualness of her response. "Listen to me. You care about the kitchen. You dry the spots from the glasses. You think nobody notices"—he tapped himself on the temple, near the eye—"but I notice. A fine employee."

Pella felt her own eyes getting moist. Humans are ridiculous creatures, she thought, or maybe it's just me: a purportedly intelligent person, purportedly aware of the ways in which women and wage laborers have been oppressed for millennia—and I get choked up because somebody tells me I'm good at washing dishes. "Thank you," she said again, this time with earnest emotion that easily matched Chef Spirodocus's own.

He dropped an elbow onto the table, squished his supple chin against his stubby-fingered hand, eyed her with a melancholy squint. "The god is in the detail, as they say. You understand this. I think you would make a good chef."

"Really?"

Chef Spirodocus shrugged. "Maybe," he said. "If it was what you wanted."

"Huh." Pella imagined in a flash the restaurant she would own: small and white, all painted white but warmly so. And every so often she would take a white chair or a white table and paint it according to her mood, paint a door frame or a section of filigreed molding, hang a canvas on the white wall, so that bit by bit the whiteness of the restaurant would emerge into color. So as customers sat there over the course of weeks and months and years the place would slowly bloom and change before their eyes, sliding from whiteness into something ingeniously raucous, a riot of green and mango and orange. And then when the job was finished she'd obliterate what she'd done with a blizzard of white paint and start again. That was the kind of restaurant she'd like to own. The food being served was fuzzier in her mind: she saw the white plates move and clatter but couldn't tell what was on them. She could see the clean sharp arrangements on the plates, the contrasts of color and texture, but not the foods themselves. She'd have to learn a lot about food. And really when the restaurant actually opened she'd be so busy cooking, running the kitchen, that she wouldn't have time to paint. So really she'd have to develop a whole new idea of restaurants and how they worked, not an interior decorator's idea but a chef's idea, and this was an idea she didn't yet have, but would maybe someday like to have. Or maybe she didn't want to be a chef at all, but the possibility of doing *something,* pursuing something, seemed, for the first time in a long time, not only appealing but real.

"Now go home," ordered Chef Spirodocus. He pushed back his chair and resumed glaring at his clipboard. "And if you don't quit after a month, the way all these children quit, maybe I can teach you something about food. I'm not some hack, after all."

38

Owen hadn't come. Had not yet come. Had not yet executed his light backhanded *tap tap tap* against the presidentially heavy walnut of Affenlight's door, slipped into the room and locked the door behind him, slid out from under his messenger bag and clasped Affenlight's hands and planted an ironically chaste peck on his lips.

It was 4:44 according to Affenlight's watch, 4:42 by the clock on the wall. Had Owen ever come this late before? Affenlight didn't think so. He yanked open the central drawer of his desk. The drawer's wheels jerked and screeched on their ill-fitting tracks. He rummaged through a scatter of pens and staples, cigarette boxes, neglected silver sheets of Lipitor and Toprol, and pulled out a wallet-size trifold Westish Baseball schedule with a picture of Henry on the front.

Affenlight had the schedule nearly memorized; had become the Harpooners' most ardent fan after a lifetime of benevolent indifference to the game. He went to watch Owen, of course, but the team as a whole, led by the dogged Mike Schwartz, had an aura of competence that might have been unknown in the history of Westish sports. And what absorbed Affenlight most, during his hours at the diamond, was the hope that Henry Skrimshander would get better. *Would get better* — that phrasing said it all, as if Henry had some terrible malady that might never lift. The empathy Affenlight felt for him surpassed anything he'd ever felt for a character in a novel. It rivaled, in fact, the empathy he'd ever felt for anyone. We all have our doubts and fragilities, but poor Henry had to face his in public at appointed times, with half the crowd anxiously counting on him and the other half cheering for him to fail. Like an actor in a play, his inner turmoil was on display for everyone to observe; unlike an actor in a play, he didn't get to go home and become someone else. So raw were his struggles that it felt like an invasion of privacy to go to the games, and at the worst moments Affenlight felt guilty for being there and wondered whether spectators should even be allowed.

Affenlight flipped over the schedule. **HOME** games in bold caps, Away games in a regular roman font. He was hoping to find a **HOME** game today, a game he'd failed to note before, because that would explain Owen's absence, which otherwise couldn't be explained, and Affenlight could hustle over to the diamond and settle in for a few innings. But today was the last day of April and it wasn't listed at all. No reason for Owen not to come. Affenlight folded the schedule and shoved it back in the drawer.

Something happened yesterday. At least now, in retrospect, it seemed like something happened yesterday. At the time it hadn't seemed like much, certainly not a turning point—just one of those moments that force you to admit, because you're not insane or utterly fanatical, that you and your lover are different people whose views of the world will some-times differ. But maybe it was more than that, maybe Affenlight had erred badly somehow, because here it was 4:49 by his watch, 4:47 by the wall clock, and Owen had not yet come.

Yesterday Owen discovered the long row of Westish Registers that spanned the length of the bottom shelf behind the love seat. They were arranged by year, their navy spines growing less faded, their gold-leafed letters richer, as you scanned from left to right. The registers were like furniture to Affenlight—not since his first nostalgic days as president, nearly eight years ago, had it occurred to him to look at one. Until Owen, sprawled idly on the love seat while Affenlight finished a memo, plucked out the '69–'70 edition and flipped to a half-page photo of a tall young man walking a bicycle across the quad. The young man's shoulders were broad. He wore pleated gray-wool pants and a wide-collared dress shirt, the sleeves of which were rolled in a recognizably dapper way, the only sign of rebellion his hair, which was far enough removed from two years' worth of Coach Gramsci–mandated crew cuts to have reached a suitably leonine, collar-brushing length. Leaves lay underfoot, their robust crackle almost audible in the photograph as the young man steered the bicycle down a path not fifty yards from where they were sitting now. The young man wasn't smiling, but he looked quite pleased to be free, free of football practice on a fall afternoon. He'd not yet begun his beard.

"Hubba hubba," said Owen. "Who's *that?*"

"Ha-ha." Affenlight shifted in his chair. He realized that Owen was using a different one of Mrs. McCallister's coffee mugs: DON'T TAKE YOUR ORGANS TO HEAVEN — GOD KNOWS WE NEED THEM HERE. "What happened to KISS ME, I'M IRISH?" he asked, taking care to sound nonchalant.

Owen glanced up from the photo, his expression not unkind. "I just grabbed this one," he said. "I can wash it when I'm done."

"No, no. No need," Affenlight said. "You just seemed to be growing attached to that IRISH mug, that's all."

"Mm-mm-*mm*." Owen pointed to the photograph, just below the roll of Affenlight's sleeves. "Check out those forearms."

"That's just because I'm gripping the handlebars." Affenlight couldn't resist glancing down at the current version of those same forearms: not nearly as impressive.

"This is what, your senior year?"

"Junior."

"Junior year. My goodness. You must have had the whole campus in a kind of choreographed group swoon. Boys and girls alike."

"Not really," Affenlight said. "I was awkward, behind the times. A bit of a loner." It sounded like false modesty, considering the stately swagger of the kid in the photo, but it was true.

"Sure you were." Owen flipped to the back, failed to find an index. "Are there any more like this?"

"I don't think so."

Owen, hungry for more, paged through the entire register. Then he pulled down the registers from Affenlight's other three years and piled them in his lap. He smiled at Affenlight's football pictures, his crew cut and shoulder pads and tight pants; chuckled at the Whitmanesque beard he began to cultivate senior year; couldn't resist returning, in the end, to the photo with the bicycle. On most occasions Affenlight sensed a hint of irony in Owen's attentions; now he seemed thoroughly absorbed. Affenlight sipped his cooling coffee and shifted in his spindle-backed chair. Why was Owen using a different mug? Why was he staring at pictures, when the real-life Affenlight was right there? Maybe he should have been flattered by Owen's oohing and ahhing, but instead he felt cut out of whatever emotional transaction was passing between Owen and the young man on the page. "I wish I'd known you then," Owen said wistfully.

"Then instead of now?"

Owen, eyes still on the page, reached out to give Affenlight's socked ankle a squeeze. "Then *and* now," he said. "Always."

"I was different then. You might not have liked me."

"I'm sure I would have liked you plenty. What's not to like?"

"I was different," Affenlight repeated. For some reason he felt keen to get this point across. The kid in the photograph wasn't simply his current self with better forearms and flowing hair. Hell, he could grow that hair now, and it'd look all the more striking for being flecked with silver. But the hair was not the point. "Back then," he said, "I wasn't *me*. Not like this. I . . . I could never have fallen in love."

"Well, sure." Owen, still looking at the photo, continued absently to caress Affenlight's ankle. "Look at you. Why would someone like that bother to fall in love?"

Why indeed. Owen asked if he could borrow that junior-year register, said he'd like to try making a copy of the photograph, and Affenlight had little choice but to say sure, why not, go right ahead. And they smooched awhile and read aloud a bit from Lear, and Owen left. And that was yesterday. And now today the chapel bells were tolling five, with no Owen. Affenlight stared again at the bold type on the baseball schedule, hoping in vain that another home game would materialize. He pushed back his heavy chair and went to the window, looked up toward Phumber 405. It had begun to rain in fierce sheets, a potent spring storm. Affenlight saw no movement behind the herbs and twisting miniature cacti that lined the sills of Owen's room. He pulled open his office door — he would make the coffee himself, Owen be damned. Standing there in the hall, sopping wet, fist poised to knock, was a bearded man Affenlight had never met before but recognized instantly, from the photograph on his firm's website.

39

Affenlight didn't hate David, not anymore. Not that he had much regard for the man, but he'd spent more time thinking about David in recent years than about anyone in the world besides Pella and Owen, and that kind of constant mindfulness, over time, could mellow into sympathy. He would never forgive David, but David had become a part of life, and Affenlight had achieved a grudging acknowledgment of the fact that David would continue to live and breathe whether he wanted him to or not. He used to think of him as a selfish lothario and borderline pedophile; now he thought of him more as a man with whom he had a quarrel. Almost — perish the thought — as a son-in-law, albeit an unpalatable one.

Even Affenlight's moral indignation had cooled recently, for obvious reasons. He himself had always observed a strict rule against liaisons with students, both as a sought-after boyish section leader and as a sought-after dapper professor, and even during that period of CNN-level celebrity when the *Crimson* ran his photo with the caption HEARTTHROB OF THE HUMANITIES. This resistance to constant, often blatant temptation had given him a strong footing from which to criticize someone like David, a grown man who'd seduced a vulnerable, huge-hearted girl. But what could Affenlight say now? How could he know that David hadn't succumbed to something similar, a feeling as sweet and fortuitous that steamrolled him just as fully? Plus, of course, Pella claimed that their marriage was over, and victory could make a man magnanimous.

And so Affenlight felt almost sorry for David when he found the latter in the hallway outside his office, fooling with his cell phone, looking forlorn and agitated. He naturally thought of Menelaus, come to reclaim Helen, but David suffered a bit in the comparison. It was pouring outside, and though he was wearing galoshes and a waterproof jacket, his head and trousers were soaked. Affenlight wondered what kind of man brought galoshes on a mission of this nature.

"David," he said. "Guert Affenlight. You look like you could use some coffee."

"Where's my wife?" David said.

Affenlight felt suddenly calm. It was a situation he had often seen in dreams: his nemesis here, in his office, on his terms. But the desire to assert and avenge himself had subsided.

"Did you call the line upstairs?"

"Repeatedly."

"She's probably still at work." Affenlight nodded toward his open office door. "Come in. Have a seat."

In person, David looked less substantial than the fellow in the photo on his firm's website, who wore a turtleneck beneath his sweater and leaned back from his drafting table, mechanical pencil in hand, smiling benevolently. He had, at least in the picture, the punctilious self-possession that Affenlight associated with a certain kind of evangelical Christian, tightly groomed beard and all. Today he looked significantly less composed.

"I suppose you're pretty pleased about all this," David said, his voice soft but strident, as Affenlight, having made the coffee whether David wanted it or not, handed him a steaming mug.

The room contained another Westish-crested chair of the sort David was sitting in; when Affenlight wanted to make a guest feel equal and at ease, he arranged himself in it. Now he slid behind his vast desk, which was cluttered with paper. His job performance lately had been decidedly second-rate. "Depends what you mean," he said. "I'm worried about Pella."

"She's my *wife,*" David said, shivering and still dripping. He set the full mug of coffee down on the edge of Affenlight's desk with an air of finality. Perhaps he was exercising his right to refuse hospitality, or maybe he took milk. "We've been married four years."

"I know. Though of course I wasn't invited to the wedding."

"I have a right to speak to her."

"She'll be here," Affenlight said.

Spring thunder grumbled softly, sans lighting, quite unlike the violent whipcracks of July and August. David lifted his mug from the corner of the desk, taking care not to slosh any coffee onto Affenlight's papers, and took a tiny, temperature-gauging sip. It seemed to relax and compose him. He looked around the room, eyeing the framed diplomas and accolades, the spines of the books that lined the walnut shelves. "Nice woodwork," he said.

"Thanks."

"They don't build them like this anymore. Too expensive. These shelves are from the twenties?"

"Twenty-two, I believe."

David nodded. "The year *Ulysses* was published. And Moncrieff's translation of *Du côté de chez Swann.* And *The Waste Land,* natch."

Affenlight wasn't sure whether this represented an attempt to engage him on his own terms, or was the way that David habitually talked. "Correct," he said.

"Is she okay?" David asked, helping himself to another, fuller sip. "You said you were worried."

"She's fine," Affenlight said. "Much better than when she arrived."

"What was wrong when she arrived?"

Affenlight was surprised by the question; he'd meant the remark as a mild dig at David, not a topic to be pursued. "Well, you know. She looked pretty...beat-up."

David sat up indignantly, gripped the armrests of his chair. "Surely you're not suggesting—"

Affenlight held up a placative hand. "No no no."

"I would never."

"Of course," said Affenlight. A knock at the door—could it be Owen? Better late than never. Of course Owen couldn't stay, not with David here, but that didn't matter, what mattered was that he'd chosen to come. Affenlight pushed back his chair, but the door swung open before he could reach his feet.

Pella stood in the doorway, still dressed in her dining-services uniform. Affenlight hadn't seen her in a baseball cap since she was a child. Maybe that was what made her seem suddenly young, or maybe it was the way she hovered anxiously in the doorway, as if waiting for the grown-ups to finish. "No blood on the floor," she said. "That's a good sign."

Affenlight smiled. "We went outside for the messy stuff."

David was up out of his chair. *"Bella."* He took a step toward her. Affenlight tensed, ready to hurl himself between them, but he was still behind his desk and it was a silly impulse anyway. They kissed on both cheeks like good cultured people while Affenlight studied his daughter's face for signs of love.

David held Pella at arm's length by the shoulders. "What happened to your finger, Bella?" His tone was that classic romantic-parental blend, as admonitory as it was solicitous.

"I walked into a tree."

"I suppose that's a common hazard here," David joked. "Too many trees. At least it's turned a pretty color." He was still holding her by the shoulders, observing her proprietarily. He looked pointedly at her stained collared shirt. "I thought we were going to dinner."

"We are."

"Am I overdressed, then?"

Affenlight was familiar with the kind of man who wilted around men but bloomed when dealing with women — supremely heterosexual, indifferent to or disdainful of or afraid of other men, but also supremely attuned to women's needs and interests. David had bloomed just that way when Pella walked in.

"I have to get ready," Pella was saying. "Did you check into your hotel?"

"No, Bella. I came straight to you."

"I made a reservation for eight o'clock at Maison Robert. I'm sure you'll hate it, but it's all we've got."

"I'm sure I'll find it delightful," David said.

"Right." Pella looked at Affenlight. "So should David come back and pick us up? Or what?"

"*Us?*" said David.

Us? thought Affenlight. During their early-morning tête-à-tête Pella had said she needed him during David's visit, but Affenlight hadn't figured that that would involve eating dinner with the man. Not that he was unwilling; if Pella wanted him there as a buffer, he was glad to comply. It was flattering, a hopeful sign, that she wanted him there.

"Us," Pella said. "My father and me."

"*Bella,*" David began to murmur in low pouty tones meant to exclude Affenlight, "I mean, really —"

Affenlight's eyes flicked out to the quad and saw through the dwindling rain that the twin dormered windows of Phumber 405 were alight. Someone was home, Henry perhaps — but then that unmistakable slender silhouette appeared against the windowlight, lifted the window with two hands, leaned out appraisingly over the misty quad. He disappeared into the room, reappeared with two small slender items between his fingers. One he placed between his lips, the other he sparked between cupped hands and used to solicit a prick of orange light from the first. And Owen leaned out over the darkened quad, elbows against the sill, and commenced to smoke his joint. Seeing him there made Affenlight terribly sad. Not only because Owen hadn't come but because he looked so satisfied and self-contained as he leaned and smoked and thought his thoughts, as needless of help or company as some gentle animal feeding in the wild. It made Affenlight feel not only superfluous but also, by comparison with such wholeness and serenity, hopelessly agitated in his soul. He needed Owen, but Owen — being himself whole, or never farther than one well-rolled joint from whole — would never need him.

40

David went to the hotel, Pella upstairs to change. Affenlight dialed the five digits of an intracampus call. It rang once, twice, three times. Owen might have been in the shower — but, no, there went his shadow past the lamp.

Four rings. Five. The machine picked up.

Maybe he'd been a terrible lover. He'd been told he was a good lover, or, by his British lovers, of whom there had been a few — women were always trafficking back and forth between the Cambridges — a brilliant one. Back in the day, British women were always rolling apart from him and sighing: *Brilliant!* But he was older now. And those women, whether British or American or whatever else, were all women. It wasn't a given that the skills would translate. A good friend didn't necessarily make a good father, a good professor didn't necessarily make a good college president, and a good performer of oral sex on women couldn't necessarily turn around and start giving blow jobs without submitting to the logic of learning curves.

Oh boy.

Affenlight listened to the answering machine's message all the way through, just to hear the wry mellow tones of Owen's recorded voice, but he couldn't leave a message. It would seem pathetic, for one thing, to chase after Owen after a single day's absence — and what if Owen declined to listen, and Henry heard it instead? Why, why, didn't he know

Owen's cell phone number? The fact that they didn't communicate by cell phone, didn't chat or text, could reasonably be chalked up to the fact that they didn't need to, they lived fifty yards apart and saw each other five days a week, but then again the students did little but chat and text, text messages were their surest form of intimacy, and to never have texted or been texted by Owen, not to know Owen's number even for emergency purposes, not that this was an emergency, seemed suddenly to expose a great gulf between them. Affenlight set the receiver down in defeat. The shadow went past the lamp again.

He walked out of his office and into the quad. Half-lost in anxious thought, hardly aware of what he was doing, he found himself entering Phumber Hall and climbing the stairs, precisely at the dinner hour when traffic in and out of the dorms was at its peak. He encountered no one on the staircase, thank goodness, passed no doors propped open in neighborly cheer, though anyone at all could have seen him crossing the quad and ducking inside.

"Guert," Owen said when he opened the door. His eyes were glassy from marijuana, but he also seemed startled or surprised. Affenlight realized it was a reckless thing to do, coming here, and not just because he might get caught. At least in his office he maintained some semblance or illusion of control over the situation. Not here. Here he was bound to seem absurd. He couldn't bear to wonder how old, how unfit he looked in this harsh undergraduate hallway light. "Hi," he said.

"How are you?"

"I'm okay." A door swung open and closed on the floor below. Feminine shoes swift-clicked down the stairs. "Do you mind if I come in?" Affenlight asked. "It'd be a little awkward if anyone..."

"Of course." Owen closed the door behind him, gestured to the rose-upholstered easy chair that straddled the room's imaginary center line, the one unique, neutral piece of furniture nestled among the mirror-image school-issue desks, beds, dressers, bookshelves, and closets. Affenlight remained standing, admired the paintings on the walls, the climbing tendrils of the hook-hung plants, the collection of wines and scotches on the mantel. He could smell the way Owen's life and habits — weed and gingery cleaners; bookbinding glue; stiff white soap and the garlicky tang of his skin; hardly a trace of Henry except for a faint bouquet of ribbed gray sock — had ingrained themselves deep in the walls and floorboards of the place. He'd made the place home. By comparison Affenlight's own quarters, which he'd lived in three times as long, reeked of bachelor transience. His whole life had been bachelor transience, rootlessness, one noncommittal night after another in the cosmic boardinghouse. Life was temporary, after all. But to live with Owen, to let Owen make his home their home — that would really be the thing.

Owen plugged in the electric teapot that sat above the squat refrigerator, set about making tea.

"I tried to call," Affenlight said. This was somewhere between an accusation and an apology for showing up unannounced. "You didn't pick up."

"I just got home a few minutes ago."

"I saw you in the window while I was dialing."

Owen's eyebrows lifted in what Affenlight hoped was genuine puzzlement. "You did?"

"Yes."

Owen snapped his fingers. "Henry." He walked over to the phone, inspected the console, flipped a switch. "He's been turning off the ringer. He comes home and doesn't want to talk to anyone. Not the scouts, not his parents, not even Mike. It's worrisome."

"Mm." Affenlight didn't want to talk about Henry, not right now.

"I went to practice today," Owen said.

"You did?"

"I'm going to play tomorrow against Coshwale. Or rather, it's unlikely I'll play, because I've missed so much time, but I'll wear my pinstripes and warm the bench. Dr. Collins cleared me this afternoon."

"You went to St. Anne's?" Affenlight said. "I would have driven you."

"That's why I didn't ask. I take up enough of your time. You have a college to run."

"Bah." Affenlight's knees wobbled, and he sank into the plushy rose chair. "This place runs itself." It was dawning on him that they'd reached the end of something, something that began when that errant baseball hit Owen in the face, and would end now that he'd rejoined the team. They'd had their time together, the time of Owen's convalescence, his holiday from baseball. Their time out of time. And now that time was over. And he had stupidly turned up here to speed things along. "That's great news," he said. "About being cleared to play."

Owen smiled gently. "Then why do you look so glum?"

"No reason. I just missed you today."

"I missed you too."

Owen handed Affenlight a cup of tea, tousled his hair, leaned down and kissed him on the forehead. Affenlight couldn't help feeling consoled, like a child whose goldfish has died. "I wish you had told me," he said.

"Told you what?"

"That you were going to practice. You must have known ahead of time."

"I didn't know the doctor would clear me. And then Mike and I went straight to practice."

"Mike took you to the hospital."

"Yes."

There was nothing especially interesting about that bit of information, but every syllable Owen spoke felt portentous. "You come every day," Affenlight said. "It makes me expect you'll keep coming."

"It's just one day."

"Well, carpe diem, as they say. A day is a day. There are only so many of them."

"Guert, don't get upset. I mean, why be upset? Because there was one afternoon when my schedule didn't conform to yours? You've never visited *me,* you know. This is the first time you've even called, and you only called to chastise me."

"I'm not chastising you. That's not—"

"Are you under the impression that this is really what I want? Covert oral sex in an office, like some scene from a seedy movie?"

Affenlight was baffled. "I hardly think it's like that."

"What do you think it's like?" Owen was standing in front of his desk, his tailbone and the heels of his hands resting against its wooden edge, his long legs crossed at the ankles. Affenlight recognized the posture: that of the lecturer in command. Which made Affenlight, fidgety and underprepared in his borrowed chair, the student. "I show up, we read and make small talk, we suck each other off, we smoke a cigarette, I leave. You wash the couch with Windex and we do it again. It's like a gay-porn *Groundhog Day.*"

"We...I don't wash the couch," protested Affenlight. "I...we drink *coffee.*" He sounded pleading and inane, trying to imbue these three simple words, this one banal act, with all the import and sentiment it held for him.

"Everybody drinks coffee," Owen said.

Affenlight, as he glanced longingly toward the bottle of scotch on the mantel of the deactivated fireplace, noticed a familiar navy volume propped beside it. That damned register, he thought. That damned twenty-year-old me. He imagined his junior-year self strolling the crosshatched walkways with Owen's fingers entwined in his, the two of them sharing a joint on the library steps, pouring out cuplets of tea for each other at Café Oo, basking in the cinematic light of their campus celebrity. It was hard to imagine, but painfully easy to imagine Owen imagining it.

"Guert? Are you hearing anything I'm saying?"

"Yes," said Affenlight gloomily.

"And?"

"And I'm sixty years old. I'll be sixty-one next week."

"That's true," said Owen. "But I'm not sure how it relates to what we're talking about."

"Which is?"

"Which is the fact that we have nothing resembling a normal relationship. We've never been to dinner. We've never been to a movie. We've never even *rented* a movie."

"I don't like movies."

Owen smiled. "That's because you're an Americanist and a philistine. But I feel like a prostitute, showing up at your office every afternoon. A poorly paid one, to boot."

"It's not like I don't *want* those things," said Affenlight. "I do."

"But?"

"But... it's delicate."

"I know it's delicate. I know we can't just walk around holding hands. There are restrictions. My worry is that you find these restrictions convenient. Or even necessary. What if we were in New York, or San Francisco, or even down the road in Door County? What if you came to Tokyo with me? Would you walk down the street with me then? Could you look in a store window and see us holding hands? Or would that be too gay for you? Better to stay right here, in the heart of the problem, where your restrictions will protect you."

"You've been reading too much Foucault," Affenlight said.

"That's impossible. And anyway don't be glib."

The mention of Tokyo, those words in that order — *What if you came with me?* — scrambled Affenlight's thoughts. It was possible, really it was. He could take a year's sabbatical, pretend to be writing a book, wander around Japan with Owen as his fearless guide, Buddhist temples, neon kittens, tea, Mt. Fuji, the tiny island where two of his uncles died. Bill Murray in that movie he'd never seen, just like he'd never seen *Groundhog Day,* the one with the curvy blonde and the hotel bar, May–December in a far-off land.

"Don't get me wrong," Owen added. "I'm not trying to stake some ominous claim. I'm not even saying I like you. But why would I want to be with someone, for whatever length of time, with whom I can't go *any-where?* I want to live, Guert. I don't want to hide in your office. It was fun the first week."

He folded his slender arms, to indicate that he had finished steering the discussion and was willing to wait for Affenlight's response. He would make a first-rate pedagogue if he chose that route; then again he would make a first-rate anything. All that remained of his injury was a makeup-like swipe of steel blue that traced the outer and under curve of his eye socket. Affenlight shifted in the rose-colored chair. He knew that this was his exam, he was supposed to be answering questions and not asking them, but he felt exhausted, buried in his chair, and he couldn't help it. "What should I do?"

Owen uncrossed his arms, unfurled himself from his lecturer's perch. His eyes flashed darkly. "If I were you I'd ask me out to dinner. I'd put on a nice shirt that matched my eyes and I'd pick me up in my silver Audi and teach me about opera while I drove me out through the dark countryside to some Friday-night fish fry in some little town in the middle of nowhere."

"You don't eat fish," Affenlight said.

"I know. But I'd be so smitten by the invitation that I wouldn't care. And then I'd take me to a motel and turn off the heat and crawl into bed with me and watch cable television into the wee hours, the way that consenting adults are sometimes entitled to do, even if they normally detest television. And I'd hold me all night and kiss me on the ear and recite whatever poems I knew by heart and feed me awful processed snacks from the vending machine, since I wouldn't have touched the fish. And then in the morning I'd have me back nice and early, so I could make team breakfast before the game."

41

Pella, having showered and dressed, dried her hair and done her makeup, was pacing the apartment waiting for David to return. Amid the scatter of papers on her dad's desk in the study lay a half-full pack of Parliaments. He really was smoking again, as she'd suspected; something was up with him. She needed to make him stop, even if that meant calling his doctor and tattling on him; smoking was *streng verboten* in the Affenlight family.

She'd never smoked much herself, not since junior high anyway, but a cigarette right now would calm her nerves. She tapped one out with her uninjured hand and managed to light it with a match without smearing her still-wet nails. She opened the study window. No sooner had she leaned out to exhale than her father emerged from the front door of the building kitty-corner to Scull Hall. She didn't have a very good handle on the campus layout — the buildings all looked alike, with their weathered gray stone — but she was pretty sure that one was a dorm, the same dorm Henry pointed to last night when he offered to go get her ice. Her dad looked left, right, left, like a noir character who thought somebody might be tailing him. Then he headed across the quad toward the alley behind the dining hall, where he kept his car.

Three and a half minutes later, as she stubbed out the cigarette on the window frame, Owen Dunne emerged from the same door — which made sense, since Henry and Owen were roommates, though it didn't explain why her dad had been in there. Maybe it was a mixed-use building; maybe he'd needed that ice machine.

The downstairs buzzer rang; David was here. Cue ominous music. She ran to the bathroom to gargle some mouthwash.

42

They drove in David's rented hybrid to Maison Robert, the upscale, slightly flagging French place she used to go with her father during her vacations from Tellman Rose. It felt nice to be among adults, even if the adults in question were David and a bunch of past-their-prime-if-they'd-ever-had-a-prime academics bleached white by one too many northern Wisconsin winters. Maison Robert served as a kind of de facto Westish faculty club. Bald pates shone in the yellow-puddled lights, wire-rimmed glasses peered at the immutable black menus, snifters of amber brandy clicked against bulbous goblets of deep red wine. Pella's oral history professor, the preposterously chic, thoroughly un-Wisconsiny Judy Eglantine, dined alone in one corner, dressed in narrow black, an open book before her. A feathery lime-green boa flopped over the opposite chair in place of a companion. Pella caught her eye and waved shyly as David pulled back her chair with his usual wooden courtesy. Professor Eglantine smiled.

David beckoned the waiter with an impatient gesture and, without having looked at the list, began quizzing him about the wines. The waiter was Pella's age but had wispy albino-blond hair, as if the winters had aged and bleached him too. He mumbled *oaky* and *spicy* a few times. David ordered a red Bordeaux.

"How do you know what I want?" Pella said. "Maybe I'd rather have white."

"It's good." David glanced up at the hurriedly approaching waiter, whom he'd already frightened into submission. *"Ah, merci — la dame le goûtera,"* he said, though there was little chance the poor guy spoke French.

Pella leaned back so the waiter could pour, let the wine's oaky spices roll around in her mouth. David knew wine the way he knew architecture and Ancient Greek, the way he knew how to wire a kitchen and choose a mutual fund. She nodded at the waiter. "It's good," she said.

"That's a lovely dress," David said.

"Thanks." It was the lilac dress her father had bought her. She had yet to wear it on a date with Mike; she and Mike hadn't been on a date since that first night at Carapelli's, unless you counted eating crackers in bed as a date, or watching Mike scarf down dollar pitchers at Bartleby's.

"The color rather matches your finger," David said. "What did you say happened?"

"I walked into a tree."

"Ah, yes. The hazards of college life."

David's sense of humor was awkward and mechanical, as if he'd learned it from a book, but over time this mechanical quality could come to seem funny in itself. He seemed to be dressing better too — maybe somebody else was dressing him. Or maybe he just dressed well compared to Mike: his socks matched, and he was wearing a jacket. He was slight of frame, especially compared to you-know-who, but the jacket was new and it fit him well. The waiter appeared to silently top off her wine; she liked when that happened, because you couldn't count how many glasses you'd had.

The table was set for four, though the reservation had been made for three. Pella hoped that when her father arrived he would invite Professor Eglantine to join them. Not only because her presence would ensure that the conversation stayed on solidly neutral ground but because Pella admired her immensely, and since attending her first oral history lecture had begun to harbor a hope that Professor Eglantine and her dad might get together. It hadn't happened in the past eight years—or maybe it had, and ended—and so presumably never would, but she couldn't help hoping. Professor E was just too striking and sexy, with her rare-bird eyes and that Sontag streak of pale gray in her hiply cut hair. Not conventionally sexy, perhaps—she was slight enough that you could fold her up and carry her like an umbrella—but her dad was capable of unorthodox appreciations. If there was a suitable match for him within fifty miles, this was it.

"So you're really planning to stay here," David said. "Shoveling slop at frat boys."

"That's one way to put it."

"I guess I'm not sure how else to put it."

"Chef Spirodocus isn't a hack," she said. "He's the real deal."

David smiled that tight, tolerant smile. "I'm sure he's a master of his craft. If he wanted to be running a first-rate kitchen somewhere, he would. He just happens to prefer making runny eggs for runny-nosed kids."

Pella smoothed and tugged the hem of her dress. Where was her father? Why wasn't Mike flinging a brick through the restaurant's tinted picture window and slinging her over his shoulder to carry her away? What was all that muscle *for* anyway? Just because they'd had one little fight, he was going to sulk in his house and let David try to win her back? How wimpy was that? She slugged down some wine. Getting saved by men, finding a new mother—her fantasies were becoming more regressive by the second, a known hazard of being around David, who induced a strange powerlessness in her.

"I do think it's wonderful," he was saying, "that you want to study cooking."

"You do?"

"Absolutely. I think much of the anxiety you've been suffering from these last few months has had to do with the lack of a creative outlet. No, not an outlet—a real sense of creative purpose. If you're really through painting, perhaps this could fill that place in your life. And it would be a useful social corrective as well. All the first-rate chefs in this country are men. So many women slaving away in kitchens, so few of them allowed to be considered artists. It's shameful."

This was the way it had always been—everything David said so multiplicitous, so full of broad assessments and tiny recastings of truth, that to begin to dig in and issue corrections seemed petty and futile. Of course he'd believe that her "anxiety" stemmed from not painting, instead of from being married to him; of course he'd believe that her "anxiety" had lasted a few months and not the bulk of their curdled marriage. It maddened her that he still tried to cast her as an artist, when she hadn't picked up a brush in years; the whole idea of art felt like a remnant of adolescence. Might as well call her a swimmer, because she'd once held the Tellman Rose freshman record in the 100 butterfly. The wine was good. She was drinking it down.

"Although of course I'd be disappointed if you truly gave up painting," David went on. "You're amazingly talented."

"No one is 'amazingly' anything," Pella said. "When have you ever been amazed?"

"I was amazed by you, Bella. By your brilliance. It was one of the chief reasons I fell in love with you."

"We were living together before you ever saw one of my paintings. We were living together before I found out you were married. I still don't know how you pulled that off."

"I didn't keep my marriage from you any more than you kept your painting from me. We were discovering each other. We were young and in love."

"*I* was young," Pella said.

"And I was in love. Anyway, Bella, my point is this: If you want to become a chef, I support you fully. But I think you should go about it in the proper way. And I'm not sure that living with your father and scrubbing pots for ten dollars an hour—"

"Seven fifty."

"My God. Really? Seven fifty, then. Is even remotely the way to blossom as a chef. Art, academia, cuisine — whatever you choose, the only way to become the best is to immerse yourself with the best." David, as he said this, speared a forkful of gray, weary escargot and wagged it as evidence. "I don't have to tell you that the Bay Area has some of the best and most adventurous chefs in the world. The Asian and the European; seafood, which I know to be a particular favorite of yours; not to mention a fair amount of actual thoughtfulness about matters of sustainability and ecologi—"

"So I should come home. Why not just come out and say it?"

"I don't think I was being terribly circumspect. You're living amongst children, Bella. What are you going to do, wash their dishes until you're thirty? While this country has problems you could be helping to solve."

Pella had fallen in love with David's rectitude, and she still found it hard to disregard. She wanted to be a good person, and that meant she should do something good with her life. Yes, from a certain vantage the Westish dining hall was a wasteland, a supporter of slaughterhouses, an exploiter of immigrant labor, a treadmill of routine and repetition and industrial foods delivered over long distances to be prepared and consumed hastily with great amounts of waste. But she felt comfortable there. Wasn't that a prerequisite, a place to start? How could you learn anything, accomplish anything, build any kind of momentum toward becoming a good person, unless you felt at least a little bit comfortable first?

Professor Eglantine signed her check and wrapped her lime-green boa around the collar of her black jacket like a scarf. She picked up her large hardcover book, tiptoed toward the door on her five-inch heels, somehow seeming both exquisitely composed and as if the book's torturous weight might pitch her over and pin her to the floor. Pella sent a pleading look in her direction, hoping against hope that she would tiptoe over to engage them in charming, heartfelt conversation that would demonstrate once and for all that Westish was a place where an elegant, useful life could be led, but it didn't happen, and Professor Eglantine was gone. So much for romance, Pella thought, so much for a new mother-in-law. Where the heck was her father?

"Don't know what to tell you," she said. "I like doing dishes."

David ruffled his tightly trimmed beard with his fingertips, sighed an ennui-riddled sigh meant to indicate that he didn't much care what Pella did but wished she wouldn't be so exasperating. "You know, if you wanted to leave, Bella, you could have done so in a slightly more civil fashion."

"I thought it was fairly civil," Pella said. "No flashing blades. No bloodshed."

"Maybe *mature* is the word I'm looking for, then. You're not a teenager anymore, Bella. You can't keep running away from home every time you feel frightened about the future. Whatever the trouble, I wish you had talked to me about it. I'm sure we could have worked it out like adults. I'm sure we still could."

Pella slugged back the rest of her wine. She was shifting into the blame-David phase of the evening. "Right," she said. "I can imagine how that conversation would have gone. 'Uh, David, I'm leaving you because you're controlling and unreasonable and debilitatingly jealous. You don't want me to work, don't want me in school, don't even want me to learn how to drive. So, uh, whaddya think, sweetie?'"

David drummed his fingers against the base of his wineglass and looked at her with oh-so-reasonable bemusement. "Bella, don't twist my words. I didn't want you to take driver's ed while you were on certain medications. That's all."

"What medications? Ambusal? Kelvesin? What year do you think this is? Every person on the road is on something or other."

"Those people already know how to drive. You were in a fragile state at the time. And San Francisco is a difficult place for a novice. Heavy traffic, constant changes in elevation. I thought it would be dangerous."

"We could have gone somewhere quieter. You could have made some accommodations. But instead you used it as another excuse to isolate me. Who knows what kind of trouble I'd have gotten into if I'd had a *car*."

David thrived on these arguments, his manner growing calmer and saner by the second as Pella tipped toward madness. Except of course that he was the mad one. "Bella, I'm surprised at you. When we first got married, I wanted you to start college right away, remember? And you told me that love and your art were all that mattered to you. So we decided you shouldn't work."

He was mocking her, throwing around these big little words — love, work, art. "That was at the beginning," she said.

"And a fine beginning it was. Remember when I met Marietta and invited her to dinner? And we took your best piece, the big collage with the salmon colors, and hung it facing her chair? I felt like a criminal mastermind when she took the bait. That was quite a night."

Marietta Cheng owned a gallery; she'd bought *Sea-Spray* for four thousand dollars, Pella's first and only real sale. Pella had almost backed out of the deal, for reasons she couldn't quite express, but David convinced her that though they didn't need the money, it was important for her to establish herself as a commercially viable artist. Soon thereafter Pella's ill feelings began. She blew Marietta's money on vintage dresses and other long-gone trivia — she'd have been better off keeping the one thing she'd made that she actually liked.

"In the beginning you would have let me work," she said. "But later..."

"Later you were sick, Bella. I wanted you to get well. That's all." He took her hands. "Look. If you want a divorce, you can have a divorce. I'm not going to dissuade you. But this" — with a flick of his eyes he took in not just the escargot and the aging patrons but the school and the town and the whole Midwest — "is not for you, Bella. You can live in the loft. I'll rent an apartment. You can get a job at a restaurant, apply to culinary school, go about this the proper way. Who knows? Maybe someday you'll let me design a restaurant for you."

Shit, thought Pella. David wasn't going to win her back—and oh what a prize she was—but he *was* going to destroy whatever tenuous momentum she'd been building. If she was going to enroll at Westish, she needed to believe that she *should* enroll at Westish, that living near her father, working for Chef Spirodocus, studying with Professor Eglantine, was the way to start to build a life. If she entertained doubts about whether she belonged here, she'd wind up back in bed, paralyzed by those doubts. The circumstances were tipped in Westish's favor—she could enroll without finishing high school, her tuition would be free, she was already here and so far felt okay. But how could she not have doubts, what with the sad-looking entrées arriving, the slumped-over patrons departing, her father AWOL as usual, Mike off petting Henry somewhere? If tonight was a referendum on her presence at Westish, the results weren't good. She didn't love David anymore, but love had trained her to see the world through his eyes, and through his eyes this place was a vapid dump.

The wine was white, which meant they'd switched.

She depended on men too much, Mike this Daddy that, needing one to rescue her from the next; even Chef Spirodocus was a man, of a sort. Maybe she needed more women in her life, that was why her mind latched on to Judy Eglantine, but she'd always gotten along better with men and that was unlikely to change much here, where most of the women were younger than she and would no doubt shun her and be scared of her and call her a slut no matter what she did. Was that too pessimistic? In any case, she'd have to rely on herself.

Something buzzed. David pulled his BlackBerry out of his pocket, glanced at the screen. "It's your father," he said.

"So don't ans—," she said, but David already had. He handed her the phone.

"Pella. I'm so sorry. I can be there in fiftee—"

"Don't worry about it," she said chipperly. "I think you were right not to come. David and I needed to hash some things out by ourselves."

"Really?" said her dad, not believing her.

"Really."

"You're not mad at me?"

"Next question!" Chipper but honest. Chipper, honest, and drunk.

"Okay…it's not going *too* well, I hope?"

"That's proprietary." Pella could hear noise in the background—voices, a kind of clinking, faint music. "Are you in a restaurant?"

"Me?…No, no, of course not. I got waylaid by Bruce Gibbs…A president's work and so on…Are you sure there's nothing I can do?"

"I'll see you tomorrow," Pella said.

It could barely have been nine thirty, but around the room checks were being paid, jackets donned. Midwestern living: the ten o'clock news and up at dawn. Pella grabbed the neck of the wine bottle, no longer willing to wait for the waiter's invisible hand. She looked at David. "I'm sleeping with someone."

"I don't believe you."

She knew he meant it: he didn't believe her. "It's true."

"I don't believe you," he repeated. "I don't even know why you'd say that. What about us?"

"What *about* us? It's not like *we're* sleeping together. We haven't had sex in a year."

He glared at her. "That's not true."

"Of course it's true," Pella said. "A year at least."

"Bella. You don't remember the last time we made love?"

Pella tried to remember. But why should she remember? They'd made love less frequently, and then they'd stopped. It wasn't like there'd been some kind of ceremony, or even a conscious decision.

"It was Christmas Day," David said. "The day I gave you these." He reached into his inside jacket pocket and pulled out a tiny manila envelope. He undid the flap and shook out onto the tablecloth two gorgeous teardrop earrings, sapphire and platinum. Pella had never seen them before. Or had she?

"You're crazy," she said.

"I thought you might want to keep them. I don't have much use for them myself."

Pella resisted the urge to pick one up. "We did not have sex on Christmas," she said.

David fixed her with a calm, pitying expression, the kind that usually preceded some calmly phrased suggestion — that she should *calm down,* or *drink some water,* or *consider seeing someone.* "Bella," he said reprovingly. "You know I hate it when you do this."

"Do what?"

"Pretend that you don't remember things. As if memories were just a matter of convenience, and you could throw them away if you didn't want them. Although why you wouldn't want such pleasant memories is beyond me. We woke up. It was sunny. I cooked breakfast. We listened to Krebenspell's Second. We made love. We went to dinner at Trisquette. I gave you these." His voice was obnoxiously calm. Pella's need for a sky-blue pill was through the roof, but she wasn't sure where her purse had gone. She looked for the bottle of wine, but it was gone too, hauled off by the waiter with the hairless hands. She'd probably drunk the whole thing herself. David always stopped at two glasses. She'd have to be crazy not to remember those earrings, and she was clearly not crazy. Opaquely not crazy. Not not not crazy. She vaguely remembered dinner in late December, an awful afternoon walled in by the platinum sun, the bizarre creakings of Deskin Krebenspell, whom David regarded as the quote "only living composer." No making love — no way. But people believed what they wanted to believe. She'd told David that she was sleeping with Mike, and he refused to believe it, had forgotten it instantly, because his brain couldn't stand to know such a thing. If he wanted to believe they'd slept together on Christmas, let him believe it.

But the earrings were something else. The earrings *existed.* They lay there on the table. They did look vaguely familiar — no doubt they'd seen them in some boutique in Hayes Valley, and Pella had oohed and ahhed, and David, having taken note of her oohing and ahhing — he'd never been stingy with gifts—bought them before flying out here. And now was pretending that he'd given them to her before. She picked one up to put it back in its manila envelope. A nice touch, that: to hand them over in their brand-new box would make them seem brand-new. It was a classic David maneuver to try to win her back this way, by making her think she was crazy. *He* made her crazy, no one else. He did have good taste, though. The earring squirted from her hand and landed in her empty wineglass amid the pale grit. She should drink it, swallow it— now *that* would make her crazy. And it would make him crazy too.

She lifted the wineglass, clicked it against David's, which was still half full. She met his eyes meanly, lifted the glass to her lips. *Fuck Mike Schwartz* was the toast that arose in her mind. *Fuck Mike Schwartz, whom I live to fuck.* Never too drunk to use *whom.* Funny that she'd thought *live to fuck* instead of *love to fuck* or *like to fuck. Like to fuck* would have been the most accurate, but it didn't make much difference. David was speaking and reaching. She leaned away. She had the wineglass nearly inverted, but the earring hung up in the little hollow that led down to the stem. She tapped the glass with her injured hand. The earring rattled free and skied down the goblet's concavity into her mouth. She rolled it around, cold metal and stone. She tested it with her teeth, slipped it under her tongue. It felt right.

"Spit that out," David said, alarmed.

She stuck her tongue out at him.

"You could be seriously injured."

A thousand-dollar dinner. A piece of performance art.

"You're acting like a five-year-old," David said. "It's not becoming."

"You said you had no use for them."

"Quit performing. Spit it out."

She showed him the inside of her mouth, like a five-year-old who's finished her spinach: clean. When she'd gone to swallow she felt a thrill and then a fear—what if it stuck in her throat? But it was small and went down without a problem.

David looked terrified. He pulled out his phone.

"What are you doing?"

"I'm calling an ambulance. That thing will shred your intestines."

"Oh, relax." Pella shoved back her chair, a bit unsteadily, and walked away from the table. Relying on yourself wasn't easy; it could involve strong measures. There were two stalls in the women's bathroom, both vacant. She'd never really been bulimic, but it was one of those things a girl just knew how to do. The earring came up in a tide of pink wine and snail sauce. She held her hair with her left hand and fished the beautiful blue teardrop out of the toilet with her right. She went to the sink to rinse her mouth and then the earring. A wicker basket of woodchip potpourri sat beside the basin. In the mirror she looked blanched and haggard, thirty at least, but the wine was gone from her stomach and she was starting to feel better already. She wouldn't even have a hangover tomorrow.

43

Schwartz, still wet from his post-practice shower, was standing in his weirdly clean kitchen, chasing a couple Vicodin with some flat ginger ale, when he heard the gate's jingle and footsteps on the front porch. The bell rang. *Pella,* he thought wishfully, but she was off somewhere with The Architect. Schwartz had fantasized about hunting them down, about putting a scare into The Architect if not pummeling him into submission, but Pella didn't have a cell phone, he didn't know where to find her, and he needed to get some sleep before tomorrow's games.

"Gentlemen." He nodded, shaking Starblind's hand and then Rick's. "Can I get you something to drink?"

"No thanks," said Starblind. Rick shook his head solemnly, his pink anvil chin describing a long slow arc.

"Something wrong?" Schwartz asked. "O'Shea looks ready for a funeral."

Rick stared down at his Birkenstocks. Starblind gave the lid of the mailbox a few apprehensive flips, not meeting Schwartz's eye. "There's something we wanted to talk to you about."

"Well, here I am."

"Right." Starblind sucked in a breath and steeled himself. "We talked it over at practice today, and we think that Henry should sit out tomorrow."

Schwartz's whole big body tensed. "Who's *we?*"

"Rick and myself. Boddington and Phlox. Jensen. Ajay. Meat." Starblind glanced at Rick. "Who else?"

Rick looked like Starblind had just asked him to name a Jew. "Sooty Kim," he muttered.

"Right. Sooty was there."

"You had a meeting," Schwartz said.

Starblind shrugged. "Not officially. It was just the juniors and seniors. No need to get the younger guys involved."

"Was the Buddha there?"

"Buddha hasn't been around much lately."

"What about me? Was I there?"

"No," Starblind conceded. "You weren't."

"Sounds like some meeting." A dangerous calm suffused Schwartz's voice. "What else did you geniuses do? Elect yourselves captains?"

"Schwartzy, please. Hear us out." Rick's normally ruddled face was drained of color. His left thumb flicked at an imaginary lighter, tapped at the filter end of an imaginary cigarette. "It wasn't a meeting. How could we have a team meeting about this? What would we do, get everyone together to talk about what's wrong with the Skrimmer? With him sitting right there?"

"So you did it on the sly," Schwartz said. "Behind my back."

"It wasn't like that. It was an impromptu discussion that led to a consensus. And here we are right afterward to tell you about it. As our captain."

"How big of you."

"I'll tell you what's big," Starblind said. "This weekend. These four games. We beat Coshwale, we win UMSCACs. We go to the regional tournament."

"You think we're gonna beat Coshwale without Henry?" Schwartz said. "Even if we could, you want to go into regionals with him riding the bench? You're nuts."

"He cost us that game yesterday," Starblind said.

"The whole team played like shit the whole game! Rick here dropped a pop-up, Boddington booted two grounders, I struck out with a runner on third. That play of Henry's was one play. We should have been up by twelve by then."

"We should've been," said Starblind, "but we weren't."

Rick sighed miserably, riffling his ginger hair. "Schwartzy, you know how I feel about the little guy. I love him and I'd go to war for him. He's like the brother I never had, and I have four brothers. But what's going on with him is messing with all of our heads. Why do you think we looked so shaky yesterday? I'm not saying it's Henry's fault, but..."

Rick lifted his arms and let them drop. Schwartz stayed silent, waiting for him to finish. "Nobody knows how to talk to him anymore. It changes the whole atmosphere. When we win nobody wants to celebrate, because Henry's our leader, you and him are our leaders, and obviously he's hurting. And when we lose... well, we shouldn't lose. We shouldn't have lost to Wainwright. We're too good a team."

"Izzy looks sharp at practice," Starblind added. "He could step right in. We'd barely miss a beat."

A pickup rolled by with two kegs in the bed, blasting the rap anthem of the moment. Friday night, for nonathletes, was under way. Schwartz felt a splinter from a cracked porch board pierce the meat of his foot. "Tomorrow's the Skrimmer's day," he said. "His family'll be here. Aparicio'll be here. You think he's just going to take a seat?"

"He might not want to," Starblind said. "But he should. For the team."

"Hell, he can play first base if he wants," Rick said. "*I'll* sit. Anything so he doesn't have to make that throw from short to first. It's killing him, Schwartzy. You know that. Anyone can see it."

"He's just pressing. He'll be fine."

"If he was pressing before," Starblind said, "what do you think's going to happen tomorrow?"

It wasn't like it had never occurred to Schwartz. It hadn't escaped his notice how smooth Izzy looked at practice, how confident an athlete he was, how much he'd already learned from Henry about playing short-stop. Izzy couldn't hit like Henry, not even close, but on defense it would actually be—Schwartz felt like a traitor to think it—an improvement. And maybe Starblind was right; maybe it would be not just foolish but cruel, sadistic, to send Henry out there tomorrow when the pressure would be cranked up ten times higher than ever before. Maybe the kid would crack wide open. Maybe it was Schwartz's job to head that off before it happened.

"Why are you coming to me with this?" he said. "Coach Cox decides who plays and who doesn't."

"You know Coach Cox," Rick said. "Loyal to a fault."

Starblind nodded. "Remember Two Thirty? Guy was a head case. But Coach Cox wouldn't bench him. He was convinced Toovs would suddenly start crushing in games the way he did in practice. How many wins did *that* cost us over two years?"

"Hardly the same situation," Schwartz said.

"Skrimmer's lost his confidence. Toovs never had any to begin with." Starblind shrugged dismissively, thrust his hands into the pockets of his shiny track jacket. "They're both fucked."

"So you want me to decide that Henry can't play tomorrow."

"You're the captain," Starblind said, a hint of snideness in his voice. Schwartz squeezed his right hand into a fist, then uncurled his fingers slowly, like a man warding off a heart attack. Thinking of cracking a few of Starblind's blinding arctic teeth.

"Just one day off might do the Skrimmer good," Rick said. "He could relax, take it easy, come back stronger on Sunday. He might even feel relieved."

Starblind eyed Schwartz levelly. "Just don't forget what you're sup-posed to put first, Schwartzy. It's not Henry, and it's not Henry's pro career."

It's this team.

It wasn't a given that sitting Henry would be the best thing for this team — how far could they possibly go without their best player? — but Starblind's words gave Schwartz pause. It was true that he'd gotten locked on Henry, Henry's feelings, Henry redeeming himself to the scouts. Not necessarily to the detriment of the team thus far — Henry's success and the Harpooners' had always gone hand in hand — but it was possible, it could happen. It was possible that the younger Schwartz, the hard-ass sophomore who'd galled Lev Tennant into punching him to get Henry into the lineup, would now decide to do what it took to get Henry back out of it. Sometimes you needed a rupture; sometimes you had to clean house. The younger Schwartz had known that. It was easy to know that when you weren't in charge.

"You guys have a shitload of theories." Schwartz meant to say this loudly, bitterly, but he could feel the emotion leaking from his voice like air from an old balloon. He sighed, rubbed a hand over his beard — but his beard wasn't there. His hand found freshly shaved skin that was starting to burn like hell. "I can't do it," he said. "We live by the Skrimmer, we die by the Skrimmer."

44

He wanted to talk to Owen, but Owen wasn't home. Sometimes it seemed he could talk freely at only two times in his life: out on the diamond and here, in the dark, across the room from Owen. Lying here, ear on pillow, it was easy to figure out how you felt and say it out loud. Your words wouldn't come back to haunt you but would land softly on Owen's ears and stay. That was the good thing about having a roommate, a roommate like Owen, but Owen wasn't home.

He picked up the phone and dialed Sophie's cell.

"Henry," his sister whispered. "Hang on." For twenty seconds the phone banged around. "Sorry," she said. "I went out in the hall."

"Where are you guys?"

"Dad's back hurts, so Mom was driving, and Mom got tired. We stopped at a motel like fifty miles away. It's kind of gross but I have my own bed. What are you doing up?"

"Couldn't sleep."

"Henry, big brother, don't be nervous. You'll be great."

"I know." It comforted him to talk to Sophie—she had an interest in his happiness and none in baseball—but he always feared she'd say too much to their parents, whom he'd told almost nothing about his troubles. Luckily he'd also told them almost nothing about the scouts and the agents and the huge sums of money that loomed, that used to loom, in

June. As far as they knew he was just Henry, their college boy, who'd tied Aparicio's record and was having a pretty good season.

"*Aparicio Rodriguez,*" Sophie said. This was the only baseball player whose name she knew. "Are you excited?"

"Sure."

"Don't be nervous," she advised. "Just relax and enjoy it. Soak it in. You'll be great."

"I know," Henry said. "I will."

"And then we're going out tomorrow night, right? You promised that when I was a senior we could."

"Soph, this is a really busy weekend. We have two more games on Sunday."

"*Henry.* You promised. You can't make me spend the whole weekend with Mom and Dad again."

"In a few months you'll be in college. You can go out all you want."

"Yeah, at SDSU. But Westish is so cool. I bought a dress. Don't tell Mom."

Henry couldn't help but smile. "Okay, okay. We'll go out."

When he hung up the phone he still wasn't sleepy. If Owen offered him some kind of pill tonight he'd take it for sure, but Owen wasn't home. Henry slipped out of bed and into his warm-up pants and Harpooner windbreaker, slapped his Cards cap on his head, and walked down to Westish Field.

He sat down on the damp sandy dirt between second and third, the spot where he'd spent so many hundreds of hours, and pulled *The Art* from his windbreaker pocket. The worn spine flopped open to a favorite page.

99. *To reach a ball he has never reached before, to extend himself to the very limits of his range, and then a step farther: this is the shortstop's dream.*

He flipped again.

121. *The shortstop has worked so hard for so long that he no longer thinks.*
Nor does he act. By this I mean that he does not generate action.
He only reacts, the way a mirror reacts when you wave your hand
before it.

He wasn't in a box he could think his way out of. Nor was he in a box he could relax his way out of, no matter how many times Coach Cox or Schwartzy or Owen or Rick or Starblind or Izzy or Sophie told him to relax, stop thinking, be himself, be the ball, don't try too hard. You could only try so hard not to try too hard before you were right back around to trying too hard. And trying hard, as everyone told him, was wrong, all wrong.

During grade-school winters back in Lankton, his sister and Scott Hinterberg would run ahead, yanking open the mailboxes that lined the streets, and Henry would trail behind to peg snowballs into the mailboxes' waiting mouths, never missing, never, unless there was mail inside waiting to be sent, in which case he would knock down the little red flag with his snowball, then politely run over and lift it again. How did he make those throws? It seemed amazing now. A kid in a puffy coat that hindered his movement, his fingers numb and raw from packing snow, perfect every time.

The shortstop has worked so hard for so long that he no longer thinks — that was just the way to phrase it. You couldn't choose to think or not think. You could only choose to work or not work. And hadn't he chosen to work? And wasn't that what would save him now? When he walked onto this field tomorrow he would carry a whole reservoir of work with him, the last three years of work with Schwartzy, the whole lifetime of work before that, of focusing always and only on baseball and how to become better. It was not flimsy, that lifetime of work. He could rely on it.

If he relied on it, he'd be fine. April had been awful, but tomorrow was the real test, like a class where only the final counted. Dwight had told him that though his draft stock had dropped, it hadn't dropped nearly as far as Henry assumed. "Teams care about potential," Dwight said, "even more than performance. You're young, you're fast, you're hitting the heck out of the ball. There'll be twenty teams there on Saturday, I promise. Put on a show for 'em." And as for the Harpooners, they were only one game behind Coshwale — they would win their first-ever conference title, would go to regionals, if they won three out of four this weekend. Redemption was there for the taking. It didn't matter that Aparicio would be in the stands, that his parents and Sophie would be there too, that it was Henry Skrimshander Day. He just needed to play baseball, to enjoy it as he always had, to help his teammates beat Coshwale. Everything else would fall into place.

React, the way a mirror reacts.

He climbed to his feet, dusted the damp sandy dirt from the butt of his pants. He turned to the book's penultimate paragraph. Clouds engulfed the low-hanging moon, so that he could barely see the words at all, but it didn't matter.

212. *It always saddens me to leave the field. Even fielding the final out to win the World Series, deep in the truest part of me, felt like death.*

Ah, Aparicio!

45

ffenlight parked the Audi on a side street a few blocks from campus. Owen reached past the gearshift and tugged at the corner of
Affenlight's pocket with his thumb; they couldn't kiss in front of the
Westishers out weeding and mowing their lawns. "I've got to go," Owen
said. "I'm late."

"I'll be at the game," Affenlight said, eager to cement some tiny portion of their future.

Owen smiled. "Me too." He shut the passenger door softly and
strolled off toward the north edge of campus, where the athletic fields
lay. As he turned onto Groome Street, just before passing from view, he
took a few steps in a sashaying, rolling-hipped way—a caricature of a
gay man's walk. Affenlight glanced around, nervous that someone else
might have noticed, but even if anyone had noticed they couldn't possibly
have cared. The hip roll was a joke meant for him alone—Owen knew
he'd be watching. It wasn't quite a joke for his amusement, and it wasn't
quite a joke at his expense. More like a joke Owen wanted him to live up
to. Don't take this too seriously, Guert. Don't be dour about it. Straight
gay black white young old—it's not going to kill you or let you live.

The silence that filled the Audi seemed profound. Affenlight rolled
down the windows so he could hear the roar of lawn mowers and patted
down his jacket in search of a smoke.

They'd driven far out into the country, headed nowhere except somewhere where nobody knew them, and wound up at a fish fry in a greenly lit basement with no nonsmoking section. The place served pale beer in small glasses, nine or ten ounces each, and every time Affenlight looked down his glass was empty, and every time he looked up the coughing blue-haired waitress had filled it again. They ordered two fish fries — *So as to seem polite,* Affenlight said, and Owen raised his eyebrows and said, *You mean not gay,* and Affenlight glared at him reprovingly, flicking his eyes toward the nearby tables, and Owen said, *Down, tiger.* Owen ate both their salads of iceberg lettuce, pale pink tomato wedges, and sliced cucumbers. Affenlight ate his beer-battered cod and Owen's beer-battered cod, so as to seem polite and not gay, and then the waitress brought more because it was all-you-can-eat, and Affenlight ate that too, cholesterol be damned. By the time he'd remembered that he was supposed to be at dinner with Pella and David he was already half-drunk. God, what a terrible father. She'd sounded surprisingly un-angry on the phone. Affenlight believed her at the time, but he needed to believe her; he was forty minutes away, a cigarette lit, several lagers in his bloodstream, his shoe tips pressed against Owen's beneath the table. He should have hustled back for dessert no matter what she said. The motel he and Owen found, forty miles west of Westish, was called Troupe's Inn.

Now he decided to leave the Audi where it was and take his stroll along the lake, which he'd missed this morning. The pressure in his temples was that of a genuine hangover. How many beers had he drunk? How nervous had he been to spend the night with Owen, share a bed, make love? Pretty nervous, apparently. It had been forty-two years since he'd lost his virginity. He'd never thought then that he would lose it again. He felt a touch of sadness now that it had happened, now that he knew what it was like. Not because it wasn't enjoyable, or wouldn't be repeated, but because one more of life's mysteries had been revealed.

46

The Harpooners were lounging in the outfield under a mellow late-morning sun, pitching Wiffle balls to one another — a favorite Coach Cox drill — when the Coshwale bus arrived. "Here come the douchetards," grumbled Craig Suitcase, the Harpooners' third-string catcher, swinging so hard in his hatred of Coshwale that he missed the Wiffle ball entirely. "What a bunch of douchetards."

For once no one disagreed with Suitcase. They looked like douchetards in their spotless beet-red satin Coshwale jackets, worn despite the pleasant weather, with their spotless beet-red Coshwale bags slung over their shoulders, and their spotless beet-red cross-trainers — which they would swap in a moment for their spotless beet-red spikes — on their feet. The Harpooners, apart from the freshpersons, knew from experience that there were spotless beet-red Coshwale batting-practice shirts beneath the jackets, and that these would be worn throughout Coshwale's omnicompetent warm-up routine and removed in unison just before game time, revealing — what else? — spotless beet-red Coshwale jerseys, with the players' surnames stitched between the shoulder blades. Henry didn't know how they did it; whether they had some kind of professional laundry service or just got brand-new equipment before every game. Three games into any given season his own beloved pinstripes were stained and dingy, his spikes, which he paid for himself, scuffed and fraying before they were even broken in. Coshwale had won UMSCACs eight of the last ten years.

Soon Coshwale's army of fans began to arrive, dressed in their beet-red attire. They set up their spotless beet-red seat cushions and sun umbrellas in the visiting bleachers, then headed back to the parking lot to set up their grills. "Douchetards upon douchetards," muttered Suitcase.

Rick appeared at Henry's side. "Where the Buddha?" he asked. "Thought he was dressing today."

"Me too." Owen hadn't come home last night, and he'd missed breakfast with the team. It was probably time to start worrying, at least a little, but Henry didn't have room for any more worry. "He'll be here."

Coshwale took the field first for infield-outfield drills. The Harpooners spread out near the home dugout, stretching, chatting, pretending not to be nervous, pretending not to watch. Owen once called the Muskies' drills as crisp as Petrarch's sonnets; Rick compared them to the North Korean army. Three burly beet-red-clad coaches slugged balls at once, puffing out their beet-red cheeks with the effort. Thirty-one players—a dozen more than the Harpooners had—fielded balls and fired perfect throws to one another in complicated, constantly shifting patterns. Cut two, cut three, cut four, third to first, first to third, 5-4-3, 6-4-3, 4-6-3, 1-6-3, 3-6-1, charge bunt, charge bunt, charge bunt. Always three balls aloft at once, never a missed cutoff, never an errant throw. When their fifteen minutes were up they jogged cockily off the field. You got the sense they might come back for an encore. The Coshwale fans were returning from the parking lot to their cushioned seats with plates of hors d'oeuvres. The home-side bleachers were filling too, faster and earlier than Henry had ever seen.

Just as the Harpooners took the field, Owen came ambling down the first-base line in full navy-on-ecru pinstripes, cleats on his feet. He slung his bag into the dugout, greeted Coach Cox with a jovial bow, and trotted out to right field to swap turns with Sooty Kim. Henry smiled. To see Owen wearing his 0 jersey for the first time since his injury was like waking from a bad dream. Everything that had happened between then and now could be forgotten. Today was big, big was good. The sun shone overhead. Fans in the stands. A chance to do some winning.

He slapped gloves with Izzy. Izzy took a cutoff from Loondorf in left, whipped it to Boddington at third. "Izz Izz Izz," Henry chanted. "What izz what wuzz will be!"

"Let's go, *vendejos!*" shouted Izzy. "Let's go!"

"Cut four, cut four!"

"We ain't letting these *vatos* walk into our house and take our shit! No sir!"

"Here, now!" yelled Quentin Quisp from left, as he fielded a Schwartz-struck fly ball and fired it toward home plate. "Right here right now!" These were by far the loudest, most emphatic words anyone had heard from Quisp all year.

"Somebody woke up Q!" Henry yelled. "Somebody woke up the Q!"

"Q Q Q!"

"Somebody woke up the Q!"

"Somebody woke up Henry!"

"Somebody brought back the Buddha!"

"Buddha Buddha Buddha!"

"O O O!"

"Our house!"

"Nuestra casa!"

"O O O!"

It felt good to yell, to repeat, to shout nonsense at the bright spring air. Everyone was nervous and it came out as a clean high giddiness. Henry's arm felt light like a bird, light and lively, about to take flight from his body. He fired pellets to Arsch, pellets to Rick, pellets to Ajay. Everyone fired pellets to everyone — Henry looked around for what felt like the first time and saw how good this team had become, how good a chance they had to beat Coshwale today. "Izzy," he yelled, though Izzy was standing beside him, "how come the good guys are *vendejos* and the bad guys are *vatos?*"

"That's how it goes, *vendejo!* That's how it goes!"

The outfielders finished their portion of the drill and sprinted toward the dugout, whooping like madmen as they ran. As each infielder left the diamond he fielded a faux bunt rolled out by Coach Cox. Henry nudged Izzy before his turn. "Watch this." He charged at full speed, barehanded the ball, and whipped it behind his back to Rick, never looking or breaking stride as he ran off the field and down the dugout stairs. Perfect.

Owen was already folded into his favorite corner of the dugout, reading light clipped to the brim of his cap, book in hand. He looked up at Henry and smiled. "How's the wing, as the natives say?"

Henry nodded. "Wing's A-OK."

"Shall we do our elaborate handshake?"

"Let's."

Owen stood, tenting his book on the bench — *The Art of Fielding.* Their handshake involved both hands and both elbows, a kiss on the cheek, mock punches to the stomach, something resembling patty-cake, and a lot of kung fu–style bowing. Henry took his eye black from his bag and drew a line beneath each eye. He removed his cap, gave the sweat-softened brim a single squeeze, and placed it back on his head. He spit a few drops of saliva into Zero's well-worn pocket and kneaded them in with his fist. Ready. The home-plate umpire strapped on his chest protector. "Two minutes, coaches."

Coach Cox wasn't much for pregame speeches. "Here's the lineup, men. Starblind Phlox Skrimmer. Schwartz O'Shea Boddington. Quisp Guladni Kim. No reason we can't handle these guys. Schwartzy, you got anything to add?"

Schwartz reached down and plucked an index card out of his shin-guard knee-flap. "Schiller," he said. " 'Man only plays when in the full meaning of the word he is a man. And he is only completely a man when he plays.'" Schwartz paused and passed his eyes around the huddle slowly, allowing them to settle on each of his teammates' faces, intense but benevolent. Whatever remained of the Harpooners' nervousness burned away like gas when the pilot's lit. "We've done the work. We ran and lifted and puked our guts out. We built this program out of nothing. We made ourselves proud to put on this uniform. We don't have a single goddamn thing left to prove to anyone. We're proven. Today we play." He extended a hand into the center of the huddle. He looked at Henry and smiled. "*Play* on three. Onetwothree —"

"*PLAY!*"

"Kill the douchetards," Owen said.

47

Pella swam six laps, rested on the edge of the pool, swam six more. Chlorine sluiced neatly through her sinuses. Her head felt clear. She used to swim miles at a time, used to have a sleek stomach and slender, powerful arms—but oh well. She hoisted herself from the pool, triceps quivering, and stretched on the deck while she dripped dry. She could feel the lifeguard watching her half surreptitiously from his high perch, ignoring the splashing faculty brats in the shallow end for as long as it took her to cross the slick tile toward the locker room. As she passed his chair she peeled off her bathing cap and shook her hair down over her shoulders. Pride goeth.

She showered and dressed and headed outside, hair still wet, Westish windbreaker zipped to her chin. She'd never been to the baseball diamond but she could see the crowd gathered there in the distance, past the grassy practice fields. A copy of the new Murakami novel, its cover an opulent yellow, poked out of her jacket pocket, bought at the campus bookstore to commemorate her first-ever paycheck.

All over campus the flyers were taped to windows and maples and bulletin boards: WESTISH VS. COSHWALE! SUPPORT THE HARPOONERS! APARICIO RODRIGUEZ! The students who came through the dining-hall serving line lately talked about little else. Pella was going as a conciliatory gesture—she wanted to support Mike, and she wanted him to see her in the stands, supporting him, and to feel a little remorse at the way they'd fought. She certainly wasn't going to watch baseball, which among team sports struck her as singularly boring. It was so slow, so finicky. This one a ball, that one a strike, but they all looked the same. When she was young, her dad had taken her a few times to Fenway Park, and she remembered the trips fondly—the sizzle of onions and peppers on vendors' carts along Lansdowne, the beach balls bounding gaily through the bleachers, the thrilling crush of impossibly tall, squawking women in the foul-smelling bathroom while her dad was forced to wait outside—but those Sunday afternoons weren't really about baseball, for her or for him; they were cultural sallies, like trips to the symphony or the MFA.

"Hey," someone yelled amid a flurry of voices, "watch yourself!" A checkered ball skidded toward Pella, and she realized she was trespassing on an intramural soccer game. "Sorry," she mumbled, mostly to herself. She was about to kick the ball as a kind of apology, but the girl who'd yelled was closing in. *"Move!"* she shrieked, baring her tiny teeth. Pella sidestepped the ball, then the girl, and hurried toward the safety of the orange cones that marked the out-of-bounds. She sighed, feeling glad to have averted catastrophe, then fifty yards later realized she'd dropped her book on the field.

WESTISH 2, VISITOR 0. Hooray, hooray. The field was ringed with people, not as many as at a Red Sox game, but lots—a thousand, maybe more. Pella spotted a few empty seats in the west-facing bleachers, which were otherwise full of people dressed in a fierce beet red. She climbed up to an empty patch of aluminum in the fifth row, her windbreaker catching snotty glances from the people she squeezed past on the way.

She scanned the field for Mike. There he was, sandwiched between the beet-red-clad hitter and the black-clad umpire, squatting on his haunches in the dirt, his face hidden behind a grid of metal bars. The pitcher—the handsome blond guy from Professor Eglantine's class who thought he was God's gift—threw the ball. It looked like a good pitch, then dropped suddenly into the dirt. The batter swung and missed. The

Westish fans cheered. Mike flung himself down to smother the ball. It bounced up and hit him square in the chest. This was fun? No wonder his knees hurt all the time. And with that bat flashing inches from his face.

On the next pitch, the batter, one of the VI ITORS, lofted a fly ball far into the outfield. Pella felt sorry for the poor outfielder as he listed in uncertain circles—who could catch a ball like that, a speck in the shredded clouds?—but at the last moment he lifted his glove, and the ball, improbably, dropped in. Pella jumped to her feet to cheer. Her bleachermates shot her dirty looks.

As the Westish players jogged off the field, Mike flipped up his mask and Pella saw that he'd shaved his beard. He looked as handsome as she'd imagined he would, even with that weird black makeup smeared beneath his eyes, even with his cheeks strafed red with razor burn. He wasn't one of those guys who needed a beard to disguise a weak chin or acne or the fact that he had no lips. He had gorgeous, model-caliber lips, and cheekbones too. But why had he done it *now*? She'd hinted at it a hundred times, made a joke of it, even while trying not to seem to care too much. And he'd just grunted, that famous Mike Schwartz grunt. And then as soon as they stopped seeing each other he went and did it. For the next girl, maybe. Or the new girl.

"We need to start hitting some balls at Skrimshander," said the man sitting behind Pella. "Let him boot a few."

His neighbor chuckled.

"I'm not kidding. Apparently the kid's lost it. You don't read Tom Parsons's blog?"

"We're talking about the shortstop with the streak? The kid all the scouts are after?"

"Not anymore they aren't. According to Tom Parsons the scouts started sniffing around and he started thinking about it. You know what happens when that happens."

"Think yourself out of a job."

"Bingo."

"I bet the kid pulls it together, though. He's the best I've seen in this league. He's like an acrobat out there."

"Care to put your money where your mouth is?"

"Meaning?"

"Hundred says he chucks one in the stands before this game ends."

The second guy thought about it. *Come on, second guy!* Pella silently cheered. *Show that first guy who's boss!* "Guess not," he said at last. "Shame, though. Kid was fun to watch."

Before she knew what she was doing, Pella had whirled toward Guy #1: "You're on."

He looked like you'd expect him to look: an overfed shiny-cheeked guy in a beet-red golf shirt. He clutched his plastic plate of grilled shrimp in his stubby arms and leaned away like she was feral: "I'm what?"

Pella patted the thin sheaf of twenties in her windbreaker pocket. Easy come, easy go. "You're on," she said evenly. "Hundred says Henry won't chuck one in the stands." She held her hand out to shake. It hung there in the air.

Guy #2 grinned and winked at Pella, clapped Guy #1 on the back. "Cat got your tongue, Gary? Sounds like a wager to me."

Gary arranged his pudgy features into something resembling a smirk. "Fine. You're on." His handshake was either naturally effete or a form of condescension to the fact that she was a woman. Pella made a show of wiping her hand on her jacket afterward.

"Good luck to your boyfriend," Guy #2 said, referring to Henry.

Pella flicked her eyes toward Gary. "Good luck to yours." Several people sitting nearby guffawed. Nothing like some casual homophobia to win over a crowd.

As she turned around she glimpsed through the fence, over on the Westish side, that oh-so-familiar head of silver-flecked hair. He was so extravagantly busy all the time, holed up in his office from four a.m. till evening every day, too busy to show up to dinner last night—and yet he had an awful lot of time to spend watching baseball. He'd been out later than Pella, and then up and out the door before she awoke—unless he hadn't come home at all. Who knew what his personal life was like these days? He never spoke of it, and even her gentlest teasings about Genevieve Wister had been met by a colorless silence.

He was sitting in the front row of bleachers behind the home dugout, flanked by a big Nordic guy in a leather jacket and a slender Latino man who, like her father, was dressed in a jacket and tie. Her dad looked dashing as always, he ruled the school, but among their trio it was the Latino man who seemed somehow to be the leader. He had the graceful, upright posture of a monk, shoulders back, hands folded placidly in his lap. When he spoke, the two taller men leaned toward him, straining to hear, and nodded eagerly. Pella imagined him divulging great truths with extreme modesty, and at extremely low volume.

After a few minutes her father excused himself. He stood and stretched and walked along the chain-link fence, shaking hands with parents and students, exchanging pleasantries, in full baby-kissing mode, until he reached the spot where the fence abutted the far end of the dugout. There, leaned against the inside of the fence as if waiting for him, stood Owen Dunne.

Pella felt intensely compelled by whatever was about to occur. Her father slowed his steps, paused, said something. Owen, his eyes on the field, index finger preserving a spot in his book, replied from the side of his mouth. Her dad declined his head and smiled a smile that threatened to bloom into laughter but didn't, quite. They stood and looked out at the field together.

Something happened in the game—a cheer shot through the Westish bleachers while the beet-red people around Pella groaned. Owen broke the tableau with a single sidelong word and disappeared down the dugout steps. Her dad lingered at the fence, as if savoring the spot where Owen once stood, the look on his face a pensive one of puppy-dog love.

Could it be? At first she tried to dismiss the thought—it seemed less an intuition than a flash of insanity. But it wouldn't go away. It wasn't just the look on his face, though that look said all that could be said. It wasn't just the way he and Owen had stood there at the fence, communicating so subtly, alone among a thousand people. It was her dad clambering into the ambulance to accompany Owen to the hospital; his obvious jitters when Owen and Genevieve came for drinks; his obvious indifference to Genevieve thereafter; his emergence from that dormitory last night, with Owen moments behind; the fact that he hadn't been home when she awoke this morning. If you swapped out just one premise — the premise that her dad was straight — it was just too obvious. Of course, that was literally the premise on which her life was based.

A woman in a Westish sweatshirt approached her dad and tapped his elbow. Absently, reluctantly, he left off thinking about Owen and turned to engage the woman. Pella, watching him there on the other side of the diamond, two lengths of fence between them, was awash in anger and fear. Her dad had lied to her, had lied and lied, had caused everything to change. But he was also in danger — he'd forgotten himself, made himself too vulnerable, or else he wouldn't be taking these foolish risks, talking to Owen in public, falling in love. She felt exhausted. She wanted to curl up on the bleachers and go to sleep, but there wasn't any room.

Gary stuck his face over her shoulder, his breath reeking of shrimp and Tabasco. "You lucked out on that one," he said.

48

The throw was high and fluttering higher. Henry wanted it back as soon as it left his hand; even as he finished his follow-through his fingertips grasped after the ball, as if he could bring it back. *Motherfucker.*

It seemed destined to sail over the fence and into the bleachers until Rick O'Shea somehow detached his two-hundred-plus beer-bellied pounds from the earth — it was impressive, how much air that leap put beneath his spikes — and snow-coned the ball with the fringe of his extralong mitt. Rick landed, spun, and slapped a tag on the hustling runner. One out.

Henry lifted two fingers in sheepish gratitude. Rick nodded and winked — *No sweat, little buddy* — and whipped the ball back to Henry to begin the around-the-horn.

Henry spun the ball in his throwing hand. It felt cold and slick and alien. He tucked his glove under his arm and worked the ball over with both hands, trying to knead some life into it. Technically illegal, only pitchers could do that, but the umps weren't going to stop him. A minute ago he'd felt fine, or thought he felt fine, but now the possibility of failure had entered his mind, and the difference between possible failure and inevitable failure felt razor slight. His lungs clenched like he was standing in the lake to his armpits.

Relax, let it go. He'd had one bad throw in him and he'd gotten it out of his system. Rick had saved his butt. They were ahead 2 to 0. He pushed the bad throw aside, steadied his breathing, tossed the ball to Ajay. Turned around and flashed an index finger at Quisp in left: one out. He could see without seeing Aparicio in the stands, his sister, his parents, Coach Hinterberg in the bright-green cap of Lankton High, a private bit of rooting amid all the red and blue. Owen's voice came floating out over the grass: "Henry, you are skilled! We exhort you!"

He pummeled his glove with his fist, dropped into his shallow crouch. Starblind threw a backdoor curve that looked like it caught the corner. The ump called it a ball. "Lookedgoodlookedgoodlooked*real*good!" cheered Henry. Stay up, stay vocal. Don't wither, don't withdraw. "That's your spot, Adam, that's your spot. Won't get robbed again." *The more guys Starblind strikes out, the fewer ground balls get hit to me.* Henry caught himself thinking this and chastised himself, caught himself chastising himself and tried to quiet his mind.

The next hitter rapped a single to center. *At least if it's hit to me now I won't have to throw to first, I can flip to Ajay for the force. If it's hit to Ajay I cover and make the turn. I haven't had trouble making the turn.*

Quiet quiet quiet.

The Coshwale fans were standing, whistling, stomping their feet. Ready to rally. Sweat poured down Starblind's temples as he took the sign from Schwartz. He checked the runner and fired a wicked two-seam fastball that was tailing in. The batter's front foot lifted and Henry knew where the ball was headed before the swing was half finished, a sharp grounder three steps to his left, ideal for a double play. He was there waiting when the ball arrived. Ajay darted over to cover second. Henry, still low in his crouch, pivoted and whipped his arm sidelong across his body, just as he'd practiced so many thousands of times, but at the last moment he sensed the throw would be too hard for Ajay to handle, so he tried to decelerate slightly, but no, that was wrong too, but it was too late, the ball left his hand and began sliding rightward, out into the path of the charging runner, and Ajay, all five-foot-five of him, tried to stretch to make the catch, but the ball caught the tip of his glove and scooted into short right field as the hard-sliding runner took out his legs and sent him flying ass over teakettle. By the time Sooty Kim chased down the ball the runners were coasting into second and third. Ajay lay flat on his back in the dust, groaning. A voice rang out from the Coshwale dugout: "Thanks, Henry!"

GARY STUCK HIS FACE OVER Pella's shoulder again. "We won't count that one."

Her dad had returned to his seat between the blond guy and the self-possessed Latino man. "How could we count it?" Pella said angrily. "It didn't go in the stands."

"Plenty of time for that. It's only the third inning."

AJAY POPPED TO HIS FEET and waved off the trainer. Schwartz called time and moseyed out to the mound, his leisurely pace meant to convey and instill a sense of calm. He motioned for the infielders to join him. "Play back," he instructed. "We'll give up that one run."

Starblind gave a curt caustic chuckle, stared a hole in Henry. "We'll give up more than that, we don't get our shit together."

"Just keep throwing like you're throwing," Schwartz said mildly. "We'll make the plays."

Starblind spat on the ground between them. "Aye aye, Captain."

The next batter struck out. Two down. *Let's just get out of this inning,* Henry thought. *Get back to the dugout, regroup.*

First pitch, fastball. Henry saw, with his usual prescience, where the ball was headed: right at him. Easiest play in the world. He charged and fielded it at sternum height, just at the lip of the infield grass. Rick stretched toward him, offering his huge mitt as a target. The batter was barely a third of the way down the line. Plenty of time. Henry slide-stepped, pumped his arm.

He pumped his arm again, gripped and regripped the ball. By now he was well within the infield grass, not far from the mound. Rick's mitt looked near enough to touch. Still time.

The batter crossed first base. The runner from third crossed home and bent to pick up the jettisoned bat. The runner from second reached third and stopped. Henry turned his palm up and looked at the ball emptily, his mind finally quiet.

He walked toward Starblind, who was standing in front of the mound. Starblind was yelling, his mouth moving, white teeth visible, but Henry couldn't hear him. He handed him the ball. As he walked toward the dugout he kept his gaze angled up at the blue of the sky.

PELLA HAD NEVER HEARD so much silence from so many people. A tear ran down her cheek, pushed forward by the one behind it, and the one behind that, and who knew how many more. She turned and glared at Gary. "You owe me a hundred bucks," she said.

49

The Harpooners in the dugout — Arsch, Loondorf, Jensen, and on down the line — lowered their eyes as he came down the steps. It was eerie, the calm he exuded. The fans had fallen silent. The players on the field stood frozen, dumbfounded, staring into the dugout. The umpires stared too. Coach Cox's jaw worked at his wad of gum. No one knew what to do. It wasn't clear that they could continue without him; it wasn't clear what the other options were.

Henry stopped in front of Izzy, laid a hand on the freshperson's shoulder, waited for Izzy to look up and meet his eyes. "Get loose," he said. "You're going in."

Izzy looked at Coach Cox. Coach Cox, remembering himself, yanked his lineup card from the back pocket of his uniform pants. "Avila!" he barked. "Hustle up, goddamnit!"

Izzy grabbed his glove and trotted up onto the field, blinking at the sunlight.

Henry walked to the far end of the bench, sat down beside Owen. Owen closed his book and laid it in his lap, but he couldn't find anything to say. Henry pried off his left cleat and then his right, knotted the laces lightly together, looped them around the strap of his bag. He slid his plastic sandals on over his sanitary socks.

Coach Cox conferred with the umpires while Izzy bounced around, windmilling his arms, trying to get loose. The way he shimmied his

shoulders; the erect, almost princely carriage of his head and shoulders —
it was uncanny. It seemed like some kind of tribute. Rick tossed him a
warm-up grounder that he gobbled up with lazy grace.

Henry unbuttoned his jersey and folded it neatly into quarters, so
that the Harpooner on the left breast faced upward. As always, he was
wearing his faded-to-pink Cardinals T-shirt underneath. He laid the
jersey in his bag, placed his glove gingerly on top, zipped the bag, and
pushed it underneath the bench between his feet. He sat back, hands on
his thighs, and looked out at the field. The game resumed.

50

Affenlight was still seated between the two baseball men.

"Blass," Dwight Rogner said, breaking a long and awful silence. "Sasser. Wohlers. Knoblauch. Sax."

"I played against Mr. Sax for years." Aparicio's voice was always soft, so you had to lean in to listen, but even more so now. "A good man, though of dubious politics."

"Chuck Knoblauch and I were teammates. His only full year in the minors — one of my ten."

Aparicio nodded.

"And then Rick Ankiel, of course, for our organization."

Affenlight didn't know the names. They proceeded from Dwight's tongue with respectful reluctance, like a litany of friends killed in war.

"They call it Steve Blass Disease," Dwight explained to Affenlight. "After the first player it happened to. A pitcher for the Pirates. That was a little before my time."

"Those were the Pittsburgh teams of Clemente," said Aparicio. "They won the Series in seventy-one. Clemente was named Most Valuable Player, but the honor could easily have gone to Mr. Blass. He had an exceptional ability to control the baseball.

"A year later, on New Year's Eve, Clemente was killed in a plane crash while delivering aid to Nicaragua. When spring training began, Mr. Blass could no longer do what he'd always done. It happened very suddenly. Walks, wild pitches. One year later, only two years removed from the height of his career, he decided to retire."

"You think this was related to Clemente's death?" Affenlight asked.

Aparicio touched his chin. "I suggested as much by the way I told the story, didn't I? But in truth I have no idea. Clemente's death affected *me* deeply, and I never met him. But I was a child, a child from that part of the world. Clemente was a hero to us. Teammates are not inevitably so interested in one another."

The Coshwale batter laid down a bunt. Rick O'Shea, remarkably spry for his size, charged and fielded it neatly, but his throw to third sailed wide, and the left fielder failed to back up the play. Two more runs scored. It was now 5 to 2 in favor of the VI ITORS.

"Your pitcher is throwing his heart out," Dwight said, as Adam Starblind banged his glove on his thigh in disgust. "Talented guy too. But the rest of the team looks done for."

They were sitting directly behind the Westish dugout, so that they couldn't see Henry inside. "Do they ever recover?" Affenlight asked. "The players with this disease?"

"Steve Sax did. Of the big names, he might be the only one. Knoblauch moved from second to the outfield, where the longer throw gave him less trouble. Ankiel moved to the outfield too."

"But a longer throw is harder," Affenlight pointed out.

Dwight shrugged. "Sometimes harder is easier."

It comforted Affenlight to have this conversation, to try to wrap his mind around what had happened to Henry, to try to contextualize it, but Aparicio's eyes were quietly trained on the field, even the eager and garrulous Dwight seemed reluctant to say much, and it seemed clear that to discuss such matters at length, in such proximity to someone to whom it was actually happening, violated one of baseball's codes. He decided to risk one last question.

"Did it really never happen before that? Before seventy-three?"

Aparicio breathed in and out—a kind of ethereal idea of a shrug. He waited a very long time before answering, as if registering a dignified protest against the demand Affenlight had placed on him. "How many times does something happen before we give it a name? And until the name exists, neither does the condition. So perhaps it happened many times before but was never named.

"And yet. Baseball has many historians, including among its players. There are statistics, archives, legends, lore. If earlier players had experienced similar troubles, it seems likely the stories would have been passed down. And then the name would be applied in retrospect."

Nineteen seventy-three. In the public imagination it was as fraught a year as you could name: Watergate, *Roe v. Wade,* withdrawal from Vietnam. *Gravity's Rainbow.* Was it also the year that Prufrockian paralysis went mainstream—the year it entered baseball? It made sense that a psychic condition sensed by the artists of one generation—the Modernists of the First World War—would take a while to reveal itself throughout the population. And if that psychic condition happened to be a profound failure of confidence in the significance of individual human action, then the condition became an epidemic when it entered the realm of utmost confidence in same: the realm of professional sport. In fact, that might make for a workable definition of the postmodernist era: an era when even the athletes were anguished Modernists. In which case the American postmodern period began in spring 1973, when a pitcher named Steve Blass lost his aim.

Do I dare, and do I dare?

Affenlight found this hypothesis exciting, if dubiously constructed. Then he glanced at Aparicio, hands folded mournfully in his lap, and his excitement curdled to embarrassment. Literature could turn you into an asshole; he'd learned that teaching grad-school seminars. It could teach you to treat real people the way you did characters, as instruments of your own intellectual pleasure, cadavers on which to practice your critical faculties.

"Doubt has always existed," Aparicio said. "Even for athletes."

51

The Harpooners lost 10 to 2. Between games, no one mentioned the ceremony that had been planned and advertised in Henry's honor. Instead the Westish players headed down to their usual spot near the right-field foul pole, where they spread out on the grass and listlessly munched the sandwiches that had been delivered from the dining hall. It had become a gorgeous, sun-kissed afternoon. There were even a few ambitious tanners laid out on the practice fields in bikinis. Henry, marked out from his teammates by his faded red T-shirt, lay on his back with his eyes closed, inviting them to carry on without him. Starblind stewed bitterly, muttering to himself and glaring at his bare right arm as he rubbed Tiger Balm into it. Nobody else broke the funereal mood, or even glanced at the spot behind home plate where Aparicio was signing autographs.

Henry tapped Izzy on the knee. "Play their three hitter toward the hole a little more. You could've had that last ball he hit."

Izzy nodded.

"Especially with Sal pitching. Compared to Adam, play everybody a step to pull against Sal. Unless he has his changeup working. Then you have to watch Mike's signs and play it more by feel."

Izzy looked down at his yogurt.

"*Comprende?*" Henry said.

Izzy nodded. "*Comprende,* Henry."

Henry hauled himself to his feet and walked over to the fence, where a skinny, coltish girl with long wavy sandy hair was waiting for him. As he approached she poked her index finger through the fence. After a moment Henry touched it with his own.

"Who's that?" asked Starblind.

"I think it's Skrim's sister." Rick looked to Owen. "Buddha?"

Owen nodded.

"Huh," Adam said. "Not bad."

52

Izzy scored the winning run in the second game of the doubleheader when, with the score tied 6 all in the bottom of the tenth, Schwartz hammered a double into the left-field corner. The Harpooners poured out of the dugout to greet Izzy as he crossed home plate, trading fist bumps and man hugs and muted words of praise. The split left them one game behind Coshwale in the UMSCAC standings, with another double-header tomorrow at the Muskies' home diamond. "Tomorrow," someone said, and it became a refrain to nod to and repeat.

"Tomorrow."

"*Tomorrow.*"

Back in the locker room, they set about their private postgame rituals, stretching and heating and icing, showering and shaving and scraping off eye black, slathering on the stinging menthols of Icy Hot, Tiger Balm, Fire Cool, detonating sneezy white puffs of foot powder, baby powder, fungus powder, crotch powder. Schwartz headed into the whirlpool room to soak. He turned off the lights, lowered himself into the rattling tub, and tried not to think about baseball for a few minutes, tried not to think about Henry, while the salts and churning water did their inadequate work on his body. He'd spotted Pella in the stands today—she hadn't hopped a plane back to San Francisco with The Architect. It had been sweet to see her navy windbreaker amid all that ugly red.

When he returned to the locker room it was empty. His back hurt as much as it ever had. It took two minutes to put his underwear on. He popped a handful of Advil — he was fresh out of anything better — and finished dressing as quickly as he could.

By the time he emerged onto the broad stone steps of the VAC the sun had set, and the evening had turned spring cool. Through the semi-darkness he could see someone wandering the parking lot in mothlike circles — she stopped and looked up as the wooden doors creaked shut. "Sophie," he said.

"Mike?"

She trotted over, backpack bouncing on her shoulder, and gave him a commiserative hug. Schwartz felt like he knew her well, though they'd only met once. She looked distinctly like her brother — same slender neck and elegant posture, same soft features and pale-blue eyes. She looked older than the girl in the faded photo above Henry's desk, more nearly adult, but also as skinny and credulous as Henry had been when he arrived at Westish. The Skrimshanders were late bloomers. "Where's Henry?" she asked.

"Probably at Carapelli's, with the rest of the team. I'm late to meet them."

"I *saw* the rest of the team," Sophie protested. "Henry wasn't with them. I figured you two were together."

Goddamnit. Schwartz reached for his phone — his first impulse was to call Owen, but he didn't want Sophie to know that he didn't know where Henry was. Instead he tapped out a text: *is H w u?* "Your brother likes to use the fire door," he lied. "One of his rituals. Where are your folks?"

Sophie rolled her eyes. "My mom dragged my dad back to the hotel to keep him from yelling at Henry. He's, like, half a second away from an aneurysm." She deepened her voice to a growl. *"Kid just quit. Quit on his team. Deserves what he gets."*

"He'll cool off."

"Someday. Anyway we're all in one room. I'm keeping away from there."

Schwartz wasn't sure what to do. He could take Sophie to Carapelli's for dinner with the team, she could meet Aparicio Rodriguez, nobody would object — but he was already beginning to understand that Henry might not be there. That he might be gone. Whatever *gone* could mean, on this little campus.

His phone trilled in his hand. He assumed it would be Owen, but the caller ID showed his own home number.

"Hello?"

"Hey," said Pella. "Where are you?"

"In front of the VAC."

"In your favorite towel?"

It took Schwartz a few beats to remember what she was talking about.

"I really need to talk to you. Will you be back soon?"

"I have to go to team dinner. I'll be back around ten."

"Could I come meet you? I'm sorry, Mike. I know you've had a rough day. I just really need your advice. It's about my dad."

"I'm sorry," he said. "I'll be home by ten."

Pella sighed. "Okay. Is it okay if I wait here?"

Sophie had wandered a few yards away and was sitting on the bottom step, staring at the tapping toes of her laceless sneakers. Schwartz couldn't send her back to her parents, couldn't take her with him, couldn't leave her here. He was about to hang up the phone when an idea struck him.

"You want me to what?" Pella said plaintively.

"You heard me."

"You're kidding. Mike, it's been a really weird day."

Schwartz wasn't kidding. "Go get dressed," he told Sophie as he hung up the phone. "Pella's going to meet you here in half an hour." He pressed two of Coach Cox's C-notes into her palm. "Tell her you want to go to Maison Robert."

53

After dinner Schwartz and Owen searched the library and the union—nothing else was open on Saturday night—and found no sign of Henry. Nor was he in the room, nor with his parents; Henry's mom had called Owen's cell in search of him, and Owen told her that Henry had gone for a walk.

They went to the VAC and scoured the building from the bottom floor up, turning on all the lights as they went, and then from the top floor down, turning them off again. Schwartz locked the door as they left. A delicate frigid breeze blew due west off the water. "I don't like this," Schwartz said. "I don't like this at all."

"Henry's an adult," Owen said. "Or close enough. He probably just wants to be alone right now."

"He's not *allowed* to be alone right now. Not without telling us where he is." Schwartz held his watch up into the cool blue glow of a security lamp. "Bus to Coshwale leaves in eight hours."

"Maybe we should return to the scene of the crime."

They checked Westish Field, and then the big stone bowl of the football stadium. Nothing. There weren't many electric lights nearby, and the moon that hung between banks of clouds was as slender as an eyelash. Schwartz had never experienced this kind of darkness before enrolling at Westish; in his first days on campus he'd been afraid to fall asleep, as if the night and the quiet might swallow him whole. Now he wondered whether he could ever live in a city again.

"I don't suppose he's out drowning his sorrows," Owen said.

Henry never went to the bars unless he was forced to, like on a teammate's birthday or the Harpooners' annual Freshperson Initiation Night. But Schwartz and Owen found their steps tending toward Bartleby's anyway. Westish was only so big, and there were only so many places to try.

It was prime drinking time for all non–baseball players: midnight on a Saturday in early May, with finals still two weeks away. The line to get into Bartleby's snaked through the amusement-park ropes and continued down the block. Girls shivered in flimsy dresses, huddling together two to a thin black jacket. Guys jammed their hands in their pockets and tried not to look cold.

Schwartz unclipped the rope from its ball-topped metal pole and moved to the head of the line, Owen behind him. One of the young Harpooner linebackers perched on a tall wooden stool beside the door, toying with his clickable crowd counter. Schwartz gave him a friendly whack on the chest. "Lopez. I figured you'd have dropped out by now."

Lopez shrugged. "Not yet."

Schwartz peered into the tinted glass door. "Pretty packed in there."

"Stuffed," said Lopez. "I'm not even letting girls in right now."

"You seen the Skrimmer at all?"

"Henry? Here?" Lopez squinted and scratched at his chin as if he were being forced to consider some complex riddle. "Guess not. Adam's inside, though."

"Starblind? What's he doing here? We've got games tomorrow."

Lopez shrugged. "Got me. He's with some chick."

"Great," said Schwartz. "Outstanding." Seven hours till the bus departed for the biggest and—if they lost, which they wouldn't—the last games of his Westish career. Not only was he not asleep, not only was he out of meds and pissed about it, not only could he feel every beat of his pulse in his half-destroyed knees, not only was his best player despondent and AWOL, but his second-best player was breaking curfew to chase tail. "Mind if we take a peek?"

Lopez leaned into the glass door with a fleshy forearm, letting them bypass the line and the two-dollar cover. Bartleby's was full of bodies and flashing lights. Neon cursive signs glared down from the walls, advertising the old local beers—Schlitz, Blatz, Hamm's, Pabst, Huber, Old Style—that were now owned by a Southern tobacco conglomerate. NBA playoff games on the TVs, crappy hip-hop on the jukebox, two beefy townies aiming plastic guns at the console of Big Buck Hunter IV. Owen leaned forward to yell in Schwartz's ear.

"What?" Schwartz yelled back.

"I said, I'm standing in beer."

"We're all standing in beer."

"But why? It's disgusting."

It was too loud to explain heterosexual courtship to Owen, even if he'd wanted to, so Schwartz kept pushing through the crowd, peering out over the baseball caps and the glossy hair of girls, unable to stop looking for Henry even though there was no way Henry would be here. God, that beer smelled good. He tried not to drink before games, but in the absence of Vikes—he'd run out this morning—a few beers were a near necessity.

Owen tapped him on the shoulder. "I see Adam."

"Where?"

"End of the bar."

His face was obscured by the abundant wheat-colored hair of the girl he was kissing, but the shimmering silver jacket was unmistakably Starblind's. When the kiss was finished he plucked a lime rind from his mouth, dropped it in a squat glass, and held up two fingers to signal the bartender for another round. The girl draped one arm around his neck, her head resting against his shoulder in drunken worship.

"Oh my," said Owen.

Schwartz elbowed his way through the heaving, half-dancing crowd, fists clenching and unclenching in a slow alternating rhythm. The bartender poured out two more shots of tequila. Sophie stood up, gathered her hair in a two-handed sheaf, and presented her neck to Starblind, who licked it slowly, then picked a salt shaker off the bar and sprinkled some whiteness on Sophie's wetted skin. Sophie took a wedge of lime from the bartenders' condiment bins and placed it between her teeth, pulp side out. She closed her eyes and tipped her head back. Starblind leaned in, licked the salt from her neck in a leisurely, lizardly way, and with a surreptitious flick of his wrist as he moved in for the kiss tossed a strobe-lit shot of tequila over his shoulder and down the front of Schwartz's shirt.

"Hi guys," Schwartz said.

Starblind blanched. "Mikey-o!" Sophie crowed, flinging her arms around Schwartz's neck and swooning in to peck his cheek. She had the same fish-belly complexion as her brother, minus the windburned tan that came from spending winter mornings running stadiums, plus the mottled tequila flush that spread from her cheeks to the neckline of her butter-colored sundress. "Owen-o!" she cheered, doling out another hug.

The Buddha smiled the sort of untroubled smile that had earned him his nickname. "Hello, my dear. Having fun?"

"*Yes.* Where's my brother? I need to find my brother. Let's all do a shot."

"We were hoping you guys had seen him," Schwartz said. "Where's Pella?"

"Pella," said Sophie, "is *beautiful.*"

"I agree. Buddha, would you order Sophie a cup of coffee? I need to confer with Adam for a moment."

"Aye aye, Captain." Owen wrapped a slender arm around Sophie's shoulders and led her away, gesticulating with his other hand as he embarked on some complicated story. Sophie nodded hypnotically, her brow furrowed to show that, no matter how drunk, she was smart enough to keep up with whatever Owen was saying. Good old Buddha.

Schwartz looked at Starblind, to whose cheeks the color had mostly returned, though the arctic Starblind smile was nowhere to be found. "Where's Pella?"

Starblind shrugged sullenly. "I bumped into them on the street. Pella said she wasn't feeling well."

"She left you in charge of Sophie?" Schwartz could get only so pissed at Starblind; Starblind was Starblind the way a dog was a dog and a shark was a shark. You didn't expect moral distinctions from a shark. But Pella — what could she have been thinking, handing Henry's sister over to a shark? Why, why, why? How irresponsible could she be? He trusted her, wanted to trust her, wanted to hold her to the same standard he held himself. And then she pulled something like this. "Team curfew is midnight," he said.

"I could say the same to you."

Schwartz stared him down in a way that emphasized his height advantage. "I don't recommend it."

"I wasn't drinking," Starblind said. "If that's what you're thinking. Just showing Sophie around."

"She's Henry's sister."

"So what? You never hooked up with anybody's sister?"

"She's seventeen."

Starblind shrugged. "She told me eighteen. Anyway, Skrim owes me one. Little bastard cost me a win today."

Schwartz picked up Starblind the way you pick a baby out of a bathtub, under the armpits, holding it at arm's length so it won't drip on your shirt, though Schwartz's shirt was already wet with tossed tequila. Starblind's feet kicked and flailed. Schwartz jacked him up against the side of the Buck Hunter machine. The machine rocked and shuddered. The two beefy townies turned to register their displeasure but stopped when they saw the warning ire in Schwartz's eyes.

Schwartz fired his left forearm into Starblind's collarbone to pin him to the machine. Starblind's head snapped back and cracked against the plastic. The pain made Starblind angry, and being angry made him smile. One thing about Starblind was he wouldn't back down. "Fuck's wrong with you?" he said. "You've been getting sucked off by Henry for years. I just wanted a little Skrimshander love."

Schwartz slid his forearm up from Starblind's chest into his Adam's apple. Starblind, coughing, twisted his head to the side to try to breathe. He brought up a knee into Schwartz's balls — a glancing blow but a blow nonetheless. Schwartz crumpled, straightened, drove the palm of his hand into Starblind's forehead, cracking his head on the plastic again. Starblind's eyes rolled. He squirmed and twisted, freed one hand well enough to take a few wild swings.

Even in the haze of his rage Schwartz could tell that awareness of a fight was spreading through the packed noisy bar. He had to finish this before some cop he didn't know showed up and there was hell to pay. He felt like killing Starblind but instead he cocked his fist and drove it low, as hard as he could, into Starblind's solar plexus, where no one would have to know, and where the pain wouldn't keep him from playing tomorrow. The breath whooshed from Starblind's body as he slid down the side of the machine to the beer-slick floor. He looked up at Schwartz and sneezed pathetically.

"Hey," Sophie protested as Schwartz lifted her drink-leaden arm, looped it around his neck, and steered her toward the exit. "I thought we were doing shots. Where's Henry? Where's Adam?" She leaned in to confide in Schwartz's ear. "He's *hot*. I mean like seriously."

"He's a dreamboat." Owen held the front door, Lopez saluted, and they passed out into the night.

"My car's down the block," said Schwartz. "This way."

Before they even reached the Buick, Schwartz's phone began to ring. Or more likely it had been ringing all along, but he hadn't noticed amid the din of Bartleby's. He glanced at the caller name: HOME.

"Hey."

"Hey," said Pella. "Any luck?"

"We found a Skrimshander. But not the one we were looking for."

"What do you mean?"

"I mean Sophie. Remember Sophie? Sweet kid you were supposed to watch out for? She was at Bartleby's, totally ripped, with Starblind sucking on her face. So I dropped him, which I maybe shouldn't have done, but hey." Schwartz, riled afresh, banged a paw on the hood of the Buick. "What'd you do, get her drunk and raffle her off to the shadiest guy you could find? What were you thinking? Where *are* you?"

"I'm at your house."

"I know where you are!" Schwartz yelled. "Why aren't you with Sophie? Why do I have to babysit the whole goddamn school? Why can't I just worry about what I have to worry about?" His voice carried down the windswept street. A gaggle of sophomore girls wavered by in their heels, en route from Bartleby's to some house party. No two of their tube tops or flouncy miniskirts were precisely alike, in cut or in color, and these slight variations made the outfits look all the more carefully orchestrated as they linked arms and passed by, pretending not to listen. Schwartz tried to comfort himself with a long look at their ten slender thighs turned pink by the cold, the good odds that he'd been between four or six of those thighs on oblivious drunken nights, but it was useless, the girls looked absurd to him now, and it no longer seemed that the universe contained an endless supply of anonymous pink thighs to which he could escape from his troubles. Pella would never dress like that.

"Sorry," Pella said, sounding more sullen than sorry. "After dinner we bumped into Adam, and I asked where the hotel was, and he said he was headed that way, he'd walk Sophie back. And why wouldn't I believe him? And then I came to your place to see you." She paused and, when Schwartz didn't fill the void with yelling, ventured a change of subject. "Still no word from Henry?"

"Nope."

"Now what?"

"I don't know," Schwartz said. "First I have to put Sophie somewhere. I can't take her back to her parents like this."

"Do they know Henry's still missing?"

"I'm going to call them now. I'm going to tell them both their children are sleeping sweetly."

"Okay." Pella sighed that wounded-kitten sigh into the phone again. "Mike, I know it's not a good time, but I really need to talk to you. It's about my dad."

"I'll be there," Schwartz said. "Just hang tight."

By the time he phoned the Skrimshanders and climbed behind the wheel of the Buick, Sophie was curled up asleep on the queen-size backseat, site of most of Schwartz's high school conquests. Her knees were drawn close to her chest, sunlight-white calves flashing out beneath the hem of her rumpled dress. If she wasn't sucking her thumb, she at least had her thumbnail hooked thoughtfully between her teeth. Drunk and asleep, her face drained of its teenage-girl defiance and willful sophistication, she looked even more like her brother. Schwartz fired the engine as softly as possible, tried to get into gear without creating the usual impression of the undercarriage dropping out, and nosed away from the curb.

"I'm worried," he said.

Owen nodded. They idled down Groome Street, Schwartz's foot never touching the gas, silently scanning the bushes like a couple of cops who've been partners forever.

"We'll take Sophie back to your room, if that's okay."

"Sure."

Schwartz parked in the service bay of the dining hall. Sophie showed no signs of waking as he scooped her weightless bird body into his arms and carried her across the Small Quad, the heels of her laced-up sandals banging gently against his thigh. The front door of Phumber Hall was propped open by a crate of art-history books, causing the swipe-card box to twinkle an inviting green. The hip-hop anthem of the moment blared from a ground-floor window, accompanied by a chorus of blurred and delirious voices. The song faded out and immediately began again, the bass line kicking in.

"Beer?" Owen offered.

"I don't see why not."

Owen ducked into the party and returned with two bright-blue plastic cups topped by foam. "Naked," he reported.

"Girls too?"

"Everyone."

Owen carried the beer upstairs. Schwartz followed with Sophie. The unspoken hope was that Henry would be there, lying in bed reading back issues of *Sports Illustrated*. Whereupon Schwartz would lace into him like never before—he'd been scripting the tongue-lashing in his mind all night, phrase by delectable phrase—and everything would be fine. But the room was dark and empty. All the anger leaked from Schwartz's body, taking what remained of energy and hope along with it. He lay Sophie down on Henry's unmade bed, covered her with a quilt, and folded back its bottom edge so that he could unlace her complicated sandals and set them by the door. Owen handed him a warm, overly frothy beer, which he accepted wordlessly and drank in one long slow gulp. The ten blocks back to Grant Street, where Pella was, might as well have been a thousand miles. He lay flat on his back on the blood-colored rug and dreamed about God-knows-what.

54

After the game ended, Henry briefly joined his teammates' celebration at home plate. Meanwhile he kept one eye on the first-base bleachers, where Aparicio was signing an autograph for Sal's little brother. He, Aparicio, who might soon become the president of Venezuela, was wearing a coat and tie, had come all the way from St. Louis, had put on a coat and tie to watch Henry humiliate himself once and for all. He looked just as Henry had imagined, as trim and fit as during his playing days, his neck long and regal, his skin almond brown, his shoulders no wider than Henry's own. Dwight Rogner stood nearby, speaking into his cell phone, and Henry didn't need lip-reading skills to know what he was saying: "Forget the Skrimshander kid."

Henry grabbed his bag and slipped into the crowd, ostensibly to shake the hand of President Affenlight, who was standing there alone, and who gave him the sort of commiserative look he'd need to spend the rest of his life avoiding. When President Affenlight looked away, Henry scuttled around the backstop and safely traversed the no-man's-land between Westish Field and the football stadium. There, in the shadow of an arch, amid the cool, sweet smells of moss and rot, he sat and cried.

Afterward he felt much worse. What at the diamond had been a sharp adrenal anxiety, fueled by purpose—*Get me out of here, away from everyone*—was settling into a flat, sullen expanse of awfulness. A moment would come, and then another, and then another. These moments would be his life.

He opened the crate where he stored the weighted vest he wore to run stadiums, put it on over his Cards shirt, buckled the straps over his sternum. The game had ended near dusk, and now it was dark. He cinched the straps tighter until the vest dug into his chest.

He left the stadium and walked eastward across the practice fields toward the lake. The wind came straight off the water, stiff and chill. He scrambled down the little scree-clotted slope to the beach, clutching at scraggly bushes for balance, and started north along the water's edge.

Where the beach ended a path began, cutting through thatchy rain-flattened grasses humming with insects. After two miles the path ended in a kind of meadow, mowed by the county during the summer months, out of which the lighthouse rose. On his usual weight-vested jog, Henry circled the lighthouse, slapping the repoussé letters of the plaque the Historical Society had fixed into the stucco, before returning the way he came. Farther north lay only a high razor-wire fence that ran from the water's edge all the way back to the highway, however far west. On the other side of the fence was a privately owned forest. On the other side of the forest lay the next town north. Henry didn't know the town's name; he'd never been there.

The lighthouse was a tall white tapering cylinder, no longer in use but kept in good repair. Paintings and photographs of it hung in every shop and restaurant in Westish. The wide-planked doors sat back in an alcove. He pulled at the arrow-shaped iron handles, but the place was locked tight. He dropped his bag in the alcove and waded out into the chilly water.

Just as the slow rolling waves touched his chin he reached a sandbar that exposed him to his hips again. The wind bit through his wet shirt and flak jacket. His teeth chattered loudly. The water, though freezing, felt more comforting than the wind. He sank to dunk his head. His Cards cap stayed on the surface when he went under, as if refusing to participate in whatever asinine shit he was getting into; the waves carried it beyond arm's reach, into the darkness. He leveled his body to the water and began to swim.

The first dozen strokes felt hard, almost impossible, because of the drag of the vest. But once he'd reached a good speed the vest didn't hamper him much. He swam past the first buoy, past the second buoy. The campus lights receded behind him. He kept swimming.

When he'd gone what felt like halfway across the lake he slowed to a paddle, his chin atop the dark water, atop of which was dark air. All he could see were stars. There were no gulls out here and nothing to listen to. It seemed possible no one had ever swum to this spot before, so far from shore. Or maybe hundreds or thousands of years ago people did it all the time. Maybe that was their sport. The water seemed to groan beneath the weight of itself, the weight of other water.

He turned around to face the campus, those few little lights pricking the distance. He let his bladder go, peed into the water. It calmed his whole body, if only for a moment.

All he'd ever wanted was for nothing to ever change. Or for things to change only in the right ways, improving little by little, day by day, forever. It sounded crazy when you said it like that, but that was what baseball had promised him, what Westish College had promised him, what Schwartzy had promised him. The dream of every day the same. Every day was like the day before but a little better. You ran the stadium a little faster. You bench-pressed a little more. You hit the ball a little harder in the cage; you watched the tape with Schwartzy afterward and gained a little insight into your swing. Your swing grew a little simpler. Everything grew simpler, little by little. You ate the same food, woke up at the same time, wore the same clothes. Hitches, bad habits, useless thoughts—whatever you didn't need slowly fell away. Whatever was simple and useful remained. You improved little by little till the day it all became perfect and stayed that way. Forever.

He knew it sounded crazy when you put it like that. To want to be perfect. To want everything to be perfect. But now it felt like that was all he'd ever craved since he'd been born. Maybe it wasn't even baseball that he loved but only this idea of perfection, a perfectly simple life in which every move had meaning, and baseball was just the medium through which he could make that happen. Could have made that happen. It sounded crazy, sure. But what did it mean if your deepest hope, the premise on which you'd based your whole life, sounded crazy as soon as you put it in words? It meant you were crazy.

When the season ended, his teammates, even Schwartzy, gorged themselves on whatever was handy — cigarettes, beer, coffee, sleep, porn, video games, girls, dessert, books. It didn't matter what they gorged on as long as they were gorging. Gorging didn't make them feel good, you'd see them wandering around, dazed and bleary, but they were free to gorge and that was what mattered.

Henry knew better than to want freedom. The only life worth living was the unfree life, the life Schwartz had taught him, the life in which you were chained to your one true wish, the wish to be simple and perfect. Then the days were sky-blue spaces you moved through with ease. You made sacrifices and the sacrifices made sense. You ate till you were full and then you drank SuperBoost, because every ounce of muscle meant something. You stoked the furnace, fed the machine. No matter how hard you worked, you could never feel harried or hurried, because you were doing what you wanted and so one moment simply produced the next. He'd never understood how his teammates could show up late for practice, or close enough to late that they had to hurry to change clothes. In three years at Westish he'd never changed clothes in a hurry.

He treaded water for a long long while, feeling an endless spontaneous power unspooling from his limbs. It seemed he could do it forever. Finally he turned toward the shore and let his limbs swim him in, aided by the waves that lapped at his back. When he reached the shore he knelt on all fours and slurped at the funky algal water like an animal. He couldn't see the lighthouse, and he wasn't sure whether it lay to the north or the south. His body gave out all at once. His teeth were chattering, really clacking away. His shoulders convulsed, his lungs heaved. He had his whole life ahead of him; it wasn't a comforting thought. He peeled off his wet clothes, nestled into the sand as deeply as he could, and fell asleep.

55

He awoke with the birds before the sun could breast the water. The low clouds made the dawn all the more beautiful, catching and spreading the soft colors across the sky. He watched it dumbly, his body shaking. Sometime in elementary school his class had read Anne Frank's diary, and Henry, terribly alarmed, asked why Anne hadn't simply pretended not to be Jewish. The way Peter escaped from the Romans by pretending not to be Christian. Peter got in trouble for that in the Bible, but if you put it in the context of poor Anne, who was not only real but also a kid, didn't it make sense? What difference did it make what religion you were if you were dead? So said a very alarmed Henry, in what remained the most passionate and probably the longest speech of his academic career.

His teacher said that St. Peter *was* a real person, first of all, and in any case being Jewish wasn't something you could put on and take off like a sweater. This ended the discussion, but it didn't satisfy Henry. He didn't see how a religion, which was a freely chosen thing, could mark people so irreparably.

It wasn't clear why he'd woken up thinking about that—the remnant of some bad dream, no doubt. If it meant anything, it seemed to mean that he was who he was and there was nowhere to go but back to Phumber Hall. The bus would be leaving for Coshwale soon. He could go to his room, take the phone off the hook, and sleep. Coach Cox would suspend him from the team, but that didn't matter because Schwartzy was going to kill him, and that didn't matter either because Henry was tired and he deserved it.

Now that it was nearly light he could see that during his swim he'd drifted a hundred yards south of the lighthouse. He bent down, scooped up a handful of greenish water, tasted it, spat it out. Then he trudged back to the lighthouse, collected his bag, and departed. The two miles to campus seemed like twenty. He was barefoot, having lost his plastic sandals in the lake. Every rock or root that forced him to lift his heels felt like a hardship. He hadn't eaten since Thursday, not that he wanted to eat.

When he got home, he unplugged the blinking answering machine, poured himself a glass of water, and went to sleep.

He was awakened in full daylight by a frantic drumming on the door. He pulled the covers over his head — *This too shall pass* — but the drumming didn't stop, and a female voice yelled his name as an angry question. He stumbled to the door in his boxer shorts, fumbled with the knob. There stood Pella Affenlight. "Henry," she said. "You look terrible."

You don't look so good yourself, Henry thought, and she did look bleary, like she'd been up all night, but that wasn't the sort of thing you said to people.

"Sorry, I didn't mean it like that. Mike's furious, you know. He's been calling me every ten minutes, not to talk to me, of course, but hey … let's see. What am I supposed to tell you? His keys are in his car and his car's at the VAC. Pump the gas if the engine won't turn over. What else? Oh yeah. Directions to wherever you're supposed to be right now, on the front seat."

Henry nodded. "Thanks."

"Oh, many welcomes. What else would I do with my Sunday morning? Messenger to the stars." She looked down at Henry's feet, which were still pruned and past white. "Sorry about the game. That was rough luck."

"Luck," Henry repeated.

"I guess *luck*'s the wrong word. Anyway, I just...if you ever want to talk, I'm around."

"Thanks."

"You're fairly monosyllabic, you know that?"

"Sorry."

"That's better."

Henry expected her to leave, but instead she just stood there fooling with her sweatshirt strings, alternately looking down at his feet and past him into the room. He tried to come up with something polite and polysyllabic to say. "Would you like some tea?"

Pella shrugged. "You're probably in a hurry. Directions on the seat and all that."

"I'm not going anywhere."

"Oh. Well. In that case. Sure. I'll have tea."

Henry had never made tea before; that was Owen's department. He tried to arrest the electric kettle at the proper gurgle, and he tried to add the right amount of English Breakfast to the porcelain pot, not that he knew what the right amount would be. Pella stood in the middle of the rug and looked around. "This place is pretty nice," she said. "For a dorm room."

"It's mostly Owen's stuff."

"Did Owen paint this?" She pointed to the green-and-white painting that hung over Henry's bed, the one Henry liked because it resembled a smeary baseball diamond.

"When I first moved in I asked Owen that same question, and he said, 'Sort of, but I stole it from Rothko.' I thought Rothko was like Shopko—that he'd really stolen it, from a store. I was amazed, because it's so big. How would you steal it? Then I took Art 105."

Pella laughed. Henry regretted the anecdote, which made him seem dumb. The effort required to speak was immense, like hauling stones up out of a well, but he'd decided to try his best. At least she seemed cheered up a little.

"You really like it here," she said, "don't you?"

"What do you mean?"

"I mean, all of you guys—you, Mike, my dad. Maybe Owen too, though I don't really know Owen. You all just seem to love it here. Like you never want to leave. Part of me suspects that Mike didn't *want* to get into law school, that he sabotaged himself in some subconscious way, so that he has no reason to leave this place, the only place he ever felt happy. I mean, why'd he only apply to six schools? The six best schools in the country? It makes no sense."

"He's graduating either way," Henry pointed out. "He can't stay here."

"He can't stay but he can't leave, not without a destination. And, well, maybe it's the same for you. Maybe you're just not ready."

Henry looked at her.

"Sorry," Pella said.

"Everybody else thinks I wanted to go pro too much. You think I didn't want it at all."

"What do *you* think?"

"I think you should all go fuck yourselves."

Pella grinned. "That's the first step to recovery." She walked over to the mantel, where a baseball, Owen's lone bottle of scotch, and a slim, leather-bound navy book Henry didn't recognize sat in close proximity. "There's not even any *dust* in this place," she said. She unsheathed the amber bottle from its cardboard cylinder. "May I?"

Henry nodded. Pella poured some into a tumbler, took a sip, rolled it in her mouth appraisingly. "Mm. Not bad." She held it out toward Henry.

Henry took the glass and sipped the light-shot fluid, which perfectly matched the color of Schwartzy's eyes. The taste overwhelmed his sleep-deprived senses; he coughed and spit it out on the rug.

"Hey, don't waste that." Pella arranged herself cross-legged on Owen's bed. She pulled down the navy book—it looked like an old register — and opened it. After a moment she looked up at Henry, her eyes inscrutable. "My dad and Owen are sleeping together."

"Your dad?" Henry said. "President Affenlight?"

Pella handed him the open book. "Top left." It looked like a youthful shot of some now-famous poet or playwright, the kind of thing Owen might frame to fill one of the few empty spots on their walls. Then Henry noticed that the pair of maple trees in the midground looked familiar; and the building behind the tree, if you ignored the pale shade of paint on the front door, could easily be Phumber Hall. And then the facial features of the tall man walking the bicycle coalesced into something familiar too. A torn strip of purple Post-it marked the page.

"Your dad went to school here?"

"Class of seventy-one. So be cheery, my lads and all that jazz."

Henry thought of the time he'd come upstairs carrying two glasses of milk, and President Affenlight was in their room.

"What's that look?" Pella said. "You knew about this?"

"No . . . no."

"But."

"But . . . your dad's been at a lot of our games this year."

Pella nodded. "I told myself it was all in my head. But here's this yearbook, right on cue. And look at you — you're not even surprised. How much proof do I need?"

She took the register from Henry's hands and flopped down on the bed, her head on Owen's pillow. She looked at the photograph for a long time, saying nothing. Beneath the window the quad lay in the soundless trough of a late Sunday morning. No birds, no crickets, no rustle of breeze in the mitt-sized leaves of the maples. When Henry's throw hit Owen in the face, his teammates, the fans, the umps, even the Milford players, fell totally silent, as if their silence might help Owen or undo his injuries. And then again yesterday, when he handed Starblind the ball and walked back to the dugout, there wasn't a sound in the park, not even a *You suck, Henry!* from the Coshwale fans. His teammates couldn't even look at him, pretended to be engrossed in the smashed paper cups and sunflower-seed shells on the dugout floor. Why not say something, something rude or obtuse or irrelevant? If the silence was for his benefit, it wasn't helping. He wanted to scream and wail his way through these false silences, wanted to put an end to them forever. Yet here he was, trapped in another such silence, a tiny two-person silence, and he couldn't even put an end to that.

One stray strand of Pella's wine-colored hair stretched out across the pale-green pillow, like a flattened sine curve or a trail that ants might follow. He reached out and touched it with his fingers, a weird thing to do.

Pella's whole body tensed, then relaxed.

"It's a great photograph," she said. "I'd like a copy for myself."

Henry could see, beneath the loose waist of her jeans, a thin shiny sliver of snow-blue fabric. His fingers wavered a little as they left her hair and traced the soft line of her cheek. She tilted back her chin to see him from the tops of her eyes. "Nervous?"

"No."

"Don't be." She grasped his wrist and guided his hand down the front of her body, toward the icy blue. "Tell me what it felt like, when you were walking off the field."

56

A trace of afternoon light still hung in the sky when Henry awoke. Cold air flooded the room from the wide-open window. His penis hurt, up near the root. He reached down under the blankets and found the lip of a condom digging into his skin. The rolling coastline of Pella's leg and hip lay alongside his own, radiating warmth. He tried to unroll the condom — it had been in his desk drawer for a year, two years, more — but it stuck to him like a Band-Aid. Finally he shut his eyes and ripped it free.

Pella, he realized as he opened his eyes and flicked the spent condom down between his legs, was awake and watching him. And now she probably thought he was playing with himself. He met her eyes, and she smiled a rueful knowing fraction of a smile.

"What do we do now?" he asked.

"What do you mean?"

"I mean...now what happens?"

"Nothing happens. I go home. You stay here. Maybe you'll do your roommate a favor and change his sheets."

"Oh."

"Were you expecting something else?" she said. "Some kind of sex-induced apocalypse?"

"No." Henry thought about how far he'd gone out into the lake in his flak jacket, how long he'd stayed there, treading water with thirty pounds of lead and nylon strapped to his chest, listening to his own breathing. He'd swum out where nobody had ever been before, but it didn't matter because *he'd* been there. "You're not going to tell Mike, are you?"

"God, no. I'll have to keep my distance for a while, though. You bruised the hell out of me."

"Me?" Henry said, alarmed. "No I didn't."

She pushed aside the duvet and pointed to the front of her shoulder: a coppery, greening mark, almost literally a thumbprint. Henry's stomach did a queasy flip.

"I've got a few more, I'm sure." She twisted away, and Henry saw the corresponding fingerprints near her shoulder blade. "And this big one on my hip."

"I'm really sorry," said Henry.

"Don't worry about it. Part of the social contract, right?"

Owen's sheets felt silky and rich. Henry wasn't sure whether he had the strength to stand. His swim, his night in the cold, had exhausted him like never before. Pella climbed over him, out of bed, and poured a finger of scotch into each of two tumblers. "When will they be back?" she asked.

To judge by the windowlight, it was nearing six o'clock. "Coshwale's pretty far," he said. "Probably two or three hours. More, even." He let the scotch scorch his throat and warm his empty stomach.

"Well, you can't be too careful these days." Pella already had her jeans and flip-flops on. Now she knelt down and felt around beneath the foot of Owen's bed. She lifted her T-shirt into view and shimmied inside. "Look how white this still is," she said. "There's not even any dust under the *beds*."

"There might be some under mine," Henry said. "But I think Owen cleans there too."

"What a guy." Pella half zipped her sweatshirt and began pacing around the room. "I don't know what I'm so worked up about," she said.

"I mean, if my dad's gay, and he's happy, then it's no big deal, right? Or even if he's gay and unhappy, it's still not that big a deal. A certain number of people are gay, just like a certain number of people have blue eyes. Or lupus. Don't ask me why I just said lupus. I barely know what it is. And I know being gay's not a disease. The point is, it's all just probabilities. Numbers. How can I be upset about numbers?"

"You can't," Henry said.

"He's a grown man who can do what he wants. And actually, it might be worse if Owen were a girl. If he were a girl he might turn my dad in for harassment, and it'd turn into a scandal and my dad would lose his job. *That* would be bad." She poured herself another finger's worth of scotch. "I guess Owen could turn him in too. But it seems less likely somehow. Maybe that's sexist of me.

"But even if Owen doesn't turn him in, they still might get caught. What would happen then? All hell would break loose."

"I don't think they'll get caught," Henry said. "Besides, Owen's going to Japan."

Pella was still pacing the room, looking distressed. Even if she'd been sitting next to him on the bed, he probably wouldn't have had the guts to hug her, or to pat her on the shoulder and say, *There, there.* They barely knew each other. He'd probably never touch Pella Affenlight again.

"Maybe you should talk to your dad." Henry hauled himself to his feet, tugged on warm-up pants and a T-shirt. He was shivering. "It seems like the two of you are pretty close."

"*Close*," she said, spitting the word like a curse. "We're close, all right."

Having lived in Phumber Hall for three years, Henry had become expert at distinguishing among different people's footsteps. As soon as these passed the second-floor landing, he knew that they didn't belong to any of the girls on the third floor, nor to either of the Asian Steves across the hall. Owen was back. But there was a second set of footsteps too. Henry stood up. Pella stopped pacing and looked at him, puzzled by what had no doubt become a very grave expression on his face. If he'd had more energy he might have shoved her into the shower or under his bed, which might have led to an even stupider sort of farce.

What really happened was that he was standing dumbly in the center of the room when Owen's key scraped in the lock. Pella flopped down into the overstuffed armchair, her legs hooked over one side, and plucked a book from the shelf beside her. Henry looked down at his feet and thought, I'm not wearing socks. I always wear socks.

Schwartz remained at the threshold while Owen stepped into the room. "Hi, guys," Pella said, glancing up from her book — *The Art of Fielding* — with an actress's aplomb.

"Hi," Schwartz said.

"Good day?"

"Not bad."

Emboldened by the banality of this exchange, Henry did something he regretted instantly. He spoke: "How'd we do?"

Schwartz glanced at him, then at Pella, then back at Henry. "Buddha," he said.

"Yes, Michael."

"Forget to make your bed this morning?"

Owen scrutinized the bed, his lips pressed tightly together, his eyebrows contracted into an expression of total concentration. "It's possible," he said after a long moment, nodding gently. "It's very possible."

"Mm-hm." Schwartz pointed toward the nook between Owen's bed and the mantel. "And is that yours too?"

There in the nook's convergent shadows lay a rumpled piece of silk or rayon or some other satiny fabric, icy blue in color. Owen gazed at it for a long time, as if willing it to disappear, or at least to become a more ambiguous version of what it so unambiguously happened to be. "No," he said finally, his voice soft and thoughtful, after it became clear that Schwartz intended to wait for a response. "I suppose not."

Pella started to speak, but Schwartz waved her off. "I'm not mad," he said, his voice loud and cracking. "I think you're a goddamn saint.

Coming in here and laying on hands. Laying on mouth. Laying on whatever. I should have sent you sooner."

"You could have sent somebody else," Pella said. "Christ, you could have done it yourself."

"What's that supposed to mean?"

"You know what it means. I don't have to be the middleman. Mike, Henry. Henry, Mike."

Owen stepped into the center of the room, held up a hand. "Okay," he said in his best, most caramelly mediator's tone. Why don't we jus—"

"Not you." Pella glared at Owen. "I know about you."

Owen looked at her. A flicker of understanding, of consternation, crossed his face, and he subsided to the corner of the room. Henry just stood there, feeling invisible. Maybe that should have been a relief, in the wake of what he'd done, but instead it was making him angry, the way Schwartz and Pella were squared off as if he weren't even there.

"I'm sorry," Pella said, her voice changed and soft.

"For what? For fixing everything?" Schwartz shook his head. "No." His amber eyes were unfocused, vacant, as if he'd gone blind. He turned and walked down the stairs.

57

Mrs. McCallister stood at the beautiful old washbasin in the hallway, the one whose coiled brass tubes, like those of a sackbut or trombone, she kept buffed to a pristine shine. Her thick gray hair was just long enough to be put up in a pencil-spit bun. She poured a capful of white vinegar into the glass coffeepot and swirled it with an elbowy motion as Pella approached. "Ah, bella Pella," she sang, "wherefore art thou? Where art thy fella?"

Pella had her wicker bag slung over one shoulder and her Westish-insignia backpack slung over the other. Together they contained everything she owned. "You're in an awfully good mood," she said. "Is my dad around?"

Mrs. McCallister rolled her eyes toward Affenlight's office door. "For once," she said. "My dear, you do have an effect on him. Ever since you arrived he's been as hyper as my nine year old grandson. Can't focus on anything. I told him I'm going to start putting Ritalin in his applesauce, the way they do for Luke."

"I'm sure he'll calm down eventually," Pella said.

"Of course. And of course it's wonderful that you're here. There's nothing like family."

"Thank God for that."

Mrs. McCallister laughed merrily. "You two are lucky to have each other."

Her dad's heavy wooden door was shut tight. Pella knocked once. Her dad cracked the door open and peered out, his cell phone tucked between shoulder and chin. Maybe he was talking to Owen—maybe Owen was telling him, in benignly neutral Owen-words, that his daughter was a whore.

"Pella." He clapped the phone shut. "There you are."

"Here I am."

It was Monday; they hadn't spoken since Friday, here in this office, with David sitting between them. She'd spent last night on Mike's broken porch swing, waiting for him to come home, but he never did. She knew he was at the VAC—he was always at the VAC—but there was no way to penetrate that fortress after hours. He hadn't returned her calls, not that anyone could blame him; it was possible he'd never speak to her again.

"I'm so sorry about dinner," Affenlight said. "I got hung up in my meeting with Bruce Gibbs and..."

"So you said."

"Well, I meant it. And I'm sorry. I wanted to be there to support you."

These lies made Pella feel more guilty than angry—here she was, arms folded, foot tapping, paying out rope for her dad to wrap around his neck.

"And then all weekend when you didn't come home I was so worried. We need to get you a new cell phone. I thought something terrible had happened."

"Like I went back to San Francisco."

"Well, yes. That was one scenario. Though I thought up more frightening ones, as I lay awake." He did look haggard—his shoulders slumped, the lines around his eyes pronounced. "I know you're not obliged to apprise me of your whereabouts. But when I didn't see or hear from you for so long, my mind began to—"

"I saw *you*," Pella interrupted. "On Saturday."

He looked surprised. "Where?"

"At the baseball game. You were talking to Owen."

Affenlight froze. "Owen…," he said as if trying to place the name. When he began to speak he spoke fast, as if to induce Pella to forget what she'd said. "Yes, Owen's doing much better. Wish I could say the same for Henry Skrimshander, the poor fellow. You know, I wrote a few pieces for *The New Yorker* when you were quite young, after my book came out. They had a fellow on staff everyone called the Gray Ghost. He'd written some wonderful pieces in the sixties — one about veterans of Korea I remember in particular — and ever since, he'd been showing up at the office every damned day, Monday to Friday, summertimes too, without ever turning in a single draft of a single article. You could hear his typewriter going great guns behind his door, and of course there were rumors about what he was working on, the opus to end all opera, but nobody ever saw a word of it. I'd come in to be put through the fact-checking wringer and he'd be wandering the hallways with this blank, stricken look on his face. He was done for and he knew it. That's what Henry's face reminded me of, when he walked off that field. The Gray Ghost." There were two kinds of incompetent con men. Those who talked too much and those who didn't talk enough. Affenlight, who was clearly of the former school, paused and shook his head. "Poor kid. I wish there was something that could be done —"

"Already taken care of," Pella said acridly. "Look, Dad, we need to talk. I can't live here anymore. I'm moving out."

"What?" Affenlight looked baffled. "Now? Is this about David?"

"No." The straps of her bags were cutting into her shoulders. She moved into the room and let them slide down onto the love seat, a temporary defeat. "I just need to get out of that apartment. It's not big enough for both of us. It's not even big enough for you. Books piled everywhere, closets stuffed full of junk. You're sixty years old. Do you really want to live in a dorm for the rest of your life?"

Affenlight looked dumbly up at the ceiling, above which his apartment lay. "I like it here."

Pella tapped a flip-flop on the floorboards, annoyed at herself for the obliqueness of her approach. When she complained about her dad's living arrangement, what she meant was that he should live in a way that was quote-unquote "normal" for a man his age—id est, without Owen. Still, she kept at it, unable to bring herself to be more direct. "Why not buy a house?"

Affenlight smiled ruefully. "Where were you eight years ago? The school wanted to sell us the outgoing president's place for pennies on the dollar. But I figured I'd get too lonely, rattling around in a big old house all by myself. Instead it went on the market, got snapped up by some physics professor who made a killing on tech stocks in the nineties. Like I should have done."

"You've done all right."

"I've done all right," Affenlight agreed.

"Anyway," Pella said. "I'm not a kid anymore and we're not a married couple. I think things will go more smoothly if we each have our own place. Okay?"

Affenlight nodded slowly. "Okay."

"Don't look so glum," she said. "Now you can have guests stay over."

Affenlight chuckled, or tried to. "Yeah, right," he said. "Like whom?"

It was the classic criminal error, that *like whom*—the longing to get caught, to take credit for the crime. Pella steeled herself. "Like Owen."

A profound, interstellar kind of silence filled the office. Eventually Affenlight said, "I was planning to tell you."

"When, on your deathbed?"

"Maybe," he said. "Or a little after that."

Pella felt a return of that same urge she'd felt at the baseball diamond—the urge to protect her father from onrushing harm. He was so naive, so boyish. She remembered how he looked while talking to Owen by the fence: Like the thousand other people in the park didn't exist. Like if they existed, they couldn't see how he felt about Owen. Like if they could see how he felt about Owen, they'd condone or forgive him.

But people didn't forgive you for doing what felt right—that was the last thing they forgave you for.

"How long has this been going on?" she asked.

"Not long."

"Not long with Owen, or"—she didn't know how to put it—"in general?"

Affenlight lifted his eyes from the floor. "There is no *in general,*" he said. "Just Owen."

He wasn't old but he looked it now, his arms limp at his sides, deep lines of worry scored into his forehead beneath his mussed gray-silver hair, his expression sad and beseeching. Why was the younger person always the prize, the older person always the striver? Ever since adolescence Pella had been gathering experience in the role of the younger person, the clung-to one, the beloved. That was the idiot hopefulness of humans, always to love what was unformed. Really it made no sense. What were the old hoping the young would become? Something other than old? It hadn't happened yet. But the old kept trying.

By *the old* she meant everyone who loved something younger—her dad but also David, and even the twentysomething guys she'd hooked up with in high school. Everyone always reaching back through the past, past their own mistakes. You could say that young people were desired because they had smooth bodies and excellent reproductive chances, but you'd mostly be missing the point. There was something much sadder in it than that. Something like constant regret, the sense that your whole life was an error, a mistake, that you were desperate to redo. "He's a kid," she said. "He's younger than I am."

Affenlight nodded. "I know."

"What if somebody finds out? Then what happens to us?" The *us* was a touch melodramatic.

"I don't know," said Affenlight.

"But you're in love with him."

"Yes."

"Well, great," Pella said. "Amor vincit omnia." What she was thinking was even crueler: *He's going to break your heart.*

She hoisted her bags and moved toward her dad. For the happiest and splittest of seconds Affenlight thought she planned to embrace him, but her hands were wrapped tightly around the straps of her bags, and in fact he was simply blocking her way. He shifted aside, leaving several inches of troubled air between them as his daughter ducked her beautiful port-colored head and slid past him and down the hallway and out of sight.

58

If you pretended not to know Coach Cox and you walked into his empty office, sat in the only visitor's chair, and glanced around apprehensively, you'd never guess that he'd been coaching Westish Baseball for thirteen years. He might as well have moved in yesterday. The door was never locked. The walls were a plain industrial white, the metal schoolteacher's desk a lackluster military green. The main signs of life were a taped-up baseball schedule and a wastebasket overflowing with pinched Diet Coke cans. A half-sized fridge, its top littered with fast-food napkins and mustard packets, completed the furniture. The narrow window didn't overlook the lake.

The desk's glass-topped surface held only a phone and a small framed photograph of Coach Cox's two children. They were sitting in a kiddie pool full of raked-up leaves, the girl with her arm around the boy in that protective way of older siblings, mugging for the camera. Henry picked it up for a closer look. Both kids wore earth-toned autumn jackets and had messy midlength hair. The boy looked about four and the girl seven, but the picture had been there as long as Henry could remember, its inks had faded, and they were no doubt much older now — maybe older than he was. Strange how little Coach Cox talked about his family; strange how little you wound up knowing about the people around you. Henry thought maybe the daughter's name was Kelly, but maybe her face just reminded him of some Kelly he'd gone to school with. Kelly and Peter, he thought aimlessly, replacing the photo on the desk in its original position, so that it faced Coach Cox's chair and not his own. Peter and Kelly.

Coach Cox came into the room, took a Diet Coke from the fridge, and plunked down in his pleather desk chair. The hinges screeched; they were so loose his whole body tipped back like he was about to get some dentistry done.

"Coach Cox," Henry said, "before you say anything, I want to apologize for what I did yesterday. I abandoned the team. It was a terrible thing to do. I'm really sorry."

The Harpooners had won both of Sunday's games against Coshwale, the first by the score of 2 to 1, the second, 15 to 0. The second game was halted after four innings in accordance with the UMSCAC's mercy rule, which was how Owen and Schwartz made it back to campus so early. The Harpooners were conference champs for the first time in their 104-year history of playing baseball. The regional tournament was days away.

Coach Cox leaned back in his chair even more, so that he was almost lying down, and stroked his mustache. "You realize I'm going to have to suspend you, Skrim. I don't especially want to, but there's no way around it. Team rules. You missed two games, so two more should be a reasonable punishment. With luck we'll win one of them. Consider it a chance to get your bearings."

"Actually," Henry said, "I was planning on something longer."

Coach Cox frowned. "What do you mean?"

"I mean ... I'd like to resign from the team."

Coach Cox's frown deepened into something else. He rocked forward to a seated position, planted his feet on the ground, glared into Henry's eyes. "I'd like to be twenty years old and have your kind of talent," he said. "But we can't always get what we want. Permission denied."

"But Coach, you don't understand. I'm quitting the team."

"You're not quitting anything. In fact, you're unsuspended, effective immediately. Practice starts in fifteen minutes. Go get dressed."

"I can't do that."

"Bull*shit* you can't. And wear old clothes. I don't care how fit you are. I'm going to run you until you puke."

"Coach," Henry said quietly, "I'm through."

Something in his voice convinced Coach Cox he was serious. The older man resumed stroking his mustache and eventually said:

"Have you talked to Mike about this?"

For a split second Henry thought that Coach Cox had heard what had happened with Pella. His throat seized tight, even as he realized the question meant something else. What Coach Cox was driving at was that Schwartzy would never let him quit. "No," he admitted. "I haven't."

"Well, let's get his input on this." Coach Cox tipped his head back and drained his Diet Coke decisively. "Come on."

They walked out to the elevator together. Henry could have refused to go down to the locker room—could have pressed the first-floor button and walked through the VAC's front doors and never come back. But something wouldn't let him. Maybe he was too used to obeying Coach Cox's commands, or maybe there was a part of him that wanted to go down there. Last night, Mike had just turned his back and walked down the stairs.

"Schwartzy," barked Coach Cox. "Can we see you for a minute?"

Schwartz, who was sitting in front of his locker with a bag of ice on either thigh, glanced up somberly at the word *we,* took one earphone out of his ear. "What is it?"

The other Harpooners in the vicinity—Rick, Starblind, Boddington, Izzy, Phlox—stared into their own empty lockers, pretending they hadn't noticed Henry come in. And they don't know the half of it, Henry thought.

"Out in the hallway." Coach Cox jerked his head toward the door. "Let's go."

"I'm icing," Schwartz said. "What is it?"

You could tell by his quick snort of breath that Coach Cox was about to start yelling, something he rarely did. Henry cut him off. "Here's fine." He steeled himself and took a step toward Schwartz. "I'm sorry about what happened, Mike. I let you down, I let everybody down. I made a mistake and I'm sorry. I'm really, really sorry..." Technically he was apologizing for ditching the team yesterday, which was its own unpardonable sin, but of course it didn't feel like that. "Coach Cox wanted me to let you know that I've decided to quit the team."

Schwartz was staring dead into his locker, his hairy shoulders slumped, those huge bags of ice on his knees. He reached inside for a stick of deodorant, pulled off the cap with a suctioning *pop,* and lifted one arm above his head. "Izzy's our shortstop," he said. "You can't even throw."

"I know. That's why I'm quitting."

Schwartz switched to the other armpit. "That's interesting," he said. "I thought it was because you nailed my girlfriend."

"I nail all your girlfriends!" Henry yelled. It made no sense, but he yelled it anyway, fists balled, feeling like he might fall on Schwartz and start swinging. "Who the fuck cares?!"

Schwartz, with infinite slowness, pulled a Westish Baseball T-shirt from his locker, poked his head through the hole, and unfurled it over his massive torso. "Maybe nobody," he said, his eyes still fixed on his locker's innards. "Rick, you care if Skrimshander nails my girlfriend?"

Rick, whose locker was adjacent to Schwartz's, looked up cautiously, his pink face grim. "I guess not," he said.

"Starblind, how about you?"

"Nope."

"Izzy?"

Silence.

"Izzy?"

"No, *Abuelo.*"

Schwartz went around the room, name by name. Each guy murmured in turn that no, he didn't care if Henry nailed Schwartz's girlfriend. At least Owen wasn't there. Henry didn't know who to feel worst for, but he knew who to blame—himself.

"Well, that's fine," Schwartz said. "Let's go practice." He removed the Ziploc bags from his knees, dumped the ice onto the circular grated drain between the benches, and, as guys pressed against their lockers to avoid his bulk, rumbled creakily, bowleggedly, out of the locker room.

"This is great," Coach Cox said, his voice growing from a mutter to a drill-sergeant shout. "This is goddamned out*standing.* Everybody to the football stadium *now!* You're all gonna run till you *puke!*" He looked at Henry. "You coming?"

"No," Henry said.

"You really want to do this, Skrim? You really want to goddamn do this?"

Henry nodded. "I do."

59

Affenlight sat in the Audi, surreptitiously smoking a cigarette, looking out across quiet Main Street at the Bremens' place, its expansive porch, its uneven cupolas, its manicured lawn sliding from green to gray in the thickening twilight. After Pella left he'd remembered that Professor Bremen was retiring from the Physics Department this spring; was moving to New Mexico to play golf, walk around in the desert with his wife, teach for kicks at an online university. Bremen was a few years younger than Affenlight, but he'd made a killing.

Sure enough, there it was on the lawn, a FOR SALE sign.

Pella had found a room for the remainder of the semester, with some Westish girls off campus. She'd left Affenlight a message to this effect, on the apartment's voice mail when she knew he'd be in his office. There was a landline there, but she hoped he wouldn't call it soon. She wanted some time alone.

Affenlight stubbed out his cigarette in the Audi's ashtray, stared at the Bremens' facade. It was a big white whale of a house, fit for a president, but there was something appealingly quirky about it as well, a kind of ad hoc austerity. Even when it seemed a foregone conclusion that he'd stay at Harvard forever, he'd never come anywhere near buying a place. Rented halves of Cambridge houses had always seemed permanence enough.

He'd intended only to drive by, to see whether there would indeed be a sign on the lawn, but now he found himself strolling up the front walk to the porch steps. The silhouette of Sandy Bremen, Tom's wife, appeared behind the front door before he could ring the bell.

"Why, Guert," she said. "Fancy meeting you here." A large dog shot out of the small gap she'd made by beginning to open the door, reared up to paw at Affenlight's chest. "I was just about to take Contango for a walk." She grabbed the dog by the collar and yanked him backward. "Sorry. He's awfully rambunctious today."

"Quite all right." Affenlight offered the dog his hand to sniff. He was a beautiful animal, old and noble, a sugar-furred husky with one blue eye.

"Tom's out for a run," Sandy said. "Is it something urgent?"

"No, no. Not urgent at all. You see, actually...I stopped by because I was curious about the house."

"Ah-ha." Sandy smiled in the slightly flirty but mostly proprietary way that the faculty wives, at least the more secure ones, liked to smile at Affenlight. She was a seal-sleek woman in a monochrome tracksuit and fresh white sneakers. He wondered, not for the first time, what it would have been like to spend a few decades with a woman like that—a woman who turned family life into a smooth-running corporate entity, whose genius was to take a sizable income and make it seem infinite, who knew how to convert money into pleasure and pleasantry. "You're finally thinking of taking the plunge?"

Affenlight shrugged. "I saw the sign," he said. "It made me a bit curious."

"Well, come on in. I'll give you the grand tour. Contango, buddy, I'm sorry—false alarm on that stroll of ours." She shooed the dog through the door, planted a hand in the small of Affenlight's back to do the same to him. "Is beer okay? I can't join you because I'm halfway through a juice cleanse, faddish girl that I am, but I'm sure Tom will partake when he gets back. He's been logging a lot of miles these days."

Affenlight, clutching the sweaty neck of his Heineken, dutifully trailed Sandy throughout the first floor and then the second as she explicated the virtues of California Closets, natural light, their recently remodeled kitchen. The Bremens' two children were both graduated from college and gone, their bedrooms converted into spruced-up, stripped-down pieds-à-terre for holiday and summertime visits. "Lucy's wedding is in October," Sandy said as they stood on the threshold of the more extravagantly pillowed of the two rooms. "Old time she is a flyin'." She turned to lead Affenlight back down the stairs. "As you can see, the place is big but not *that* big. Three bedrooms, Tom's office, one bath up, one down. It's really a very functional house, because it's so old — it's more on the model of the farmhouse than the mansion. Not outlandish for one person." She gave Affenlight that sly look again. "You *are* still living alone, aren't you, Guert?"

"More or less."

"Ah, the ambiguities! Meaning what?"

They sat at the kitchen table. Affenlight accepted the second beer Sandy handed him, reached down to ruffle the dog's belly. Pella had begged for a dog throughout girlhood, but they'd never quite gotten around to it. "My daughter's considering enrolling at Westish," he said, knocking a knuckle softly against the wooden table so as not to jinx that prospect. "We wouldn't necessarily be living together, but..."

"Ah, but she'd need her own room, certainly. Pella, is it? Such a lovely name. But I thought she was at Yale? Or even finished by now?"

Affenlight had for years brought a deliberate vagueness regarding Pella's whereabouts to cocktail parties. It felt like a betrayal now. "Yale didn't entirely pan out," he said.

Sandy nodded sagely. "Few things do," she said, her beaming, impossibly hale face suggesting just the opposite. "So what else can I tell you?"

Affenlight gazed through the patio door at the groomed and moonlit backyard, the lake beyond. It was a beautiful house. Big but not outlandish, as Sandy said. But why even consider it? He'd been in the quarters for eight years, had hardly felt cramped or dissatisfied. If the garbage disposal broke or there was a problem with the heat, he just called Infrastructure and they sent someone over. Here there was no Infrastructure. He'd have rooms to paint, a furnace to replace, property taxes to pay. Not to mention the fact that he owned so little furniture, not nearly enough to fill so many rooms. What kind of condition was the roof in? That was the kind of question he needed to ask Sandy, the kind of question that, if he bought a house, he'd be asking himself forever.

Hadn't the myth of the glory of home ownership been debunked once and for all? Did he really want to trade his free time—and a formidable chunk of his savings—for a big white symbol of bourgeois propriety? Well, maybe so. And he couldn't help thinking Pella would love the place. The entire upstairs could be hers: one room for sleeping, another for a study, the third small one for a studio, or a walk-in closet, or whatever. He himself would have plenty of space downstairs. She could take a room in the dorms too—a place where he could assume her to be when she wasn't around, thus saving him plenty of worry and compromised sleep. She was upset with him now, and rightly so, but she'd love this place, he could feel it. Not that this was a plan to win her back.

And though it had been decades, he himself was no slouch mechanically—he'd grown up on a farm, spent years on board a ship. He wasn't some kid who'd been raised by the internet. He could take care of a house. The Bremens maintained their yard in the familiar American style, a lush immaculate carpet, but that didn't mean he'd have to do the same—he could dig up all that lushness and plant tomatoes, rhubarb, beans. Garlic in the fall. Hell, pumpkins. He could plant pumpkins, his favorite boyhood crop, crazy as that seemed. Who could stop him? Was there some rule that said a lawn had to be a lawn, with a prim staked garden tucked in the corner? Yes, most likely—the town of Westish probably had no lack of pointless regulations and nitpicky neighbors to enforce them. But those people would be confronted, stared down, chased off, by the grumpy Thoreauvian president with the pumpkins and the beans...

His phone trilled in his pocket. Maybe it was Pella, maybe he could convince her to come over now and look around. He smiled apologetically at Sandy, slid it out to peek at the caller ID: Owen.

"Don't mind me," Sandy said. "I know how in demand you are."

But Affenlight let his voice mail absorb O's melted-butterscotch voice. If this extempore scheme appealed to him partly as a declaration to his daughter—*I'm here, I'm reliable, rely on me, I love you*—it could only mean something entirely different with regard to Owen, something Affenlight wasn't ready to formulate. Owen would be going to Japan in September, would come back to Westish for his commencement ceremony and little else. There was nothing for him in this part of the country, nothing at all. Whereas Affenlight had a college and a daughter, at least for the next four years, and then he'd be sixty-five. To buy a house would be a declaration that he could conceive of living without Owen—or at least that he was resigned to try.

Contango settled down on the pale kitchen floor inches from Affenlight's chair, noble head on noble paws. The two of them watched as Sandy washed and peeled carrots and oranges and prepared to feed them into a juicer. "Looks like somebody's made a friend," she said. "Now, not to be crass, but should we talk about money?"

"I suppose it couldn't hurt."

She told him the list price. He whistled. "I thought the housing market collapsed."

Sandy laughed. "You get what you pay for."

Except when buying suits and scotch, Affenlight habitually thought and acted as if he were poor; this was one consequence of his upbringing he'd never quite kicked. But in truth he had plenty of money; his expenses were nil and his salary went straight in the bank. The Audi, his last extravagance, was six years old. The lake, through the patio door, felt near enough to touch.

"We can make this work!" shouted Sandy over the hum of the juicer. "If we move fast we can pull it from the realtor—the sign just went up this morning—and do it ourselves, chop off six percent that way. Lord knows Kitty Wexnerd doesn't need the money. And all the red tape we can just leave in ribbons on the floor. I would so love to have you and Pella fall in love with this place. It pains me to leave it."

The front door banged open and in came Tom Bremen, fit and bald and drenched in sweat. *"Herr Doktor Presidente,"* he said. "Let me wash my hand before I shake yours."

"Guert stopped by to talk about the house."

"Really?" Tom kissed his wife, took two beers from the fridge, set one down in front of Affenlight. "Did you gild the turd and gloss over all the flaws in this dump?"

"I certainly did not. Because there aren't any."

"I knew I could count on you. Like a sexy Ricky Roma. ABC, baby. Dump needs a new roof, though."

Sandy rolled her eyes. "We put on a brand-new roof last summer," she explained. "Tom and Kevin did it themselves."

"Five weeks of fourteen-hour days. Almost cost me my life. And my relationship with my son." He sat down at the table, clinked his Heineken against Affenlight's. "Good to see you," he said, plucking his sweat-wicking shirt away from his chest. "Did Sandy tell you the unburdened beast comes standard?"

Affenlight looked at Contango, who looked back. Maybe it was the third beer that made the latter's expression seem so companionably wise. "Really?"

"How about I translate?" Sandy said, joining them with her juice. "Contango is Kevin's dog. And Kevin's going to be in Stockholm for a length of time he refers to as 'indefinite to permanent.'"

"To what end?" Affenlight asked politely, reaching down to pat the dog again.

Tom, catching Affenlight's eye, mimed a plenteous Swedish bosom.

"Thomas, please. And I'm actually terribly allergic to pets of all kinds, though I've been keeping a stiff upper lip about it. And Contango has grown very comfortable here in the past few months. So if the buyer of the house, whoever that may turn out to be, were really and truly interested in such an arrangement..."

"We'd throw in a year's supply of Purina and flea shots," Tom concluded. "How's that for sweetening the pot?"

"Huh," said Affenlight. "Wow."

60

The Harpooners finished dressing and followed Schwartz outside to run stadiums till they puked. No one made a sound. Izzy lingered until he was the last one there, tugging on his wristbands extra slowly, fiddling with the gold crucifix he wore around his neck. It seemed like he might try to say something, but instead he just dropped his head and left. As he passed into the hall he popped his fist loudly into his glove's webbing, a one-smack salute to Henry's career.

Henry sat down in front of his locker. His outburst at Schwartz had surprised him; what surprised him more was the way his anger wasn't subsiding. He, not Schwartz, had messed everything up. He, not Schwartz, was to blame. And yet every memory that popped into his head as he sat there in that underground room thick with memories was a memory of Schwartz causing him pain. He was angry at Schwartz. He kind of hated Schwartz. Remember when he arrived at Westish, friendless and adrift, and Schwartz, who'd brought him here, who'd led Henry to expect he would guide him, had left him hanging for twelve long lonely weeks before he'd finally called, and said by way of excuse that he'd been busy with football? Back then Henry had felt too pitifully grateful to mention his distress, but now the pain of those early days broke over him. He pretty much hated Schwartz for that. Hated him too for every weighted stadium he'd made him run, every five a.m. workout, every thousand-pull-up workout, every torturous toss of a medicine ball...it was pain that Henry had craved and demanded, purposeful pain, or so it had seemed, but what broke over him now was all that pain in its purest state, pain that meant nothing, could not be redeemed, because it all led only here, and here was nowhere. God, how he hated Schwartz. Hated him for his attention and hated him for his neglect. Lately, since Pella, it had been neglect again. Without Schwartz pushing him, torturing him, he wouldn't be here. Schwartz had brought him here and now he was fucked. Before he met Schwartz his dreams were just dreams. Things that would peter out harmlessly over time.

Time to leave before somebody returned and found him here. He took the fire stairs, slipped out a side door, headed away from the campus toward downtown. The streets looked odd and purposeless as they basked in the afternoon sunlight. He'd never come this way in the daytime except while jogging.

Next to the Qdoba on the corner of Grant and Valenti stood a bank, recently closed for the day. Henry walked up the drive-through ATM lane, his sneakers slurping through the sticky deposits of oil left by idling cars. He punched in his PIN and withdrew the last eighty dollars from his account. He pocketed the bills and headed back up Valenti toward Bartleby's.

Another place he'd never seen in the daylight. It was empty except for two middle-aged couples gathered around a table littered with half-eaten burgers, half-full beer mugs, broken mozzarella sticks with the cheese stretched out like taffy. The bar was being manned by Jamie Lopez, a football player Henry sort of knew. He leaned over an open textbook, a white bar rag slung around his neck. He was wearing a black Melville T-shirt, the concert-style one with the list of the dates of Melville's travels on the back. Henry took a stool.

Lopez raised an eyebrow in surprise. "Hey Skrim." He marked his place with a swizzle stick. "What are you doing here?"

Henry shrugged. "Chillin'."

Lopez nodded approvingly, frisbeed a cardboard coaster to a spot by Henry's elbow. "What can I do you for?"

Henry looked down the long row of taps. He'd drunk enough beer at baseball functions to know how bad it tasted. But everything else tasted worse.

"Tell you what," said Lopez. "Let me mix you up something. It's my first day behind the bar. Got to practice my craft."

Henry studied Lopez's face for a sign that he knew what had happened on Saturday. He found none. And yet Lopez had to know. Everybody knew. Half the school had been there, and the other half would have heard right away. Deep down Henry despised this pleasantry, this *Hey Skrim,* behind which Lopez was feeling sorry for him, or superior to him, or something. Why didn't people just say what they were thinking? Then again Henry didn't want to talk about it either, and Lopez's acting job, if that's what it was, could be considered a form of kindness. Or maybe Lopez really didn't know. A pint glass appeared on the coaster, filled with ice and an inky liquid. Henry sipped at the fat blue straw.

"How'd I do?"

Henry coughed as he swallowed, covering his mouth so Lopez couldn't see his expression. "Good." He nodded. "Perfect."

Lopez grinned proudly. "It's my take on a Long Island Iced Tea. Kind of nudging it toward the more masculine end of the spectrum."

Henry stared at the strongman competition on the huge TV behind the bar and listened to Lopez hold forth about bartending school. The shifting lights on the screen held his eye, Lopez's voice droned softly in his ear, and his drink disappeared in thoughtless pulls at the straw. Lopez made another, set it on the coaster. It grew dark outside. Pool balls clacked together. The bar began to fill with people. Lopez dimmed the house lights until the place was sunk in a greenish nighttime glow, punctuated by the bright red and blue of electric beer signs.

"Hey Skrim," he said. "Would you fire up the jukebox for me?" He slid a ten-dollar bill across the bar. "Maybe err on the mellow side. It's early."

Henry made his way to the jukebox, fed in the ten, pressed the buttons that turned the plastic pages. The only band name he recognized was U2—that was mellow, right? He punched in a bunch of U2 and still had twenty choices left. Flip flip flip. The only songs whose names he knew were the ones Schwartz played while they lifted weights, and those weren't mellow at all. He gave up and headed for the bathroom.

Pinned to a corkboard above the urinals were the sports pages of *USA Today* and the *Westish Bugler*. "Home at Last!" read the *Bugler*'s banner headline, above a half-page photo of the Harpooners storming Coshwale's diamond with raised arms and mouths in midscream. Even Owen looked excited. The article, like every article about the baseball team, bore Sarah X. Pessel's byline:

COSHWALE, IL—They had never, in over one hundred seasons, won a conference title. Their opponents, the Coshwale Muskies, had captured twenty-nine in that same time span, including four in a row. Their star shortstop, Henry Skrimshander, was nowhere to be found.

It didn't matter.

Sunday afternoon, the Harpooners put an exclamation point on a century of frustration, fishhooking the favored Muskies 2–1 and 15–0 to don their first UMSCAC crown. Senior captain Mike Schwartz spearheaded the redemption with two home runs and seven RBI, while junior pitcher–center fielder Adam Starblind, he of the blond locks and movie-star swagger, chipped in four hits and earned the save in the opening game, despite what he described after the game as severe abdominal soreness, lifting his jersey to reveal a bruised but impressively sculpted six-pack.

Freshperson Izzy Avila filled in more than admirably for the absent Skrimshander, scoring a brace of runs and patrolling the middle of the diamond the way Crockett and Tubbs patrolled Miami in the age of early Madonna: with flair. One or two sublimely acrobatic plays even had bystanders murmuring the name of the shortstop he replaced—a man many deemed unreplaceable. "Izzy looked sharp," intoned mustachioed skipper Ron Cox, a manly man with a nose for understatement.

Schwartz, meanwhile, shrugged off the suggestion that Skrimshander's apparently unexcused absence, one day after walking off the field midinning after a long battle against waning confidence, would hamper the team as they prepared for their first-ever regional tourney. "Skrimmer'll be back tomorrow," Schwartz growled. "You can bet your god- [CONTINUED ON 3B]

Henry ripped down the page, tore it into thin strips like confetti, and peed on the strips. In the mirror as he washed his hands he saw how he looked in his filthy sweatshirt. He hadn't shaved or showered in days. Lopez wasn't just being nice—he was humoring him the way you humor a crazy person.

His knees felt wobbly. He lingered by the bathroom doorway until Lopez made his way to the far end of the increasingly crowded bar. He slipped a twenty under his empty pint glass and hustled out the door, crossing the railroad tracks into the heart of deserted downtown, where few students had reason to go.

Walking toward him, or trying to, was Pella Affenlight.

She didn't see him at first. She was struggling to move a four-legged piece of furniture down the sidewalk. She hoisted it off the ground, clutching its flat top to her chest so the legs pointed straight at Henry. Once she had it in the air she could only stagger a few steps forward and, with a flurry of soft curses, let it drop.

When he reached her, he couldn't not stop; they were the only two people on the street. They looked at each other across the desk.

Pella pulled a pack of cigarettes and a lighter out of her sweatshirt pocket, tapped out a cigarette and lit it. Henry reached out his hand. Pella looked at him. "You sure?" she said.

Henry nodded. She handed him the cigarette. "Careful. They're strong."

Henry didn't know strong from unstrong. He put it between his lips.

"This isn't as stupid as it looks." She nodded at the desk as she lit a second cigarette for herself. "Or actually no — it *is* that stupid. I knew I couldn't carry this home. But I really wanted it."

The cigarette wasn't having much effect. Henry tried to imitate Pella's approach, really sucking on the end this time. His head exploded into dizziness, and he put his cigarette-holding hand on the desk to steady himself. He lifted the other to his mouth and coughed a little fluid into it.

"Henry, are you all right?"

He nodded.

"Come on. Let's sit you down for a minute." Pella took him by the hand and guided him to the curb, where they sat with their feet in the street. "I got a new place," she said, to distract him. "It's over on Groome Street, with two juniors named Noelle and Courtney. They had a third roommate, but she left midsemester — five to one she went into rehab for her eating disorder, to judge by the general vibe of the place.

"When I went to pawn my ring to pay the rent, I saw this writing table in the shop next door. I figured it'd be nice to have one piece of furniture that was mine. So I bought it."

"It's nice."

"Thank you. The owner asked when I wanted to pick it up. And I said, Do you deliver? And he hemmed and hawed and said, Well, he didn't have his truck, maybe he could bring it by on Saturday. And I said, Saturday? It's Monday! And he said he knew what day it was. So I said, Forget it, I'll just take it now. I carried it out of there and got a block away and nearly collapsed."

"I can help," Henry said.

"You just take it easy for a minute."

They sat there in silence while Pella finished her cigarette. Then she helped Henry to his feet and they began lugging the desk toward Groome Street. Henry had to walk forward to keep from getting dizzy, which meant Pella had to walk backward, and her tiny mincing steps, combined with the fact that he kept getting dizzy anyway, made for slow progress. Every half block they had to stop and rest.

Finally they reached Groome and turned east, toward the lake. "It's on this block," Pella said. "I think."

"What's the number?"

Pella couldn't remember. "Why do all these houses look alike? And don't say because it's dark. Oh wait—maybe this is it." They set down the table, and she darted up onto the porch and peered in the window. "They really do all look alike," she said.

Henry hiccuped. The street was tilting under him. "Try your key."

"I forgot to get one." She climbed the porch steps again and tried the door—it was unlocked. She peeked inside. "This is it," she said. "Let's be quiet."

They carried the table onto the porch, into the darkened living room, and then into Pella's room. She flipped on the light to reveal an empty carpeted room with dust bunnies in the corners and a futon mattress on the floor, the contents of her wicker bag and backpack spilled out across it. On the floor beside the futon sat a fresh-from-the-box digital alarm clock, its cord still kinked as it snaked across the rug. "Voilà," she said. "Mon château."

They carried the writing table to the obvious spot, kitty-corner from the futon, and worked it up tight to the wall. Pella stood back and appraised it with folded arms, used her hip to shove it a half step closer to the window. "I think that's it," she said.

Henry walked down the hall to use the bathroom. On the way back he peeked into the kitchen, where a dim light shone above the sink. On the counter stood a bottle of wine with a rubber stopper in it. He'd never tasted wine before; even in church he skipped that part. The bottle was a little more than halfway full. He pulled out the stopper and glugged it down in two long pulls. He shoved the bottle as far down in the trash as it would go.

The kitchen table had a blue Formica top and four matching chairs, but there were only three people living there. And Pella didn't have a chair for her new desk. Therefore he picked up one of the chairs and carried it back to Pella's room, trying not to bang it on the hallway walls as he walked.

"Oh," Pella said. "I probably shouldn't use that."

"What? Why?" Henry felt himself wobble a bit. "Do whatever you want." He pushed the chair under the desk with a flourish.

"Hm." Pella folded her arms beneath her breasts and assessed the setup. "Maybe you're right. It does look pretty good."

He turned to face her, held out his arms. "*You* look pretty good."

"Henry. Cut it out. You're drunk."

He belched discreetly into his hand. "I love you."

"No, you do not."

"Uh-huh."

"You moron. How'd you get so drunk? You were drunk before, but not like this."

"I drank the wine."

"The wine? What wine?"

"Kitchen wine."

"You drank kitchen wine? Okay. You drink all the kitchen wine you want. You've earned it. But don't go around telling people you love them. Deal?"

Henry nodded. Then he closed his eyes. Pella took him by the hand and led him out into the living room. When he awoke a few hours later, he awoke in darkness, the room spinning, his face pressed into the couch. A hand was shaking his shoulder. *"Henry,"* Pella whispered.

He grunted.

"It's almost five thirty. I'm leaving for work. Go sleep in my room so my roommates don't get mad."

61

On the day before the regional tournament began, Schwartz drove out to see his orthopedist. The clinic was tucked into a redbrick strip mall between a cell phone outlet and a Christian bookstore. Schwartz parked the Buick in the handicapped spot, a little in-joke with himself. Julie, the receptionist, held up two fingers, indicating which exam room he should head to. He always scheduled the first appointment after Dr. Kellner's lunch so he wouldn't have to wait.

"Mike." Dr. Kellner gave him a strong handshake, held the grip. Orthopedists, in Schwartz's experience, were serious alpha males; hard-charging, broad-chested guys much like himself, except better at math. "I've been keeping up with the team. Conference champs. Congrats."

"Thanks."

"It's a banner year for Jewish ballplayers. That Braun kid for the Brew Crew is going like gangbusters."

"The Hebrew Hammer," Schwartz said gamely. Dr. Kellner liked to connect with him on an ethnic level; understandable in this part of the country, where the natives were blond or German or both.

"So what have we got today?"

"Just here for my monthly tune-up."

"Well, good. Hop up on the table, Captain Crepitus."

Schwartz hoisted himself onto the padded exam table, lay on his back, yanked his sweatpants' gathered elastic hems up onto his thighs.

Dr. Kellner tested his range of motion, prodded each kneecap, applied valgus and varus stresses. "Where does it hurt best?" he asked, an old joke of theirs.

Crepitus: the noise produced by rubbing irregular cartilage surfaces together, as in osteoarthritis. With each stretch Schwartz's knees snapped and popped at increasing volume, as if trying to outbid each other. Within a minute Dr. Kellner had heard enough. He plopped down in a chair, scratched a meaty arm under his short-sleeved scrub shirt. "Nothing we don't already know," he said. "Normal people have cartilage, you've got ground beef. Every game you catch brings you that much closer to a couple TKRs."

"I'm almost done," Schwartz said. "Just regionals this weekend." And nationals too, if they won — *when* they won — but not much point in saying so.

Dr. Kellner was making marks on Schwartz's chart. "Can't hardly wait," he said without looking up. "We'll get you in the OR, knock your ass out, clean you out good. Cartilage, scar tissue, the works. Get you ready for life after baseball. No more of this stopgap bullshit. How's the back? You've been seeing your chiropractor?"

"Every week."

"You want me to have a look?"

Schwartz shrugged. "Not much point right now."

Dr. Kellner nodded. "Keep going with the anti-inflammatories. Twelve hundred milligrams three times a day is fine for a guy your size."

"I have been." Schwartz paused, pretended to study the kitschy framed posters of strongman stretches that hung above the exam table. "But as long as I'm here...maybe we should go one more round with the Vicoprofen."

Dr. Kellner cocked his head. "We've talked about this, Mike."

"Just a dozen or so. Enough to get me through these games."

"We agreed that your attachment to these painkillers was borderline problematic."

"It's not an attachment. I'm in pain. Pain I would like killed."

Dr. Kellner cocked his head further. "I believe you about the pain, Mike. Believe me, I believe you. I quit doing marathons because one of my knees looks half as bad as both of yours do, and you're half my age. How's that for bad math? If I gave you an MRI right now and looked at the results I'd have to shut you down for good—you and I both know that. But a person can be in legitimate, significant pain and still be attached. These are habit-forming drugs."

"I don't care about the drugs per se. I just don't want the pain to affect my play."

"So we'll do another shot. Cortisone with the lido."

"It's not enough," Schwartz said. "It did shit last time."

Dr. Kellner leaned back in his chair, arms folded, and contemplated Schwartz. "When did you last take any pain meds?"

Schwartz counted back the days. It was now Wednesday; he'd run out on Saturday, the day Henry walked off the field. This season had been rough, painwise; much worse than previous years, worse even than this past football season. Until recently, he'd been getting painkillers both from Dr. Kellner and from Michelle, a nurse at St. Anne's whom he'd dated on and off since sophomore year. But Schwartz had stopped answering Michelle's texts when he met Pella, and now—of course—Michelle wasn't answering his. Stupid, stupid, stupid.

"Have you been having trouble sleeping?"

"Only a little," Schwartz lied. "Because of my back."

"Any chills or excessive sweating?"

"My sweating is always excessive." Good thing he'd left his windbreaker on. Kellner couldn't see that his T-shirt was drenched.

"Have you been feeling unusually anxious or irritable?"

"Me, irritable?" Schwartz joked.

Dr. Kellner didn't laugh. "You drink with the meds? A few beers here and there?"

Schwartz ignored the question. "We're not talking about habits," he said. "We're talking about a well-defined short-term situation. I just need to make it to Sunday. To give my team a chance to win."

Julie poked her blond head around the door. "Doctor K. Your two o'clock is here."

One of her eyes had a sleepy tic, but otherwise she was cute enough. No doubt she had a steady stream of meds at her disposal, working here. Schwartz should have laid the groundwork a long time ago; too late now. He'd asked around at school, steering clear of his teammates, who might get the wrong idea, but all anyone had was Adderall and coke, coke and Adderall.

Dr. Kellner shooed Julie away. Schwartz went on: "In moderation these aren't dangerous drugs, right? They're legitimate treatment for lots of people. People in way less pain than me. I mean, you can walk into any dentist's office in town holding your cheek and they'll write you a scri—"

Dr. Kellner shook his head. "Stop right there, Mike, or I'll call every doctor, dentist, and pharmacist in a fifty-mile radius and tell them to be on the lookout for you. *Moderation* means small, non-habit-forming amounts. That's not you. You've got a problem with these narcotics. Period. You're going through withdrawal, and the sooner you ride that out the better. I should ship you over to St. Anne's to see a counselor, but I know you won't go and I don't have time to play babysitter. You want cortisone, I got cortisone. You want to tell me what else is going on in your life that makes a little oblivion so appealing — I'm all ears. Otherwise I'll see you next month."

Doctors were the most self-righteous people on earth, Schwartz thought. Healthy and wealthy themselves, surrounded by the sick and dying — it made them feel invincible, and feeling invincible made them pricks. They thought they understood suffering because they saw it every day. They didn't understand shit. Plus they could prescribe themselves what they knew they needed without having to listen to lectures about the meaning of moderation from people who hadn't even read the goddamn *Ethics*.

Dr. Kellner stood up, looked at his watch.

"Fine," Schwartz said. "Give me the goddamn shot."

62

On the way back to campus, Schwartz told himself that he wouldn't. Then he turned the Buick down Groome Street anyway, to see if what he'd heard was true. He parked on the far side of the street, one house down, in the shade of a massive maple. The curtains in the front room weren't drawn. A TV flickered bluely, but as far as Schwartz could tell there wasn't anyone watching it. He cut the engine. The cortisone helped; he had to admit it. He felt like horseshit, he was sweating like crazy, his heart pounded constantly, but his knees would make it through the weekend's games. He took off his watch for no particular reason and strapped it around the uppermost segment of the steering wheel. Ten minutes passed. Fifteen. If he didn't leave now he'd be late for practice.

As he unclipped his watch from the wheel, someone walked up Groome Street and entered the low chain link gate of 339. Long dark hair, knee-high leather boots, Burberry coat. It was Noelle Pierson. This was the place, then; he'd heard they were at Noelle's place. But no sign. Schwartz fired the engine. Noelle climbed the three stairs to the porch. She was a junior, a history major; they'd hooked up a few times his sophomore year, when she still lived in the dorms. As her boot heel hit the porch, the TV ceased to flicker. A figure in a faded red T-shirt jumped off the couch and hurried from the room. He'd been there all along. Schwartz nosed the Buick away from the curb.

63

That afternoon, for the second straight day, the Harpooners had a flat, desultory practice. Even Coach Cox seemed lethargic. Schwartz, unable to practice because of his knees and unwilling to watch anymore, headed back to the locker room to soak. He was in the whirlpool tub when his teammates wandered in. The door was half open, so he could hear what was being said.

"How good you think these teams are?" asked one of the young guys, probably Loondorf. "Compared to Coshwale."

"Put it this way," Rick replied. "Coshwale's won conference, what, eight times in ten years?"

"Okay."

"And they've never gone to nationals. It's always some team from the River Nine. Or else WIVA. But mostly River Nine. Those guys are beasts."

"Who's the River Nine team?"

"Northern Missouri."

"Shit. Northern Missouri."

"In oh-six they won the whole shebang."

"Are they in our half of the bracket?"

"I think so. I think we play them if we beat McKinnon."

"Crap. Northern Missouri. When you put it that way."

"Yeah."

"Man, we could sure use Henry. Even just to DH."

"Amen to that."

"It'll be good experience, either way."

"Who knows? Maybe we'll beat McKinnon. Starblind on the mound. Then see what happens."

"Could use Henry's bat, though."

"One thing I know. We're gonna party when it's over. Regardless."

Schwartz wasn't in the whirlpool anymore. He was through the door, naked and dripping, closing fast, feet slipping on the concrete floor. He jacked Rick up against the lockers, two hands twisted into Rick's T-shirt for leverage. "You want to throw a party?" he was screaming, his voice less a voice than a visitation from some very dark place. "Is that what you want?"

Rick shook his head no. He was trembling a little and had his gut sucked in, afraid to breathe, as if Schwartz might hurt him badly. He was right. This wasn't college-boy Schwartz getting riled up for effect. This wasn't Schwartz Lite. This was full-bore Schwartz, the kind of Schwartz these prep-school pansies didn't know they'd never seen. Nobody moved to intervene. Nobody moved at all.

"This weekend is not the end!" Schwartz let go of Rick; he was addressing them all. He bashed his fist against a locker, not even remembering to use his left. He dented the metal, bloodied his knuckles. "Anyone who thinks otherwise, anyone who'd rather go play for McKinnon, or Chute, or Northern Missouri, can clear the hell out. I'm winning a regional title, and then I'm winning a national championship. And guess what? You motherfuckers are along for the ride."

Coach Cox had wandered into the locker room and was watching dispassionately, hands in his pockets. Through the haze of his rage Schwartz saw a glass Snapple bottle in little Loondorf's hand; he grabbed it and sent it flying a foot or two over Coach Cox's head, just because. It was a fucked-up thing to do but he needed their attention. Coach Cox ducked. The bottle exploded against the dingy tile wall between the clock and the water fountain. Shards of glass rained over the room.

"You want to have a party?" Schwartz beat lockers, beat his chest, beat anything stupid enough to be near. "Then it's going to be a goddamn national championship party. That's the only kind of party anyone in this room is going to. Because we're not fucking this up. We're the Westish Harpooners. Do you hear what I'm saying? *Do you hear me?*"

He sank down on a splintered bench. His shoulders rose and fell as if he were sobbing, but without any tears or noise. He felt pathetic. Always before, his rants and speeches had had an element of performance in them, an element of calculation. But this was pure need. After the season there was nothing. No baseball no football. No meds no apartment no job. No friends no girlfriend. Nothing. And it had to be that way for all of them, down to the last man. They couldn't just want to win. The other teams wanted to win, and the other teams had more talent. The Harpooners had to feel, like he did, that they would die if they lost.

64

Pella woke into the charcoal hum of predawn. Her hand shot to the alarm clock before it could complete even a single screechy *beeeep* that might wake Henry. His T-shirt and socks and warm-up pants, which he'd worn every day since she — since *they* — moved in, lay balled on the rug on his side of the bed. She scooped them up and carried the tiny bundle down to the dank half basement, shoved it into the ancient washing machine, added a half scoop of one of her roommates' Tide. She brushed her teeth and slipped out the front door, taking her usual detour around Mike's block. When she clocked in, Hero clicked his tongue at her jokingly: three minutes late.

The students kept dirtying dishes and mugs and glasses and silverware; the cooks kept scalding food to the bottoms of pots; the other dishwashers kept quitting because it was May, the weather was heavenly, and finals were looming. Pella kept picking up shifts. She wasn't going to classes anymore. You never knew who you'd run into in the lecture halls or out on the quad, and anyway she wanted the money she earned here, in the safety of the noisy, humid kitchen. She missed Professor Eglantine, but she wasn't going back into oral history class to face all those baseball players. She'd already bought the books for the seminar Professor E was teaching in the fall. By then Mike and Owen would be gone and the rest of them would have half forgotten her. Who knew what'd happen to Henry.

When the breakfast dishes were finished she headed to the VAC, her sweatshirt hood tugged up around her head like a burka. This didn't keep anyone from seeing her, of course—but it kept her from seeing them. She swam fifteen laps at her slowly improving pace, showered, and headed back for the midday shift.

Toward late afternoon she helped set up the salad bar for dinner. Chef Spirodocus emerged from his tiny office, where he'd been holed up doing paperwork. "Today," he said, "we make my favorite. Eggs Benedict."

Their first lessons had been elementary: how to stand in the kitchen without straining your back; how to hold a knife; then how to slice, chop, dice, mince, carve, julienne. Pella had nicks and cuts all up and down her hands—her still-swollen middle finger didn't help—but her skills were improving day by day. Chef Spirodocus had told her she could graduate to prep cook by fall, which was good, because the dishes were getting boring.

The hollandaise turned out perfectly, creamy and smooth but not too heavy. Pella plated the finished product and shared it out among the dinner shift's workers, who nodded approvingly. She wanted to take some home for Henry, but she knew he wouldn't touch anything so rich. He'd barely been eating. Instead she filled an empty plastic tub with soup from the salad bar's big crock and stuck it in her backpack.

When she arrived home, Henry was sitting on the living room couch, the television off, the remote control by his side, no book or magazine in sight. Pella touched the top of the TV to see if it was warm—yes. What kind of weird pride was that, that let you sit around someone else's house all day long, doing nothing, but kept you from wanting to be caught watching TV?

"Anybody home?" she asked peppily.

"Just me."

"How was your day?"

"Not bad."

"That's good."

She was the wrong caretaker, or coach, for someone so depressed: she was too indulgent, too empathetic. He'd be better off with someone tougher, someone who'd never really been depressed and didn't know what it was like. At least he'd managed to get his clothes from the washer to the dryer and back on his body. That was something.

His caved, vacant expression reminded her of all the days she'd spent pinned to her and David's bed by the white sunlight that streamed through the high windows of their loft (*There's a certain slant of light . . .*). Bad days, those. "Are you hungry?" she asked. "I brought some soup."

He hesitated, weighing his aversion to food against the mild censure he'd face if he declined. "I'll heat it up," Pella said, and headed for the kitchen. She dumped the soup in a saucepan, cranked the gas, waited for the pilot to catch.

Henry, having followed her into the kitchen, went to the sink and filled his Gatorade bottle with water. He carried that thing everywhere. Or at least he carried it from the bedroom to the bathroom to the living room to the kitchen — those, as far as Pella could tell, were the only places he went. He took a long gulp that drained the bottle, refilled it, and screwed the orange plastic cap back on. The scruff was thickening on his face and neck. Men and their beards. "You did the dishes," she said.

"Yeah."

"Thanks."

"Sure." He unscrewed the cap and took another gulp. "Your dad called."

"When?"

"While I was at class. He left a message."

Pella doubted that Henry had gone to class — in fact, she realized, it was Saturday. Which meant tomorrow was Sunday, her day off. She swirled a spoon through the bubbling soup and headed for the living room to check the voice mail.

"I erased it," Henry said. "Like you told me to."

"Oh." It was true she'd told Henry to do that, days ago—she wanted not to think about her dad for a little while, and she didn't want Noelle and Courtney to hear any forlorn messages that might lead them to gossip about their school's president—but it seemed presumptuous and maybe even cruel of Henry to have actually *done* it. "Okay."

"He said he wanted to talk to you about something. He said he was going to the baseball game tonight, but he'd have his cell."

"Okay. Thanks."

Henry's fingers twisted the orange lid back and forth on its threads. Something had occurred to him. "What day is it?"

"Saturday."

"Oh. Wow. Really?"

"Does that surprise you?"

He sank down at the table, twisted the orange lid. "Saturday night's when they play the final. They made the final. They could go to nationals."

There was little Pella could say to that. She set out two bowls from the wire dish rack and tried to pour the soup over the lip of the pot without spilling. There was probably a ladle in one of the drawers, but she didn't know which. It was annoying to live in a place where nothing was yours, where every move you made felt like thievery. Noelle was already annoyed with Henry's constant presence; kept making pointed jokes about splitting the rent four ways. Pella needed to talk to Henry about that, but it could wait till morning.

Even after the eggs Benedict, Pella was ravenous; she'd been eating more lately, a side effect of all the work and exercise. The soup was mulligatawny. It tasted delicious, and it would have been useful to try to parse the ingredients, but her first thought was that it would be too rich and spicy for Henry. Sure enough, he sipped a few mouthfuls and laid the spoon down beside his bowl. Something like chicken noodle would have been better, blander. Not that she'd had a choice: the soup of the day was the soup of the day. Something like Stockholm syndrome was going on here, or reverse Stockholm syndrome, depending on whom you considered the captive and whom the captor — she couldn't even taste the soup for herself but imagined it on Henry's tongue.

She finished her bowl. Then she finished Henry's. They put the unwashed bowls in the sink and walked to the bedroom. Pella stood on one side of the floor-bound futon and stripped down to her underwear, while Henry did the same on the other side. Her arms were growing less flabby from swimming and scrubbing pots; it made the lines of her tattoo look sharper, better drawn. Someday soon she would make up with her father once and for all. They'd been fighting half her life, and yet the fights always felt like aberrations. No matter how bad things got between them, she could always reach forward through time and grasp the moment, however distant, when they'd be as close as they were when she was six or ten.

She lowered herself to the futon from one side, Henry from the other. They faced each other under the cool dry sheets, their heads on separate pillows. They were the previous tenant's sheets and pillows, left in the hall closet: Pella had washed them twice instead of buying new ones. Part of the new frugality. She lay on her left side, facing Henry, her body pressing into the mattress with a pleasant weary weight. She knew that his stifled yawns meant something different from hers, were the signs of a caged, stymied energy turned inward and devouring itself, and she felt for him. They were like children or invalids, in bed at seven o'clock. Her hand slid onto his hip. He flinched and then relaxed.

Tonight was different, stranger than the first time, a kind of surrender to the tender meaninglessness of adulthood. She wasn't going to let him kiss her, with that beard, and he didn't try. Apart from the beard his body was like a Platonic ideal of a body, a smooth white marble statue, though already a little less muscular than she remembered. Like a statue, he didn't smell like much of anything. They clung together loosely, eyelids open, watching each other. He came quietly, with just a hint of a whimper. People thought becoming an adult meant that all your acts had consequences; in fact it was just the opposite.

Outside a springtime Saturday evening was just beginning—crickets chirped, speakers thumped, frat boys shouted from porch to porch. Pella reached down and felt for her book on the rug. She was reading Proust, something she'd never done before. For years she'd been planning to get her French in shape to read him in the original. But who knew when that would happen.

Henry pulled on his boxers beneath the covers, part of their weird routine of modesty, and left the room, shutting the door quietly behind him. As sleep closed over her Pella heard water running in the tub. He'd lie there until he heard Noelle or Courtney come in, which, tonight being Saturday, might be in six or seven hours or not at all.

65

ffenlight's meeting with the trustees ran long, and the drive, even at dangerous speed, took more than two hours, so he didn't arrive at Grand Chute Stadium until the top of the eighth inning. Beer, no matter how fervently one wished for it, was not being sold at the concession stand. He bought two hot dogs, applied mustard and relish, and found an available seat—not a swatch of corrugated bleacher but an actual flip-down seat—behind home plate. The UW–Chute Titans' colors were navy and gold, with emphasis on the navy, so that when Affenlight looked straight at the field and squinted, the seas of people filling his peripheral vision could easily be mistaken for Westish fans.

The Harpooners were trailing by the very respectable score of 3 to 0. They had played admirably to reach this, the regional championship game, winning three of their first four games in the double-elimination tournament, far exceeding the expectations of everyone involved, especially their opponents, who'd expected to crush them—and yet, as Owen told Affenlight on the phone this morning, to dream of winning this game was probably folly. The University of Wisconsin–Chute was on another level, a state-funded university with an enrollment of fifteen thousand and an extraordinary investment of pride and money in their baseball program, as evidenced by their lush, cozy, pro-style ballpark, suitable for hosting a regional tournament. Not to mention, Owen added, that this would basically be a home game for them.

"Excuses, excuses," said Affenlight, half joshing.

"Oh, we'll come to play," replied Owen. "Mike wouldn't have it otherwise. The real problem is pitching. We've never played so many games in so few days. Remember the old poem *Spahn and Sain and pray for rain?* For us it's *Starblind and Phlox and then get rocked.*"

"*And lots of walks.*"

"*And poor Coach Cox.* I don't know how long we can keep it up. Adam has already pitched two complete games. His eye contains that crazed I-can-do-anything look, but I don't know if he can lift his hand above his shoulder."

For as many games as Affenlight had attended this season, he'd yet to see Owen actually *play*. Now, as he settled into his seat, that beautiful creature was settling into the left-handed batter's box, a clear plastic face-mask attached to his batting helmet to protect his damaged cheek from further injury. Owen had complained vociferously about the contraption, which he considered unflattering and potentially performance-disrupting, but Coach Cox — good man — turned a deaf ear.

Whereas some hitters twitched and stomped while awaiting the pitch, chopping their bats into the strike zone, Owen exuded a listless calm. He might have been standing in the quad, pursuing a postlecture discussion, holding an umbrella against a light spring rain. The first pitch blazed past the inside corner, inches from his hip, and struck the catcher's glove with a sound more powerfully percussive than any Affenlight had heard at Westish Field, even when Adam Starblind was pitching. Affenlight flinched in fear for Owen's safety, leaving fingerprints in his hot-dog bun; Owen merely turned to watch the pitch go by, cocking his head in contemplative disagreement when the umpire called it a strike.

The second pitch came in just as fast but more toward the center of the plate. Owen, after waiting what seemed to be far too long, dropped his hands and swung. It was a baseball commonplace, dimly remembered from Affenlight's childhood days as a halfhearted Braves fan, that left-handed batters had more graceful swings than righties, long effortless swings that swooped down through the strike zone and greeted shoe-top pitches sweetly. Affenlight didn't see why this should be so, unless the right and left sides of the bodies possessed inherently different properties, something to do with the halves of the brain, but Owen's languid, elliptical swing did nothing to deflate the hypothesis.

The ball looped over the third baseman's head and landed squarely on the left-field line, kicking up a puff of chalk. Fair ball. The home crowd let out an anguished sigh that seemed all out of keeping with an empty-bases hit in a three-run game. As Owen loped safely into second base, they rose, almost in unison, and began to clap. Affenlight thought them very magnanimous to cheer so heartily for an opponent; somehow Owen inspired that kind of behavior in people.

Affenlight stood to clap as well, but it was the pitcher who, as the noise continued to mount, sheepishly tipped his cap. Affenlight, flummoxed, asked the woman beside him, who was wearing a gold-and-navy CHUTE YOUR ENEMIES sweatshirt, what happened. "That lucky twit," she said, indicating Owen, "just broke up Trevor's no-hitter."

Out on the electronic scoreboard in center field, the 0 in the Westish hit column had changed to a 1. Affenlight reproached himself; a real fan would have noticed that immediately. He reproached himself again; he'd gotten a dab of mustard on his Harpooner tie. Not that he didn't have three dozen more at home. "I don't know," he said. "I thought it a rather skillful play."

The woman chuckled. "I'm pretty sure his eyes were closed."

The next batter, Adam Starblind, drew a walk. "Your pitcher seems a bit rattled," Affenlight noted.

"Trevor? Please. These rich preppy kids couldn't hit him with a ten-foot pole."

Affenlight wanted to point out that several of the Harpooners came from extremely modest or even straitened circumstances, and that the team didn't have a baseball facility anywhere near this luxurious—how on earth did a public school afford it?—but it would be hard to make the case while wearing his best Italian suit, and anyway the game had reached a critical moment, two runners on, the tying run at the plate. The batter was the Harpooners' replacement for Henry Skrimshander at shortstop—Affenlight prided himself on knowing the students' names, but the freshpersons often eluded him. The Latino non-Henry, whatever his name, performed several rapid signs of the cross as he stepped into the batter's box. He took one strike, then another. He gamely fouled off two tough pitches, then slapped a ground ball that glanced off the fingertips of the second baseman's glove. Bases loaded.

"Al*most!*" cheered Affenlight, with what amounted to a kind of sneering glee. Remorse quickly followed. What if that second baseman was this woman's child? In any event, he was somebody's child.

"Do you have a son on the team?" he asked, trying to atone, but the woman simply shushed him and pointed to the field. Mike Schwartz, his daughter's cuckolded lover, was walking toward home plate.

The catcher called time and jogged out to calm Trevor, who was storming around behind the pitcher's mound, talking to himself. Affenlight focused his attention on the lovely Owen, who, while standing with both feet on the tiny island of third base, reached into his uniform's back pocket and produced a roll of mints. He offered one to Coach Cox, who declined with folded arms, and then to the third baseman, who shrugged and held out his palm.

Mike Schwartz, by comparison to Owen—or, really, to anyone— had a snarling, hyperactive mien in the batter's box, like a barely restrained bull. His back foot gouged at the dirt until it found a purchase it liked; his hips twisted, screwing his knock-kneed stance more tightly into the ground; his shoulders bobbed while his fists made curt, jerky motions that slashed the bat head through the air. He crowded close to home plate, smothering it with his bulk, daring the pitcher to find a place to throw the ball. Affenlight couldn't tell whether all this kinetic menace came naturally to Schwartz or was a performance designed to intimidate; probably any such distinction would be false. Only in the instant of the pitch's release did he quiet himself, and then the swing became compact and dangerous, and the pitch — a high fastball, probably in excess of ninety miles per hour — shot off the bat with a pure loud *ping* of aluminum. Affenlight leaped to his feet, thrust a fist in the air. The ball landed in the tall firs beyond the left-field wall, and all four Harpooners — Owen, Starblind, not-Henry, and Schwartz — stomped joyously on home plate in turn. Four to three, Harpooners.

Adam Starblind, who had been playing center field, came in to pitch the last two innings. The Titans stranded a runner on third in the eighth, and in the ninth not-Henry and Professor Guladni's son Ajay turned a handsome double play to end the game. Affenlight wended his way through the stands toward Duane Jenkins, the Westish athletic director, who was standing behind the Harpooner dugout, filming the celebration with his cell phone.

"Nationals," Duane said, beaming. "South Carolina. Can you believe it?"

"I can now." Affenlight held out his hand. "Congratulations, Duane. A lot of hard work went into this."

"I'd like to take the credit. But we all know who to thank." Duane jerked his head toward the field, where Mike Schwartz had somehow obtained a folding chair and was sitting quietly apart, undoing the buckles of his shin guards while his teammates jitterbugged around Adam Starblind, who thrust the big faux-gold trophy aloft.

Affenlight wrapped an arm around Duane's schlumpy shoulders. "That's precisely what I wanted to talk to you about."

66

Alcohol was banned from the locker room by NCAA decree, but Schwartz had bought three cases of champagne with the last of Coach Cox's money — he'd also paid his May rent and his Visa bill — and, with Meat's help, smuggled them into an empty locker at Chute Stadium and covered them with bags of ice. When the Harpooners returned to the locker room after accepting their trophy and hugging their families and posing for pictures and plenty of jumping around, the ice had melted and seeped out the locker's cracks, forming a giant puddle on the fancy slate navy-and-gold checkerboard floor. Meat undid the lock, and a few moments later they were having the victory celebration they'd seen on TV so many times, dancing shirtless in their sliding shorts to the Spanish hip-hop that blared from the boombox Izzy brought on road trips. Only the cameras were missing.

Schwartz took a long slug from his personal bottle of champagne, which he wasn't going to waste by spraying around, and sought out Owen, who was shimmying on top of the locker-room bench, his Harpooner cap twisted and cocked like he was from the hood. He paused in his gyrations to give Schwartz a high five. "I'm wearing my cap askew," he said.

"Looks good." Schwartz leaned in to be heard above the music without shouting. "Listen, Buddha. After your surgery — they gave you something?"

Owen nodded. "Percocet."

Schwartz belted back some more bubbly. "Huh."

Owen reached into the locker, unzipped his bag, and produced a translucent orange cylinder. "This is what's left." He slipped the bottle into Schwartz's palm and closed Schwartz's fingers around it, like a grandparent distributing dollar bills or illicit stores of candy.

Schwartz, not wanting to seem eager, didn't shake the cylinder, but he gauged its near weightlessness with dismay. "Thanks, Buddha."

"Aye aye, my captain."

Schwartz retreated to a bathroom stall, just to be by himself for a minute, and popped two of the remaining three capsules, hoping to keep one in reserve for later, but it seemed silly to let that lonely little thing jitter around in there like that, like some kind of keepsake, so he swallowed it too. Three Percs weren't going to do shit anyway.

Even in the best circumstances his enjoyment of moments like this was bound to be partial, muted, hedged; he was already thinking about the next game and how not to lose it. It was a coach's mentality, a field general's mentality, and it was his mentality too. Permanent vigilance, because disaster always lurked. The best he could hope for was an instant of peace before the planning began again, a moment when his muscles unclenched and he thought, *Okay, fine, we did it.*

But today he couldn't even have that. All he could have today was a sickly champagne-and-Percocet high, and the knowledge that there'd be at least two more games — because nationals were double elimination — before he had to face his fucked-up life. If Henry were here, Henry's joy would be total, his holy-fool dancing would put the Buddha's to shame, but Henry wasn't here. He hadn't pushed through that one last barrier, his fear of succeeding, beyond which the world lay totally open to him. Schwartz would never live in a world so open. His would always be occluded by the fact that his understanding and his ambition outstripped his talent. He'd never be as good as he wanted to be, not at baseball, not at football, not at reading Greek or taking the LSAT. And beyond all that he'd never be as *good* as he wanted to be. He'd never found anything inside himself that was really good and pure, that wasn't double-edged, that couldn't just as easily become its opposite. He had tried and failed to find that thing, and he would continue to try and fail, or else he would leave off trying and keep on failing. He had no art to call his own. He knew how to motivate people, manipulate people, move them around; this was his only skill. He was like a minor Greek god you've barely heard of, who sees through the glamour of the armor and down into the petty complexity of each soldier's soul. And in the end is powerless to bring about anything resembling his vision. The loftier, arbitrary gods intervene.

Working with Henry was the closest he'd ever come, because Henry knew only one thing, wanted only one thing, and his single-mindedness made him — made both of them — pure. But Henry had tried to beat himself, had inserted himself into the equation, had started to worry about being perfect instead of simply becoming the best goddamn short-stop ever, and now he was no better than Schwartz. He was just like Schwartz, a fucked-up guy with a fucked-up life.

"Schwartzy!" yelled Rick. "Get the bleepity bleep out here!"

Henry, Schwartz thought, hauling himself up from the sink over which he'd been hunched, staring at his sunken but shaven face through a mess of dried toothpaste and spit flecks. *Henry's here.* He headed back into the locker room, still throttling his empty champagne bottle. The Harpooners had gathered in a huddle in the center of the room, undressed and dripping champagne, arms draped around one another's shoulders. Rick and Owen stepped apart to open a spot for Schwartz, and the circle expanded to accommodate his girth. Henry wasn't there. The rest of them pressed their temples together and swayed back and forth like junior high school kids at their last-ever junior high school dance, singing the school shanty at the top of their lungs.

67

L ate that night, after the team returned from Chute, Owen came. And as they made love, and afterward, as they lay together in the dark, Affenlight kept one ear open, listening for Pella. It was unlikely she'd show up unannounced, after so emphatically declaring she wanted a few weeks to herself, and now past midnight it grew less likely with each passing moment. Even if she did come she wouldn't barge into his darkened bedroom. And yet. Every voice that floated up from the Small Quad seized his senses. Every standard nighttime sound produced by the apartment—the crack of frost in the back of the fridge, the chiropractic groans of walls and floors, the scratch of the mouse Affenlight had never seen but knew existed—caused his breath to catch, just for a second. His breath caught a lot; there were lots of sounds.

"Are you all right?" Owen asked. "You seem tense."

"I'm okay." He felt guilty more than anything. Guilty to Pella for having Owen here; guilty to Owen for the way he himself was absent, his attention scattered like pollen over the quad.

"Tell me about the house."

Now that he was no longer *in* the house, knee-deep in the Bremens' belongings, distracted by Sandy's superior saleswomanship, surrounded and perplexed by their superfluously detailed lives, the place had begun to take shape in Affenlight's mind. He began to talk about it to Owen, haltingly at first, but as he got rolling he started to remember and describe the shapes of rooms, the size of windows, the shaved-wood smell of the kitchen's ancient buckling cedar floor. Soon he was verbally ripping up carpets, repainting rooms, converting the Bremens' den into a proper library with custom bookshelves. The backyard was even expansive enough that you could build a little writer's shed there at the back edge of the property, overlooking the lake; perhaps that would be profligate, given how big the house was already, but it might also be fun, and clarifying to the mind, to have a spartan outpost back there, a spot without comforts or distractions, in which to sit and write. Perhaps — he couldn't believe he was saying this aloud — he would even be moved to revive the novel he'd begun so long ago, *Night of the Large Few Stars,* the 153 pages of which were still sitting in a drawer somewhere. Or, better yet, to begin something new — no use chasing the dreams of so long ago. But to have the shed, to bundle up and stoke a tiny stove and look out at the lake and write, would be good. And if visitors with writing projects to pursue — here he glanced at Owen — would make use of it too, well, all the more reason.

"Sounds like you want to buy it."

Affenlight hesitated. "I do." His eyes flicked anxiously to Owen's face. He felt like he was suggesting that they break up, though Owen looked supremely unconcerned, and in truth Affenlight knew that he was as capable of breaking up with Owen as he was of sawing off his own leg with his letter opener: he'd do it to save Pella's life but probably not his own.

"I think it's a great idea," Owen said.

"You do?"

"Certainly. This apartment is, as my mother has noted, a bit dismal. I think you'd benefit from having some more space to roam around in. Space that's brighter, and really yours. And Pella would like it too. Especially if you let her decorate."

"What about us?" said Affenlight, stressing *us.*

"What about us?" replied Owen, stressing *about.*

"I mean . . . you're going away."

"That doesn't mean you shouldn't buy a house. Unless you'd like me to talk you out of it? Is that what I'm supposed to be doing?"

"Yes please." Affenlight lay on his side, one hip rolled over on top of Owen's thigh, one cheek on Owen's shoulder. It was a quintessentially feminine posture, or had been throughout his forty years of sharing beds — the man on his back with hands behind his head, the woman nestled against him — and yet he slipped into it naturally now. With his free hand he caressed Owen's belly, which itself felt almost feminine, not muscled but soft with the strong, invulnerable softness of youth. His senses remained on high alert, but for the moment the quad had slipped into silence. It was too late for the students to go out to the bars, too early for them to come home.

Owen assumed his lecturer's tone. "That's easy, Guert. What you so blithely call a house would better be termed an ecological disaster. How many barrels of oil does it take to heat a big old place like that through a bad winter, not that we have bad winters anymore? Just to keep a couple of bodies warm?"

Affenlight couldn't help wondering which couple of bodies he meant. Two Affenlights? An Affenlight and a Dunne? " 'I have heard that stiff people lose something of their awkwardness under high ceilings, and in spacious halls,' " he said, quoting Emerson's *The Conduct of Life*.

"I'd hardly describe you as a stiff person." Owen slid a hand down between Affenlight's legs, toyed with him gently. "At least not right now."

"We just finished," Affenlight protested, not wanting to be mentioned even jokingly in the same breath as that particular ailment of age, but in fact he was already thickening under Owen's touch.

"Thoreau's journals," Owen said. " 'When a philosopher wants high ceilings, he goes outside.' He doesn't buy an oversize house that requires massive amounts of dwindling resources to heat in the winter. And to cool in the summer — let's not even talk about air-conditioning. Why not just buy a McMansion out by the freeway, install a helicopter pad in back? Do you think you get a free pass because the house is old and lovely? It doesn't work that way, Guert. Waste is waste, sprawl is sprawl. Your good taste doesn't count. If there's any kind of exclusionary, private-club-style afterlife, St. Peter won't be asking questions at the gate. You'll just be lugging all the coal and oil you've burnt in your life, that's been burnt on your behalf, and if it fits through the gate you're in. And the gate's not big. It's like eye-of-a-needle-sized. That's what constitutes ethics these days — not who screwed or got screwed by whom.

"Perhaps you're better off here, Guert. This place suits your spartan tendencies, which I much admire. You're an especially unencumbered type of soul."

"Jeez, O," said Affenlight glumly. "You didn't have to do quite such a good job."

"Sorry." Owen released Affenlight's half-hard penis, kissed him on the forehead. "I get worked up."

Sometimes Affenlight worried that Owen dallied with him solely so that he could whisper in Affenlight's ear about campus-wide environmental initiatives. But that was probably reductive, if not downright paranoid, and anyway such things were worth being whispered to about. The schools Affenlight had been affiliated with — Westish in the late sixties and recently; Harvard in the eighties and nineties — were places where environmentalism had a modest presence, academically and publicly, and his work had tended in other directions, toward questions of political and social selfhood, male identity mixed with sex and a smidgen of Marx. But he was a farmer by birth, a biologist by undergraduate degree, a hippie by year of birth, and a diligent student of Emerson and Thoreau, and so Owen's growing and insistent interest in ecology was easy for him to assimilate. Perhaps he was a trend jumper, in terms of intellectual preoccupations, a humanist back when humanity was popular, now moved on to bigger things, but certain trends were better jumped late than never.

"Now that I think about it," Owen said, "this whole building's on one thermostat, isn't it?"

"Yes."

"So every night and all weekend, when there's nobody downstairs, the whole building gets heated just for you. And for me, sometimes. Which must be terrifically wasteful, given how drafty this place is and how old the furnace must be. You'd be better off with the house."

"Yeah," said Affenlight, "but they'd probably leave the heat on all the time anyway."

"Who's *they*? It's your college."

It wasn't quite that simple, but Affenlight couldn't disagree with the principle. Owen began enthusiastically concocting plots for the further greening of Westish, and for the installation of solar panels on Affenlight's new house. Affenlight loved it when Owen grew enthusiastic, he even loved the plots, but his mind kept drifting away, away, away. Away to Pella. He was buying the house for her, in hopes that she would stay with him for four years. Or three—she might want to graduate in three. And then she could move on to grad school at Harvard or Yale, or even Stanford if she wished. Affenlight disliked the thought of sending her back to California, against which he harbored a grudge even though it was the source of Owen, because California had already once swallowed up Pella and kept her for four long years.

Not that grad school was the only respectable path in life; perhaps Pella would devise other plans. Affenlight, for his part, planned only to not be overbearing. She could visit the house whenever she liked—could come over for dinner, for pumpkin soup. Her rooms upstairs, should she choose to use them; his rooms down. Owen was right, it was a lot of space for two people, one of whom didn't even live there, but the solar panels! He would install the solar panels, cost be damned, even if the cost-benefit analysis declared that they wouldn't pay off until long after his projected life span had expired. He would outlive the actuaries' projections, would leave the actuaries dejected and abashed at their own uselessness, would remain on this marvelous earth until his ingenious, responsible, not-quite-prohibitively-expensive solar panels had done the work of a thousand, of ten thousand, barrels of criminal oil. And by that time Owen and Pella would be nearing middle age themselves, and global warming—as Owen was now saying, though Affenlight was no longer more than half listening—would have accelerated its decimation of the world's poor equatorial regions, and the true geopolitical shitstorm—as Owen was now saying, and Affenlight's ears perked up because Owen rarely cursed—would be under way. Even as sleep closed in on Affenlight and expanded the realm of what was possible to include the stuff of dreams, there was no real way to incorporate Owen's words into a rosy picture of what the world would be like after he, Affenlight, was gone, a world in which Pella and Owen, and any children Pella might someday have, would have to live, but at least he could bequeath to her (and maybe to them both, to share in some way, because who knew but that they'd eventually become close friends) a pretty white solar-paneled house near the lake in northeastern Wisconsin, and as the summers spoiled and the coasts flooded and the monocrops failed and the powers that be squabbled and panicked, as Owen was now describing in fearsome detail in his sonorous butterscotch voice, northeastern Wisconsin would probably not be the worst place to be.

68

Henry was standing in Pella and Noelle and Courtney's kitchen, washing the dishes, drinking the first cup from a pot of coffee he'd made. He'd started drinking coffee since he'd been here. It was something to do. When he'd finished the dishes — there were just a few glasses and mugs; Pella ate at work, and Noelle and Courtney subsisted on red wine and Red Bull — he sprayed down the sink with a bleachy cleanser and wiped it with a sponge. Through the window the late-afternoon light was dimming steadily but still more gold than tea colored. This was the fragile hour of the day when he felt okay. The hour when he got out of bed and, if he sensed that Noelle and Courtney weren't home, out of Pella's room entirely.

He wrung out the sponge, propped it on the sink's back. Only a few minutes left before the light would fade. If he'd begun his day earlier — at eight, say, or even ten or noon — he might have felt all right today. It would be smart to get up early tomorrow. *Tomorrow I'll get up early,* he thought, and then smiled to himself, because the coffee was making him feel okay, and because he'd promised himself the same thing yesterday and the day before and the day before that, so that it had become a private running joke.

He cleaned the coagulated orange soap out of the little crown top of the dish-soap bottle. When Noelle and Courtney were home, or when he sensed they might be home, he stayed in Pella's room, lying low, peeing in a Gatorade bottle. Pella didn't seem to mind. Not about the pee — she didn't know about that — but about his presence in general. She seemed okay with it. He thought of the *Odyssey*, which he'd half read in Professor Eglantine's class — Ulysses trapped on Calypso's island, wasting time, but he was no Ulysses, had no Ithaca to get home to, even though his beard had come in darker and fuller than he'd expected, a harsh brown beard that after a month or two would be the sort you might see on a statue of Ulysses, or that you did see on the statue of Melville that stood in the corner of the Small Quad, peering out to sea.

He opened the pantry out of boredom. There wasn't much there. Olive oil, salt and pepper, girlie protein bars in pastel foil. Protein-enhanced whole-wheat vermicelli. Four-packs of sugar-free Red Bull. A can of black beans. There used to be two cans of black beans: in his first days here, when he was still adapting to his lack of appetite, he'd eaten the other can. He'd also eaten a girlie protein bar. Once he'd even tried to cook vermicelli on the stove. He'd never cooked pasta before, and the job was made more difficult by the fact that he had to keep running to the living room window to make sure that Courtney and Noelle weren't about to come in and catch him stealing their food. He didn't boil enough water; then he put in way too much vermicelli; then he cooked it way too long. The water evaporated from the pot, and the pasta sat there in a dull lump like an animal's brain. Now he preferred not eating. Not because not eating meant not stealing, not because not eating meant not cooking, but just because.

I should stop drinking coffee too, he thought. He'd almost thought *give up* coffee, but that was a misleading phrase. There seemed to be meaning in it, meaning that didn't exist. When you gave something up, who or what did you give it up *to*? Giving something up implied that your sacrifice made sense, and Henry knew that this was untrue. The days did not accumulate and turn into something better than days, no matter how well you used them. The days could not be used. He did not have a plan. He'd stopped playing baseball and eating beans and now he would stop drinking coffee. That was all.

The front door opened.

Henry froze, listened to his heart. He was a rat or a roach in this house — owned the place when he was alone, roamed the rooms like a roach god, and then scurried to safety when one of the humans walked in. Now he was trapped. He grabbed a pot he'd already washed, sudsed the sponge, and began to wash it again. It was too early to be Pella, who was working the dinner shift, and even Pella might be a mixed blessing. She'd urged him to go out more during the daytime, and he'd nodded in agreement. He never knew what to say to her.

He kept scrubbing the clean pot, pretending not to be able to hear footsteps in the living room over the running water, pretending not to feel the heat of the eyes of the person who stood in the doorway.

"Henry."

He could plausibly ignore a soft voice like that.

"Henry."

He could not-so-plausibly ignore a not-so-soft voice like that.

"HENRY."

He left the water on, turned around, his hands covered with suds. Pella's hair was pulled back and her ears were flushed pink. She sighed and let her wicker bag full of soup and swim gear bang down on the linoleum.

"We need to talk."

Maybe he'd left a pee-filled Gatorade bottle next to the bed. He'd tried to be careful about that, tried to remember to dump the bottles in the toilet and rinse them every day, but part of him, the truest Henry-part, didn't *want* to remember, wanted to keep the pee forever, and maybe he'd let that part get the best of him. It was the one real freedom he had, waking at noon with his bladder full of water and coffee and pissing a long clear stream into the bottle in the bedroom without having to go down the hall and worry that someone would be in the bathroom, or would knock on the bathroom door while he was peeing and be annoyed with him because it wasn't his bathroom at all.

It was a three-year-old's freedom, yes, he recognized that. Like peeing in the lake on those August evenings after Schwartz had worked him like a dog and he'd swum way out and turned back to look at the few lights winking on the Westish shore. He didn't want to rinse out the Gatorade bottle, okay? He wanted a permanent collection of all his pee and shit, not that he ever shat anymore, now that he'd stopped eating.

"Sure," he said. Bubbles scudded down the backs of his hands. "Let's talk."

"Good." She gestured toward the Formica table with its three matching chairs. "Sit down."

Henry sat down. Pella took a mug from the cupboard and poured herself coffee. She sat down at the table, cupped her mug with two hands. Her face looked leaner than when Henry first met her, leaner but also healthier. He thought of asking her to marry him. The thought came idly, in a what-if way, the way that sometimes when his face came close to Owen's he wondered what would happen if they kissed.

"Henry, what are you doing here? And don't say the dishes."

He looked at the sink, the sponge, the still-dripping faucet. "I like it here."

"No, you don't," Pella said. "But that's not the point. We talked about this, remember? We agreed that you can't hang out here all day. You're going to get us kicked out. And then where'll we be?"

Henry nodded.

"Why are you nodding?" Pella said, her voice rising. "It wasn't a yes-or-no question."

He stopped nodding. Pella looked down at her coffee. "Sorry," she said. "What I meant to say was, I talked to Chef Spirodocus today, and he said it would be great if you wanted to come back to work. You know how much he likes you. And you know how everybody quits this time of year. Nice weather. Finals."

Henry looked at her.

"It wasn't even my idea. Chef Spirodocus brought it up."

He shook his head. "I can't."

"I know you don't want to bump into anyone. But you wouldn't have to. We'd be on shift together. I'd take care of the salad bar and the juice machines and all the other dining room stuff. You could just stay in the back and do dishes. Get a little exercise. Make a little money."

"I can't," Henry said. "Not yet."

"Okay," Pella said. "Okay. Then I have one other suggestion. Hear me out, okay?" She reached into her sweatshirt pocket and pulled out her little vial of sky-blue pills, removed the cap, and tapped one into her hand.

Henry shook his head.

"They work," Pella said. "I should know."

"I don't want them to work."

"There's nothing to be afraid of. It doesn't, like, change your personality or anything. You're still you. You're *more* like you." Christ, Pella thought, I should be in a commercial.

"It does something."

It was getting dark in the kitchen. Pella got up, brought over the coffee pot, refilled both their cups, sat back down.

A pill was the opposite of what he wanted. A pill was an answer that somebody else had worked hard to come up with. He didn't want that. A pill was small and potent. He wanted something huge and empty. He'd decided not to drink coffee anymore and just like that the smell of it wafting up from the mug nauseated him. He covered the mug's opening with his hand, let the steam condense on his palm.

"Say something." Pella rested her cheek on her hand, looked at him. "Talk to me."

He'd never been able to talk to anyone, not really. Words were a problem, *the* problem. Words were tainted somehow — or no, *he* was tainted somehow, damaged, incomplete, because he didn't know how to use words to say anything better than "Hi" or "I'm hungry" or "I'm not."

Everything that had ever happened was trapped inside him. Every feeling he'd ever felt. Only on the field had he ever been able to express himself. Off the field there was no other way than with words, unless you were some kind of artist or musician or mime. Which he wasn't. It wasn't that he wanted to die. That wasn't it. That wasn't what not eating was about. It wasn't about perfection either.

What would he say to her, if he was going to speak truly? He didn't know. Talking was like throwing a baseball. You couldn't plan it out beforehand. You just had to let go and see what happened. You had to throw out words without knowing whether anyone would catch them — you had to throw out words you *knew* no one would catch. You had to send your words out where they weren't yours anymore. It felt better to talk with a ball in your hand, it felt better to let the ball do the talking. But the world, the nonbaseball world, the world of love and sex and jobs and friends, was made of words.

Pella was sipping her coffee, watching him, waiting. You couldn't predict what she'd look like in three or thirteen or thirty-three years. Maybe she'd sprout a third eye, or the strange purply hue of her hair would turn paper white overnight. More likely she would just become more weirdly beautiful with each passing year, though it was impossible, at least for him, to predict what path that beauty would take. Which made her different from all the other girls at Westish, all the other girls he knew. Not that he loved Pella. He didn't. But he could imagine how someone could love her, and that someone was Schwartzy. They were pretty much perfect for each other. If he, Henry, way back in the days before he arrived on campus, had been able to picture what the women of Westish would look like — twelve hundred girls of the sort Mike Schwartz would date — he would have pictured twelve hundred Pella Affenlights.

But if Pella and Schwartz made a perfect whole, like the yin and yang on Owen's favorite pajamas, or the two halves of a baseball's cover, two infinity-shaped pieces of leather stitched together with love's red thread, then there was no room for Henry. If you were a boy and you loved a girl, you could make plans together. And if you were a boy and you loved a boy — he thought of Owen and Jason Gomes on the steps of Birk Hall, heads bowed together, sharing a joint; he had no comparable image of Owen and President Affenlight to call upon — then you could make plans together too. The world would be against you, would threaten you and call you names, but at least it would understand. It had words for what you were doing. But if you were Henry and you needed Mike you were simply screwed. There were no words for that, no ceremony that would guarantee your future. Every day was just that: a day, a blank, a nothing, in which you had to invent yourself and your friendship from scratch. The weight of everything you'd ever done was nothing. It could all vanish, just like that. Just like this.

"I told myself," Pella said softly, "that if you wouldn't come back to work, and you wouldn't try the pills, and you wouldn't agree to see someone, then I was going to kick you out."

Henry nodded, stared at the back of his hand, the hand that was blocking the coffee smell.

"And you're not going to do any of those things. Am I right?"

He moved his hand, looked at the trembling surface of the coffee. He thought, *I'm not going to drink coffee anymore.* It was too dark, too dirty. Too much like food. The thought of no more coffee and no more food made him momentarily happy. He wanted to follow that happiness where it led — wanted to and would. It was a journey he was embarking on. Had already embarked on: how many days since he'd eaten more than a spoonful of soup? And each day, each hour, each minute furthered the journey. He knew what would happen if he ate: his body would churn up the food, piss it and sweat it and shit it out, stack little segments of protein on his shoulders till he looked like the guy on the SuperBoost jar. He knew how to participate in that whole cycle. But not-eating was new. It was new and just for him: he couldn't tell Pella about it. She wouldn't understand.

"Am I right?" Pella repeated.

Henry nodded. "I can't."

"Okay." He watched her gather her resolve. He felt bad that he was making her do this. "Okay," she said. "Then I think you should probably go."

Henry shoved back his chair and stood. His knees wobbled a little, not in an unpleasant way: he felt loose and light, like a parade balloon. When he got back to the room Owen wasn't home.

69

Practice had ended an hour before, and now it was just the two of them together in the dimness of the third-floor gym, the smaller man crouched in the batting cage, unleashing swing after swing like a repeatable toy, the other standing behind the cage's netting with his chin declined and his arms crossed over his chest. After a dozen line drives in a row, Izzy fouled one straight back. Schwartz reached out and snared it barehanded, strands of nylon netting between the ball and his hand.

"Keep your hands up," he said.

"Aye aye, *Abuelo.*"

Schwartz didn't mind the nickname, which all the freshpersons had adopted. It referred to his widow's peak and his creaky knees, his crotchetiness, his penchant for dispensing pearls of wisdom like an old man on a porch, but there was a more interesting meaning in there too. For Izzy and the other young players, Henry was the father figure, the guy who'd harassed and cajoled and counseled them day by day, bucked them up and called them out, made them memorize passages of Aparicio — taught them, in his own imperturbable way, the lessons Schwartz had taught to Henry and Rick and Starblind. Henry was their father and Schwartz was *abuelo.* But now their father had abandoned them, as fathers often did, and the old man was back in charge.

"Keep your weight back," he said. "You're lunging."

Ping.

Ping.

Ping.

"Goddamnit, Izzy. Quit slapping at the ball like that. This isn't a catfight."

Ping.

Actually, the kid looked good. He wasn't Henry, but he was going to be one hell of a college ballplayer. Better than Starblind, most likely. Better than Schwartz, for sure.

His batting stance was pure Skrimmer: the easy sink of the knees, the sense of prevailing silence, the dart of the hands to the ball. Good players tended to be good mimics; old footage of Aparicio, if you were as familiar as Schwartz with Henry's movements and mannerisms, was downright eerie to watch. And now, in a similar way, it was eerie to watch Izzy. The lineage was clear.

Duane Jenkins, the school's AD, was standing at the far end of the gym, hands in his khaki pockets. "Hey Mike," he called. "You got a sec?"

Schwartz gave Izzy a fist bump through the nylon. "Strong work," he said. "We're going to need that this weekend."

"I'm done, *Abuelo?*"

"You're never done. Go get dinner."

Schwartz followed Jenkins up to the AD's office, tried to arrange himself in a tiny cloth-covered chair. If big men ran the world, as was often supposed, you'd think they could get the furniture right.

"*Nationals.*" Jenkins shook his head in wonderment. "How's it feel?"

"It'll feel pretty good if we win."

Jenkins smiled. "Win or lose, it's been a heck of a year. Especially for you. Conference champs in football. A regional title in baseball. Academic all-conference. School record for home runs."

Schwartz looked at his watch. He wasn't in the mood for a Mike Schwartz retrospective.

"Westish sports are having an unprecedented amount of success across the board, Mike, and that's mostly your doing. Coach Cox's been here for thirteen years, Coach Foster for ten. Somehow I don't think they suddenly turned into geniuses four years ago. And I can't say I'm getting a heck of a lot smarter either. You've changed the culture of this entire program."

"What's your point, Duane?" Schwartz liked Jenkins, he'd always liked Jenkins, because even though Jenkins didn't know what he was doing, he tended not to bullshit. But this sounded suspiciously like bullshit.

Jenkins smiled sheepishly. "Sorry. I was trying to lead into this slowly, but I should know better by now, with you.

"I don't know if you've locked in any plans for next year, but I've been authorized to offer you a job."

Schwartz's back spasmed, just above his ass. He squeezed the arms of the too-small chair and lifted himself a few inches off the cloth, grimacing.

"Assistant football coach, assistant baseball coach, and assistant athletic director in charge of recruiting and raising funds. Basically you'd be doing what you've been doing for the past four years. Except instead of paying for the privilege, you'd be getting paid." Jenkins opened a folder on his desk, took out a sheet of paper covered in tiny type, and handed it to Schwartz. Circled in ink, halfway down the page, was a number.

Schwartz had spent enough time trying to finagle money for the football and baseball programs that he knew the AD's budget down to the dollar. "You can't afford this."

Jenkins smiled, shrugged. "It's authorized."

It wasn't graduate-of-Yale-Law money, it wasn't first-round-draft-pick money, but it was okay. Surprisingly okay. A person could pay his rent, his Visa bill. He could even, before too long, put down a payment on a car that could hold a quart of oil, get the Buddha off his back about his carbon footprint.

"The funding's locked in for three years minimum," Jenkins was saying. "But if you wanted to leave sooner, to go back to school or to do whatever, you'd be free to do so. I'd say however many years we could keep you around, whether one or three or thirty, would be a blessing for us."

Schwartz wondered where he'd gotten the money. Jenkins wasn't the kind of mover-shaker who could drum up funds where there weren't any. That was why he was the athletic director of a school that had always taken pride in the mediocrity of its athletics: he wasn't a mover-shaker.

"So?" Jenkins asked.

Schwartz shook his head. "No thanks."

Jenkins looked confused, maybe even crestfallen. "What do you mean?"

"I mean, no thanks. I don't want to coach."

Jenkins scratched his thinning auburn hair above one ear. "But you already *are* a coach," he said. "You're the best coach this school's ever had, and we've never paid you a penny. Might as well let us make it up to you, at least for a year."

"Can't do it, Duane."

Jenkins leaned back in his chair, tried to regroup. Glanced around the office as if trying to take in the big picture. "Can I ask what you plan to do instead?"

"Don't know."

Jenkins nodded. "But you're sick of the grind. Road trips. Two-a-days. Supervising workouts. Half your life inside this building. The whole deal."

"I'm not sick of it," said Schwartz. "I just—" Just what? Just didn't want to wake up in twenty years and see behind him a string of lives he'd changed, stretching out endlessly, rah rah go team, while he himself stayed exactly the same. Stagnant. Ungreat. Still wearing sweatpants to work. He who cannot, coaches.

"There's benefits there," Jenkins said. "Health insurance, dental. As for vacation, we shut down for most of July. Plus you can eat for free in the dining hall. Not sure how appealing that is."

"It's a nice offer."

"I could probably tack on another grand or two," Jenkins said. "But that's about it."

"It's a nice offer," Schwartz repeated. "I wouldn't want more."

"So you'll think about it?"

"No."

"Think about it." Jenkins took the contract, which Schwartz was still holding, and put it back in the folder. He put the folder in his desk. "The job starts August fifteenth. There are no other candidates."

70

Affenlight, as he sat at his desk, slid one socked foot from its bur-
gundy loafer and rubbed his instep, which itched, on the rigid
heel of the shoe. Competing versions of the coming year's budget were
spread out before him, along with the official proposals of Students for a
Responsible Westish and transcripts of discussions Affenlight had had
with environmental consultants and activists and architects, the people
who'd undertaken these sorts of transformations at wealthier, more on-
the-ball-type schools. He'd been toiling hard enough lately that Mrs.
McCallister had resumed greeting him in song.

Beside him on the rug, not toiling at all, lay Contango, his regal head
at rest on his white paws. This was a trial run, while Sandy Bremen was
in Taos decorating their new place.

Affenlight felt bleary; the numbers blurred and shifted before his
eyes. A cup of coffee would perk him up, but it was already 4:37, 5:37 in
South Carolina, where Owen was, and Mrs. McCallister would have
dumped the day's sludge before she left. He would need to make a whole
fresh pot. Perhaps he should take the dog for a walk instead, refresh
himself that way.

He extracted something small and dry from the corner of a nostril
and flicked it toward the wastebasket. Then he lifted his hindquarters,
grasped the arms of his antique leather chair, and shuffled ninety degrees
left to face the window. The chair was sturdy and comfortable, suitably

presidential — it had supported the buttocks of every Westish president since Arthur Hart Birk himself — but sometimes Affenlight pined for a sleek modern one, with casters and a medial axis on which you could spin. Having shuffled the big chair to the window, he leaned his forehead against the glass, which felt cold despite the sunlight, and dragged his neatly trimmed nails across the exposed portion of the screen, producing a scratchy metallic sound. The word for what a chair should do had been escaping him: *swivel*. Melville had once called America a seat of snivelization; what Affenlight wanted was a seat of swivelization.

Outside the window, a dining-hall worker in a navy smock and cap hurried out for a smoke. A girl in navy shorts with Greek letters across the butt tossed a pink Frisbee, bending it expertly between the trees. A skein of geese passed overhead. Scaffolding had been appended to the side of Louvin Hall, which had a leaky roof. Yellow rope strung between white stakes protected a newly sodded corner; Infrastructure loved to try to make the place seem idyllic for commencement, sometimes going so far as to spray-paint dead patches of grass bright green. Piano notes wafted like smoke, mixed with bland chirpy birdsong. A pizza deliveryman emerged from Louvin, rezipped his red insulated hamper.

Affenlight felt expansive, as if he'd had one scotch and was angling for a second. Pella didn't know about the house yet — he didn't want to unveil the surprise over e-mail, which was the only way they'd been communicating — but negotiations were proceeding apace with the Bremens. And, happily, Pella had decided to become a full-time student for the fall semester. He missed her, more so when she was a mile away than a thousand, but he sensed that they'd made a renewed commitment to each other, he by buying the house, she by enrolling at Westish. His future as a father seemed more secure than it had in a decade. Things were moving ahead. Mike Schwartz hadn't accepted Jenkins's offer, but that was his prerogative. And in any case, it wasn't for Pella's sake that Affenlight had fought hard to apportion the money for a job for Schwartz. It wasn't even because Schwartz would repay his salary twenty times over, in the funds he'd raise directly and in the improved PR that athletic success would bring, though that was indubitably true.

It was because Affenlight could tell that Schwartz felt the same way about Westish College that he did. If Affenlight were to list the things he loved, he wouldn't include Westish—that would seem silly, like saying you loved yourself. He spent half his time frustrated with, ambivalent about, annoyed at the place. But anything that happened to alter the fortunes of Westish College, however small; anything that was done to or even said about Westish College, Affenlight took more seriously than if it were happening to himself. He would protect Westish from any danger. That attitude was taxing—it kept you ever vigilant—but it was invigorating as well. It served to expand the self far beyond its usual confines. And Mike Schwartz felt like that about Westish too. Schwartz might not realize it yet—hell, it had taken Affenlight thirty years to figure it out—but he felt like that too.

Contango had fallen fast asleep: so much for their constitutional. Affenlight went to the hall and brewed a pot of coffee. As he sipped a steaming mugful—MAMA AIN'T HAPPY—he decided to reward himself for a week well spent by setting aside the budget and working on his commencement remarks. The end of the academic year, after all, was fast upon them. He shuffled his chair to a neutral position—desk on one hand, window on the other—and opened a fresh legal pad. *"We can make liquor to sweeten our lips,"* he mumbled. *"Of pumpkins and parsnips and walnut tree chips."*

Commencement tended to be a wicked bit of fun for Affenlight. The hired keynote speaker—usually some middling politician or author or corporate head; they never pulled a big name—pontificated, told laborious stories, and displayed strange notions about the fears and desires of the newly minted graduates. By comparison—not that it was a competition—Affenlight always came out ahead. He kept his remarks brief and stuffed them with dubious Westish in-jokes and puns, to which the students, having been subjected to such groaners from their convocation onward, now responded with raucous laughter. These were *their* puns, this was *their* college, *their* president, and no one else could understand. Affenlight lifted a somber hand, pretending to admonish them for their laughter, and this made them laugh all the harder.

He knew from his own student days how the most formidable professors always garnered the biggest laughs; the slightest display of levity, however forced, was enough to send spasms of giddy relief through a lecture hall. See, Professor X is human too! Affenlight himself was now, and had been for a couple of decades, the beneficiary of such easy laughs. People vested him with a certain nobility—they saw him, rightly or wrongly, as the finished product of sixty years of devoted study. It wasn't a bad position to be in—not so much worse, perhaps, than being young.

Then at the end of any address he would shift, just for a moment, into high oratorical mode. Quote a little Latin, thank the professors and parents, invoke the never-ending search for understanding—it was almost too easy to conjure up strong sentiment, but that was because he meant every word. The students would start to cry; so would some of the parents.

The students' mistakes lay ahead of them, were prospective and therefore glorious. His own lay in the past. They might have been glorious too, his own mistakes—at least, he would not change them for anyone else's. He regretted only a single loss—those years he'd missed of Pella's life, and the string of errors that led to a loss like that was so thick and knotted that he'd never found one end of the string, so that he could follow it in and up and around and figure out why. Perhaps he'd been too permissive and tolerant a parent, and thereby forced Pella to grow up too fast. Or perhaps he'd never been tolerant enough to accommodate a girl of Pella's talents. Or perhaps he'd raised her perfectly, but every other parent in the world had miserably erred, and so Pella, precisely because of her perfect upbringing, had been forced to find her own way.

This last was a joke, and Affenlight smiled. Most likely the string of errors was perfectly looped, without any ends at all. There were no *whys* in a person's life, and very few *hows*. In the end, in search of useful wisdom, you could only come back to the most hackneyed concepts, like kindness, forbearance, infinite patience. Solomon and Lincoln: *This too shall pass.* Damn right it will. Or Chekhov: *Nothing passes.* Equally true.

He followed these thoughts down his legal pad for a few moments, then set aside his pencil and inspected his fingertips, which had acquired half-moons of pale grime from the window screen. The sentences he'd scribbled down were a bit gloomy, a bit equivocal for commencement, but they could be brushed into shape. The keynote speaker, the middling politician, would give the rah-rah, use-your-many-talents-and-advantages-for-the-benefit-of-all exhortation. Affenlight would stick to humor and resignation.

His cell phone ring-a-ding-dinged. Contango lifted his nose inquisitively. Affenlight waited a few beats before answering, so as not to seem too eager.

"We did it again," said Owen, over the din of a locker room. "Eight to seven."

"Hot damn!" Affenlight slapped the twill of his thigh. "Amazing."

"You don't know the half of it. You should see the teams we're playing against. There must be a large allocation for steroids at these schools. And their fans do coordinated dances."

"And yet the Harpooners keep carrying the day."

"Well, we carried today. Sal pitched beyond his talents. And Adam and Mike each hit a home run. Those two are playing like men possessed."

"Amazing," Affenlight repeated. "And you?"

"I may have contributed a hit or two."

"Two?"

"Two," Owen confirmed. "Coach has me batting third."

"Amazing," Affenlight said for the third and, he resolved, final time. Sometimes talking to Owen rendered him extremely eloquent; sometimes it reduced him to slack-jawed stupidity.

"So you'll be here tomorrow?" Owen asked. "For the championship?"

"I booked a flight already. I didn't want to tell you, in case that consti-tuted some kind of jinx. It leaves at the crack of dawn."

"Perfect. You know, Guert, I've never been nervous before a game before. I've never even understood the concept of nervousness before a game. I mean, what's the worst that could happen? You could win, or you could lose. But now I'm thinking about tomorrow, the national championship game, live on ESPN, and it's like..." He lowered his voice as if making a shameful confession. "I want to *win*."

Affenlight smiled. It was a joy to hear Owen, he of the preternatural calm detachment, cop to a strong feeling of any sort.

"Have you checked on Henry?" Owen asked.

"I knocked on the door last night," Affenlight said. "And again ear-lier today. He never seems to be home."

"Oh, he's home," Owen said. "He's just not answering the door. You'll have to surprise him. Can you get a key from Infrastructure?"

Affenlight reached into his pocket, fingered the key he'd borrowed when Owen was in the hospital. He carried it like a talisman. "I think so."

"You're a sweetheart, Guert. You don't mind, do you?"

"Not at all."

Affenlight hung up the phone. Beyond the window, the quad had entered that afternoon hiccup between the end of classes and the dinner rush. The sun lay below the tree line, the light cinema soft. No one, as far as Affenlight could discern, ever accomplished anything at this time of day, although many of the students were compulsive accomplishers, and the gymnasium treadmills, if not the library carrels, were probably packed. Mrs. McCallister's yellow roses were budding, just barely, in the narrow space beside Scull Hall; he pulled out his daybook and made a note to praise their beauty. A knock came at the door.

71

E*ntrez you,"* called Affenlight, an old malapropic joke, if you could call it a joke, from Pella's elementary school French class.

In came Evan Melkin, the dean of Student Affairs. Melkin was still half a student himself—Class-of-'92-and-Never-Left, cherubic and chinless, a true Westish lifer as opposed to a recidivist like Affenlight. He wore what the kids wore, the prep school kids who couldn't get into more prestigious seaboard institutions: rumpled khakis and a blue oxford shirt and moccasins. The only thing missing was the baseball cap, though a baseball cap would have served Melkin well; the sole feature that revealed his forty years was the ragged retreat of his wispy blond hair. Affenlight stood to shake his hand. This seemed to throw Melkin off somehow. He lingered in the doorway. Bruce Gibbs pushed past him and hobbled into the room.

Bruce, at least, knew how to shake a man's hand. "Guert."

"Bruce."

"Handsome animal you have there."

Contango scrambled to his feet, ears perked; he seemed wary of their visitors. He pressed his snout into Melkin's crotch and growled. Melkin edged backward. "He belongs to Tom and Sandy Bremen," Affenlight explained.

"Who'll be leaving us soon," said Gibbs.

Affenlight nodded. "But the dog may be staying with me. This is something of a trial period."

Contango growled at Melkin again. Gibbs reached down and stroked the dog between the ears, shushed him expertly. "Handsome animal," he said again. "What's his name?"

"Contango."

"A Brazilian husky?"

"Actually it's an economic term," Affenlight explained. "A recent coinage. But the word *tango,* interestingly enough, isn't derived from the romance languages, as I also used to think — it's a Nigerian word, which..."

By the time he reached the end of this little lecture, Affenlight knew that something was afoot. Melkin was too twitchy, Gibbs too calm and somber, Contango too suspicious.

Bruce cleared his throat. "I'm afraid we've got a problem, Guert. Or what appears to be a problem, from my vantage, unless you have some way of clarifying it that would render it unproblematic."

Affenlight's mind went blank. Bruce's voice seemed to emanate from everywhere: "It's no concern of mine what a person does with his personal time. I have no particular prejudices in that regard. But as you know the college does observe a strict and carefully delineated code with regard to student-teacher interactions, and administrators fall under that rubric. Especially when that administrator plays a very public role in terms of the college's relation to the surrounding community."

"How'd you find out?"

Bruce looked at him. "That sounds like an admission, Guert. We're not necessarily asking you to admit anything at this time."

"Just tell me how."

Melkin opened the folder he was holding. Affenlight hadn't noticed the folder before. There's a folder, he thought. Melkin cleared his throat nervously and began to read: "The subject was first raised by Parent X. Parent X was en route to Westish to attend the baseball doubleheader on May first, and stopped for the night at the Troupe's Inn on Route 50. On the morning of May first, Parent X saw you, President Affenlight, leaving a room at the aforementioned motel with a student. Parent X subsequently phoned me at Student Affairs to report this incident. The report clearly required follow-up through the proper channels. However, I didn't want to disseminate any allegations that could damage your reputation and then turn out to be false. So I decided to conduct an informal pre-investigation on my own."

Melkin produced from the folder a photocopied page from the Troupe's Inn license-plate log. "Is that your handwriting, President A?" He pointed to the name *O. Bulkington* beside the Audi's plate number. Affenlight nodded.

"I thought so." Beneath Melkin's somberness you could see he was proud of his literary detective work. "Having confirmed that you were indeed at the motel in question, I spoke to the student proctor of the dorm of the student in question, using as much discretion as possible. She reported having seen you enter the dorm on the afternoon of April thirtieth in what she described as an agitated state.

"A few days later, I personally witnessed the student in question leaving Scull Hall via the private entrance early in the morning. At that point I called Chairperson Gibbs."

Melkin, in other words, had staked out the quarters. Affenlight looked down at his tie. His chair was still angled forty-five degrees from his desk, so that he had to turn his head to see Bruce and Melkin. He felt like a child banished to the corner, but he lacked the strength to shimmy around to face them. "Have you talked to Owen?"

"The student in question is traveling for an athletic competition. As of yet there has been no—"

Bruce lifted a hand to silence Melkin. "I wanted to talk to you first." He rested his walking stick against the arm of the love seat and sat down heavily. "Guert, even if Owen denies any kind of impropriety, we'll still be obliged to investigate. My hands are tied in that regard. This isn't a criminal situation where we're going to use the language of victim and predator and dig into people's private lives. It doesn't matter what went on in that motel room. The mere fact that you were there with a student, in full view of other students' families, is already a serious breach of the school's honor code and its definition of professional conduct.

"If we do investigate," Bruce went on, "that investigation will be handled by the Administrative Committee, and the committee will be required to interview a variety of people."

"Meaning what?"

"Meaning the situation will become public. The students will know about your relationship with Mr. Dunne, and so will the parents and the alumni. This is a liberal arts college, but you and I both know that it's not *that* liberal."

"Don't make phrases at me, Bruce." Affenlight's whole body had been limp; now anger surged through him and he brought a sudden, useless fist down on the arm of the chair.

Gibbs lifted a hand in apology. "I know this is difficult for you, Guert. My point is that I'm finding it hard to envision a scenario in which it would be feasible for you to remain in your current position."

"You want me to resign."

"I'm asking whether you might prefer to seek other opportunities. As opposed to subjecting both yourself and Westish College to an unprecedented amount of scrutiny and derision. This kind of publicity could seriously affect our fund-raising capabilities. If you think it's difficult to find money for your 'green' initiatives now, just wait till this gets out."

"Is that what this is? You don't like my budget?"

"Guert, don't be absurd. This isn't a conspiracy."

"No, no. Of course not. It's a convenience."

Bruce, looking for the first time a bit beleaguered, leaned back into the love seat and sighed. If you knew what went on there, Affenlight thought meanly, you wouldn't get too comfortable.

"In terms of conveniences," said Bruce, "I feel obliged to mention the following. Convenience one. The student in question has, in three years, paid no tuition or fees as the winner of the Maria Westish Award, an award whose selection committee is chaired by you. Records of the committee's deliberations suggest that you forcefully championed the student in question, despite his undistinguished grades in math and science."

"His essays were brilliant," Affenlight said. "He's brilliant."

"Convenience two. The student in question is a member of several environmental groups as well as the student-faculty committee that drafted the carbon-neutral legislation of which you, rather abruptly to my way of thinking, have become a forceful champion."

"Everyone should champion those measures," Affenlight said. "They're an ethical duty."

" 'Ethics' is not your angle right now, Guert."

Affenlight fell quiet. He could quibble about the details—Owen was the best student Westish had seen in a decade; the budget proposals were fair and sound—but it didn't matter. He'd done so many rash things—he'd forgotten himself and his position. Visiting Owen's dorm, going with Owen to a motel—they were the crimes of a careless, foolish man. And he'd done them with all his heart.

He knew it wasn't really the budget; he knew Bruce didn't want him out. As presidents went he was a good one. Bruce felt he had no recourse. And yet, and yet! What kind of conversation would they be having if Owen were a girl? Bruce would be using the same legalese, the expression on his face would still be stern, but he'd be pouring himself a scotch. The gleam in his eye would say, *Good for you, Guert. Still got it, eh?* Because it happened all the time, a hundred times a day. Sleeping with an alluring female student was the second great topic of American literature, after plain-old infidelity. It happened to everybody, and you couldn't fire everybody.

Of course, it happened plenty this way too, the same-sex way—had always happened plenty. Affenlight hadn't made a major innovation in human relations by falling for a bright young boy. But then again people got fired all the time, people resigned, and rarely did you find out why.

We can run away, Affenlight thought. We can just *go*. Owen and I.

Me and O. I can pull my bid on the house. We can move to New York, get an apartment in Chelsea, walk up and down Eighth Avenue holding hands. We can be free.

"Does Genevieve know?" he asked, though he wasn't sure why it mattered. *If Mama Ain't Happy...*

"Parent X has not communicated directly with Ms. Wister. That communication has been entrusted to us."

"But if this parent has a son who plays baseball, then this parent must be in South Carolina, with Genevieve. All the parents are there."

Melkin looked up from his notes. "Parent X does not currently have a student traveling with the team."

"What?" said Affenlight. "But how is that even possi..." He trailed off as he realized what Melkin was telling him. What he wished Melkin hadn't told him. "Oh. I see."

This was how the world worked: Implacably. Irrevocably. But always through particular people. Affenlight felt faint and peculiar. He looked at Contango, who'd settled back into his own version of implacability, head on paws on rug on floor. The dog's black nose and one blue eye seemed to be receding from him, racing away at the Audi's top speed. Affenlight gripped the arms of his chair. "What about Pella?"

Bruce cocked his head. "Excuse me?"

"His daughter," said Melkin.

"My daughter. She's been accepted for the fall term. But only informally. Her situation is a bit unorthodox. She's a few credits short of requirements."

"That shouldn't be a problem."

"What about her tuition?"

Bruce hesitated. Affenlight couldn't tell whether he was being bold or not nearly, nearly bold enough. Shouldn't he throw punches? Shouldn't he rage against this smugness, this goddamned smugness, this hypocritical fucking smugness? Contango's blue eye raced out to some terminal point and then stopped and switched and raced back in. Bruce was speaking.

"I can't imagine the daughter of a former president paying tuition to Westish College. Or his grandchildren, or his grandchildren's grandchildren. That's not how the system works."

The system. Affenlight nodded, looked down at his tie, lifted a shaky hand to smooth it uselessly. He tried to think of Chelsea, an apartment in Chelsea, he and Owen on Eighth Avenue holding hands, or else Tokyo, what about Tokyo, but the image wouldn't come. His hand dropped into his lap. He was pressed deep into his chair, unable to move, unable to muster his strength. In an instant he'd become an old man, a wilted and pliant old man.

"If you tender your resignation, effective at the end of the academic year," said Gibbs, "no further investigation will be made by the trustees, in whose stead I am acting as a unilateral representative. You'll be free and clear to seek a professorship or a presidency elsewhere. Dean Melkin will put that folder of his through a shredder."

Affenlight felt a strong, dull pain where his neck met his shoulder. He found his cigarettes in his jacket pocket, fumblingly lit one while Bruce was still speaking. That much, at least, they couldn't deny him.

"Mr. Dunne has been retained by the Drama Department as an instructor for the summer term, which begins June twelfth. If you intend to remain in your current position past that date, we will have no choice but to inform Ms. Wister and conduct a thorough investigation." Bruce looked up at Affenlight. His bureaucratic composure faltered, and for a split second his confusion, his desolation, seemed almost to rival Affenlight's own. "Are we understood?"

72

Affenlight rapped on the door. No answer. He pulled the pilfered key from his pocket, slipped it into the lock.

A dense stench, like that of a fetid locker room, assailed him before he could cross the threshold. He retreated to the stairwell, sucked in a breath of clean air, and entered the room, which was shrouded in evening gloom. No Henry. He raised the drawn shades and threw open the windows. Scattered across Henry's blond-wood desk were several cylindrical plastic tubs of the kind yogurt or margarine comes in. Dotlike fruit flies buzzed about the lidless ones. They looked to be full of different kinds of congealed soup. Affenlight shooed the flies, picked up two of the containers, and carried them toward the checkerboard-floored bathroom, intending to dump them down the toilet.

The bathroom lights were out, but there in the tub lay Henry, naked, submerged to his neck in water tinged a pale unpleasant yellow. His diaphragm rose and fell, trembling the water. He was asleep.

Affenlight glanced down at the soup in his hands. Chicken noodle on the left, with a thin scrim of fat on the surface, split pea on the right. Henry looked ghastly pale, except for his scruffy brown beard and matching pubic hair. His slack hands were shriveled like white-grape raisins, his internal liquids leached out into the larger body of the tub. His jaw clenched and unclenched. Crammed inside that undersize tub, his cheeks drawn, flaccid muscles submerged in the stagnant water, he seemed both too large and too small for himself, precisely the wrong size.

Affenlight stealthily exited the bathroom, set the soup on the desk, and lit a cigarette. The pain had vanished for a while, but now it returned, this time in his chest. He sat down on the arm of the rose-colored chair to smoke and wait it out. It was strong, but not especially worrisome — he'd had a similar sensation a few times lately after serious exertion, whether with Owen or on the treadmill upstairs, and he knew that it would pass. When it did he tried to decide what to do about Henry.

There seemed to be no clean clothes in Henry's dresser, so he opened Owen's and pulled out the most masculine-looking pair of briefs. He dug around further until he found a clean white T-shirt and a pair of drawstring pants. He took a towel from the closet shelf, wrapped the clothes in it, and, having removed his shoes so as to make less noise, slipped into the bathroom to set the bundle on the checkerboard floor beside the tub. Then he shut the bathroom door and knocked on it. "Henry?" he called. "Are you there?"

Sloshing noises came from behind the door. *"Minit,"* Henry groaned, sounding weakened and annoyed. Affenlight heard water draining from the tub, gurgling through the pipes and finishing with a slurping flourish. He stubbed out his cigarette and flicked it through the open window. A minute later Henry came through the bathroom door, dressed in Owen's clothes. His eyes looked sullen and uncommunicative, as if trapped behind thick glass. "Hey," he said.

"Hey," replied Affenlight with false chipperness conjured from who knew where. "I hope I didn't disturb your bath. I just wanted to let you know that —" How to phrase it? The Harpooners? The baseball team? You? We? Affenlight was even less a part of the *we* than Henry now, though Henry didn't know that. "— we won today."

"I know." Henry's voice was flat and dull, like hammered steel. "Owen called."

"Oh. You spoke to Owen?"

"He left a message."

"Ah." He looked awful, emaciated, his cheeks concave and gray above his beard. "When did you last eat?" Affenlight asked.

Henry thought about it. "I don't know."

"What about the soup?"

He shrugged. "Pella leaves it."

"But you don't eat it."

"No."

The Westish payroll was packed with professional counselors, people schooled in the art of connecting with students who were bulimic, anorexic, alcoholic, depressed, distressed, drug-addicted, suicidal. Presumably the proper course would be to deliver Henry to such a counselor. There had to be a campus hotline, someone on call around the clock at whatever they called the infirmary nowadays. A Person To Talk To. An impartial person: Affenlight had spent maybe ten minutes total with Henry, but their lives were too entwined. Owen. Pella. Henry's parents. All that knowing filled the room and threatened to make talking impossible.

There was that damned register, still sitting on the mantel above the fireplace. Affenlight picked up the baseball that was resting against it. The ball's smooth white flesh was marred by a few scuff marks that gently abraded his fingertips. Amid his confused and wounded thoughts it struck him that a baseball was a beautifully designed thing — it seemed to demand to be thrown, made him want to give it a good strong toss through the open window and across the dove-gray quad. As he bandied it from palm to fingertips and back, he realized that he had spoken.

"You're flying to South Carolina in the morning."

Henry looked at him dully.

"I already bought your ticket," Affenlight said.

Henry lay down on the unmade bed, laid his ear on the pillow. His body was curling and closing into itself, like an old arthritic hand or a daylily at nightfall. "Can't," he said. "I've got a final tomorrow."

"Tomorrow's Saturday. Only freshpersons have finals."

"Today," Henry said wearily. "I had a final today."

"You can take it later. When the rest of the team takes theirs."

It was getting dark. Affenlight stood in his socks in the center of the rug, tossing the baseball from hand to hand. "You can't stay here forever," he added sternly. "The dorms have to be clear by next weekend."

Henry's face collapsed and he started to sob, so loudly that Affenlight had no choice but to sit down on the bed beside him and pat his shoulder and whisper what he hoped were calming words, words like *sssh* and *hey* and *it's okay*. Henry slowed to a whimper and seemed on the verge of regaining his breath, but then the sobbing crescendoed again and he became almost hysterical, his head tipped back and his mouth agape. He started to hiccup. Snot bubbled out of his nose as he sucked hard at the air. A dark sheen of sweat arose on the back of his neck. "Sssshh," Affenlight said softly, rubbing his back in clockwise circles between the shoulder blades. "It's okay. It's okay." He felt a coolness in the room, especially on the strip of skin where his pant cuffs had ridden up above his socks.

"Sorry," Henry said, wiping his eyes, once the several waves of sobbing had passed.

"Hush now," Affenlight said. "You just take it easy."

Affenlight brought Henry a wad of toilet paper with which to blow his nose. On the windowsill sat a bunch of bananas, an outsize box of Rice Krispies, and the proper dishware. Affenlight opened the mini-fridge and found a half gallon of milk—Owen's way, no doubt, of trying to provide for Henry in his absence. Affenlight poured a bowl of cereal, carved off banana slices with the spoon, added milk. He didn't quite spoon-feed Henry, but he did sit beside him with a hand on Henry's shoulder, murmuring his approval at each swallowed bite. With his free hand he lit a cigarette, lit another when it was done. Henry grimaced at the first spoonful, and as it reached his stomach he looked like he might vomit, but after a few bites things went more smoothly. He made it most of the way through the bowl and lay down drowsily.

"You have to leave early to make the flight," Affenlight said. "I'll set your alarm."

Henry nodded.

"I'll drive you to the airport. Meet me outside by the statue. Six o'clock sharp."

Henry yawned and nodded again. It wasn't clear whether he was really listening or whether Affenlight would have to come here tomorrow morning and drag him out of bed; either way was fine. Affenlight took the cereal bowl and the fly-clotted soup containers to the bathroom, dumped them down the sink, rinsed them, and set them on Owen's desk to dry. On his way out he snapped off the light.

"President Affenlight?" Henry said.

Affenlight paused in the doorway. "Yes?"

"G'night."

Affenlight smiled. "Don't forget your uniform."

73

As the door swung shut his foot kicked something, knocking it over — a squat container like the ones he'd just emptied. Luckily the seal on the lid was tight and it didn't spill. As he picked it up he could feel the heat of the soup through the plastic. He carried it down the stairs with him, lit a cigarette as he stepped outside.

The evening was cool and dry. Affenlight sat down on the broad stone base of the Melville statue. The warmth of the soup container felt good between his hands; he peeled off the lid and let the steam waft up to his nose. Chowder, Boston clam. It smelled marvelous. He lifted the container and took a sip, parted his lips to let through a cube of potato, a chewy dollop of clam. The texture, the richness of the cream, the proportions of salt and pepper, which seemed so simple but were often skewed — Affenlight had eaten his share of chowder, and this was a nearly ideal specimen. The lake spread out before him, better than any ocean. Was this what they were serving in the dining hall these days? It couldn't be. If it was, they should cut costs. If it was, he should have eaten there more often.

When the soup was gone he lit another cigarette. The pain had returned to his chest, and in addition he could feel it in his shoulder, or his collarbone — somewhere around there. Each drag on the Parliament seemed to exacerbate it. If it didn't pass, if it came back again, he might have to think about calling the doctor.

By the time he entered his office his chest felt better. Contango greeted him warmly. Affenlight scratched the back of the husky's sugar-furred neck, opened the office door and the outside door so Contango could wander out into the quad. Then he called the airline and converted his plane ticket to Henry's name, called his car service and scheduled a trip to the airport for six o'clock. There was no need to drive Henry to the airport. Henry could decide whether he wanted to go to South Carolina, just as Mike Schwartz could decide whether he wanted to take the job in the AD's office. These children weren't his children; they weren't children at all.

He loosened his tie, poured a sizable scotch, put Gounod's *Faust* on the shiny executive stereo that was tucked into the bookshelves. He lit a Parliament and sat down at his computer to write Pella an e-mail.

Dear Pella,
I just wanted to tell you that I saw Henry today. He looks a little rough, but he'll be fine.

He paused, unsure of what else to say. He wanted to write a truthful message, and yet regarding the biggest, most intractable matter of all he had no intention of telling the truth. If he told Pella the truth, she would leave this place and never forgive it. He wanted her to stay. For practical reasons, he told himself: She had been accepted. Her tuition would be nil, provided Gibbs kept his word. Given her disciplinary record at Tellman Rose, her expired SAT scores, her lack of a high school diploma, it would probably take two years to get her into any other decent school.

But there were selfish reasons too, and maybe those were the ones he really cared about. He needed her here. They'd erase him from the memory of this place as quickly and thoroughly as they could; she was the part of him that would be allowed to stay. That was the deal. Even if he was elsewhere — God knew where he would be — he needed her here. Was that insane? Probably it was, after what had happened today.

But he couldn't change what he wanted just because it was insane. He couldn't hate this place just because it had cast him out. And he couldn't have Pella or Owen hating it either. It was no worse than anyplace else, and it was theirs.

Contango wandered back inside, did a lap of the office, and settled down on the rug, head propped on his paws. Affenlight finished his scotch, lit another cigarette. He wasn't sure what to say to Pella; maybe the safer course, for the moment, would be to say nothing. He'd get his story straight first. With Owen too. That would be even more difficult — how to give up Owen without Owen knowing why? Owen would almost certainly figure it out, there were clues enough to piece it together, but Affenlight couldn't *let* Owen figure it out. He couldn't let any of the weight or blame of his banishment settle on Owen's shoulders. He couldn't become burdensome or pitiable in Owen's eyes. The thought of such a thing sent a pain through his chest that was worse than the actual pain, unless that *was* the actual pain and he was confusing the two. In any case he'd have to get his story straight before he talked to Pella. Early retirement, doctor's orders, stress, a longing to travel, to write, to teach again — some bullshit like that. He closed out of his e-mail and shut down the computer, as he did every night.

When the screen went dark he felt so deeply and sweetly tired that even to walk upstairs seemed impossible. With effort he pushed back his massive chair and made his way over to the love seat. He sat down and laboriously unlaced his wing tips. Contango was asleep on the rug. Affenlight lay down, crossed his long legs at the ankles, and spread his jacket over his torso so as not to get cold. He'd taken to turning the building's thermostat down, way down, at the end of the working day.

The music that entered his dream wasn't Gounod or Mozart or anything Affenlight loved. It was the first few notes of the old Westish fight song, sentimental, unassuming, played by a flute or some other trilling woodwind. The band kicked in, brassy and strong. Eighty-six maple go. Eighty-six maple go. Hut *hut*. The ball came back between Neagle's gold thighs, snapped into Affenlight's hands. The pleasure of pebbled leather against his palms. Cavanaugh on the go route, fastest man on the team, a wonder of speed but with terrible hands. Affenlight drop-stepped, scissored, dropped, scissored. The end would come from his blind side. Cavanaugh loved the go route, ran it like a big-college guy though he couldn't catch anything, what a tease that made him, a purveyor of false hope with his racehorse strides, neck and neck with his man but not for long, no safety ever deep enough to be there to take credit when Cavanaugh dropped the ball. Still there was always the chance that this would be the one. The next one was always the one.

How many days since Affenlight found that sheaf of papers in the library basement? Now with the scrum of linemen snorting and collapsing around him, he remembered the music of H. Melville's words. How odd. His concentration was usually total, everybody's was, needed to be, that was what made it work, the common agreement that the game was all-important, but now the encroachment seemed lovely, an intimation of a world beyond the world of the green-and-white field. It was then, as he finished his seven-step drop and heard Melville's words and saw Cavanaugh gaining separation from his man, that Affenlight knew he was through with football, through for all time, he wouldn't be back next year. Other things awaited. It was good to be young and to know it for once. So much unfolding to do. He had the laces, he patted the ball. Footsteps pounded toward him from behind. There was no hint of wind, a ship captain's nightmare, a quarterback's dream. *I won't be back next year.* He pushed off and threw as high and as deep as he could, the ball arcing through blue toward Cavanaugh's terrible hands, but he no longer cared whether Cavanaugh caught it or not, and as the end arrived and his breath left him he couldn't remember or imagine ever having cared. He was five or six, he was cutting pumpkins in the sun with his father. The tiny sere needles of stems bit through his cotton gloves and stung his hands. Still he loved the pumpkins, he could not lift the big ones, and the field all around was autumn brown.

74

The Harpooners queued along the third-base line, shoulder to shoulder, their caps clapped over the spearmen that adorned their pinstriped chests. Schwartz gazed out at the emerald diamond, which was part of the Atlanta Braves' spanking-new AAA facility in Comstock, South Carolina. The field breathed magically beneath the high-banked lights, the grass precisely mowed in starburst rays of lighter and deeper green. Down the first-base line the Amherst fans were already on their feet, chanting and cheering and waving their purple pennants. A beefy man in a size-too-small tux clambered out of the stands' first row and swaggered to home plate, cordless microphone in hand, followed by a crouching cameraman in an ESPN polo. The betuxed guy turned to face the crowd, doffed his white ten-gallon hat, and pressed it to his beefy chest.

"Why's he in the batter's box?" Izzy muttered. "He's messing up the chalk."

Suitcase, who was standing beside Izzy, nodded and spit. "It's the national championship, for Chrissake. They could've at least gotten a chick to sing the anthem."

"Yeah, word. A chick in a dress. How hard is that?"

"*Sssshhh,*" hissed Loondorf. "That's Eric Strell."

"He's what?"

"Eric Strell. 'Don't Fence Me Out'? Remember?" Loondorf, who sang tenor in the Westish Wails, began to croon in a quiet voice: *"Don't . . . fence me out / In my heart there is no doubt . . ."*

"Country's gay," said Izzy.

"It's a good song," protested Loondorf. "I might solo on it."

"Gay."

"It's about Mexican immigrants. Like your *dad.*"

"Ga-a-*ay.*"

Owen cleared his throat.

Izzy covered his mouth with his cap. "Sorry, Buddha."

"Can it, all of you." Schwartz's voice was sharp, but inwardly he felt pleased that the younger guys were loose enough to goof around. He himself had already puked twice out of nervousness — once discreetly in a locker room sink, once less discreetly by the left-field foul pole during warm-ups. If any balls got hit down into the corner, Quisp or the Amherst left fielder would be in for a messy surprise.

Eric Strell was really belting it out. He wasn't a small guy — only one notch smaller than Schwartz, and he was crammed into that tux with the boots, the bolo tie, the whole bit, his cheeks the alcoholic color of steak tartare, especially when he reached for the sky with his hat's crown in his right hand and brought down the *HOME . . . OF THE . . . BRAAYYYYYVE* in a tumid drawl that lasted so long it left him doubled over, crumpled and spent like Arsch after a jog to the lighthouse. The crowd exploded. Eric Strell straightened, waved his ten-gallon hat at the stands. He brought the mike close to his now-crimson face, beefy hand cupped tight around the windscreen, and gazed into the camera lens, making sweet love to each and every American who'd tuned into ESPN2 hoping to see bowling or billiards reruns and instead got the D-III college baseball championship game. "Puh-*lay baawwwl!*" he purred.

Schwartz put his hat on, blinked back a renegade drop of salt water. He'd always been a sucker for the anthem, and then there was the almost unfair beauty of a professional ballfield, the expensive riotous green of the grass, the scalloped cutouts around the bases, the whole place groomed like living art. As he turned back toward the dugout and glanced into the stands, it seemed as if the little contingent of navy-clad fans were composed entirely of mothers — Rick's mom flanked by the gawky ten-year-old O'Shea twins; Sal Phlox's mom ancient and white-haired and leaning into Papa Phlox's elbow; Meat's mom seated because of her gout while everyone else stood, spilling out over her chair, a ripe blueberry of a woman in her triple-XL Westish T-shirt. Owen's and Izzy's waving their Westish pennants like cheerleaders. Loondorf's mom, who'd brought them so many kringles over the course of the season; Ajay's tiny Indian mom with her many bracelets; and on down the line. An endless supply of mothers, though of course the one you wanted was never there.

He plunked down on the bench to don his chest protector. A cell phone buzzed nearby. He glanced around, ready to cuss at someone — no phones in the dugout — then recognized the ring as his own. He unzipped the side pocket of his bag, peeked at the display: Pella's new number. There were several missed calls too, all from her. What a great time to get in touch. He powered down the phone, grabbed his mask and mitt, and headed up the dugout steps to join his gathered teammates.

Coach Cox read the lineup in his usual way, but you could tell by his rapid mustache-stroking that his nerves were up. "Starblind Avila Dunne. Schwartz O'Shea Boddington. Quisp Phlox Guladni." He paused, examined their faces, stroked his mustache some more. "Big game today. Real big. But you guys are ready. Play together, and you'll be fine. I'm not one for speeches, as you know, but I just wanted to say that... I'm really proud of you all. You guys are ballplayers all the way." Coach Cox glanced around, stroking his mustache, embarrassed at his own floridity. "Mike, you got anything to add?"

Last night, as he lay awake in the hotel room listening to Meat snore — at least they had separate beds this trip — Schwartz had developed a strong premonition that Henry would show up today. It made no sense, there was no way, and yet the premonition had only grown stronger as the day went by, so that now Schwartz was surprised not to see the Skrimmer's blue eyes as he scanned the huddle. Not that Henry had any business here. His presence, even as a spectator, would have been disruptive. Schwartz looked around the circle, cranked The Stare up to a 7, a 7½. He himself was clean-shaven, his razor burn finally gone, but his teammates had been cultivating playoff beards. Individually the beards ranged from wispy and pathetic to lush and shampooable; taken together they made the Harpooners look like a tough, grizzled group. Yes, Henry had helped them get here, whatever they accomplished they owed in part to him, but to win these last twelve games they'd had to fill the gap left by his absence as quickly as possible, and once you healed the Henry gap you had no place for Henry. Even Owen had a layer of soft grayish fuzz on his face.

While Schwartz lay awake, he tried to concoct a pregame speech that would whip his team into a frenzy. A real fire-and-brimstone number, based on his favorite theme, that ageless angelic theme, of the underdog outlasting the favorite, the oppressed bitch-slapping the oppressor. He was going to start by bringing up the namby-pamby Amherst mascot: Their team was called the Lord Jeffs, after Lord Jeffrey Amherst, the eighteenth-century British general who advocated using smallpox-infected blankets against Native Americans. And—so went the speech—not much had changed in three hundred years. The Amherst players were still Lords, still hip-deep in old-school power and privilege—imagine the practice facilities they had! Imagine the jobs they'd be given when they graduated! By comparison the Harpooners might as well have been sucking on smallpox blankets. They were going to answer to guys like the Amherst guys for the rest of their lives. Their average postgraduation starting salaries were miles apart—Schwartz had looked it up. So were their acceptance rates at places like Harvard and Yale and Stanford Law. Their first, best, and last chance for preemptive revenge was here, now, tonight. Crush the Lords or be forever crushed.

That was the sort of convoluted crap Schwartz kept coming up with, as he stared at the ceiling of the surprisingly cushy Comstock Inn while Arsch sawed logs. But pregame speeches didn't depend on statistics or cute transitions. There wasn't another Harpooner who cared about the relative socioeconomic status of Amherst and Westish grads, except maybe Rick, who'd beer-bonged himself out of his Ivy birthright and been banished to Westish. None of Schwartz's teammates had Schwartz-ian ambitions. They just wanted to win a baseball game. Which was fine, better than fine, perfect, but it left him without a speech. His nerves were shot. It all came down to this.

He tried to take The Stare to an 8, let it level off when he noticed that the stares coming back at him were like 9, maybe 9½. Plus beards. Star-blind was pawing a cleat at the dirt like a coked-up bull. Even Owen's soft gray eyes above his soft gray fuzz expressed a deathly intensity. Schwartz had talked an awful lot of warrior bullshit in his athletic career, especially at football halftimes, but this was the first time he'd ever felt like one of his teammates—*any* of his teammates—might haul off and punch him in the throat. The Skrimmer had been their tran-scendent talent, but now that he was gone the other eighteen Harpoon-ers had found something new inside themselves. A paradox better left unconsidered: they might never have made it here with their best player. Schwartz cast his gaze around the circle one more time. What came back was something beyond confidence, a sense that the game might as well already have happened. He didn't know if *he* was ready to play—his mind was everywhere, sleepless and scattered and sentimental—but they sure were. If he was the Ahab of this operation, this tournament the target of his mania, then they were Fedallah's secret crew.

"You guys," he said softly, the respect in his voice legit, "are some scary motherfuckers."

Nobody even smiled at this, much less laughed; they just nodded and took the field.

75

Henry wasn't wearing his uniform, and despite the absurdly large Westish bag slung over his shoulder, the usher wouldn't let him into the stadium without a ticket. "Game starts in five minutes," said the usher, who was old and wiry with long white sideburns, as he stepped in front of Henry to block the gate. "The players have been here for hours."

"Look at this huge bag." Henry wearily slapped the Westish logo. The bag really did feel huge, a burden, today. "Would I carry this around if I wasn't on the team?"

"Don't know."

"Look at it. It's a baseball player's bag. This part's extra long so you can fit your bat."

"I don't see any bat."

"I don't *have* a bat," Henry said.

"Don't see why not." The usher waved Henry aside so that he could rip the tickets and pat the heads of two young girls in flower-dotted dresses. Then he pulled a program out of his back pocket and unrolled it. "Which team do you play for?"

"Westish. Look, there's my n—"

The usher jerked the program away. "Who's first on the roster?" he demanded. "And how much does he weigh? I'll give you five pounds leeway. Either side."

Henry scrolled alphabetically through the squad in his mind. "Israel

Avila. Shortstop, number one. Chicago, Illinois. Weighs... I don't know what he weighs. One-fifty."

"Sorry, kid. It's Demetrius Arsch. Two-sixty." The usher rolled up the program and waved it toward the parking lot. "Go find another sucker."

Not until Henry unshouldered and unzipped his bag, dug around inside, and produced his rumpled jersey top did the old man wave him through, grumbling as if the whole exchange had been Henry's fault. Henry stepped uncertainly through the pavilion's milling crowds, bag flopping against his back. This was a brand-new, top-of-the-line minor-league ballpark — the kind of park he'd seemed, just a few weeks ago, to be destined to be playing in soon. His uniform still in hand, he waved it at a second usher and emerged into the first-base stands.

The teams had finished infield practice and were gathered in front of their respective dugouts while the head coaches conferred with the umpires. The wide number 44 on Schwartz's back faced Henry. He had one arm around Arsch and the other around Izzy, his head turning slowly from side to side as he delivered the speech he'd been waiting all his life to deliver.

Henry sat down in an empty aisle seat. There was no way he was getting any closer to the team than this. He was already wondering why he'd come this close. He didn't want to be the bad-luck charm, the albatross that doomed the Harpooners' streak. They'd lost the last two games he played in and won the last twelve he didn't. Those kinds of numbers spoke for themselves.

"Pardon me, young man." A rotund man in a coat and tie tapped Henry importantly on the arm. "I believe you're in our seats."

A woman with dyed-blond hair and a gauzy shawl thrown over her shoulders was standing behind the man, her hands wrapped helplessly in the shawl, as if the weather were cold. She towered over his balding head.

"Sorry," Henry said, and squeezed his bag back out into the aisle. As he rose, the Harpooners' huddle broke. Owen caught Henry's eye and waved, smiling broadly. Several other guys turned to look. Owen was beckoning him with his glove. So was Rick. So was Izzy. If there'd been an empty seat nearby, he might have been able to wave and stay put, but there wasn't, he was stranded, standing, and finally there seemed to be nothing to do but descend the stairs to the front row and clamber onto the concrete top of the Amherst dugout, on which was painted the navy-and-lime-green logo of the NCAA World Series. He tossed his bag down first, then, light-headed, lowered his sneaker-clad feet to that beautiful, beautiful field.

The Harpooners, having won the coin toss, would be the home team and bat last. The PA announcer boomingly introduced the Harpooner starters, who jogged to their positions as the crowd cheered amiably. Amherst fans far outnumbered Westish ones, but the bulk of the crowd was unattached — locals, or fans of one of the six already eliminated teams.

Henry, having hopped down into foul territory, froze. Coach Cox had spotted him too, was waving him over, but to reach the Westish dugout he would have to go right past Schwartz, who crouched behind home plate catching Starblind's last warm-up throws. Henry stalled there, feeling more exposed and roachlike than he ever had in Pella's kitchen, an ESPN cameraman two steps away and what felt like ten thousand eyes upon him. Finally Schwartz, without turning around, lifted his right hand and gestured toward the Westish dugout. *Come on, come on.*

Henry scuttled by. Obviously he hadn't thought this through. If the Harpooners lost they would blame him, rightly blame him, blame him forever, for dragging himself halfway across the country to jinx them. What had he been thinking, coming here? What had President Affenlight been thinking? He couldn't blame President Affenlight, it was his own bad decision, but President Affenlight had proposed it and when the president of your school proposed something it was awfully easy to comply. Albatross, he thought. Crap, crap, crap.

Coach Cox greeted him at the mouth of the dugout with a happy, bone-crushing handshake. "Go get dressed," he growled.

"Oh, I don't think so," Henry said. "That wouldn't be—"

"I need you to coach first base. Get your damn uniform on."

Henry headed into the dark corridor that led to the locker room to change. His gear was dirty and a little gamy, unwashed since the Coshwale game, but he dressed with his usual slow solemnity, or at least in imitation of it, in an effort to appease the gods of fate. Coaching first wouldn't be bad—it would give him a way to contribute, however minimally, and it meant that when the Harpooners were batting and Schwartz was in the dugout, Henry'd be out on the field.

Starblind had already gotten two quick outs when Henry entered the dugout. The reserves were perched on the narrow upright back of the bench, glaring out at the field. No one had shaved since regionals began, though with Loondorf and Sooty Kim you could barely tell. They all wore the same expression, as fierce as if they were pitching. Henry made his way down to the distant end, where anyone who didn't want to see him wouldn't have to, and took a seat on the far side of Meat.

"Adam better throw a doggone shutout." Arsch flipped sunflower seeds toward his mouth. "We've got no pitchers."

"Who's left?" Henry asked.

"Sal went eight yesterday, so he's finished. Quisp's been throwing a ton too. Even Rick had to pitch a few innings—can't believe we survived *that* shitstorm. So for relievers it's Loonie..." Arsch scanned the dugout. "...and Loonie, basically."

"My wing's pretty sore," Loondorf reminded him. "I've got nothing."

"Loonie's got nothing," Arsch repeated, shaking his head sadly.

Starblind struck out Amherst's number-three hitter and stalked toward the dugout with a steely fist pump. Henry stepped onto the field beneath the high-banked lights and made his way toward the first-base coaching box. His knees wobbled; he had to concentrate. Coaching first base wasn't hard, but you could certainly screw it up.

Starblind lined a first-pitch single to left. Izzy laid down a perfect sacrifice to move him to second, headed back to the dugout to receive his long line of congratulations. So far, so good. Owen settled into the batter's box, politely stifled a yawn with the back of a batting-gloved hand. On the fourth pitch he chopped a single back through the middle. Starblind wheeled around third at sprinter's speed and slid home as the throw veered off target. One–nothing, Westish.

"You're the man!" Henry told Owen.

"I'm the man!" Owen squinted up into the stands. "Have you seen Guert?"

"Something came up," Henry said. "He couldn't make it." He was lying without really knowing why. When his alarm went off this morning, he'd grabbed his bag from under his bed, unsure whether he'd hallucinated his entire encounter with President Affenlight the night before. In a way, it was that uncertainty that propelled him; he'd gone downstairs more to see whether Affenlight's visit had been a dream than because he was sure he wanted to fly to South Carolina.

President Affenlight hadn't been by the Melville statue, where he'd said he'd be, but a black town car lurked in the service bay of the dining hall. The driver rolled down the window. "Skrimshander?"

"Yes."

The driver popped the trunk. Henry told him he was waiting for someone. The driver said, *You're Skrimshander, right?* The chapel bells tolled once, lugubriously, to indicate that it was six fifteen, President Affenlight had said six. Maybe Henry had misunderstood; maybe Affenlight hadn't intended to join him. It only took a moment to lift his bag into the trunk and climb into the backseat. Once the driver shut the heavy, sound-muffling door behind him, there was no turning back.

"He told me to wish you luck," Henry said to Owen.

"Luck? I require no luck. That's unfortunate, though, that Guert couldn't come."

The Harpooners' lead held until the third inning, when Amherst pieced together a hit batsman, a single, and a sacrifice fly to tie the game. It could have been worse for Westish, but with runners on the corners and two down, Izzy made a diving grab of a shot up the middle and, while lying flat on his belly on the outfield grass, flicked the ball to Ajay for the force.

"He's no Henry Skrimshander," Arsch said. "But he's pretty damned good."

Izzy came sprinting toward the dugout, thumping his fist into the web of his glove and yelling, the way you do when a great play gets your blood up. As Henry trotted out to first base, he slapped Izzy on the rump. "Good play," he said.

Izzy beamed. "Thanks, Henry."

Behind the Amherst dugout stood a row of six female students, purple decals painted on their cheeks, wearing oversize purple T-shirts that spelled out A-M-H-E-R-T in white letters. Four of the girls were stout and blocky and more or less butch. The fifth — letter *E* — stood six-foot-something and swayed in the wind, hair pulled back in a dark ponytail. The sixth — letter *A* — was petite and blond, with her own ponytail slipped through the slot at the back of her purple baseball cap. Henry could tell they were Amherst softball players who'd road-tripped south to support their male counterparts. Their missing *S* was probably back at the motel, passed out after a too-hard day of partying.

A, despite being half the size of her teammates, was the ringleader; she started the foot-stamping cheers, and she was drinking the most impressive quantity of the pink liquid being distributed by letters *M* and *R,* with eroding secrecy, from smuggled-in plastic bottles into stadium-issue Pepsi cups. She strained forward over the railing, her face bright red from booze and yelling. She'd caught Henry's attention right away. Then in the fourth inning, to Henry's dismay, he caught hers.

"Hey, Henry!"

This startled him, but he couldn't turn around or in any way acknowledge it.

"Hey, Henry! Why won't they let you play?"

He felt quite certain that the voice, shrill and demanding, with an undercurrent of malicious playfulness, belonged to *A*. His heart sank a long way. A second voice, deeper but less assured, chimed in:

"Maybe he's a choker."

"A choker?" asked *A*, feigning surprise. "Henry's a choker?"

"That's what I heard."

"Why does Henry choke?" *A* demanded.

"Maybe he can't take the presha," someone suggested, in a strong Boston accent.

"The pressure?! Henry can't take the pressure?" *A* sounded utterly flummoxed, as if she'd known Henry a long time and had never in her wildest dreams believed it would come to this.

Henry stared intently at the vivid white square of first base, pretending to ignore them while straining to hear every word. Schwartzy walked to lead off the inning. He tossed his bat aside, removed his forearm guard, and ran hard to first. Henry clapped once, kept his eyes on the bag.

A had found Henry's four-line bio — the longest on the team — in the glossy tournament program. "Henry Skrimshander," she announced. "Junior. Lankton, South Dakota. Five-foot-ten. One hundred and fifty-five pounds. As a sophomore, was named Conference Player of the Year. Batted .448 this year, with nine home runs and nineteen stolen bases. Shares the NCAA shortstop record for consecutive errorless games with Hall of Famer Aparicio Rodriguez."

Henry was painfully impressed by the flawless, fiber-optic clarity with which she delivered this information to a significant portion of the ballpark. The first-base stands had fallen quiet; they were listening to her.

"Hey, Jen, don't those sound like pretty good stats for a first-base coach?"

"I'd say so," replied Jen.

"Maybe Henry's too *good* to play for this sorry team. Do you agree, Jen?"

"I do."

"Maybe *Henry* would rather stand there and waggle his little butt in our faces."

"Yes!" yelped Jen, her voice fracturing into shards of laughter. Henry mentally checked his butt cheeks to make sure they were perfectly still.

"Tough crowd," said Schwartz, not to Henry but to the first baseman.

The first baseman shrugged. "That's Miz."

"Miz?"

"Elizabeth Myszki. Second baseman for the softball team."

"She's a charmer," Schwartz said.

The first baseman shrugged again. "She's got a thing for middle infielders."

Rick O'Shea laced a one-hopper to the Amherst third baseman, who set in motion an easy double play. Boddington flied out to center for the third out. Henry, not wishing to seem too eager, paused a quarter beat before sprinting back to the dugout. Once safely inside, he could finally turn around and have a long look, albeit from afar, at the very pretty, incredibly unpleasant Elizabeth Myszki.

Top of the fifth. The scoreboard read 1-3-0, runs-hits-errors, for each team. The field was a sapphire storybook dream. Starblind walked the first batter on four pitches, none of them near the strike zone.

"Uh-oh," said Arsch. "Here we go."

Starblind walked the next batter too. He was taking a long time between pitches, muttering to himself, laboriously wiping sweat from his golden forehead. Schwartz called time and trudged out to the mound for a heart-to-heart. Coach Cox stroked his mustache and looked up and down the dugout. "Loonie," he said. "How's the wing?"

"Don't know, Coach. I can sure give it a shot."

Coach Cox was staring at Starblind with fervid intensity, as if trying to see through his pinstripes and into his soul. "Meat," he said. "Take Loonie down to the bullpen, play a little catch."

"Right, Coach." Arsch grabbed his chest protector, and he and Loondorf headed down the foul line. Starblind toed the rubber, checked the runners, and threw a fastball that the batter clobbered off the left-field wall. One run scored easily. Quisp held the other runners to second and third: 2–1 Amherst, nobody out.

"Goddamnit." Coach Cox picked up the bullpen phone and waited for Arsch to answer. "Get Loonie ready quick." He signaled for time and strolled out to the mound to chat with Starblind, though Henry knew that the real purpose of his visit was to give Loondorf a chance to get loose. As Coach Cox spoke, Starblind nodded forcefully and slammed the ball into his glove. Everyone on the Westish bench could read his lips. *I'm fine. I'm fine.* "He ain't fine," Suitcase grumbled, spitting a fragment of sunflower-seed shell between his front teeth. "He's out of gas."

The next Amherst hitter walked to load the bases. Up came a lefty, thin as a toothbrush, who held the bat straight over his head as if trying to catch lightning. With the count 2 and 0, he hung back on a big slow curveball and punched it the other way, just past a diving Boddington.

The runner from third scored, the runner from second scored, and here came the runner from first, rounding third as Quisp dug the ball out of the left-field corner. Quisp rose with the ball and took a momentum-gathering gallop, lifting his right knee and then his left high in the air like a Cossack dancer. He fired with all his might toward home plate, tumbling forward into the grass as he let go.

It was a throw you could dry laundry on, head-high all the way, and only a step off target. A one-in-a-thousand throw. Schwartz snagged the ball on the infield side of the plate and dove back to slap a tag on the arm of the sliding runner.

The umpire swept his hands out, palms down. "Safe!"

"What?!" Schwartz leaped to his feet, stared wildly at the umpire, fell into the baffled, beseeching, knee-buckled, disbelieving, palms-up, how-can-you-do-this-to-me crouch of the wronged and righteous athlete. He grabbed the ball from his mitt and shook it, a menacing display, as if he intended to bash the umpire over the head with it.

"Three!" Henry yelled as he saw the base runner break. "Three three three!" Schwartz whirled toward third, but it was too late, and the guy who'd hit the ball, the toothbrush-thin lefty, slid in without a throw. Schwartz slammed the ball into his mitt. His negligence had given Amherst an extra base, but at least the ugly tableau with the umpire had been broken. Another half-second and he would have done something to get himself ejected, if not arrested. Now he stalked down the third-base line, away from the ump, fuming. Coach Cox jogged out, ostensibly to argue the call, but mainly to intervene if Schwartz got riled again.

Quisp was lying flat on his stomach in left field. "What's wrong with Q?" Henry asked. Before anyone could answer, the bullpen phone rang. Henry was the nearest to it. "Hello?" he said.

"Was he out?" Arsch asked.

"Sure looked that way."

"Shit." Arsch's voice sounded soft and doomed. "Loonie can't go. He's throwing like sixty."

"Okay," Henry said.

"Coach has already been to the mound this inning. If he goes again, he'll have to change pitchers."

"Right." Henry dropped the phone, sprinted onto the field, and latched onto the arm of Coach Cox, who was headed toward the mound to pull Starblind from the game. "Phil can't go," Henry said. "Dead arm."

They were standing halfway between home plate and the pitching rubber. Henry wondered how close you had to get to the mound before it qualified as a trip to the mound. "Then we'll go with Quisp," Coach Cox said.

Henry pointed toward left field. "Quisp is down too."

"Jesus F. Christmas," Coach Cox muttered. "What the goddamn is going on?"

Two trainers jogged out to look at Quisp, who'd put so much power into that gorgeous throw that he'd torn an abdominal muscle. Eventually he was able to stand and limp back to the bench, supported by Steve Willoughby and Coach Cox. Sooty Kim grabbed his glove and jogged out to left, goose-stepping to stretch his cold legs. Five to one, Amherst. Runner on third, nobody out, cleanup hitter at the plate. The A-M-H-E-R-T girls leaned out over the railing like purple Furies, screaming through their makeshift Pepsi-cup megaphones. Albatross, Henry thought. These guys will never forgive me.

The game had already been paused for what seemed like an eternity, but just as the batter settled into his stance, Schwartz asked for time. The umpire granted the request with obvious reluctance. Schwartz hustled out for a quick word with Starblind, who nodded once and mopped the sweat from his forehead.

Starblind stared down the runner at third, fired a four-seam fastball right at the chin of the hitter, who jerked his hands toward his face as he flung himself to the ground to get out of the way. The ball caromed off the neck of the bat and toward the Amherst dugout. The Amherst coach, who was already charging onto the field to scream at Starblind, detoured to give the spinning ball a petulant kick. The umpire could easily have ejected Starblind — and also Schwartz, who'd clearly ordered the pitch — but instead, and perhaps in compensation for missing the call at home, he simply issued a warning and sent the Amherst coach back to the dugout.

The batter dusted off his jersey and stepped gamely back into the box, but a disastrous thought had been planted in his subconscious. The next pitch, a slow curve, buckled his knees for strike two, and then Starblind threw a mediocre fastball, high and outside, which he waved at unconvincingly.

Starblind hopped off the mound, pumped his fist. He looked suddenly revived — shoulders thrown back, jaw relaxed. He jammed the next batter with his best fastball of the game, inducing a pop fly to Ajay, then struck out the Amherst first baseman, stranding the runner at third. As the Harpooners ran off the field, shouting to one another that they weren't through yet, never say die, time to put some runs on the board, Henry marveled, not for the first time, at Schwartz's uncanny ability to orchestrate situations. How did he know that the ump wouldn't eject Starblind, leaving the Harpooners totally pitcherless? How did he know that that particular batter would be so readily intimidated? How did he know that one strikeout would rejuvenate Starblind, at least for the moment?

The answer, presumably, was that Schwartz didn't know any of that. But he'd thought of a plan, something to try, and he'd been bold enough to try it.

Loondorf and Arsch returned from the bullpen. "Loonie," Henry said, draping an arm around the freshperson's drooping shoulders, "I need you to go coach first."

"Okay, Henry." Loondorf trotted out toward the A-M-H-E-R-T girls. Owen sat down beside Henry and produced a library copy of *Fear and Trembling* from beneath the bench. "Protect me from errant balls," he said, tucking his bookmark under the lip of his navy cap. "I have fragile bones."

"I thought Coach Cox wasn't letting you read anymore."

"He's not. Protect me from Coach Cox too."

Neither team threatened to score until the bottom of the eighth, when Starblind and Izzy singled, putting runners on the corners with nobody out. Owen lined out to first, a bit of bad luck on a well-hit ball, and trotted back to the dugout to resume his reading.

Henry could feel a quiet, electric idea slithering through the ballpark as Schwartzy strode to the plate and pawed at the chalk-swirled back line of the batter's box with his size-fourteen spike. He was Westish's all-time home-run leader, and he looked the part. The Amherst fans, except for Elizabeth Myszki, fell quiet. The tiny contingent of Westish parents stood and whistled and clapped. The other six thousand people slid a few inches forward in their seats, together producing a subtle shift in energy that was evident throughout the park. The Harpooners, except for Henry and Owen, leaned over the lip of the dugout, yelling mild profanities to distract the pitcher while inwardly they prayed, contorting their fingers and toes into whatever configurations they felt would produce the most luck. There was a lot of superstitious fidgeting and shifting — nobody wanted to move around too much, which was itself unlucky, but nobody wanted to get stuck in an unlucky pose.

Henry too, as he sat two steps behind his antsy teammates, inches from Owen's elbow, tried to find a pose that would help. Deep down, he thought, we all believe we're God. We secretly believe that the outcome of the game depends on us, even when we're only watching — on the way we breathe in, the way we breathe out, the T-shirt we wear, whether we close our eyes as the pitch leaves the pitcher's hand and heads toward Schwartz.

Swing and a miss, strike one.

Each of us, deep down, believes that the whole world issues from his own precious body, like images projected from a tiny slide onto an earth-sized screen. And then, deeper down, each of us knows he's wrong.

Swing and a miss, strike two.

"Rally caps!" yelled Rick O'Shea from the on-deck circle. Everyone — except for Owen, who continued to bury his nose in his book — flipped his hat inside out so the skeletal white underfabric showed. Henry followed suit.

But it wasn't to be. Schwartz took a third massive swing, glared angrily at the untouched barrel of his bat, and stalked back to the dugout, head down. The Amherst fans roared. Two outs.

Rick O'Shea strode to the plate to try to redeem Schwartz, settled into his left-handed stance. *Come on,* Henry thought. *One time.* Izzy, who'd gotten a sneaky lead at first, took off. The pitch was a fastball down and in, right where Rick liked it. *One time.* Rick dropped his hands and torqued his hips mightily, his pinstriped belly trailing behind. The pitch was ankle-high, but Rick's looping swing caught it square on the fat part of the bat. The clear loud peal cut through the crowd's noise. The ball described a parabolic arc through the dark Carolinian air, climbing and climbing still higher, high above the light stanchions, so high it could only come straight down, and would either clear the fence or be caught. The right fielder drifted back, back, until his back was pressed against the wall. He flexed his knees, intent as a cat, and leaped, hooking his free arm over the top of the wall as he stretched his glove toward the plummeting ball...

"Yes!" Owen, who'd seemed not even to be watching, flung his book aside and vaulted the dugout stairs. "Yes yes yes yes yes!" The ball landed in the Amherst bullpen, a yard past the wall. Owen, the first to arrive at home plate, beat madly on Rick's helmet with both hands, leapfrogged onto his shoulders as the whole team, Henry included, danced around. *"Yes!"*

The Harpooners trailed by only one. When Boddington followed with a sharp single to right, the Amherst coach finally signaled to the bullpen for a fresh pitcher. The righty who jogged to the mound looked more like an accountant than a star pitcher — he was Henry's height, pale-haired and sunken-chinned, with slouched and flimsy shoulders. "Name's Dougal," Arsch told Henry. "Pitched a two-hitter against West Texas the other day. He is *filthy.*"

Henry nodded. The ability to throw a baseball was an alchemical thing, a superhero's secret power. You could never quite tell who possessed it.

Sooty Kim stepped to the plate. Dougal checked the runner at first, slide-stepped expertly off the mound, and drilled Sooty in the shoulder with a ninety-plus fastball. Sooty dropped to the ground and writhed there for a while. He climbed to his feet and walked down to first, wincing as he kneaded his upper arm.

"Did he do that on *purpose?*" Arsch wondered aloud, not without a whisper of admiration in his voice, as the now thoroughly disgruntled umpire warned both benches.

Henry shrugged. It certainly looked purposeful. It looked like Dougal was exacting revenge for the brushback pitch Starblind had thrown three innings before—a reckless, almost crazy thing to do in such a close game. *You want to throw at my guy? Fine. I'll put the go-ahead run on base, and then I'll get out of it.* Which is just what he did, striking out Sal Phlox on four pitches. *"Filthy,"* Arsch reiterated. "Just plain filthy."

Top of the ninth. As Starblind warmed up, Coach Cox kept scanning the length of the dugout, frowning all the while, the way a hungry person keeps opening an empty refrigerator on the off chance he might have overlooked something. He needed a pitcher, but he didn't have one. Starblind was finished, was basically lobbing the ball to home plate, but he was going to have to do that for one more inning.

The leadoff hitter smoked a double into the gap between Sal and Sooty Kim. The next batter yanked a long drive down the left field line, bringing the Amherst players surging happily out of their dugout, but it curled just foul. Starblind's whole body looked limp, spent. Schwartz lifted up his mask and looked beseechingly toward the dugout. *Even me, his eyes said. Even I might throw better than this.*

Maybe I should volunteer, Henry thought. I can throw as hard as Starblind. Harder, even. Get in there, fire a few fastballs over the plate, stop the bleeding. We come back and win it in the bottom of the inning. Storybook ending. So what if I haven't eaten in a while?

Before he could indulge the fantasy any further, Starblind threw another wobbly pitch. The hitter lined a head-high shot up the middle. The Amherst players surged toward the field again, ready to celebrate another score. Izzy came flying in from nowhere, stretched full-out in midair. The ball vanished into his glove. He landed on his stomach and reached out with his right hand to touch second base, doubling off the stunned runner. Two outs. Starblind, somehow, induced a fly ball to end the inning. The Harpooners sprinted off the field, shouting nonsense. Down by one, one last chance.

"Arsch," barked Coach Cox. "Get a bat. You're hitting for Ajay."

Arsch nodded resolutely, bat already in hand. "Filthy?" he muttered to himself, staring out toward the mound. "I'll show him filthy."

The bullpen phone rang. Coach Cox reached down into the dugout and grabbed the receiver. "Mike?" he said. "Mike's pretty goddamn busy right now." He moved to hang up the phone, then brought it back to his ear. "Hey. Whoa. Just calm down a sec." Pause. "Hang on. Hang on. I'll get him."

Henry kept one eye on Arsch as the big man stepped in against meek-looking Dougal, and one on Schwartz, who pressed the phone to one ear and a grimy hand to the other to muffle his teammates' chatter. Schwartz was watching the field too, initially — Arsch took a called strike — but his eyes quickly fell to the concrete floor. "Are you sure?" he said quietly.

Ball one. Schwartz sank down on the bench, ten feet away from Henry.

"Baby. Oh, baby. I'm so sorry."

His grimy hand made a slow pass over his widow's peak, fell helplessly into his lap. He was wearing all of his gear except for his mask. He spoke a few more words into the phone, too softly for Henry to hear, and handed the receiver to Jensen to hang up.

Meat struck out swinging. Two outs left in the season. Owen shut his book and stood, stretched his arms over his head, fingers woven together, and hummed a little ditty; he would bat if Starblind or Izzy reached base. Henry looked at Schwartz, who stared down at the squashed paper cones that littered the floor.

Owen pulled his batting gloves from his back pockets, slapped them decisively against his thighs, and headed for the bat rack. "Buddha," Schwartz said softly. Owen turned around.

Schwartz was wearing a look of indecision that Henry had never seen on him before. "Buddha," he repeated, even more softly. "That was Pella. It's about her dad. Mrs. McCallister found him this morning. He's..." Schwartz's voice caught. Deep furrows ran through the dirt on his forehead. Henry already knew—felt like he'd known all day—what he was going to say. "He's dead."

Owen froze. "You're joking."

"No."

They stared at each other, Owen's smoke-gray eyes against Schwartz's big amber ones, for what felt like forever. Starblind's bat made a loud promising *ping*. Henry glanced up to see the Amherst third baseman wrap his glove around a hard line drive. Two outs. Starblind yelped in anguish and pounded his bat into home plate. Owen, his face expressionless, lowered his eyes and nodded, as if to say, *Okay. I believe you.*

"I'm sorry," Schwartz said.

"Why? Did you kill him?" Owen swam blankly past Schwartz and sank down on the bench. Schwartz sat down beside him. Henry slid nearer, so that the three of them were in a row, Owen bent forward in the center. "You're on deck," Henry said.

"So?"

"So..." Henry looked to Schwartz for help, but Schwartz either didn't notice or wouldn't meet his eye. Henry wanted to tell Owen to go get a hit for President Affenlight, that that was all he could do right now, that they would work through the rest later, but the words were absurd and they dried on his lips. He patted Owen weakly on the back. "I'll tell Coach Cox."

Izzy had one foot in the batter's box and was performing his usual pre-at-bat ritual—five signs of the cross at maximum speed. "Izzy!" Henry yelled from the dugout steps. "Step out!" His voice dissolved into the crowd's roar. *"Izzy! Step out!"*

Izzy, confused, complied. Henry ran out to Coach Cox and tried to explain that President Affenlight was dead and therefore Owen couldn't bat. Coach Cox stroked his mustache, annoyed and uncomprehending.

"Owen can't bat," Henry said. "He just can't."

"Why the goddamn not?"

"Believe me," Henry pleaded. "He just can't."

Coach Cox looked up and down the dugout. The only guys left on the bench were the guys who rarely played — guys who had zero chance against a dealer of filth like Dougal. "Grab a bat."

"*Me?*" Henry said. "But Coach... I'm not even wearing a cup."

"You want mine? Grab a bat and get a goddamn hit, Skrimshander."

Oh Jesus, Henry thought. He didn't know what to wish for. If he didn't get to hit, it would be because Izzy made an out and the game was over. If he did get to hit, he was toast. He hurried to the bat rack to find a bat — he chose a lighter one than usual, to match his diminished strength — and took a few tentative swipes at the evening air. The bat felt like lead in his hands.

Dougal rocked and fired. The pitch was a fastball, low and outside. Izzy, overmatched, stuck out the bat. The ball looped torpidly over the second baseman's head and dropped in shallow right-center for a single. *Oh boy.*

Coach Cox pulled his crumpled lineup card from his back pocket and waved at the plate umpire. Dougal stomped pissily around the back of the mound, flipping the rosin bag with the backs of his fingers. Henry squeezed into a batting helmet and slowly made his way toward home plate. He dipped one foot inside the batter's box, as if testing the temperature of a pool.

"Let's go, son," growled the umpire. "Season can't last forever."

Henry stepped into the box, tapped the Harpooner on his chest three times. He felt less muscle than he'd grown to expect beneath the starchy fabric. Dougal peered in, agreed to a sign. The Amherst crowd started a chant. The first pitch, an absolutely filthy slider, darted by for a strike.

Henry knew that he was toast. Dougal could throw that filthy pitch twice more, and he wouldn't come close to hitting it. It was a pro-quality slider, had broken a foot or more while moving outlandishly fast. The timing required to hit a pitch like that was a matter not just of skill but of constant practice. A day off made it tough; a month off made it impossible. Schwartzy might someday have forgiven him for what he'd done with Pella, but now he'd never know — because Schwartz, standing there in the on-deck circle with two weighted bats on his shoulder, would never forgive him for this.

He decided in advance to swing at the second pitch, if only to give Dougal something to think about. Dougal wiped the sweat from his forehead, checked Izzy at first. The pitch was another slider, identical to the first. Henry swung and missed. Two strikes.

Still, he must have done something to catch Dougal's eye, because Dougal shook off one sign, and then another, and then beckoned for the catcher, who called time and jogged out to confer. The Amherst fans were going crazy. Dougal lifted his glove to his face and spoke through the latticed weave of the webbing, to keep Henry from reading his lips. A burst of affectionate sympathy surged through Henry; somehow all of a sudden, and maybe because he felt so light-headed, it occurred to him that he and Dougal were brothers, members of a tribe of unassuming, live-armed guys, guys who looked like nobodies but carried their force on the inside and were determined to beat you, would do anything to beat you, would kill themselves to beat you, and he knew where Dougal disagreed with his catcher. The catcher figured Henry was an easy mark — wanted to finish him off right away, with another slider down the pipe. The catcher was probably right. But Dougal saw something else in Henry, smelled a whiff of danger *(We are brothers, Dougal, brothers...)*, and felt a need to set him up for the kill — to show the fastball high and tight, before finishing with the slider low and away. It was flattering, in a way, that a pitcher like Dougal would go to such trouble to strike him out. And it was foolish, in a way, for Dougal to be so crafty, to insist on the pride of his craft, to try to orchestrate things, instead of simply letting Henry beat himself.

Henry set up farther from home plate than usual, to encourage Dougal to throw his high tight fastball a little tighter than he otherwise might. He went through his age-old routine—touch the far black of the plate with the bat head, tap the Harpooner on his breast three times, make a single, level pass of the bat through the zone—but it had a different meaning now, a counterfeit meaning, or no meaning at all, since he had no intention of swinging at the pitch.

Dougal checked the runner, began his elegant efficient slide-step toward home. Henry gritted his teeth. It was weird how clear and clean the air felt. His mind subsided into something like prayer. *Forgive me, Schwartzy, for quitting the team.* He stepped sharply toward home plate, dipping his shoulder as he did so, as if expecting, diving into, a slider low and away.

76

His first thought was that he was President Affenlight and that he had died, but the mere fact of thinking such a thing meant that it couldn't be true. Wherever he was was dark. He tried to lift his left arm to touch his head where it hurt, but the movement was arrested by two tubes that were taped to his forearm. A bitter taste stung his mouth. Schwartz was sitting in a chair by the bed, motionless in the dark.

The simple act of moving his jaw sent shocks of diabolical pain through his brain, worse than anything he'd ever felt. When he finally managed to speak, the words came out soft and slurred. "Who won?"

Schwartz cocked his head. "You don't remember?"

"No." He remembered the pitch, a tiny white pellet shoulder-high and rising. He remembered trying to spin away so it would catch him on the helmet rather than flush in the face.

"You scored the winning run," Schwartz said, frowning.

"I did?"

"That fastball hit you square on the earflap. Everybody in the park thought you were dead. Me included. But you bounced right up and ran to first. The trainers tried to check you out, but you wouldn't let them. *Play ball,* you kept saying. *Play ball!* Over and over again. Coach Cox tried to send Loonie in to pinch-run, but you yelled at him till he went back to the dugout."

Henry didn't remember any of that. "Then what happened?"

"Dougal got ejected. He screamed bloody murder about it, but the benches had been warned, and he was gone. They brought in their second-best guy.

"I knocked the first pitch off the wall. I almost hit it too hard, it caromed straight back to the left fielder. But you were flying. I've never seen you move that fast. By the time I got to first you were rounding third. Coach Cox tried to hold you, but you never even looked at him.

"You beat the tag by half an inch. Everybody piled on top of you, including Coach Cox. Heck, half the parents were on that pile. And when everybody else got up, you didn't."

Henry studied Schwartz's face, or what he could see of it, in the dimness. To see if he was telling the truth, not that Schwartz ever lied; to see in what ratio the sadness of Affenlight's death was mixed with the joy of winning the national championship; to see if his friend might be beginning to forgive him.

"You shouldn't have done that," Schwartz said sternly.

"Done what?"

"You know what. Eaten that pitch."

Henry's idiot lips were taking forever to form the sounds of words. "I thought it was a slider."

"Bullshit."

He tried to cover his mouth as he retched, but the tubes inhibited his movement. A few bile-wet Rice Krispies spilled over his lower lip and down his chin.

"Bullshit," Schwartz repeated. "I saw it live and I saw it on *SportsCenter* while I was sitting in the goddamn waiting room at the goddamn ER. You dove into that thing like it was a swimming pool."

Henry didn't say anything.

"You even set up away from the plate, so he'd have to come farther inside to buzz you. You baited him into it."

Henry wasn't going to admit it any more than he was going to argue with it.

"What were you thinking, Henry? How many bodies you want to pile up in one day?"

Schwartz was pissed, no doubt about that, though he hadn't raised his voice and had barely twitched a muscle, as if he'd reached such a state of exhaustion that he'd never move or yell again. "What about the Buddha? Poor Buddha. He just found out about Affenlight—and now he's got to sit there and watch you try to kill yourself? You could have just stayed home."

"I thought I'd be able to turn my shoulder into it, get a free base that way," Henry said. "I didn't expect him to throw it so high."

"Well, Dougal's a crazy bastard. Just not as crazy as you."

This was the gentlest thing Schwartz had said. An odd giddiness was tickling up and down Henry's spine, despite the intensity of his headache. "I didn't have a lot of options out there," he said.

"Swing and miss. Get us on a plane back home. That was an option."

"Aren't you glad you won?"

Behind the shut curtain of the room's lone window, a little light was beginning to appear. Schwartz's watch, glowing yellow-green in the grayness, read 5:23—Henry felt too confused to subtract forty-two, but it was four-something in the morning.

"Yes," Schwartz finally said. "I am."

The giddiness was washing over Henry from his toes up to his neck. It felt beautiful, like angel-song. Maybe in some partial way, and despite Schwartz's anger, Henry had redeemed himself in the eyes of his friend.

The giddiness deepened into bliss. His limbs lacked energy to move, but a different type of energy was moving through them, originating somewhere in his bones and organs and spilling outward, scrubbing and scouring him from within, suffusing him to his skin. Maybe it was Schwartz's presence, maybe it was the fact that the Harpooners had won the national championship—but the bliss laughed at those things, and Henry realized that they were irrelevant where the bliss was concerned. Maybe this was what dying felt like.

"Am I okay?" he said.

"Depends what you mean. You've got a concussion. A pretty bad one. Dougal throws ninety-two, you know.

"But that's not why the doctors think you collapsed. According to your blood work you've run out of pretty much every mineral and nutrient necessary for life. Even salt. It's not easy to run out of salt. I think you're going to be here for a while."

"—"

"*Tried to drown himself from the inside* was how one of the doctors put it."

Henry looked toward the white underbelly of his forearm, where a length of transparent tape kept the needles and gauze in place. "Is this morphine?"

Schwartz half smiled at this. "If it was I'd have ripped it out and stuck it in my own arm. Those are both just nutrients."

"Hm." He had begun to imagine that the bliss was a function of morphine or some other spectacular sparkling drug being shuttled into his blood. But maybe it was mere food that was making him feel like this. In which case maybe it was worth it not to eat for a few weeks, to reach this bliss at the end.

"How's Owen?"

Schwartz shook his head as if to say, *Don't ask*. "He headed back right after the game. To take care of Pella."

"How's Pella?"

Schwartz stood up, looked at his watch. "I'm going to try to catch the early flight," he said. "Some of the other guys will probably stop by later to visit, if they wake up in time. They're out partying now."

"Okay," Henry said.

"Don't mention Affenlight. They'll find out soon enough."

"Okay."

A little bit of dawn was seeping past the dense hospital curtains. Schwartz stood there, a hulking shadow in the dimness. With undisguisable difficulty he hoisted his huge beat-up backpack and slung it onto his back, adjusting the straps so they wouldn't cut into the meat of his chest. Then he shouldered his equally huge equipment bag.

"This is the psych floor," he said.

Henry nodded. "Okay."

"Figured I'd give you a heads-up. They're going to send in the shrinks to talk to you about not eating. Your anorexia, as they referred to it."

"Okay."

"I told them only cheerleaders get anorexia. You're a ballplayer — you're having a spiritual crisis." Schwartz's smile returned, rueful this time. "They thought I was being serious."

"Well," Henry said. "You're a serious guy."

Schwartz had never seemed like a college kid exactly, but now he looked flat-out old, sleepless and worn, the creases in his forehead deep. His knees wavered under the weight of his bags. He grabbed the railing at the end of the bed to steady himself. "Get some rest, Skrimmer."

His big body eclipsed the doorway and vanished down the corridor, the thump of his shambling footfalls and the scratch of his backpack against his jacket diminishing as he went.

77

T he phone rang, and he felt like letting it ring, but he'd just been talking with Dr. Rachels about handling problems as they arose, in the present, one at a time, and here was a problem he could probably handle: a ringing phone. He'd been here for ten days.

"Henry, it's Dwight. Dwight Rogner."

"Hey Dwight."

"Congratulations, my friend. It's my distinct pleasure to inform you that you've been chosen by the St. Louis Cardinals in the thirty-third round of the amateur draft."

"What?" Henry sank down on the unmade hospital bed. His first thought was that it was Adam or Rick, playing a joke so absurd it could hardly be considered cruel. "You're kidding."

"I know it's not what you were shooting for, in terms of the round. But I think it's a wonderful opportunity for you. And for the St. Louis Cardinals, frankly, to get an athlete of your caliber at this stage of the draft."

"But...," Henry protested. "I mean... I don't even play anymore. I quit the team."

"Henry, I know you haven't had the easiest season. But the draft is about one word, and that word is *potential*. And I'll be damned if the Cardinals are going to find another player in the thirty-third round with your kind of potential. Who I can easily close my eyes and imagine as a star in this league. A legitimate, long-term star."

Henry said nothing, but that seemed okay because Dwight kept talking: "You and Mike have done a great job with your training, given the available resources. But the difference between Westish College and the St. Louis Cardinals is night and day. With us you'll have the best coaches, the best trainers, the best facilities. Everything we do is designed to make you a better ballplayer."

"I've lost weight," Henry said.

"You'll gain it back. We'll bring you along slowly. Nobody's expecting you to play in the majors tomorrow. We just expect you to work hard every day. To follow your dream."

"I'm in the *hospital*," Henry said loudly. "In the psych ward. I can't throw." He slammed a hand down on the bed. Anger surged through him. He didn't want to talk about dreams. He wanted to talk about what was real.

"I know you've had a rough go," Dwight said. "It happens to the best of us."

"You're serious," Henry said. "You drafted me."

"We sure did. You have a much higher ceiling than most late-round picks, and we'll be offering a correspondingly higher bonus to convince you to sign. How does a hundred strike you?"

"Dollars?"

Dwight laughed. "Thousands. A hundred thousand dollars, up front. Anyway, we can discuss that later. You have until the end of August to sign a contract. If you don't sign, we lose your rights, and you'll go back into the draft next year. In which case I'll be tracking your progress very closely."

Henry said nothing. There was nothing to say. A hundred thousand dollars to play baseball: just what he'd always wanted.

"By the way," Dwight added, "the Cubbies picked up your buddy Adam Starblind. He's made quite an impression the last month or so."

"Wow. That's . . . wow." *Let it be after me. Just let it be after me.* "What round was that?"

"Thirty-second," Dwight said. "Right before you."

78

Pella walked through the Large Quad feeling something like herself. It was a blistering day in early August, two months since her father's death, and the busiest day she'd had since that first awful week, when flowers and condolences were arriving from all over. Mrs. McCallister handled the arrangements and the thank-yous. Pella lay in the guest bed in the quarters, Mike at her side, and refused to cry.

She'd worked a short shift in the dining hall this morning. Then she'd eaten lunch with Professor Eglantine, who'd offered to supervise her in a one-on-one tutorial for the fall, and who'd insisted she call her "Judy." Pella worried that Professor Eglantine, Judy, was just being kind, but then again she'd seemed to be enjoying herself, and it would be great to have her for a tutor and possibly, if it wasn't too much to ask, for a friend. The syllabus they'd constructed, while Professor Eglantine picked unconvincingly at her Cobb salad, centered on the letters of Mary McCarthy and Hannah Arendt. All in all, it had been a very heartening lunch.

Now she was on her way to Dean Melkin's office, on the ground floor of Glendinning Hall, to finalize the details of her enrollment for the fall. Pella wasn't sure how many details still needed finalizing, or why Dean Melkin, whom she'd never met, was so burningly eager to finalize them. Granted it was August now, but he'd been calling the quarters all summer, beginning much too soon after her dad's death, begging her to meet. Pella had put him off with a series of brief, widely spaced e-mails, saying she wasn't yet up for a face-to-face but had been in touch with Admissions, with the Registrar, with Student Health. These other departments of Westish simply e-mailed forms to her, and Mike filled out the forms and dropped them off. Whereas Dean Melkin kept leaving pleading messages on the machine.

Dean Melkin was on the phone when Pella peered cautiously around his half-closed door. He smiled and waggled two fingers to indicate how many minutes he'd need. After precisely that many minutes he invited her in, a slender man in khaki pants and a too-large houndstooth jacket with elbow patches, youthful in that slightly fetal way of certain descendants of the upper British Isles, his pale hair beating a ragged retreat from all directions at once.

"Pella." He smiled at her pinkly. "Thank you for coming in. I know this has been a very difficult summer."

Pella nodded in an unforlorn way meant to indicate that they needn't talk about it.

"If you'd ever like to chat," he went on, "morning, noon, or night, please don't hesitate. I've left my cell number on your machine, but I can give it to you now too."

"Thanks," Pella said.

They sat down. Arranged on Dean Melkin's desk, beneath a Post-it that bore her name, was a tall stack of materials — materials regarding core requirements, online registration, foreign language requirements, AP credits, dining hall plans, health insurance. He began to talk her through them, or to try to, but each time Pella, after waiting a minimally polite period of time, quietly indicated that yes, and yes, and yes, it had been taken care of. Each time Dean Melkin, seeming oddly nervous, lauded her conscientiousness and moved on to the next already-taken-care-of matter.

"Last but not least," he said. "Housing. It wasn't easy to fit you in — we have limited flexibility regarding late admits — but I did some finagling, and I found not only a room for you, but I think an excellent situation." He leaned back happily in his chair. "You'll be rooming with a young woman named Angela Fan, who was not only the winner of this year's Maria Westish Award, which as you may know indicates an extremely high level of academic accomplishment, but also recently published a chapbook of poetry with a small press in Portland. And she took a gap year last year to work on an organic farm in Maryland, so she's also a slightly more mature roommate than you might otherwise have had."

"Oh no," Pella said. "I'm so sorry. I can't believe I didn't mention this earlier. I've been making plans to live off campus. In fact I just signed a lease on a place. With my boyfriend." She didn't know why she'd added the *boyfriend* part—it seemed too louche for the dean's pink-tipped ears.

Dean Melkin looked very sad. "Ah," he said. "Hm...it's college policy that all freshpersons live in the dormitories, we find it encourages a robust immersion in college life. Even our nontraditional students..." There seemed to be a war going on within him, between his devotion to college policy and his desperate desire to accommodate her. Pella couldn't help sagging in her chair a little, to magnify her grief—damned if she wanted to pretend to live in the dorms, to hustle from her and Mike's place to weekly popcorn parties in the RA's room.

"I'm sure it can be arranged," Dean Melkin decided quickly, smiling for her benefit. "Your adjustment to Westish is the vital thing."

Pella thanked him profusely, and thanked him some more, and stood to leave. But the look on Dean Melkin's face had become so perplexed, so somehow needy, that she let her butt fall back in the chair.

"So you're doing okay?" he said.

Pella nodded.

"Your father was a very interesting man. He had a...a way about him." Dean Melkin plucked at the gold-painted buttons on the cuffs of his jacket. "Nothing meant more to him than having you here." He looked up at her, his expression only growing in perplexity, so that it could even be called tortured.

"It was very sudden," he said.

"Yes." Pella nodded with the somberness that was both expected of her and easy to muster.

"That is to say … it *was* very sudden, then? There wasn't some kind of … precipitating illness?"

"No," Pella said. "Not at all."

"Ah. Aha." Dean Melkin wrinkled his turned-up, slightly fetal nose. He seemed dispirited by the lack of a precipitating illness. "It was very sudden, then, but it wasn't … that is to say, it was …" He hesitated, pursed his lips. "It was a matter of natural causes?"

"Sure." Pella peered at Dean Melkin, trying to figure out what he was saying. "What other kind of causes are there?"

"Oh, well. None, I suppose." He looked up at her, his expression deeply pained. "But there wasn't any way in which it could have been … or been construed as … *intentional?*"

What? Suddenly it felt like their entire meeting, not to mention his summerlong pursuit of her, had been building toward this moment of anxious prying. "My father died of a heart attack," Pella said sharply. "For which my family has a strong genetic predisposition. The men, at least. The women live forever."

"Ah." Dean Melkin sank into his chair. He looked, though still uncomfortable, perceptibly relieved. "Well, then. It couldn't have been avoided, could it?"

What was going on? Did Dean Melkin think that her dad wanted to *kill* himself? Why in the world would he think such a thing? Maybe because her dad had been so ruddy and hale and energetic; maybe it was difficult for Dean Melkin to imagine him just ceasing to live. But her dad was also so cheerful, so downright life-affirming, in his public persona, that she couldn't imagine anyone thinking that he might commit *suicide.* And not just thinking it but thinking it with sufficient intensity to *ask* her about it, as Dean Melkin had essentially done, which was truly bizarre, not to mention seriously unprofessional.

Unless there was some reason for Dean Melkin to think it. Some inside info, some hurt or scandal or hidden rot in her dad's life that she didn't know about but that other people did. Was she going too far? Was she living inside her head again?

But Dean Melkin was sitting right there, acting so bizarrely, still fiddling with the buttons on the cuffs of his too-big imitation-dean jacket, not that he wasn't a real dean, but he looked more like a watery kid who wanted someday to be a dean, and her point was that she'd arrived here in an okay mood, really the best mood she'd been in all summer, and it was Dean Melkin whose agitation was agitating her, whose strange behavior and strange words were causing her to think strange thoughts. It wasn't her. It was him, and she had to get to the bottom of it. And if she thought of hurt and scandal in relation to her dad, well, she could think of only one possibility. Of one person.

"Of course," she said with great gravity, "all this has been exceptionally hard on Owen."

Dean Melkin looked more perplexed and tortured than ever. But not in a who's-Owen-and-why-did-you-utter-this-strange-non-sequitur kind of way. No, it was more the perplexity of a person trying hard to craft a reaction to news he already knew. "Of course," he said, nodding thoughtfully. "I can see how it must be very difficult."

He knows, Pella thought. He knows about Owen. The dean of students knows about Owen. He knows about Owen and he's wondering whether my dad committed suicide. And now *she* was wondering whether her dad committed suicide. Because the dean of students knew. And if he knew, he wasn't the only one. Which meant that her dad had gotten strung up, or had been about to get strung up, or something.

Could he have killed himself? Was there a way to kill yourself that looked enough like a heart attack to fool people who expected you to have died of a heart attack? Well, yes, there had to be. But it just wasn't possible. Her dad didn't have a morbid bone in his body, had always been a terrible fraidy-cat where death was concerned. He didn't like doctors, her mom at least partly excluded, and he didn't like the pills that, paradoxically, reminded him he would someday die. No, he couldn't have killed himself, though he *had* been smoking too much—she regretted not realizing that earlier, not harping on it more. When Mrs. McCallister found him his right hand was on his chest, gripped around his pack of Parliaments, which were thoroughly crushed.

"Within the administration," she said, "I suppose that pretty much everyone knew about him and Owen."

"No no no." Dean Melkin straightened in his chair, tugged at the collar of his white oxford. "No no. It was only me and Bruce Gibbs, and I believe Mr. Gibbs consulted one or two other trustees, in a highly confidential way, just to gauge what the options were. Whether there *were* any options."

There it was, then. He'd been caught. He'd been caught, and he'd been banished. Those bastards. And her father, what an idiot. He hadn't told her. Had he told anyone? Had he told Owen? No—he couldn't have. He wouldn't have. If Owen had known, if she had known, they might have been able to calm him, console him, buck him up somehow. Instead he'd kept it all on that heart of his.

She had to get out of there. Not just out of Dean Melkin's office—out of Westish, away from Westish. Like forever.

Dean Melkin was still worrying the buttons on his cuffs. Clearly he'd been waiting for this moment, had been living all summer with a weird guilt upon him.

"Pella," he said, "I'm so very sorry. I wish there was something that could have been done differently. Of course your father was my superior, I had no real say in the matter, but the idea that there may have been some sort of connection between his resignation and his passing, well, it's terrible, it's just terrible…"

"I couldn't agree more," she said sharply, a promising beginning to a rant, but she felt too miserable to make a scene. Somehow she managed to get to her feet and swim out of the room, out of Glendinning Hall, leaving her stack of catalogs and carbon copies on the edge of Dean Melkin's desk.

She had to get so far away from here. Mike was working at Bartleby's tonight, was probably there already — when she calmed down she would walk over there and drink whiskey, and tell him why she had to leave. Would he come with her? Surely he would. She was willing to go anywhere he wanted, as long as it wasn't here. Even Chicago would be far enough.

She was outside, sweating in the hazy afternoon sun, and she swung wildly around the campus in helpless, hopeless circles for a long while, down to the beach and back, out to the football stadium and back, here there and everywhere. She thought about her dad and how to avenge him. How to shun Westish in the most profound way possible. How to make the entire college and everyone involved with it know and understand that she and her father were shunning it in the most profound and everlasting way possible. She was full of rage but she wasn't coming up with much.

She didn't want to think about Dean Melkin, he was the last scourge-slash-person she wanted to think about, but something he'd said kept flitting through her mind, flitting and flitting until finally it just stuck there in the middle and nothing could get around it. "Nothing meant more to him," Melkin said, "than having you here." It was true, wasn't it. It was all too true. She'd never know what her dad's last minutes or hours or days were like, but one thing she knew was that Dean Melkin was right, and that no matter what had happened between her dad and Westish, her dad would have wanted her here. If she lashed out at Westish, in whatever impotent way she could lash out, then she'd be doing it for her, not for him. If she wanted to do something for him, it wouldn't be that.

She wouldn't tell Owen. To tell Owen would only make him feel awful and guilty, like he'd contributed to her dad's death, and for what? For the sake of the sound of her voice. And to tell Mike would be pointless. She would keep it between her and her dad. And she would keep ramming the Affenlight name down the throat of Westish College, over and over, but not like that, not in a vindictive way—she would do it like her dad would want her to do it. She would settle in. She would read the letters of Hannah Arendt and Mary McCarthy. She would be, to whatever extent was possible, at peace.

Without Pella realizing it, her wanderings had carried her, for the first time since the funeral, to the edge of the cemetery. Now she braced herself, entered the gate, and walked within sighting distance of her dad's grave. She didn't get too close; it was enough, it was hard enough, to be here, forty yards away, and to know that his flat headstone lay near that wide and knotty tree, which she recognized from the haze of the burial.

She would be here for the next four years, but he was gone, gone from this place, from every place, forever. *That's the deal,* she thought, and the thought seemed to come from elsewhere, a visitation. *That's the deal.*

She turned around, away from the headstone, and faced the lake. Waist high waves flung themselves at the breakers. She thought of what she always thought of in a cemetery: her dad's anecdote about Emerson digging up his wife Ellen's body. Then, still gazing at the water, she remembered his old Harvard e-mail password, which she'd decoded as a kid without him knowing—*landlessness,* how obvious could you be? An idea was forming in her mind. Her dad had died as the president of Westish, his funeral had been full of pomp and circumstance, he'd been buried here in a spot of honor. And all of those were no small things. But there was a falseness to it too, to him being buried here. Now that he was dead he could be here and not be here; *they,* the Melkins and Gibbses of the world, could think he was here, while she would know the truth. He belonged out there, in the water, which he loved.

Maybe it seemed silly to construe an e-mail password as a person's deepest wish, but now that the idea had occurred to her she knew that it was right. All the lashed sea's landlessness again. Of course, she couldn't do it alone. She headed back to the quarters, where they were still staying, to wait for Mike to come home.

79

Schwartz's new job would start in mid-August, when football season began and the new school year's budget kicked in. Till then he'd been working at Bartleby's, picking up as many shifts as he could, but there wasn't much need for bouncers during the slow summer months, and even when he filled in behind the bar, like tonight, he walked home half drunk with no more than forty dollars in his pocket.

When he got back to the quarters, Pella was curled in a leather armchair in what had been her father's study, asleep. Schwartz scooped her up in his arms — she was several pounds lighter than she'd been in April, a change of which he did not approve. She murmured and squirmed, wrapped her arms around his neck, but didn't awake. He supported her bottom with one hand; with the other he plucked her book from a crevice of the chair.

She groaned and rolled onto her stomach when he laid her down on the bed they shared. He tugged up the hem of her tank top and unhooked her bra, rubbed very lightly the twin pink indents where the clasp had pressed into her skin. Things were not so bad. Lately she seemed to be emerging from the deepest part of her grief, that summer-long coma during which she'd napped and read, read and napped, eyes Xanaxed and dry. A few nights ago they'd made love again, for what felt like the first time.

The night was warm, too warm to bother with blankets. Schwartz found an extra sheet in the hall closet and spread its seashell pattern over Pella's sleeping form. Now they had no parents between them.

He went to the kitchen and boiled water for instant coffee. He made it strong, the way he liked it, and added a finger's worth of scotch from President Affenlight's liquor cabinet. He'd been working through the scotch slowly, systematically, starting with the least expensive. Only in the last week had Pella asked him to pour her a little glass too; this was another good sign, the stepwise return of one appetite at a time.

It was after one. He descended the narrow staircase to President Affenlight's office, where he'd been spending his nights, his dawns, and many of his days. Contango trailed him down the stairs and curled up in his usual spot on the rug. The financial documents had been carted away by accountants and attorneys, but Affenlight's books and papers, a lifetime's worth of learning, were still here. They needed to be dealt with, or at least packed up, before late August, when the newly hired president arrived, but Pella had so far refused to come into this room, the room where her father died. So it fell to Schwartz to comb through the type-written lecture notes and yellowed journals; the coffee-stained drafts of essays and wrinkled carbons of decades-old correspondence; the grocery lists and scribbles; the copiously annotated copies of antebellum prayer-books and poetry primers, to decide what should be kept and what thrown away. Everything was paper, paper, paper—he'd brought twenty more boxes of paper from the study upstairs, and these were stacked in the corners of the room. Affenlight had kept a computer on his desk, but it seemed to have been mostly for show.

One box of 4 × 6 cards was marked, simply, SPEAKING. Some of the cards contained jokes or anecdotes, along with the dates and occasions of their use. Schwartz remembered many of the more recent occasions, and the jokes. Other cards offered aphoristic rules in Affenlight's precise hand: *With a small group, assonate, as in writing; with a large group, alliterate.*

Often Owen dropped by as late as three or four, mug of tea in hand.

Schwartz would share his recent discoveries; Owen, as he listened, would purse his lips into something like a smile. They would seal their evening by smoking a wordless joint on the front steps of Scull Hall. Tonight, though, Owen didn't come, and Schwartz, feeling rather literary, took down Affenlight's *Riverside Shakespeare* and settled in behind the desk to page through it. He scanned the marginalia, paused to read some familiar passages. He somehow felt deeply at home here, in Affenlight's office, among Affenlight's thoughts, near Affenlight's death. Deeply at home but also tenuously so; he considered it a privilege to serve as the de facto custodian of Affenlight's papers, and he felt a constant worry that someone closer to Affenlight, or at least better versed in American literature, would show up to kick him out. But it hadn't happened yet, and as the summer crept by it seemed less and less likely to happen. Which saddened Schwartz, in a way: what a smart and thoughtful man Affenlight had been, and how little he'd be remembered.

The Sperm-Squeezers was a beautiful book, the early exemplar of a critical genre; perhaps grad students would read it for another decade, and intellectual historians mention it for a decade after that. And perhaps Schwartz, as he readied all this paper for the college's library, could pull together a second, posthumous book, a collection of essays and speeches that a university press would publish. But a Guert Affenlight wasn't a Herman Melville; wouldn't burst back into prominence after death and fifty years' obscurity. His portrait would hang in the dining hall, alongside those of the other former presidents; four years from now, only the kitchen staff would recognize his face. No doubt some conference room or floor of the library would be renamed in his honor — or, Schwartz thought now, what about the baseball diamond? The current name, Westish Field, was strictly by default. Affenlight Field had a nice ring to it. Was that alliteration or assonance? The crowds there usually constituted a small group, though that might change now that they were national champs.

The office door creaked open, waking Schwartz, who'd been dozing at Affenlight's desk. Morning light leaked through the blinds. Schwartz jumped up, not wanting to get caught by Mrs. McCallister, who preferred both him and the dog to sleep upstairs. But it was Pella, freshly showered and dressed for work. She hadn't so much as poked her head in here all summer. "Hi," she said, and plunked down on the love seat, and told him what she wanted to do.

Schwartz said nothing for a while; just leaned back in the president's chair. She's been reading too much, he thought — had drifted across that line that separated what you might find in a book from what you might do. "I think we should think about this," he finally said.

"I've *been* thinking about it."

Maybe it was the morning light, or the heat of the shower still flushing her cheeks, but she looked sharpened and repaired. "We have to," she said. "We have to."

"You can't just dig up a body."

"Why not? It's my dad. It's my plot. It's my coffin." She swept a hand over the room. "You've been through all this stuff. So show me where it says, 'Put me in a box. With fake gold trim. And then stick it in the ground.' Show me where it says *that*."

Schwartz went to the love seat and sat down beside her. He zipped her hoodie up to her chin and gently knotted the strings. This gesture used to bug her — it bugged her right now — but at least she'd figured out what he meant by it: you are mine.

"It just makes sense," she said. "My dad loved this lake. He spent three years on a ship. He spent half my childhood rowing on the Charles. It's what he would have wanted."

Schwartz, having passed the summer among all this Affenlight-annotated Melvilleania, the memoirs of whaling ships, merchant ships, naval ships, couldn't disagree. "I understand why you want to do it this way—"

"We should have done it this way to begin with. If I'd had time to think it through, we would have. If I hadn't been so upset."

"I see what you're saying. But it's just not possible. It's a felony, for one thing" — Schwartz was bluffing, but he figured it could easily be a felony — "and you've got to remember how deep that hole is. And how much that box weighs. It would take forever. One person walks by and we're sitting in jail."

"Fine by me." Pella smiled, and Schwartz knew that he had lost the argument, had lost it before it began. He ran his hand over his deepening widow's peak, scratched his softening belly. He hadn't worked out once since May.

He half hoped that Owen would veto the scheme, but Owen just nodded and said, "Call Henry."

80

"Henry," Owen said warmly, wrapping his slender fingers around what remained of his roommate's biceps. "Is that you? You're skinnier than I am."

Schwartz held out his fist and Henry bumped it with his own, and Pella could tell from their somber, ceremonious expressions that their feud, or whatever you'd call it, had ended. Men were such odd creatures. They didn't duel anymore, even fistfights had come to seem barbaric, the old casual violence all channeled through institutions now, but still they loved to uphold their ancient codes. And what they loved even more was to forgive each other. Pella felt like she knew a lot about men, but she couldn't imagine what it would be like to be one of them, to be in a room of them with no woman present, to participate in their silent rites of contrition and redemption.

"Hey," Henry said to her.

"Hey." It seemed strange not to hug, so after a brief fit of school-dance awkwardness they finally did. He smelled ripe, like an adolescent boy not yet attuned to the fact that he needed to wear deodorant. It's because he's been on the bus all day, she thought, and hoped this was true — hoped he hadn't smelled this way since June. She held on to him for an extra second, long enough to detect an undertone of sticky Greyhound pleather in the scent of his skin.

They'd arranged to meet here, at the Melville statue. The afternoon had been scorching, and the dog-day humidity had compressed itself into a drumming rain that now, just after dusk, was dwindling to an ambient mist. The lake, churned-up but calm, looked like fresh-poured cement. Already the days were shorter than they'd been in June.

Two shovels, a cooler, a picnic basket, and a giant vinyl football equipment bag leaned against the weathered brick of Scull. They shouldered the gear and set off. Henry didn't ask where they were going or why; maybe he'd figured it out, or maybe he'd forgotten to care. It could be hard to tell with Henry, and Pella didn't know what effect the summer had had on him. When she'd called his parents' house in South Dakota, she'd merely said, "We want you to help us with something before Owen leaves." And he'd merely said, "Who's *we?*"

They crossed the Small Quad and then the Large in silence, walking four abreast. Contango sauntered along behind, eyeing the occasional darting sparrow with lazy suspicion. The grass of the practice fields had been burned khaki by the endless heat.

"Let's stop a moment. My arms are exhausted." Owen set down the beer-laden cooler and took from Pella the picnic basket, which he'd packed. He opened the wicker lid and took out a bottle of scotch from her dad's collection. "You first," he said, handing it to her. She lifted it to her lips and took a long slow glug. It burned nicely all the way to her stomach. Great minds, she thought, patting the flask in her windbreaker pocket as she handed the bottle to Owen, who drank and gave it to Mike. And then to Henry, and back to her. When the bottle was half gone, they put it in the basket and moved on.

Three rolls of sod had been laid over Affenlight's grave, and though the grass had grown long and damp, the edges of the rolls were still visible. One of the spades had a flat, rectangular head, while the other's was heart-shaped. Mike took the flat one and plunged it into a sod seam. The grass roots began to yield with a series of weak pops and groans as he leaned his weight on the handle. He worked his way around all three rolls. He and Henry lifted them off the grave and laid them aside.

They worked mostly in silence, Mike with the flat spade, Henry with the heart-shaped one. Owen, his reading light clipped to the brim of his cap, held the battery-powered lantern and distributed cans of High Life from the cooler. Pella sat nearby on an upright headstone, drinking scotch and stroking Contango's fur. The recent rain had softened the topsoil, rendering it easy to dig through, but beneath that the earth was pale and rock hard, and soon their progress slowed.

Sometimes a cloudless swatch of sky would blow past the moon, and Pella could see the outline of Mike's face in slightly sharper relief. It was strange the way he loved her: a sidelong and almost casual love, as if loving her were simply a matter of course, too natural to mention. Like their first meeting on the steps of the gym, when he'd hardly so much as glanced at her. With David and every guy before David, what passed for love had always been eye to eye, nose to nose; she felt watched, observed, like the prize inhabitant of a zoo, and she wound up pacing, preening, watching back, to fit the part. Whereas Mike was always beside her. She would stand at the kitchen window and look out at the quad, at the Melville statue and beyond that the beach and the rolling lake, and realize that Mike, for however long, had been standing beside her, staring at the same thing.

A light rain began to fall. Henry stopped digging and leaned on his shovel. The hole was shin-deep. The dog had fallen asleep. "Let me relieve you," Owen said, but Henry waved him off. The night was close and soupy, so that the rain didn't seem to be falling so much as oozing out of the wet air, and the sweat that trickled down Mike's and Henry's cheeks and noses mixed with the ooze as well. Henry looked exhausted. Owen declared that it was time for a break; they sat on headstones and ate pâté-and-Triscuit sandwiches, drank more beer. Pella passed around her scotch. After that, Henry held the lantern while Owen and Pella took turns digging beside Mike.

It wasn't long before Schwartz's spade banged against one of the metal runners on the casket's lid. The unexpected contact sent a rude judder through his forearms, like fouling a fastball off the neck of the bat in cold weather. At the noise they stopped and looked at one another in the moonless dimness. Their plan wasn't just a plan anymore. Schwartz felt more worried by the second. Not worried that they'd get caught; his worry, his fear, was more obscure. He was thinking about his mom. He looked at Pella, who nodded with fierce and possibly drunken resolve. "It's okay," she said.

Schwartz had planned the excavation as scrupulously as he could. First they widened and deepened the hole to free the sides of the casket; then they dug out, at the head, a space large enough for Schwartz to climb down into and stand. He knew from the funeral-home director that the oak casket weighed 240 pounds; that plus Affenlight's weight was a lot, but he needed to hoist only one end of it. He hunkered down in his deepest catcher's squat, grasped the single metal handle at the casket's head with both hands, and said a little prayer that his back would hold up. He drove through his heels, yanked with his arms and shoulders, felt the pain knife down his spine. Was this the origin of the word *deadlift?* Surely not, but it was the same motion.

That first effort was needed to free the casket from the earth beneath. The second would be the tricky one; more a power clean than a deadlift. He dropped low, rocked even lower. He exploded upward, jerked his hands toward his chin. As the head of the casket moved upward, Schwartz let go, dropped his hips, maneuvered his hands and shoulder, just barely, beneath the casket's bottom. Then it was a matter of walking it up to vertical, letting it tip over and lean, almost upright, against the far side of the hole. A little rain was falling. It wasn't a ceremonious procedure — he could feel Affenlight's body sliding inside the box — but at least it was getting done.

Henry and Pella and Owen grabbed hold of the casket's handles from above. They pulled from above while he tried to push from below. He'd imagined this part would be easier, but his friends weren't strong, and their footing on the wet grass was poor. The casket moved inch by inch, and he bore its weight from below. "On three," he said. "Owen, count." And as Owen counted Schwartz got down as low as possible, grunted, gave a last Olympian shove. Henry and Pella and Owen stumbled backward. The casket slid over the lip of the grave and, now upside down, settled beside the hill of dirt they'd made.

The rain had slowed again. Schwartz dug in his equipment bag for the sanitary gear he'd brought—facemasks, nose plugs, elbow-length rubber gloves. He handed a set of gear to Henry. Pella and Owen dragged Contango off to the opposite side of the cemetery. Mike could hear her laughter ring through the darkness; it sounded a bit hectic, but not worryingly so. He was glad she'd finally gotten drunk.

He reached a rubber glove into the cooler and produced two cans of beer, handed one to Henry. They drained them at a long slow gulp.

"Ready?" he said, and Henry nodded.

With effort they flipped the casket over. Schwartz undid the buckles. As he raised the lid he held his breath and stood as far back as possible, head turned, letting the first wave of whatever would come out disperse itself into the humid night.

"It's okay," Henry said. "We can do this."

Schwartz nodded. He wondered how Emerson had done it— whether Emerson really *had* done it, after all. It was one thing to hear President Affenlight tell the story, one thing to imagine Emerson kneeling in the dirt in his suit, tears in his beard, lifting the simple wooden lid off a simple wooden casket. Your mind stayed trained on the emotional, the intellectual, the symbolic. Emerson became a character in a play, and his act became a myth, a source of meaning. You didn't think about what Ellen Emerson's decaying body looked like, or how it smelled: you couldn't think about that if you tried.

Schwartz felt himself faltering. His face was still averted, and he wanted to keep it that way.

"It's okay," Henry said. "It's not so bad."

Schwartz, both heartened and abashed by the Skrimmer's calm, turned his head. A shock ran through him, another current of obscure

fear, but the shock passed, and Henry was right that it was not so bad —
or at least it wasn't so much worse than the viewing at the funeral. Affenlight's body had slid toward the foot of the casket and was oddly,
pathetically, contorted, but the embalming seemed to have held up
through the hot summer, and the body seemed still to be his own.

They lifted him by the lapels of his suit, the pockets of his pants.
They lowered him into the huge vinyl bag Schwartz had pilfered from
the VAC, and into which he had inserted steel bars to ensure that the
body would sink. He zipped the bag shut. They pulled off their gloves
and masks, tossed them into the casket, clapped it shut. Nose plugs still
in, they slathered their arms in diluted bleach, hoisted the bag, and carried it down to the beach. Owen and Pella rejoined them at the water's
edge, where a long rowboat awaited them. Luckily the water was calm.
They tied Contango to the little pier and rowed out into the lake, tacking
this way and that because they were drunk and none of them knew how
to row.

81

They were far, far out, dangerously far if you wanted to think of it that way, and even the few lights of Westish that pricked the distance seemed on the point of vanishing. Mike, who'd been doing the heavy rowing, grimacing in pain all the while, stopped and raised his oars from the water. Henry, behind him in the bow seat, did the same. The creak of the rowlocks ceased, as did the steady slosh of the blades, and all that remained was the slap of waves at the rowboat's hull, the black sky all around.

Pella sat in the stern, Westish at her back, the lake ahead, though most of what she could see was Mike's sweat-drenched chest, the shrug and drop of his big shoulders as he tried to catch his breath. What a face, she thought. Let it never be bearded again.

Alone at the prow sat Owen, his back to the rest of them. He looked out at the dark water, a hand laid softly on the material of the bag in which Pella's father lay.

They were drifting now, the rowboat's nose tacking softly to port, to the north. It was time, and Mike was looking at her, waiting for her to say that it was time, but even though it was her dad and her idea, she realized that she was waiting for Owen. Owen would know what to do. She found a warm can of beer beneath her seat—they'd brought the beers but not the cooler—and cracked it and handed it to Mike. Mike handed that one to Henry, and she found another.

Finally Owen turned around. He was wearing his Westish cap with the harpoon-skewered *W,* and behind the weak beam that streamed from his reading light his face was wet. He smiled, looked at Pella. "Would it be all right if I said something?"

They rearranged themselves, Owen and Henry on one bench, Pella and Mike on the opposite one, her dad in between. Owen passed the bottle of scotch.

"Perhaps we should bow our heads," Owen said. "Don't worry. I won't invoke any bread-based religions."

They bowed their heads. The beam of Owen's reading light passed over each of them, settled on the navy vinyl bag at their feet. "Guert," he began.

"At risk of becoming sentimental, let me say that you've been integral to my life for a long time. I read your book when I was fourteen, and it bolstered my courage at a moment when my courage was required.

"When we met, three years ago, it was because you selected me for the Maria Westish Award — another reason I'll always be grateful to you. Because barring that I would never have come to Westish, and I would never have met the people who are with me now. My own dear friends, as the poet said.

"But it wasn't until a short time ago that you and I became friends. And of course I regret that our time, your time, was so short."

Owen's voice wavered. He closed his eyes, opened them again.

"You told me once that a soul isn't something a person is born with but something that must be built, by effort and error, study and love. And you did that with more dedication than most, that work of building a soul — not for your own benefit but for the benefit of those who knew you.

"Which is partly why your death is so hard for us. It's hard to accept that a soul like yours, which took a lifetime to build, could cease to exist. It makes us angry, furious at the universe, not to have you here.

"But of course your soul does exist, Guert, because you gave of it so unstintingly. It exists in your book, and in this school, and also in each of us. For that we'll always be grateful." Owen looked up, lifting the beam of his reading light. It passed over each of them again. He smiled. "And we miss your corporal form, which was also nice."

Pella was weeping like crazy, as quietly as she could. That stuff about making a soul—she wondered whether her dad had really said it, or whether Owen had derived it himself, as a sort of synthesis of what her dad believed. Either way it was remarkable, and she glimpsed for the first time how close they were, how their relationship may not have been a static, one-sided kind of smitten worship, as she'd lazily imagined it, but a real and powerful thing.

She was shivering, and Mike put his arm around her. Despite the appalling heat of the day before and the day to come, despite the heat of the scotch she'd been drinking and drinking, both from Owen's bottle and her own flask, the four a.m. breeze that came over the water felt cutting and frigid. It was time for her to say *something,* to do right by her father somehow, but it was impossible, there was too much to say and no way to say it.

Owen reached across and handed her something. A piece of paper, folded into quarters. She unfolded it, but it was too dark to see.

"Here." Owen took off his Harpooners cap and, as Pella leaned forward, placed it on her head. In the beam of the battery-powered light she could see what he'd handed her: a typed copy of "The Lee Shore," the short chapter of *Moby-Dick* that was her father's favorite piece of writing, the source of his old password, and, not incidentally, the poetic epitaph of a brave and handsome man.

She'd known it by heart since she was six, and once she'd started she didn't need the page. When her dad recited it in lecture he did so with a stage actor's vigor, shouting his way through the exclamation points, as if to remind the students that old books contained strong feelings. She couldn't do that now, but in a hushed way she tried to do the passage justice. Mike squeezed her hand.

When she'd finished, Mike took a pair of scissors from his pocket and cut slits in the bag, so that it would fill with water and sink. He and Henry knelt beside the body, cradled its length with both arms, and, very slowly so as not to capsize them all, scooped Affenlight up and over the side.

82

The four of them — five, including Contango — stood on a rocky stretch of beach that had been dragged by the Parks Department earlier in the summer and still showed sweeping parallel marks, like a fresh-raked infield.

"Will you take the dog?" Pella asked Mike. "I have to get to work."

Schwartz frowned. "You promised you'd take the day off."

She handed him the leash, winked at Henry with a cried-out eye. "You can have an off day..."

She wrapped Owen in a long hug, they whispered to each other, and she padded off toward the dining hall, flip-flops slapping the packed sand.

The clouds were dispersing, and the sun had poked above the lake. Owen was leaving for San Jose, en route to Tokyo, in a matter of moments. Henry desperately wanted to say something fitting, to thank Owen for being such a good friend and roommate, to tell him how much he was going to miss him, but now his own eyes were full and he couldn't even squeeze out a *Take care* or a *See ya around*. Owen gripped his shoulder consolingly. "Henry," he said. "You are skilled. I exhort you."

And then it was just Henry and Schwartz, standing there in their gritty T-shirts. The dirt on Schwartz's face, and the mean-looking five a.m. shadow beneath it, reminded Henry of their first meeting back in

Peoria. Schwartz's widow's peak had deepened since, and his shoulders and chest had thickened and settled into a kind of premature middle age. But his eyes still held that pure maple-syrup color, that light that drew people to him like moths.

"What time's practice?" Henry asked.

"Not till seven." Schwartz checked his watch. "If we hurry we can fill in that hole."

They made their way to the cemetery and shoveled the dirt back into what had been Affenlight's grave. Once the sod had been relaid, the surface looked a little uneven, as if a mild earthquake had struck, but it seemed unlikely anyone would notice or care. They shouldered their shovels and headed back to campus.

"Where's your new place?" Henry asked.

"Grant Street. Block and a half from the old one."

They walked in silence for a while. Though it was still quite early, Henry saw one and then another Ryder truck pass by in the distance. It was freshperson moving-in day.

"The new football players aren't bad," Schwartz said as they stopped in the VAC parking lot. "I might make a few of them puke today."

During Henry's time in the hospital in South Carolina, he'd met every day with his psychiatrist, Dr. Rachels. She'd taken a liking to him, or at least an interest in him, and had come in on the weekends to continue their sessions. Sometimes they talked for two hours or more. To Dr. Rachels, the ethically dubious things Henry had done — sleeping with Pella, quitting the team — were justifiable and even borderline heroic, because they asserted his independence from Schwartz, whom Dr. Rachels considered an oppressive, tyrannical, oedipal figure in Henry's life, an assessment confirmed for her once and for all when Henry told the story of his and Schwartz's first meeting in Peoria, and the name that Schwartz had called him.

"Pussy," Dr. Rachels said, tapping her pencil against the arm of her chair with barely restrained glee. "Before you'd even *met.*"

Whereas the thing he'd done that might sound pretty brave—putting his head in the path of a whistling fastball, for the sake of the team—could even be considered cowardly.

"What comes to mind when I say the word *sacrifice?*" Dr. Rachels asked.

"Bunting."

"Decorative bunting? *Easter* bunting?"

"Bunting," Henry said, holding an imaginary bat horizontally across his chest. Dr. Rachels didn't have a couch, as he might have imagined; he sat in a stiff wooden chair. "Laying down a bunt."

"This is a baseball term? Use it in a sentence."

"Instead of bunting, I swung away."

"I found it interesting," said Dr. Rachels, "that you chose to say *Laying down a bunt* the way a person might say *Laying down my life.* You're familiar with this passage from the Gospel of John? *Greater love hath no man than this, that he lay down his life for his friends.*"

"I didn't choose to say it that way," Henry said. "Lay down a bunt. Everybody says that."

"You're always *choosing,*" Dr. Rachels answered, a hint of snap in her voice. "But who is Mike Schwartz? Why do you need to lay down your life for him?"

"I don't."

She clapped her hands together. "Pre*cisely!* So why did you? Are you some kind of pussy?"

Henry had spent a good deal of the summer pondering that question, until it came to seem more philosophically dense than *The Art of Fielding,* or Aurelius's *Meditations,* or anything on Owen's many shelves. He'd had plenty of time for pondering, first in the hospital in South Carolina, and then as he shoved snaking lines of silver carts across the Piggly Wiggly parking lot in Lankton, which he'd done just yesterday and was scheduled to do tomorrow.

Now he reached into the back pocket of his jeans and pulled out a wad of paper, handed the wad to Schwartz. "I guess you've heard about this," he said.

Schwartz unfolded the contract and flipped through the pages. There it was in black and white: $100,000.00. He handed it back. "You'd better get this in the mail," he said. "August is almost over."

"I don't want to mail it," Henry said. "I want to come back."

"So come back. You're a student here."

"I want to play ball."

Schwartz found something of interest under his left thumbnail, studied it intently.

"Starblind's in the minors," Henry said. "Owen's headed to Japan. Rick's the only senior, and Rick's a goof. You need somebody to run the team. A captain."

Schwartz kept fiddling with his thumbnail. He wasn't going to make it easy.

"You're a paid employee now," Henry went on. "It's against the rules for you to lead off-season workouts. Who's going to be on the guys every day from now until practice starts? Who's going to make them puke?"

Schwartz raised his gaze, fixed it on Henry. "So Coach Cox and I name you captain, and everything's fine for a while, and then you start having problems. What then?"

Henry tried to answer, but Schwartz cut him off. "If you mail that contract, you can think about yourself, your game, twenty-four-seven. If you're here, different story."

"I know."

"Whatever happens with your wing, whatever happens with your head, it doesn't matter. Whatever's best for the team is best for you."

Schwartz looked Henry in the eye, cranked up The Stare.

"And there's no guarantee you'll get your job back. We won a national championship with Izzy at shortstop. It's his spot as far as I'm concerned."

Henry had been nodding along with everything Schwartz said. Now his eyes dropped to the asphalt. This was the ultimate sacrifice, or indignity, or something—to not think of himself as the shortstop.

"If we need you at second, you'll play second. If we need you in right field, you'll play right field. Agreed?"

To consent to this, to submit once again to Schwartz's conditions and discipline, was maybe not what Dr. Rachels had in mind. But Henry knew that Schwartz was right.

Fog lazed at the water's edge, waiting for the sun to burn it away. He nodded. "Agreed."

Schwartz unlocked the VAC, slipped inside, and emerged moments later, carrying a bat, a five-gallon bucket, and his fielder's glove. He tossed Henry the glove, and they crossed the khaki practice fields, Contango lumbering gamely alongside. On the Large Quad, small and busy in the distance, the juniors and seniors of the Welcoming Committee were setting up rows of folding chairs, in preparation for President Valerie Molina's first convocation address.

Schwartz tied Contango's leash to the fence. Henry yanked up first base, which was anchored to the ground by a metal post, and tossed it aside. He jammed the wooden handle of the square-headed spade into the posthole. It fit snugly, and the spade head sat at sternum height, just where Rick's outstretched glove would be.

He walked out to shortstop, slid Schwartz's glove onto his hand. Not since he was nine had he worn a glove other than Zero. It felt clumsy and huge, and Schwartz, who only ever used his catcher's mitt, had never really broken it in. Henry mustered whatever saliva was left in his mouth after a night of whiskey and beer and no water, spat into the pocket, and rubbed in the spit with his fist.

It had been a summer of record heat, and last night's rain had done little to soften the infield dirt. He pawed at it with the toe of a sneaker, bounced on the balls of his feet, jangled his achy limbs.

Schwartz held up a ball. "Ready?"

Henry nodded. A lone seagull coasted by overhead. Schwartz took a lazy cut, and the ball bounded toward Henry, a routine two-hopper. Part of him could tell how slow the ball was moving, and yet it reached him so quickly he could barely respond. He flung Schwartz's glove in front of it, and the ball smacked the heel of the pocket with a painful thud. He grabbed the ball and spun it to find the seams, his fingers cramped and stiff from shoveling. He side-stepped toward the shovel head. His arm felt heavy and unfamiliar, like he'd borrowed it from a corpse. *Come on,* he thought. *One time.*

The throw sailed well wide of the shovel head, bounced to rest in the longish grass at the base of the fence. Schwartz stooped to grab another ball.

Another slow grounder, two steps to his left. Henry's legs felt heavy, he was wearing jeans, he'd been up all night. He stuck out Schwartz's glove and snagged the ball awkwardly. His throw flew high and right.

The next ball caromed off a pebble and struck him in the meat of his shoulder, or where the meat of his shoulder used to be. He picked it up and whipped it sidearm, missing badly. The balls kept coming. The morning was already thick and stifling, and after a dozen grounders he was exhausted, pouring sweat, his head throbbing with scotch and sleeplessness, but his arm was getting looser, and the throws drew nearer to the shovel head.

Schwartz stooped and rose and swung, stooped and rose and swung. He didn't have to count, because the bucket always had fifty balls in it, but he counted anyway. Eighteen. Nineteen. Twenty. As rusty as the Skrimmer looked, his sneakers sliding on the dirt, Schwartz's too-big glove slipping off his hand, his throws missing high and low and left and right, he still possessed a grace, a sureness of purpose, that was unlike anything Schwartz had ever seen, on a baseball field or anywhere.

Before long four dozen balls lay scattered at the base of the fence, a harvest of dirty white fruit. Schwartz paused between swings and held up the ball: Last one.

Henry nodded. Sweat dripped off the tip of his nose. *Come on,* he thought. *One time.* The ball screamed off the bat, a low shot toward the hole. He darted to his right, angling backward as fast as his shaky legs could go. At the edge of the outfield grass he dove. With Zero he would have missed it, but Schwartz's glove had an extra inch of leather. He snow-coned the near half of the ball, somehow held on as his stomach smacked the ground. He skidded toward the foul line on grass still slick with dew. He scrambled to his feet, planted his back heel, felt a blister rip. *Come on.* Mist or sweat fogged his eyes so he couldn't really see the shovel head, just a kind of looming not-large grayness there in the middle distance. His fingers found the seams. He spun his hips and whipped his arm, feeling nothing, less than nothing, no sense of foreboding or anticipation, no liveliness, no weight, no itch or sentience in his fingertips, no fear, no hope.

The ball bore through the morning mist on what seemed like a true path. The closer it got the more Henry expected it to veer off course, but halfway there it looked good, and three quarters of the way it looked better. *One time.*

The shovel head rang like a struck bell, continued to quiver after the sound was gone. Contango howled as if trying to match the pitch. The ball dropped straight to the infield dust. The feeling that ripped through Henry was better than that magic IV he'd been served in the Comstock hospital, better than anything he'd felt on a baseball field before. A half second later the feeling was gone. He'd made one perfect throw. Now what?

Schwartz bent down gingerly, reached into the bucket. "Just kidding," he said. "I've got one more."

Henry nodded, dropped into his crouch. The ball came off the bat.

Acknowledgments

The story of Ralph Waldo and Ellen Emerson is adapted from the excellent *Emerson: The Mind on Fire,* by Robert D. Richardson Jr.

Thank you to Keith Gessen, Matthew Thomas, Rebecca Curtis, Allison Lorentzen, Chris Parris-Lamb, Michael Pietsch, Andrew Ellner, Stephen Boykewich, Brian Malone, Timothy "Viper" Lang, the Hucks, the Blausteins, Kevin Krim, Brad Andalman, Emily Morris, Jean McMahon, and everyone at *n+1.*

About the author

Chad Harbach grew up in Wisconsin and was educated at Harvard and the University of Virginia. He is a cofounder and coeditor of *n+1*.